The Grail Conspiracies

Michael McGaulley

Published in the United States of America by Champlain House Media. ChamplainHouseMedia. com.

This is a work of fiction. Any similarity to real persons or names, living or dead, or to actual events, organizations, or locales, is coincidental and not intended by the author.

The concepts and approaches attributed to the characters in this book, or by means of the references to the embedded book, *JOINING MIRACLES,* are based on the author's research, as well as on the author's imagination in extending existing theories in quantum physics, human psychology and higher human potentials, and related fields, to the realm of what *might* be possible.

Library of Congress Cataloguing-in-Publication Data can be obtained from the publisher upon request.

ISBN 0-9768406-0-X

First Edition: 2005.

10 9 8 7 6 5 4 3 2 1

Acknowledgments

Where do ideas come from? Some of the ideas in this book I feel I can take credit for, but so many have come out of seeming nowhere, and for those — and to whoever implanted them, in whatever way — I am grateful.

On a more practical level, *The Grail Conspiracies* would not have come to fruition without the contributions of my wife, Susan, who kept things running in the pragmatic world while my head was buried in the computer screen, voyaging from one reality track to another. But even more than that, Susan contributed many breakthrough insights during our research trips to the book's locations, as well as in numerous edits of the manuscript as it came together.

Many thanks to Mariclare Beggy, who edited the final draft, and caught arrors in what I'd asummed was a prefect mannuscript. (Alas, she did not get the chance to edit this page!)

Many thanks also to graphic designer Russ Shoemaker (rshoemaker@bigplanet. com) who took some of my vague ideas and translated them into the cover and related items.

Thomas G.V. O'Connell, S.J., then an English professor at Le Moyne College, introduced me to the Grail legends, and all that lies within and beyond them.

Acknowledgments and thanks also to those who helped in producing, editing and testing the related website: TheGrailConspiracies. com.

Tom Burke, (tom@AWSinternet. com) of Adirondack Web Services, developed the web page and flash presentations. If you haven't seen them yet, then be sure to check them out — just as soon as you finish reading the book!

Thanks as well to Diane Aguilar, who edited and helped us refine and energize the slide presentations.

Rob Wray, a fellow connoisseur of sunsets, contributed some of the photos in the slide presentations, including the one that starts them all.

Howard White's *Ocean Song* makes, I think, the perfect sound track for the slide presentations on TheGrailConspiracies. com.

"*The ultimate object of magic in all ages was and is to obtain control of the sources of life.*"
— William Butler Yeats

"*Miracles happen, not in opposition to Nature, but in opposition to what we know of nature.*"
— St. Augustine

"*My own suspicion is that the universe is not only queerer than we suppose, but queerer than we can imagine.*"
— J.B.S. Haldane

"*We will first understand how simple the universe is when we recognize how strange it is.*"
— John Archibald Wheeler

Prologue

Southern England. June 6, 1944. Afternoon

"But we're deceiving him, lying to him about his mission," Webster said. "If he can't trust his own people, who *can* he trust?"

"Hell, he's just a soldier," Barrington replied. "It's not his goddam job to know the score." The three of them sat at a table, Barrington in the center — it was his operation — Webster on one side, the Major on the other.

Barrington looked, some people said, like a shorter version of Gary Cooper. But his eyes were strangely hooded. "Lizard-eyes," they'd called him in school, until he showed that it was dangerous to laugh at him.

His state's Senator pulled some strings in the first months of the war, and he got in at the start-up of the OSS, Office of Strategic Services, referred to by some as Our Spooks and Spies.

Barrington didn't really fit the OSS mold — he wasn't a New England WASP with an Ivy League degree and a background on Wall Street. But he was smart and ruthless, and spoke French.

His parents had been born in France. When they came to the United States in 1911, an immigration officer wrote their name, Bourton, as Barrington, and it stuck. His mother thought Hadley sounded more American than Henri, his father's name.

"I still don't think —" Webster began, then cut himself off. He was 36, round and balding, an associate professor of psychology at Yale on loan to the OSS.

"If you don't like what we're doing, blame goddam Hitler, not me," Barrington growled. "But right now, do your job. Tapscott is going to be here in a minute. When he leaves this room, it's essential that he believes this mission is exactly what we say it is."

He leaned forward and peered down the table at Webster. "You *are* with us on that, aren't you, Professor?"

Webster nodded. In Barrington's mouth, "professor" was an insult. There was no point in antagonizing him. Barrington had connections; Webster was having a good war where he was, and had no desire to get shipped out to some godforsaken atoll in the Pacific. Cross Barrington, and that could happen.

Besides, what was one more life in a war like this?

Barrington looked at the Major. He'd lost an arm on a B-17 raid over Hannover, and seemed to feel it was a miracle that he was still alive. He would coordinate the air-drop, and was sitting in on the briefing as a technical advisor. He nodded; he was used to following orders.

Barrington pushed the button on the table. They heard the buzzer sound, two rooms away.

Wind rattled the windows, and the rain started up again. It was early afternoon, and the troops had hit the beaches in Normandy at dawn. D-Day was finally under way.

❏

Paul Tapscott entered the room. He was a shade under six feet, lean, with curly dark hair and a boyishly handsome, open face dominated by dark, intelligent eyes beneath thick brows. He looked younger than his 25 years, unusual in a time when so many faces had been prematurely aged by war and stress. He had spent nearly two years in a Catholic seminary, preparing to be a Jesuit priest, before leaving to join the war effort.

It was OSS custom to wear the uniform of a U.S. Army officer with no rank or other insignia. Tapscott had added the set of pilot's wings he'd earned before being grounded.

"At ease, take a seat," Barrington said, pointing to the wooden chair in front of the table. His voice was husky from the daily three packs of Camels. He nodded to Webster.

Professor Webster cleared his throat, and began as Barrington had scripted. "I open with a question: Are you familiar with the so-called 'Spear of Longinus,' the alleged 'Holy Lance?'"

Tapscott wondered if he'd heard correctly. Was this some kind of a trick question, another weird psychological assessment?

But the invasion had begun; this had to be for real. Unless Barrington and the others were insane. "In the New Testament accounts, it's the lance the Roman centurion Longinus used to pierce the side of Jesus before they took the body down from the cross."

Webster steepled his fingers and said, "There was supposedly a — shall we say *mystical?* — aspect to this lance, one that made it of interest to certain military leaders. Perhaps you are aware of that?"

❑

The three men behind the table waited until they heard Tapscott leave the building.

Barrington chuckled. "The dumb shit fell for it, hook, line and sinker. Some goddam spy he'd make!"

Webster shook his head. "Such a fine young man. Innocent, naive — so rare these days. He won't last long over there."

"Starting this morning, *professor*, fine young men are dying all over Europe by the thousands. But if this operation succeeds, then we can save a hell of a lot of those lives. We sacrifice one and win the war. It's a trade that makes sense."

"But tell me," the Major said, running a finger along his moustache. "The mystical power of the Spear, and all that. Do you actually think there's anything to it?"

Barrington snickered and lit another Camel. "You asked Tapscott the same question. Hell, it's about as goddam real as Mickey Mouse."

Day One

"Perhaps you are thinking that a few words carved on an old church wall can have no real impact?"

"Something like that," I responded, trying to be polite to the old monk. He'd saved my life, after all, and it was his chapel, his little monastery, his whole world.

"Einstein wrote even less — $E=MC^2$ — and changed the way the universe was perceived."

"But $E=MC^2$ was" — I groped for a way to express it — "was only a symbolic way of expressing a much larger concept."

"Then why do you assume these messages convey less?"

From
JOINING MIRACLES:
Navigating the Seas of Latent Possibility
by "P"

1

Washington, DC. 7:15 AM.

> Greg,
>
> <u>WARNING! YOU ARE THE BUTTERFLY!</u>
>
> You're about to set off a storm that starts ITB and spreads around the world!
>
> Sending <u>very important info</u> regarding our recent conversation.
>
> Pass it on if anything happens to me.
>
> <u>Do not call me.</u> I'll call you when/if it's safe.
>
> <u>THIS IS NOT A DRILL!</u>

I'd have written the fax off as a joke if it had come from anyone else.

But this was in Cal Katz' distinctive scrawl, thick and stubby like the man himself, even more rushed and illegible than usual.

Cal was not one for practical jokes. He was a strange little guy, one day hush-mouthed and conspiratorial, the next day ready to tell you more than you ever wanted to know about what was *really* going on behind the scenes in Washington.

A conspiracy nut, but an intelligent one who did his homework.

A paranoid, forever vaguely hinting at threats he'd supposedly received.

But paranoid with good reason: people were in prison because of things he'd turned up; others had seen their careers blown.

"Sometimes even paranoids have real enemies," he'd said more than once, quoting Henry Kissinger — who certainly was no stranger to the ways of Washington.

Info regarding our most recent conversation. He'd phoned me, maybe a week ago. As usual, no preamble, no pleasantries, just asked out of the blue if I'd had a relative in the OSS during the war.

I'd told him about my Uncle Paul Tapscott — OSS, missing in action since D-Day.

"Interesting," he'd said with even more than usual gusto. "I'll get back to you," he'd said, and hung up before I could ask him what this was all about.

❑

I poured some juice and moved on to the phone message blinking on my answering machine. A number in Vermont I didn't recognize, but my father's voice: "Greg, it's me. Don't — *do not* — call me back. I'll call again in a little while. It's urgent."

Don't call me, I'll call you — the same phrase that Cal Katz had used. Mere coincidence, I thought.

However, as I was about to learn, there *is* no such thing as a "mere coincidence," certainly not on anything important, and what seem to be random events are usually anything *but* random. (As the little book I was soon to discover put it, "What appear to be unusual coincidences are merely normal happenings in a different Reality Track." So true, as it turned out.)

The two messages and two strands were about to come together in ways no one foresaw.

2

What I'd learn only later, when it came out at the trial:

Cal Katz had been up all night, pulling the material together and making copies, three sets, for redundancy. But he had no illusions about what he was up against, and three copies or a dozen might not be enough. They'd pull out all the stops, given what was at stake.

They'd been following him for days, maybe weeks, there was no way to be sure. So this morning he kept to the pattern he'd set — along Columbia Road to Starbucks for a copy of *The New York Times* and his usual *latte venti*.

Lull them into complacency — just long enough.

Back toward his apartment, as usual. But today a quick side-trip, to the post office, just off Calvert Street. He was running now, the first time since childhood. If he could get the envelopes into the post office slot then they'd be safe. The U.S. Mail was sacrosanct, nobody could grab the envelopes back. Maybe the FBI could, but these weren't FBI, definitely not.

He made it, his chest heaving with exertion, his heart pounding with fear, and slid the three thick envelopes into the slot, one by one. They'd taken all the postage he had in the apartment and he hoped to God that was enough to carry them to their destinations.

He glanced around. There was nobody running toward him, nobody even seeming to pay any attention. But he knew they were there, and that they'd seen what he'd just done.

Now maybe they'd leave him alone, now that the secret was out in the world.

But there was still risk. He raced back to the apartment, for some reason recalling the words of a *Post* profile: "Cal Katz scuttles around Washington on his stubby legs, gathering tidbits of news here, obscure reports there, to bind into his exposes." He didn't care what they said about him; only his work mattered to him.

He lived two floors above an Afghan restaurant. He glanced around once, then slid the key into the lock and made it inside fast. Up the first flight, pause, listen, then hustle up the final flight. "Fortress Katz" somebody had called it when he brought them here — four separate locks, plus an electronic alarm. Not much more than he'd grown up with on the Upper West Side, where security was the name of survival.

Adams-Morgan was safe enough, for an urban neighborhood. But he wasn't just the usual city-dweller, and it wasn't just his electronic equipment — computers, faxes, digital cameras — that made him a target. It was what he did that really put him at risk — his job was about upsetting the rich and comfortable.

The last key turned and he stepped inside. He never knew what crashed into his body, sending him tumbling before he could get the door shut.

3

I'd been up and at it since 4 A.M., crashing out an overdue report, then out for a quick jog through one of those monsoons that hit Washington in the autumn.   It felt good to pull off the wet running suit and hit the shower. There were still some loose ends to tie up before sending it to the client.

As I showered, my mind was on Cal's message. *You are the butterfly. The storm is about to hit ITB.*

"ITB," of course, was local jargon for Inside-the-Beltway — considered the Center of the Universe by many of those who live here.

"Butterfly" was from Chaos Theory, suggesting that small, unanticipated events, like the tiny puff of wind set off by the wings of a butterfly, can trigger a chain of events that bring about major, unpredictable change.

But me as the butterfly? Not likely. I was just another faceless soldier in that army of Beltway Bandits living off government contracts. I had no politically embarrassing documents to leak, no secrets the media or anyone else would find the least titillating.

So I thought then. But, as things turned out, Cal was right. A storm *was* brewing, and I, the 180 pound butterfly, was indeed about to set it off.

When the storm climaxed a few days later — the day before Election Day, by no coincidence — things would be changed forever, not just in my life, but changed as well in how we view reality, and what is possible *within* that reality.

But I didn't know that then. On this first morning, I had no more idea of what was about to happen than a soccer ball does before both sides start kicking the hell out of it.

❑

The phone rang. That same number in Vermont. I took the portable phone and some juice out to the balcony, dreading the conversation with my father. Kiss a toad first thing in the morning, and nothing worse can happen to you all day.

Looking back now, knowing how things would turn out, of course I'm sorry I felt that way, but lately every conversation with him had been a downer.

It's urgent, probably meant he wanted me to drop everything and fly up for the weekend. He'd been pressuring me since summer to come to Burlington for a visit, and I'd been putting him off, partly because things had been too hectic here. But also because he'd been in a funk for over a year now, and it was draining to be around him. He was unhappy nowadays; I could understand that. But I didn't like him taking it out on me.

He'd been a lifer with IBM, and couldn't seem to accept that there were other ways of living. In his view, it was long overdue for me to quit consulting and get a "real job" — by which he meant one where I filled a box on an organization chart, putting in the years toward a pension. As he saw things, I was *un*employed, not *self*-employed. The world had changed, but he hadn't.

I wasn't in the mood for his needling. One of his favorites: "What's a consultant? Somebody who *used* to have a steady job."

It stung because there *was* some truth to what he said. I *was* drifting — in my career, in the rest of my life. But drifting was comfortable, for the moment. I'd just turned 32, and had plenty of time ahead. I didn't need to be reminded — one more time — how much he'd accomplished by the time *he* was my age.

A couple of deep breaths of the fresh, misty air cleared my head. My apartment, on the twelfth floor, overlooks a park and a little brook that meanders through a natural growth of trees and underbrush. It's like living in a tree-house — a nice fantasy for those days when life in Washington gets to me. As apartments go, it's great, but I've been there too long — going on two years now, since the split with Laurel.

The rain had let up now. Mist hung in the trees, almost blocking the view of the apartment buildings across the park and Massachusetts Avenue, one of those broad, tree-lined boulevards L'Enfant laid out a century and a half ago when he redesigned the city, back before the days of commuters and grid-lock, back before Washington had evolved from a swampy village into the self-proclaimed center of the universe.

The phone chirped. "Morning, Greg. Did I wake you up?"

Great way to start a conversation. "Hey, Dad, I've been up and working since four this morning. I got —"

"Tell me, has anybody come around asking about Paul?"

"Paul who?"

A pause. "Your *Uncle* Paul, who else?"

"But Uncle Paul — he's been dead 60 years. Why on earth would anyone —"

Then it clicked: Cal Katz asked if I'd had a relative in the OSS, and I'd told him about Paul.

Before I could say more, Dad went on: "Two men showed up at the house last night, asking a lot of very peculiar questions: 'When was the last time we saw Paul?,' 'When did we last have contact?' Crazy stuff, and I told them so. They were from the CIA."

That stopped me. "You're joking!"

"You know I wouldn't joke about Paul. Never forget it was the CIA that kept insisting all these years that Paul was dead. Now they show up, ask questions, won't tell me diddly-squat, just that supposedly it related to a national security issue, something about a terrorist group. That's why I want you to catch that plane tonight. Let's come up with some answers on our own."

"Catch what plane? Where?"

"Because that's where he wants to meet. He set it all up, even paid for the tickets. They're being delivered directly to you."

"I'm not following you, Dad. *Who* wants to meet? Where?"

Has he been drinking this early?, I wondered.

"I don't know who he is, don't have a clue. He signed the letter P. Willoughby, but the name means nothing to me. The deal is, you catch a plane to Paris tonight, connecting to La Rochelle."

"But I can't go anywhere today. It's out of the question. Not today."

"Your passport — it's up to date, isn't it?"

"Sure, but I'm overdue on a report, and I can't leave town until I turn it in." It pained me to say that, as a trip to France sounded a lot better than pounding a keyboard. "Why don't you go? A trip would do you good."

"I can't do that, Greg. The fact is I'm not — not feeling so well these days. I really need you to do this for me."

"You're sick?"

I heard him sigh deeply, the way he used to in those grim months before Mom died. "There's something we haven't talked about, Greg. I was hoping all summer you'd come up to visit so I could tell you face-to-face. Remember that stiff neck I had last spring? Well, turns out it wasn't just from too much golf. Turned out to be a cancer, pretty bad one at that, progressing damned fast."

I felt my legs wobble, and I dropped into a deck-chair. Not Dad. He'd always been so healthy.

I couldn't get the words out at first, then finally managed, "Why didn't you tell me?"

"That was why I was hoping you'd come up over the summer. I wanted to . . . didn't want to have to break the news this way, over the phone. The doctors say I've got maybe a month, two at the most, though I'm going to be knocked out with the drugs for half that time. I really need you to follow up this lead on Paul — so I can know the truth before I go."

4

I wasn't present, of course, but from what I picked up later, the meeting that first morning must have gone something like this:

Brad Fackson had the kind of bland, chubby face no one noticed. Ride an elevator with him and you wouldn't really see him — he was the generic middle-aged white guy in a gray business suit who blended into the scenery like one of those computer-generated extras in a film.

That potato face, coupled with a mind that was definitely not average, were the assets that had made his career. A lawyer by training, he had put in his 20 years to a pension in the FBI before leaving to serve as lead investigator on a Senate committee exploring illegal foreign campaign contributions. His ability to get the goods on those who were out of favor and to be "reasonable" in dealing with those with better connections attracted the notice of law firms around the city.

Washington was full of lawyers, but Fackson had unique skills. The big law firms needed a savvy resource they could use – covertly, with deniability – to collect the kind of "dirty" information a respectable law firm couldn't risk being caught looking for. It was the same with trade associations — lobbyist organizations — and companies that did a lot of business with the government, and needed the edge that even the best lawyers and lobbyists couldn't always give.

Fackson Research Group – FRG – was smaller and even more secretive than Kroll Associates and the Investigative Group International, its two main rivals in the business of obtaining information without leaving footprints.

Close to half of FRG's business came from Hadley Barrington, either directly through the companies he controlled, or indirectly through the clients and contacts he introduced. When Barrington called, Fackson jumped.

❏

Sharon escorted Fackson to Barrington's office, then left them alone. Barrington grunted, "Sit!," and continued to look out the big windows, as he did when he was thinking.

The dome of the Capitol dominated the view down Pennsylvania Avenue; a corner of the Treasury building and some of White House grounds could be seen in the other direction. That always impressed clients, a graphic demonstration of the access the firm enjoyed at both ends of Pennsylvania Avenue.

Finally Barrington rotated the big leather chair and pulled himself to his feet — goddam these creaky old knees! — and lumbered into the secure conference room next to his office. Fackson followed.

Modeled on the secure rooms in American embassies, the special conference room was windowless, shielded in every way against eavesdropping. Sharon swept it each morning for electronic bugs. "White noise," a low hum, played constantly in the background.

"You told Sharon there was a problem with Katz?," Barrington said. "A goddam 'glitch,' you called it. I don't like the sound of that."

"Bottom line, Katz is now out of the picture. No further problem. My people have been through all his files, everything is clear in the apartment."

"About damned time. So what was that glitch?"

"It seems he may have gotten some copies off before —"

"*Copies!*" Barrington's dark eyes receded beneath the heavy lids, as they did whenever he was upset. He knew they still called him Lizard-eyes behind his back, just as they had so many years ago, back in Louisiana. Now even his skin, pale as parchment and wrinkled from so many years of heavy smoking, had shriveled to resemble lizard skin. "Christ, what a screw-up!"

"It's not as bad as it sounds. Just three copies."

"*Just* three? For Christ sake, *one* is enough to kill us! That damned little bastard, Katz! You say your folks took care of him – did he suffer?"

"Suffer? Not really, it was —"

"Too bad, I'd have fed him to a bunch of hungry 'gators. Those three copies — I hope to hell you're going to tell me you grabbed them before they got away."

"We're on top of it. He sent faxes telling the three to watch for those memos. We traced the numbers. Turns out they're people like Katz, nobody significant. We're setting up a watch on them. Chances are, we'll be able to grab what Katz sent before they even see it."

"You *get* those damned copies, y'hear? Whatever it takes, you get them. Just be discreet about it. Who are the three he sent to?"

"Nobodies, like I said. Nobody to be concerned about."

"Those nobodies have names?"

Fackson reached into his briefcase and handed a sheet across the table.

"Tapscott!," Barrington burst. "Tapscott, of all the damned ironies! If Katz links with . . . Shit, and I was thinking it couldn't get any worse!"

"I ran the name, Gregory or Greg, Tapscott, through our databases. Tried law-school for a year, then dropped out and ended up with a master's in biology — *marine* biology of all the useless damned things — along with a night-school M.B.A. Works short-term contracts with various consulting firms around the Beltway — agency reorganizations, little stuff. The same kind of crap Katz did on the side. The first —"

"Where's he from?," Barrington cut in.

"From? From nowhere, really. His father worked for IBM, so he moved around a lot in his early years."

"The father, where's *he* from?"

Fackson had to check the printout. "From Vermont. Burlington, Vermont. Where he lives now, retired from IBM."

"Hell! Then it *is* the same goddam Tapscott! I knew a relative of his, a long time ago. Back in the war. That's bad, *very* bad news."

Fackson was surprised at how troubled the old man suddenly looked. He handed Barrington a man's photo. It was a little fuzzy, blown up from an ID shot. "This is Tapscott, one we had in our files."

"I *know* it's damned Tapscott, but why is it in your files? He's been dead— Hold on! You mean this is *young* Tapscott? Christ!"

"Of course. An ID photo we had in one of our data-bases."

"Well, isn't that the damndest thing! He's the goddam image of his uncle, the one I knew back then. The same thick brows, the same nose, even the same smile. God, this takes me back!" He leaned back in his chair and stared at the photo.

Then he said, "I want you to put your best people on this, fast. I want to know every damned thing about young Tapscott, and I want him watched, starting right now. Send somebody good in to do a search of his place. Install taps, the works."

Fackson was stunned. This was the kind of full-court press they put on for corporate clients with big mergers underway . . . or on behalf of White-Collar clients in very deep trouble. The Fackson Research Group was notorious in Washington. Politicians used the Fackson Group for "oppo" work, ferreting out the skeletons in the closets of their opponents.

"Isn't that a bit excess — "

"Just goddam do what I say," Barrington snapped, his eyes dark beneath the heavy lids. "With the election so close now, we can't afford to take a chance. We can't let *anything* screw it up."

"There is one other peculiar twist with Katz," Fackson said. "Once we got into his apartment, it turned up that he'd been collecting information on Twisted Messiah and that whole — "

"Twisted Messiah, the goddam rock group? You're telling me that Katz liked their music?"

"Katz wasn't a fan, he was doing research on them. You probably aren't tuned in, but Twisted Messiah is a lot more than a rock group, it's a movement, it's — "

"You don't have to tell me, I have other sources, I probably know more about it than you do. But you're right, it's a hell of a lot *more* than just another damned rock group, with all that implies. If Katz was researching it, then the little jerk was definitely into too damned much for comfort."

Fackson nodded. A second surprise in five minutes. First the reaction to Tapscott, now this, as if Barrington had been fearing a link.

And the link was through Katz. Tapscott to Katz to Twisted Messiah. Why?

"The materials that Katz had on this Twisted Messiah — what did you do with it all?"

"Sanitized, like the rest."

"I hope to hell you're right. Now go follow up on young Tapscott. And don't screw it up."

5

I fly out of Washington just about every week, yet still get a kick out of looking down on the gleaming marble Capitol, the White House, the monuments, the museums.

And of course on the blocky office buildings that hold the government agencies, and the lawyers and lobbyists and assorted other Beltway Bandits — me included — that feed off the federal budget.

Why do I stick around this place? That's a question I've been asking a lot lately.

Willie Sutton robbed banks because that's where the money was, back in his day. These days, *Washington* is where the money is . . . if you are, as I am, "an over-educated migrant brain-worker."

The phrase came from a *Wall Street Journal* editorial a while back that deplored "the army of over-educated migrant brain-workers who work short-term contracts with the Beltway Bandit consulting firms and think tanks that cluster around the interstate that rings Washington, feeding at the government trough."

Dad had clipped the piece and sent it with a note: "To my over-educated son, the migrant brain-worker."

Over-educated? I'd spent too many years chasing degrees to deny that. But I'm definitely under-wealthy — at least by comparison with the folks in those other armies of lawyers and lobbyists and talking-head journalists who keep the Washington economy humming.

I hadn't planned to be a Beltway Bandit. It was just the way things worked out after a few years of doing various things and collecting miscellaneous degrees. A friend told me I should become a consultant, as I fit the consultant profile — somebody who doesn't know what he wants to be when he grows up.

Which was me. Still is.

You are the Butterfly. The storm is about to start ITB.

ITB. Inside-the-Beltway — the magic place I was looking down upon right now.

It made no sense.

❏

When I'd last seen Dad, in May, I'd been encouraged by what the family genes forecast for me. Despite what he'd been through losing Mom, he'd still been tanned and fit — at 76, six feet and 200, an inch shorter than I, and proud that he was only 20 pounds heavier. His hair had thinned over the years, but he still had the Tapscott features, the large eyes, the prominent brows. His only complaint had been a stiff neck that he couldn't shake.

That was then. Now, over the course of a summer, my rugged, vibrant father had turned into a shrunken, hairless old man hunched in a wheelchair. The chemo and radiation had cost him his hair, but hadn't stopped the tumor.

With his hair gone now, and his face swollen by medications, he looked like an oversized baby with a big, round head. Without the Tapscott eyebrows to shield them, his eyes seemed bigger and more expressive, and I picked up a sense of vulnerability that had never been there before.

"Why didn't you tell us?," I asked, struggling to keep my voice steady. "Did you tell Joanie?" Joanie, my older sister, lives in Colorado with a passel of kids.

"I was hoping you'd come so we could talk face to face. It wasn't the kind of news I wanted to give over the phone."

How many times over the summer had he asked me to come up for a weekend? I couldn't remember now what had been so important that I'd begged off each time.

❏

Despite the pain etched on his face, he insisted on holding off his pills, saying he wanted his mind clear while we talked. We sat on the glassed-in porch he'd installed for Mom so she could pretend to be outdoors in those final months.

"As I told you on the phone, a couple of guys in lumpy suits showed up at the door yesterday. CIA, they said. I pointed out how damned odd it was for them to suddenly come asking me about Paul, since it was their agency that'd been insisting all along that Paul died back in '44. They shrugged it off, said they were just doing their jobs."

The mystery of my Uncle Paul began with the telegram that arrived from the War Department at the end of June, 1944:

> *The Secretary of War desires me to express his deepest regret that Paul Anthony Tapscott has been missing in action in Normandy, France since 7 June 1944.*

A couple of weeks later, a letter arrived from Paul's commanding officer, assuring the family that Paul had "died a hero on the Normandy front on 7 June 1944."

June 7, of course, was the day after D-Day. Things were hectic, and the letter gave no details. As Paul had been in the OSS, there was no real signature, just a bureaucratic code: B/F-12.

That settled it for the family: it was true, Paul was dead, a reality confirmed by his Commanding Officer. Maybe his body would be found and returned home for burial after the war.

But then another letter arrived a few months later, after France had been liberated, setting off a mystery that had puzzled our family for 60 years.

The letter had supposedly been sent by a young Frenchwoman named Cecile Du Fresne, with a return address 23 Rue des Cygnes, apartment 4, La Rochelle, France. She wrote that she'd had the "honor" of meeting Paul during the "short period of 7 to 10 June, 1944, while he was in La Rochelle," and was writing to enquire about him.

Nothing unusual about a soldier making friends with a local girl. Nothing unusual, except that Paul had been on a secret mission into occupied France: would he really have given her his name and home address?

Even more puzzling, La Rochelle was 250 miles south of the Normandy invasion site. If Cecile was telling the truth, then Paul had been a long way from where his Commanding Officer had told us he died.

Further, Cecile Du Fresne claimed that she had been with Paul until June 10. If that was true – a big if – then Paul had been alive for at least three days after his official date of death.

Aunt Ursula wrote back to Cecile three times, and got no reply.

Dad had made the trip to La Rochelle once travel became possible again. He even knocked on the door of #23, but no one had heard of Cecile Du Fresne.

❏

Over the years, the family had made attempt after attempt to get to the truth about Paul.

Finally, they sent photostatic copies of Cecile's letters to one of the Vermont Senators, who passed them on to the War Department and the OSS for an explanation. By that point, the War Department was evolving into the Department of Defense, and the OSS into the CIA. Not much came back.

The Senator pressed the issue. Eventually a letter from Washington arrived, changing the government's story:

> *Due to a similarity in operational code names, the death of Paul Tapscott and another OSS member had been inadvertently confused as the result of difficult operating conditions during wartime. After thorough investigation, it has now been determined that Paul Tapscott died attempting to blow up a railroad bridge near La Rochelle, France, on 11 June 1944. The objective was to block reinforcements heading north to the Normandy area, and his effort was successful.*

Similarity in names . . . inadvertently confused . . . difficult operating conditions during wartime. That made sense. After all, the term SNAFU – Situation Normal, All Fouled Up – had come out of that War, and Dad himself had encountered enough SNAFU's to accept that a mistake like this could have occurred

Along with that letter came a black-and-white photo of that bridge, along with a photo of a plaque to the memory of *"Un Soldat Americain Inconnu."* An unknown American soldier.

Requests to have Paul's body brought home opened the next phase. Now the people in Washington claimed that it was not known where Paul had been buried.

But, as Dad put it in the letter he wrote back, "If the U.S. government doesn't know what happened to his body, and the French

don't know the name of that unknown American soldier, then why
should we have any more confidence in the story that Paul died at the
bridge in La Rochelle than the previous account that had him dying in
Normandy? Why won't you just tell us the truth? WHAT REALLY
HAPPENED TO PAUL TAPSCOTT?"

6

Roberts was waiting when Fackson got back from the meeting with Barrington. "Tapscott's travel info just came in. Get this: he's going to France today, by way of Vermont."

"Why France? Where in France?"

"La Rochelle, on the Atlantic coast. No idea why. The other interesting thing is who set up the reservations and paid for his tickets — business class, no less."

"Well, who, dammit?"

"The 3347 Group, Inc."

"Who the hell is that?"

"We've tried, can't get a handle on them. A Delaware corporation with an accommodation address in Wilmington. A dummy corporation, for whatever reason, but that's where the trail stops."

Fackson stood, shucked off his suit jacket, and settled again behind his desk. "Call in Jerry Edison for this one, he speaks a little French."

"Snowshoe," Roberts chuckled. Edison was another Bureau retiree, another invisible guy who blended in everywhere — so long as nobody noticed his feet.

"Tell him to fly up, get on that same plane out of Boston, stick on Tapscott's tail all the way to La Rochelle. Get some locals to pick it up in La Rochelle, let them do the close work so Edison can hang back and stay out of sight. We may need him later."

"Christ, this'll be expensive."

"It's the way the Lizard wants it. There's something about

Tapscott that scares the shit out of the old bastard, and I want to know what that is. Meanwhile, get some folks into Tapscott's apartment, set up the usual taps. Figure out a way to grab his mail, just in case Katz mailed him a set. Do the same in France, get somebody into his hotel room, see what he's got with him. If he's carrying a laptop, get a keystroke recorder on it, along with a transmitter, of course."

"Isn't that getting ahead of things? Assuming Tapscott already got his hands on the Katz stuff, isn't that all we want?"

"Sure, we need Katz' stuff back, that for sure. Whatever it takes. But we also need to know who's running Tapscott on this."

"Once we have Katz' stuff back, then what do we do?"

"Whatever the Lizard orders."

"I don't like this."

"I don't like it either, not a damned bit, but once you're in bed with Barrington there's no getting out."

7

Burlington

"Those CIA boys like to ask all the questions, but don't like to give much in return," Dad picked up after he had rested for a while.

"But they did tell me this much, when I asked why the hell this fire got lit after all these years. Supposedly they've been picking up Paul's name frequently in the 'chatter,' as they called it, of a certain terrorist organization. You know what chatter is? Intercepted messages and phone calls and e-mails."

I was back swimming in that sea of unreality. Had I raced up here because Dad's medications were causing him to hallucinate? Why would the name of someone dead for 60 years be of interest to today's terrorists?

He chuckled, and I saw a flash of the person he used to be, before the sickness and drugs that had bloated him. "I can still read your face, just as well as ever. No, your old man hasn't hallucinated all this. That's exactly what they said, that some terrorist group has been talking about Paul Tapscott, actually using his name."

"What group?"

"They wouldn't say." He laughed again. "They wouldn't tell me much of anything at all, so I don't feel I need to tell them every damned thing." He opened a file folder and handed me a letter. "This arrived yesterday, by messenger, not long after they left, along with your air tickets, business class, no less, all paid for."

Carston Mansions, #12
Carston Gardens
London, SW 7

Dear Frank,

For information on your brother, Paul, who was alleged to have been killed in action in France in June, 1944, perhaps your son, Greg, would be kind enough to meet with me at the Hotel de la Monnaie in La Rochelle, France, on 26 October, at ten in the morning.

Greg will find a room reserved there for him, with our compliments.

It's time the truth came out, and time is of the essence.

P. Willoughby

"Damned if I know who Willoughby is, never heard of him. But did you notice the wording? 'Your brother, who was alleged to have been killed.' Not 'killed,' but '*alleged* to have been killed.' That's why we've got to follow this up."

"If Willoughby lives in London, why not meet there? Why have us both go all the way to La Rochelle?"

But Dad didn't hear me. "Willoughby also says, 'It's time the truth came out.' We can't pass up the chance that it might just amount to something."

"But can we trust Willoughby? There have been so many false leads over the years — what makes you any more sure this is the real thing?"

When I saw the sadness cross Dad's face I wished I hadn't asked. "Fact is, I'm not sure of this one. But I know this is the last chance . . . last chance in my lifetime, that's for certain. I've spent most of my life wondering what really happened to Paul. If Willoughby can tell us that, then I can go in peace."

I can go in peace. I choked up then and turned away so he wouldn't see the tears that filled my eyes. I couldn't bear the thought that my father was dying, and I didn't want to leave him.

Day Two

"Einstein links with the message carved into that old stone wall?" Could he be serious? Did he really expect me to believe that?

Brother Freddie nodded. "$E=MC^2$ expressed Einstein's concept that what we perceive as matter and what we think of as energy are in fact ultimately the same thing."

I was regretting now that I had asked him about those carvings: Don't ask a question of a lonely old monk if you don't have all day to listen to the answer.

"Would you say this table is solid?," he asked, pointing to the battered wooden table between us. It looked as though it had been there forever.

I knocked on the wood hard enough so my knuckles stung. "It's solid, no question of that. They don't make them like this any more."

He laughed. "But it's not solid, it only appears to be solid. The wood is comprised of atoms, and atoms are 99.99 percent empty space. The solid appearance is an illusion. Now tell me about your hand: is it solid?"

"Is my hand solid?" I wanted to get out of there, away from this crazy old monk, but in this storm, with a broken ankle, there was nowhere else I could go. "As solid as ever."

He shook his head, his eyes twinkling. "Ah, but the

reality is that your hand is no more solid than the table, because your hand, like the table and everything else on this earth, is made up of atoms, and atoms are mostly empty space. No matter what everyday experience seems to indicate, the fact is that your hand, like the atoms that comprise it, is 99.99 percent empty space."

He paused, then added, "You look at the table and see solid wood. A physicist would look at the same table and see mostly empty space."

"But if both my hand and the table are 99.99% empty space, then why do they look and feel solid?"

He chuckled. "Good questions, but no one really knows the answer. Not now, perhaps never."

"Why are you telling me this?"

"To prepare you for the Knowledge."

"The Knowledge?" Something in the way he'd said it told me "Knowledge" came in capital letters.

He pointed to those words carved into the stone wall of the old chapel. "The Knowledge is there."

"Telling me my hand is mostly empty space prepares me for the Knowledge? How? By shaking my faith in reality?"

"Exactly so. Reality is not at all what it seems to be. The sooner you understand that, then the sooner you'll be free to apply the Knowledge in your life."

From
JOINING MIRACLES:
Navigating the Seas of Latent Possibility
by "P"

8

Paris. 6:50 AM

The 747 broke through the clouds in the final minute before touchdown, and we floated over flat green meadows and scattered villages. I craned to get a glimpse of Paris, but saw only patches of fog and more farm fields muddy from the morning rain.

A grim day. A day that matched my mood.

I'd brought my laptop, planning to spend the flight banging out the final details on that overdue report, but I couldn't work, not after seeing Dad. He had only a very finite number of days left, and I didn't want to be wasting any of them chasing after Willoughby's letter. I told him I thought I should be staying with him for these days.

He'd looked at me for a moment, just as I was going out the door, his eyes sad. "I'd like that, to spend these days together, but this is an opportunity we can't pass up."

❏

La Rochelle. 9:20 AM.

My spirits perked up a bit as I came to the end of the final leg, and saw the blue Atlantic sparkling in the midday sun as the plane banked to land at La Rochelle.

From the air, the core of the old town, spread around the small harbor, was as picturesque as a movie set, with arcaded streets, red-tile roofs, and a pair of medieval stone towers that flanked the entrance to a small inner harbor.

I stepped out of the terminal, and the warm air, tinged with sea-salt and the aromas of flowers, triggered images of arriving at a sea-side vacation.

This was no holiday, but at least the sun and sea air lifted my spirits. Maybe something worthwhile would come from this, and I'd be able to fly home tomorrow, mission accomplished.

A cab dropped me at the hotel in La Rochelle, just inside the old city walls, and within sight of the medieval port. According to a plaque by the entrance, the building had been constructed to serve as a Royal Mint back in the 1600's, and looked it: a grey block of granite, with walls as thick as a fortress.

But the lobby was light and airy, filled with bright morning sunshine. A fountain bubbled in a small private garden in the sun-drenched open courtyard.

Janine, the desk clerk, pulled up my reservation. "You guaranteed it with your Visa card. Will you be leaving it on that card?"

"*My* Visa?" Willoughby's letter had said the room would be with his compliments.

"You are Gregory Paul Tapscott?"

I usually sign as Gregory P., but this seemed close enough.

She rotated the monitor so I could read the card numbers. The Visa was in my name, but the account number was definitely not mine.

P. Willoughby was not waiting for me in the lobby, nor had he (or was it she?) left a message.

I asked: P. Willoughby was not registered at the hotel, nor did he have a reservation for tonight.

A bad omen? Was he going to follow through on delivering the "truth" he'd promised? Or was this going to be another in that 60-year string of false leads? A practical joke, with the travel bills charged to a phony credit card in my name?

I pulled out my business class air tickets and looked to see what card had paid for them. My new fake credit card. April Fool in October.

9

The room was spacious and airy, overlooking the bay and the pair of ancient stone towers that flanked the entrance to the old harbor. The only sounds were the wailing of seagulls and the splashing of waves thrown off as a small fishing boat chugged out to sea. As I stood there, a sailboat scudded outbound, its colorful sail flapping in the fresh breeze. Sunlight sparkled on the rich blue water, and the breeze carried scents of salt water and garlic-seasoned soups bubbling in the kitchen.

I showered away the travel grime, then plugged in my laptop and checked e-mail. Nothing that mattered.

A couple of hang-ups on my answering machine, then something that had come in yesterday evening about eight o'clock: "Greg, it's Shelly, Shelly Sherman. You've heard about Cal, about what happened to him? I'm devastated. Call me, please, I need somebody to talk to." Then she broke off, sobbing.

It was only yesterday morning, not even 24 hours ago, that Cal had sent that fax. What in hell could have happened to him that quickly?

France was six hours ahead of Washington, which meant it was still only 4:30 in the morning there — too early to call Shelly, so I went back online and checked Washingtonpost.com.

I found it in the *Metro* section:

Intruder Kills Maverick Journalist Cal Katz

I rocked back in the chair, stunned, recalling Cal's words on that fax: *Warning! You are the Butterfly! You're about to set off a storm that spreads around the world. THIS IS NOT A DRILL!*

The police theory was that Cal had been been killed by an intruder, probably an addict looking for drug money, when he returned to his apartment yesterday morning, shortly before eight o'clock.

Eight o'clock yesterday morning — not very long after he'd sent me that fax.

Still, the addict theory did make some sense. Cal lived in a 3-storey brick walk-up in Adams-Morgan.   It wasn't the safest neighborhood, but it was Cal's kind of place. Rents were cheap by Washington standards, it was trendy in a funky sort of way, it had a ferment of people not all cut from the career-driven mold, and it had ethnic restaurants from every part of the globe. For a guy from the upper west side of Manhattan it was the closest thing to home.

The *Post* termed him a "Maverick journalist," but that was not exactly accurate. Cal was a maverick, no question of that, but not so much a journalist as a person consumed by offbeat obsessions. He spent about half of every year working on consulting projects. That paid his rent, leaving the rest of his time free to indulge his passion for exploring what he was convinced was really going on behind the scenes. His articles had appeared in magazines as diverse as *Mother Jones, National Review,* and *Vanity Fair.* He had his own web-site for those who wanted more details — or who wanted to slip him leads.

But Cal was not a classic conspiracy theorist: he left the Kennedy assassinations and the UFO cover-up theories to others. His focus was more mundane: the effect of what he saw as a growing concentration of power in America, coupled with declining options for consumers.

As Cal saw things, there were only eight or ten banks that really mattered; a half-dozen airlines that called the shots for travelers around the world; a handful of media firms that were behind most of the films, music, cable and network TV, books, magazines and newspapers. There were the Big Four Accounting firms (formerly the Big Eight, probably soon just the Big Three, or maybe just Two); a handful of major consulting firms that controlled the direction of product development and marketing; a limited number of law firms in each city holding the lion's share of the major accounts; and – Cal's particular gripe – just two dominant political parties in America.

In line with his obsession with the growing concentrations of power and decision-making, he'd published a series of articles pointing out how money, compensation, and perks were being concentrated on a few fortunate executives and professionals: CEO's who made $100 per minute, while their factory workers with 20 years experience were lucky to make $100 per day. Other top executives who grabbed sound companies and bled them dry, then got Golden Handshakes –$10, $20, $30 million – as going-away bonuses for failing. The trial lawyers in a class-action who walked away with $30,000 for every hour billed — $500 per minute — while their clients ended up with a few dollars each, or maybe just discount coupons to buy a product they'd never want to touch again.

Cal was 5'6" and about 220, smoked a dozen black cigars a day, drove like a maniac in an old yellow Ford (someone had dubbed it The Yellow Peril after riding the Beltway with him), wore thick glasses that seemed to be perpetually covered with the subway dust of his native New York City, and was a strong believer in avoiding exercise.

"Burn the candle brightly at both ends," he'd said more than once, "then go out with a bang."

Now he had gone out, with a bang of sorts. But why? He wasn't harmless: his exposes had cost cushy jobs and fat contracts, and sent a few to prison. Was this payback?

And if it *was* payback, why was I the butterfly? What storm was I about to set off?

And how did that tie in with the OSS and what happened to Uncle Paul six decades ago?

10

The *Syndicat d'Initiative* — the French version of Chamber of Commerce and Tourist Information office rolled into one — was a ten-minute walk on the other side of the old harbor, past the pair of medieval stone towers that still guarded the little port.

Along the way, I stopped to buy a cheap cell-phone with some pre-paid time — something Dad had insisted on as I was leaving yesterday. Then it had seemed paranoid. But, as Cal Katz — the *late* Cal Katz — put it, sometimes even paranoids have real enemies.

❏
Then a strange thing happened with that phone.

A call came in on it not more than ten minutes after I bought it. "Greg Tapscott?"

"That's me," I said, "who's this."

"Your telephone provider, just checking the connection. Thank you. Have a good day."

That made sense, a courtesy call, good business practice.

Then it clicked: the caller had spoken with an American accent. An American working for a French phone company?

❏
The ladies at the tourist office gave me a map of the city, then checked the local directories: there was no Cecile Du Fresne. For that matter, no Du Fresnes at all.

Scratch that lead. I asked if they had reverse directories that would tell me who now lived at 23 Rue des Cygnes, #4 – the address from which Cecile had written so many years ago. They shook their heads.

I dug out a copy of the photo, supplied by the U.S. Government around 1946, of the bridge at which Paul had allegedly been killed in a skirmish. None of the clerks could place that bridge, but one of them suggested that I talk to Monsieur de Lattry, a semi-retired lawyer, who had made it his responsibility to oversee the monuments to the war dead in the area.

They called De Lattry's office; he replied that he would be "honored" to meet with me.

❏

Alphonse De Lattry was a withered man in a black suit and gold-framed eyeglasses, probably 90 years, maybe more. His office overlooked the harbor, a large, formal room furnished with what looked like antiques but were likely just things that had been there since new. Despite the warm October sun streaming in, he kept the windows tightly closed, and worked in his suit jacket. His only concession to the era was a fountain pen instead of a quill. No computers on his Louis XIV desk.

I explained why I had come to La Rochelle, sketching in the mystery that had surrounded my uncle's apparent death. I passed him that photo of the bridge where, according to the official account, Paul had been killed in a skirmish.

De Lattry studied the photo with a large, old-fashioned magnifying glass. "Yes, I know the spot, this bridge. But things are very different there now, everything has changed. There is a new bridge in that place. You would be wasting your time to go there. In any case, I can tell you that it was not your uncle who died at that place. The American who was killed, his name was Fournier. That has been known since '46 or early '47, since not long after the plaque went up. They corrected that plaque a few years later, so I do not understand this claim by your government. The Americans, they knew better, even then."

He handed back the photo, and said, "As for whether Paul Tapscott fought and died here in June of '44, let me check, to be certain."

He pulled himself out of the chair and hobbled to a black safe the size of a closet. He extracted a leather-covered book. The entries were hand-written in large, old-fashioned flowing script.

"No," he said at last, shaking his head, "my memory is still good, there is no one of the name Tapscott on the list."

"Would an American necessarily be listed in your book? Is there another directory, maybe in Paris?"

"If he died fighting the Germans, or if he was injured anywhere in this area, then he would be listed here, I have seen to that. This is the definitive listing for the *Departement*." A *Departement*, I knew, was an administrative division of France, roughly comparable to our counties, and all of France was divided into about 100 or so *Departements*.

"But he probably wasn't in uniform."

De Lattry shrugged. "A man of that age? There were not many around then. Some had been conscripted to Germany as forced labor, others were hiding in the hills. Or were dead. He would have been noticed, for certain. If a stranger died here, this Register would have recorded it."

I felt suddenly exhausted. Defeated. For half a century, the family had counted on this photo of the bridge where he supposedly died as the last contact with Paul. And it was a fake.

"But there is another possibility," de Lattry added after a moment. "The Nazis, they were particularly brutal in the days after the Normandy landings. If you drive across France, you will see monuments marking where they rounded up a dozen men, two dozen, sometimes more, and shot them on the spot. Why? Sometimes because they had been caught blowing bridges or roads. Other times, men were chosen at random to be shot or hanged in retaliation for partisan raids. It was Nazi policy to kill ten French for each German."

I'd seen a couple of those sites on a trip through Provence a few years ago, chilling reminders of a time when the French countryside was not so peaceful.

"If the dead men were known in the area, as most were, then it was possible to identify them. Otherwise we could only bury the body and mark the grave with that sad word, *inconnu* – unknown."

De Lattry leveraged himself to his feet again, and I stood, thinking the meeting was over. But he waved me back to my chair and dragged himself to a large map on the office wall. "Perhaps I may have an answer. There is one spot where an *inconnu* fell at the time your uncle was here. I will make some calls and arrange for someone to drive you to that spot so you can pay your final respects."

I hesitated, not sure whether getting into this was a good idea, then finally said, "Suppose I were to tell you that certain terrorist groups currently had an interest in my uncle and what he turned up?"

"Terrorists?" He shook his head. "Phhht! Impossible. Your uncle has been . . . gone . . . a very long time, long before today's terrorists. But what group were they, these terrorists?"

"I don't know, it's just a rumor we heard, that Paul's name came up among groups considered threats to national security."

He pondered that a moment, his expression unreadable. Then he shook his head. "That makes no sense, none at all." He peered at me, then asked, "But tell me, do *you* believe that is likely, after all these years?"

I shrugged. "I don't know what to believe."

For the first time he smiled. "Ah, a sensible attitude. Believe nothing, question everything."

11

I was half-way down the block when one of De Lattry's secretaries caught up with me. There was something he wanted to add.

He waved me back to the chair. "May an old man offer you some advice? If I were in your position, I would go back to Washington and demand that my government tell the truth about this matter. The people there know what really happened. If there are terrorist links, as unlikely as it seems, then you should be warned."

"We've been trying to get the truth for 60 years, and gotten nowhere. It appears the government either doesn't know or doesn't want to tell."

He shrugged. "Yes, perhaps it would be a futile gesture. Governments— my government, your government, all governments— they do not like to share the truth, yes?"

I nodded, not sure what point he was making.

He went on: "But perhaps it is not really the *true* government that is afraid of the truth? Governments sometimes are formed by the people, but then they take on lives of their own, and things begin to move in unintended directions. Bureaucracies grow within them, power bases develop, and subtly, over the span of years, things change. All it takes is a few determined men working silently within, manipulating the levers of power."

He paused, peering at me, gauging my reaction. "I hope you are not offended by an old man expressing his opinion? Perhaps you no longer believe it, even in America?"

"I hadn't thought of it quite that way," I said, evading a direct response.

What was he suggesting? I considered filling in more background, to get his reaction: that the CIA had been inquiring about

Paul because they had heard Paul's name mentioned in terrorist intercepts. But that was a matter of American national security, supposedly, and I wasn't comfortable sharing the information.

Besides, I really didn't know very much. What organizations were being intercepted? How did those organizations impact national security?

De Lattry continued: "All it takes to commandeer an organization, even a government, is for a few people who care, *deeply* care, to band together. Or people who have a financial interest in controlling things. And when that happens, then they soon control that organization. Not directly, not overtly. Those people are usually too shrewd to act directly. Instead, they move in subtle ways, and the rest of us, we never even realize what has happened."

"I'm not clear — " I began, then cut off, not wanting to offend the old man, yet not realizing how his words would echo in the days to come.

"Not clear what this has to do with your uncle?" De Lattry shrugged. "Perhaps nothing at all, perhaps a great deal."

Looking back, it was at that point that I should have understood just what I was dealing with, and been more alert. *All it takes is for a few people who care, deeply care, to band together. They move in subtle ways, and the rest of us never realize what has happened.*

But I was jet-lagged, an amateur among professionals, and I missed the game that was being played around me.

1 2

The few commercial fishing boats still working out of the old harbor were outnumbered by the large, ocean-going yachts. The tide was out, and the scents of sea air and pungent salt flats carried on the breeze.

I came on an historical marker near one of the stone towers: This small harbor, hardly bigger than a good-sized Vermont farm pond, had served as the main Atlantic port of the fleet of the Knights Templar.

At that point, I knew almost nothing about the Templars and their legends, and nothing at all about the treasures that may have passed through this little port on a dark week back in 1307.

The breeze pinged the cables against the masts, reminding me, in a strange way, of Swiss cow-bells. Reminding, me, too of going with Dad to the marina in Burlington, setting out for a day's sailing on the lake. Something we'd never do again.

I was dragging now, jet-lag catching up with me. I wandered up to the shopping area, a pedestrian zone of crowded cafes, patisseries, and designer boutiques a block back from the old port, and settled at a sidewalk café, the Café du Commanderie.

A quiche, a salad and some crusty bread. Then an espresso, the European version, as thick and black as old motor oil, and zip! no more jet-lag.

The autumn sunshine warmed me despite the salt-tanged breeze from the water. The scents of flowers from a *fleuriste* blended with the odors of coffee, the aromas from the neighborhood bakeries and *confiseries*, and the pungent garlic and oils simmering from the restaurants that ringed the area.

Pedestrians flowed past – locals with the pointed ends of long loaves of crusty bread sticking out of their net shopping bags, tourists ambling arm-in-arm, school-girls in uniform, fashionably-dressed ladies carrying gaudy bags from the designer boutiques that lined the street.

The Café du Commanderie, I learned from the back of the menu, drew its name from the fact that it lay in the heart of what had been the Commanderie, or headquarters, of the Knights Templar when they were at the peak of their power, close to a thousand years ago. The Commanderie was only a couple of minutes' walk from the old harbor.

The card directed my eye to the buildings across the narrow street. Behind the modern shop fronts, I saw the original buildings of the Knights Templar still in use, nearly a millennium later, marked by the distinctive Templar cross carved into the stonework just below the roofs. The Templar Cross, similar to a Maltese Cross, resembled four arrow-heads meeting at a point. It juxtaposed two symbols – the cross of Christianity and the arrow – apparently conveying the role of the Templars as warriors who were also monks.

Interesting, I thought then, but so what?, still not realizing how the story of the Templars would link with that of Uncle Paul.

I pondered that while watching a woman — a tourist, had to be American: who else would be wearing a pink backpack and matching pink shoelaces in white running shoes? — meticulously photograph the old buildings, front, side and back. Then she disappeared down a passageway in the old Templar Commanderie.

I wasn't the only odd visitor in town today.

❑

If De Lattry was right, that Paul had not died at the bridge in that old photo, then I was out of leads, and had no idea how to pick up a trail that had been growing cold for 60 years.

I used my new cell-phone to check for messages at the hotel.

"Ah!" Janine said, "It is good that you called. A fax has just arrived for you, marked urgent. Should I read it to you? It says, 'Greg, Now journey onward to *La Fin du Temps* and ask for Mr. Willoughby's package.'"

"That's it? That's all it says?"

"There was no signature," she said, then added, "It's very strange, *oui*? It's all in English, except *La Fin du Temps*. Do you understand it?"

"*La Fin du Temps?* Does that translate as The End of Time? This message seems to be telling me to journey onward to the end of time. But that doesn't make any sense."

"Alas, but I cannot help — Ah! Yes, but of course! *La Fin du Temps* — that is the name of a bookstore here in La Rochelle. It is, how do you say in English? A bookstore of the New Age."

❑

A passer-by marked the way on the map: *La Fin du Temps* bookstore was on a side street, only a couple of blocks away. The building seemed to be about the same vintage as those in the Templar area, but this one bore no Templar Cross.

A bell above the door tinkled as I stepped inside. A Mozart symphony played softly, and a calico cat lay curled on the table in front of a man at a desk in the second room. Neither paid me any attention.

I explored the shelves for a couple of minutes, trying to figure why it was urgent that I "journey onward" here, to The End of Time.

Another too-subtle practical joke? Or was there really something in this array of New Age stuff from Eastern spirituality to nutrition to channeling to UFO abductions that was relevant to a search for an uncle who had disappeared more than a half-century back?

Nothing came to me, so I approached the clerk, still busy clicking away at his computer. He was nearly bald on top, though the hair that grew from the sides was shoulder-length, blond and curly. A blue-denim shirt, ragged at the collar, was spruced up by an expensive silk tie.

"I was told to pick up Mr. Willoughby's package." The cat opened one eye to look me over, then yawned and rolled over to the other side, and I saw that she was missing one back leg.

The clerk shrugged and pulled a brown envelope from a shelf. He tore off a receipt taped to the package and slapped it on the counter in front of me. "Sign here."

"I don't know what I'm buying. What's the amount?"

"It has been paid for. Sign, and we can both be about our business."

"Who bought it for me? A man? A woman?"

He shrugged. "Who can say?"

13

I stopped back at the Cafe du Commanderie for another *espresso*, then slit the package open. It was a small book, barely more than a pamphlet: *La Rochelle and the Mysterious Treasure of the Knights Templar.*

There was no note inside, no hint of who had set it up for me.

The port of La Rochelle, I read, had been the main naval base of the Knights Templar, a mysterious band of medieval warrior-monks, founded around 1118, ostensibly to protect religious pilgrims during their travels to the Holy Land.

According to some, that was only a cover story for the Templars' true mission. But what that true mission was remains a mystery, nearly a millennium later.

They were called Templars -- officially, the Poor Knights of the Temple of Solomon -- because they were first headquartered at the old Temple of Solomon, in the heart of Jerusalem.

By some accounts, they had spent the first few years tunneling below the Temple, looking for objects unknown. For what, no one really knew — but there were legends and speculations aplenty. In some, they were looking for the Ark of the Covenant, while others claimed they had searched for, found, and guarded, the Holy Grail.

Or had they dug up buried treasure that financed their early growth?

What's not in dispute is the speed with which the order grew in members, wealth, and power.

Within a relatively short time, the Knights Templar became a spiritual force second only to the Vatican, and an economic force greater than that of any of the kingdoms of the time. The Templars also evolved into the strongest and most disciplined fighting force the world had ever known.

Rumors of the time claimed that the Templar wealth had been procured by tapping the secret occult wisdom of antiquity — perhaps found under the Temple, or uncovered during their forays into Egypt or even the Far East. In some versions, the Templars had discovered the secrets of creating "unlimited wealth."

More likely, their wealth and power grew from donations, augmented by shrewd moves into merchant shipping (protected by the Templars' military fleet), and then into international banking.

The Templars were the first merchant bankers, and created the basis for today's commercial banking system. Templar Commanderies were spread around the known world of the time. Their high-tech innovation was a break-through in that era, a system of secret codes that allowed a merchant in England, for example, to do business in the Middle East, without fear of losing payments to pirates and shipwrecks.

By some accounts, the Templars financed the wave of construction of the magnificent Gothic cathedrals at Chartres, Amiens, Reims, and dozens of other locations across France and the rest of Europe. According to some of those accounts, the Templars used the stonework of the cathedrals to preserve encoded occult messages, containing knowledge possibly going back as far as the builders of the Egyptian pyramids.

Some claimed that the Templars had been working on bringing about a reconciliation of what was termed The Three Great Religions of the Book: Judaism, Christianity, and Islam. If true, then that would have made them the targets of the powers threatened by the prospect of any reconciliation.

❑

The Templars had emerged with amazing speed for the time, and their downfall was brutally abrupt.

On Friday the 13th of October, 1307 — the original Friday the 13th, the basis of the superstition — the combined forces of the Vatican and the King of France moved suddenly against Templar holdings across France and other countries.

For a reason not understood to this day, the Templars, the

strongest fighting force of the time, surrendered without resistance.

Yet it seems they had warning of the raids to come, as witnesses described seeing caravans of heavily-laden wagons racing from Paris and the other Templar strongholds to their port here at La Rochelle in the days before the end, and of seeing boats sailing off into the nights. When the kings' men arrived on that first Friday the 13th, they found little of the material riches of the Templars, and none of the legendary occult secrets.

Although the Templars were imprisoned and tortured, none told what happened to the Templar treasures. Nor did any ever reveal just what those treasures consisted of. Thus the legends grew.

The legends of the Holy Grail — supposedly the cup from which Jesus drank at the Last Supper— came to prominence at around that same point in history. In some versions, the Templars were identified as the Guardians of the Grail.

Indeed, that version of the Grail legend, with the Knights as its guardian, found its way into the operas of Richard Wagner, including *Parzival*, a particular favorite of Adolph Hitler.

The Knights Templar, the book added, became the prototype for secret organizations including the Rosicrucians, the Freemasons, the Illuminati, and the Jesuits.

That knocked me back in the chair. *The Jesuits?* A bizarre coincidence. Paul had studied under the Jesuits for his four years at Georgetown, then had joined the order as a novice and stayed three more years.

❏

I glanced over, and saw the woman I'd seen earlier, taking photos of the old Templar area — distinctive with her flowing chestnut hair and matching pink shoelaces and backpack. Now she was at a table in the next café, tinkering with a camera.

She looked up, as if sensing I was watching her, smiled, then went back to tinkering with the camera.

Too bad this wasn't a pleasure trip. It would have been interesting to say hello and see what developed.

❏

Back to The End of Time Bookshop. The three-legged cat had somehow managed to climb to the top of one of the bookshelves, and the pony-tailed clerk was still clicking away at his computer. This time his eyes flicked with interest when he saw me, but he didn't smile.

"I was wondering about the person who left that book for me."

"Other people have been wondering the same thing."

"I don't understand."

"When you left, someone came in wanting to know—" He broke off and shrugged.

"Wanting to know what?"

"This is a bookstore.   Here we *sell* information, you understand?"

I pulled out a €5 note.

"Phht! That hardly pays for a newspaper. If you want information, then dig deeper, much deeper."

Go to hell, I wanted to say. But I needed to know. I was low on Euros, so offered a $20 travelers' check. He glanced at it and handed it back. "It needs to be signed."

"When I get my information."

"A man came in after you left, an American, from his accent. He wanted to know what you bought. I told him we sold information, just as I tell you. When I told him about the book, he also bought a copy of the same title. He was tall, glasses, a raincoat, average size, average face, not particularly attractive."

"What about the person who left the book for me?"

He pointed to the travelers check, and I signed it. "No, the man who left the book for you, he was an older man, perhaps 60, tall, like you. He had white hair. He said he was your uncle."

"I don't have an uncle — not a living uncle."

He shrugged, conveying that my family matters were of no concern to him, now that he had my money in hand.

I showed him the photo of Uncle Paul, a copy of the picture taken when he'd just won his wings, six decades ago. "Could it be this man?"

He looked it over, looked up at me, then back at the photo. "That is a very old photo, of course, I see that from the uniform. People change. But no, I think it was not this man who bought your books. No, probably not him."

❏

I was at the door when he said, "But there is one thing about the man, something of interest."

I turned back, expecting another shake-down. But this was free. "The man who came today asking questions about you, he had — how do you say in English? — he had *les pieds plus grande.*"

"Big feet?," I translated, sure I had it wrong.

"*Ah, oui*, exactly. He had the largest feet I have ever seen on a man — a man of that size, of ordinary height. But the feet of a giant."

14

A message from Monsieur De Lattry had arrived moments before I got back to the hotel. I returned the call, expecting he was following through on the promise to arrange a ride out to the spot where an *inconnu* – an unknown – had been killed around the time Paul was here.

That seemed a futile exercise.   It was possible that unknown was Paul, but probably not. In any case, we'd never know for sure. Still, I figured I needed to go through the motions, for Dad's sake, so I could tell him I followed up on every lead

But de Lattry had a surprise: "A person came to mind after you left today. He's an old man, old like the rest of us, but he was the radio operator for one of the Resistance groups. He tells me that he is certain he met your uncle in '44, and remembers him. Perhaps he may have some answers for you."

❑

I picked up a couple of bottles of wine — de Lattry's suggestion as an ice-breaker — and a taxi brought me out to one of the grim concrete apartment buildings on the edge of La Rochelle where Jacques Farentoise lived with his son, also named Jacques.

The son answered the door. He was maybe 40, not more than five-six, probably 200 pounds, dressed in a blue T-shirt and a pair of muddy blue work pants.

The father sat in a haze of smoke in the small living room, a small man with a creased leathery face. His voice was raspy, and he paused for breath every few words. Both father and son seemed glad to see a visitor, even happier to see that I had brought some good wine.

The windows were shut, and the smoke hung in the air, the

heavy cloying scent of French tobacco. I hoped I wouldn't be here long.

The son uncorked one of the bottles. Neither son nor father spoke any English, so I struggled along with my rusty college French. De Lattry had prepared the way, and the background of why I was there went easily.

Then the old man laughed and started to speak, but the laughter degenerated into a fit of coughing. "You are the nephew," he tried again, "yet you look enough like your uncle that you could be the son. You look as much like him as Peti' Jacques looks like me."

Petite — little. The son was still Little Jacques, and probably would be until death. I glanced from father to son and nodded, though the resemblance was hard to see through the hundred pounds of excess flesh the son carried.

"I'm amazed that you can remember my uncle that clearly, after all those years," I said, wishing that de Lattry had not introduced me as the nephew. Did the old man really notice a resemblance, or was that just something to make a better story?

"Of course I remember. I remember those days better than last week. We all do, those of us who lived through it. Things stuck with us then because we lived on the edge at every moment, always at risk from the Nazis. It's the eyebrows. Your uncle had thick brows, like yours. Perceval he was called, Perceval One."

"Perceval One? How did you know that?"

"Perceval was not his real name," Farentoise responded. "His real name I never heard. Perceval was his radio call, and I knew that because I served as his radio operator for the one message he sent. He didn't have a radio, and the unit he was supposed to work with had been turned by the *Boche*, so I sent the message for him."

"Wasn't he operating in code?"

The old man shrugged. "He thought he was, of course, but that code had been broken by the *Boche*, months before. London knew the code was broken, we told them ourselves, we knew this other unit had been turned. But they wouldn't listen to us, the stupid bastards. I'm telling you that his own people sent your uncle to a unit that was under the control of the Nazis, and they sent him with a code that the Germans had already broken. He had no other code, so he had no choice but to use that code."

Farentoise shook his head, coughed, then said, "Even now, after all these years, it is incredible that they were so stupid, London. It was criminal, what they did to him."

He paused for a couple of sips of wine, then said, "Your uncle, he was very lucky when he landed in France. Very lucky or very smart. Whatever, he didn't make contact with the Resistance unit to which he had been sent, because then the Germans would have grabbed him for sure. He found his way to us, through a woman, and that's how it happened that I was the one to relay his message to London."

"Why would his own people send him to be captured?"

"Sometimes in wartime . . . well, things happen. Word doesn't get to the right people in time. Or people are stupid. Or bigger games, they are being played."

"You're certain that my uncle was Perceval One?"

"As certain as I am that you're sitting there in front of me."

"Was there a Perceval Two?"

"If there was, I never saw him."

"Did you understand the message he was sending?"

"I wasn't supposed to understand, I was only the radio operator, it was better not to know. But, yes, I did know what it said, most of it. He said that he had located the most powerful weapon, and was ready to bring it back according to the original plan."

Most powerful weapon. I felt a chill, the sense it was coming together. "What kind of weapon? Most powerful? What does that mean?"

He shrugged. "I don't know."

"You said he was ready to 'bring it back according to the original plan.' Do you have any idea what that plan was?"

"I know nothing more, not even what happened to him, your uncle."

He sipped some wine, then said, "But if you ask me, what do I *think* happened to him? I'm sorry, but I think the Germans got him. That's what we all thought, the old-timers, when we talked about it after the war."

"You said he found his way to your Resistance unit through a woman. Do you know who she was?"

"The daughter of one of us, one of the men in our unit. But that man is dead."

"Do you know the name?"

"Almost, I almost had it." He snapped his fingers a couple of times, then sipped more wine. "He was a pharmacist, the father, but the name . . ."

Peti Jacques broke in. "You said before it was old Du Fresne the pharmacist, yes?"

"Du Fresne! Yes, that's it."

"And the daughter's name?"

"Celine, Celeste — something like that."

Cecile Du Fresne had sent those letters to the family inquiring about Paul later that summer of 1944.

Maybe, just maybe, things were finally going to come together.

15

I spent the taxi-ride back to the hotel trying to figure what to tell Dad.

It seems that Paul may have been betrayed by his own people, who had sent him in to contact a Resistance unit that had already been turned by the Germans.

Most likely, it was a blunder — somebody had failed to get a warning, or had been too stressed with D-Day coming up to grasp the implications.

Tough luck for Paul, tough luck for millions of other young guys who'd had the misfortune of being born into that time and place.

Still, there was that message Paul sent — that he had found "the most powerful weapon," and was ready to bring it back "according to the original plan."

But what *was* that original plan? What had he been sent here to accomplish? After all, the action was in Normandy, a couple or three hundred miles north of La Rochelle.

And what was that "most powerful weapon?" This far from the front, what kind of weapon would matter?

❑

"Monsieur?," the cab-driver said after I paid and tipped him. I thought he wanted a bigger tip. "I must tell you, perhaps you did not notice. But another car, it followed us out to where you went and waited there, and then came back here again. Did you know that?"

I shook my head, scanning the street. "What kind of car?"

He shrugged. "A silver Renault, like a thousand others. But it was the same car out and back, I am sure of that. With a woman driving. It is gone now."

❑

It was coming on dinner-time here, lunch-time back in Burlington. I phoned home from the hotel, hoping to catch Dad before he dozed off for the afternoon.

Mrs. Fox answered, her voice hushed and grim. "Your father is doing very well today. That's not a good sign."

"*Not* a good sign? Doing well is a bad sign?"

"That's the way it often happens. Often, just before the end, they have one final good spell and seem to be coming out of it. But it's only one last gift of time, then they go. You need to face that, it's a fact."

Dad came on, his voice strong and upbeat. "Never mind what she says, Greg, I'm doing okay."

I decided to tell the whole story of what I'd picked up to that point, beginning with Willoughby's no-show for the promised meeting, then what I'd picked up from De Lattry and the radio operator, and that 'most powerful weapon' he supposedly turned up.

He was silent for a while after I finished. Then he said, "Paul always had a knack of turning setbacks into successes. As for the OSS maybe double-crossing their own guy? Hell, nothing about this surprises me any more."

16

There was one final possibility.

I walked back to the Rue des Cygnes, pretending to look in shop windows along the way. If there was a silver Renault following me, I didn't see it, nor did I see anyone on foot who stayed with me.

Had the cab-driver been playing games, hitting me up for a bigger tip?

Again I rang the bell for apartment #4. Still no reply. I tried the security door leading to the upper floors, and found it unlocked. An old-fashioned staircase with wrought-iron railings and marble steps circled around an enclosed atrium. The melange of cooking aromas — garlic, fish, lamb — reminded me how hungry I was.

I knocked at Apartment 4. The door opened on a chain. "*Oui?*" a woman said through the crack.

"My name is Greg Tapscott," I managed in French. "I'm searching for information on my uncle."

"Your uncle?" She shook her head and moved to close the door. "He is not here, I tell you that for certain."

"I'm ultimately trying to trace Cecile Du Fresne," I managed as she swung the door shut.

That stopped her. "Cecile? But she is dead, for many years." She opened the door a little to look at me, leaving the chain still in place.

I slid a copy of one of Cecile's letters through the opening, glad that Dad had included it with the file he'd prepared for me to take on this trip. "It seems that Cecile knew my uncle when he was here during the war. I was hoping that she could help us —"

She looked at the letter, then back at me, and something

registered in her eyes. *"Mon Dieu! C'est incroyable!* That is her handwriting, without doubt." She pulled the chain off the door and invited me in with a sweep of her hand.

She was early 40's, thin, with long black hair pulled back in a twist, stylishly dressed for someone spending an evening at home. Her face had relaxed now; she was attractive with high cheekbones and vibrant dark eyes accentuating fair, smooth skin.

A man popped his head in from another room, nodded, and left. He was dressed in a white shirt and tie. His skin had barely more color than the shirt; his shoulders slumped in the manner of someone who lived at a desk.

The woman gestured me to a brocaded chair with wooden armrests. It probably wasn't anything they thought of as an antique, just something that had been in the family. I wondered if Paul had sat in this same chair.

"After all these years, it's hard to believe," the woman said. "But who are you? The nephew, you say?"

"I'm Greg Tapscott. Paul was my uncle. And you?"

"I am Lili. Cecile was my aunt. She died in '85." She held out her hand. It was soft and feminine, and I understood, if she was any reflection of her aunt, how Uncle Paul might have been charmed.

"My family tried writing back to your aunt several times, but our letters never seemed to get through."

"Ah, from '46 onward she would have been in Paris. But the family was here. I do not understand."

Then she giggled. *"Tante* Cecile, she had a terrible crush on your uncle. Grand-papa, he did not approve. Perhaps that is where your letters went — into his pocket."

Her face sobered. "But there may have been another reason. "The American OSS, they came looking for Paul in the spring or perhaps the summer of '45, soon after the war ended, and they were not friendly, not at all, as if he had been a traitor or a deserter — which of course he was not. My family did not trust anyone who came after that, thinking they were just more OSS agents looking for Paul and what he turned up."

That was just about the era when the OSS was insisting that Paul had died at Normandy. So why come here looking for him. Did they know something, or was it just another screw-up?

Before I could ask what it was that Paul turned up, she stood and hurried out of the room. "A little moment, please."

She returned with a glass of wine and placed it on the small round table beside me. "You will drink some wine with us, yes?"

She left again, and returned with a photo album. She pulled a chair next to mine, and flipped to a page in the album. She looked at the page, then back at me.

"It is . . . so extraordinary. You are truly the image of your uncle." She jumped up again, and fetched her husband. He came in, shook my hand without a word, then compared my face to whatever was in the book. He shook his head, his face impassive. "*Ah, oui, oui. C'est incroyable,*" then retreated to the other room.

She turned the book around so I could see, and pointed to an old black-and-white photo of a young woman and a man in a baggy, ill-fitting suit. I recognized the man: it could have been me.

Lili found a magnifying glass in a drawer. There was no doubt of it: this was Uncle Paul. "Do you know when the picture was taken?"

Lili removed the photo from the album. Someone had written in careful script on the back, "*Paul et moi, le 9 Juin 1944.*"

17

A meeting went on longer than planned, so it was after lunch before Barrington could break away for an update from Fackson.

Tapscott's apartment was in a modern building on Massachusetts Avenue with good security, so Fackson's people had rented an apartment there on a short-term lease just to get past the front desk. Once in, with a base to operate from, it was easy enough to get into Tapscott's place. They set up taps on both the phone and fax lines, along with a keystroke transmitter on his desktop computer so everything he wrote would be sent to a receiver in the flat they had rented. They copied his hard drive, and went through his papers.

"That's all well and good," Barrington said. "But get to the damned point. Did you get the materials Katz sent him?"

Brad Fackson shook his head. "It wasn't there. Maybe he got it before he left and took it with him. We did find the key to Tapscott's mailbox; we'll check it daily. But there's something else about Tapscott's apartment, something that blew my mind."

"What? Don't play games."

"When we got in, we found all the lines, phone and internet, already had taps — before us. Someone else is keeping watch on him, not just us. No way of knowing who that is."

"Christ! That can only mean one thing: they *know*, they *already* know! Shit!"

Fackson waited silently. You didn't probe Barrington, you waited for him to share information. "They" obviously meant the opposition. But for which son, which candidate?

Or was he bothered by something else altogether — something going back to the War?

After an interval, Barrington sipped some water, and said, "It's what we were talking about. Tapscott goes back to the war, he and I. It's bad news if they've gotten wind of it. They'll use it against the boys."

Barrington's oldest son, Harmon, 50, was running for a second term in the Senate; the younger one, Henley, 41, was in a tight race for governor. Fackson's team had been doing Oppo research on the Barrington sons' opponents, hoping to turn up useful dirty laundry to use at the right time. It was no surprise that the other sides had been doing their own Oppo. That was the way the game was played.

But why the hell could something the father had done back in the war have any bearing on elections these days?

❑

"What else have you turned up about young Tapscott?"

Fackson began with what they had learned yesterday, that Frank Tapscott was terminally ill, yet had insisted that his son fly off to La Rochelle.

"As for Greg Tapscott in France, my people have him under a full-time watch, and have also effected entry into his hotel room there, and set taps on the phone, as well as another keystroke transmitter on his laptop. They copied a file of old family information, and it seems that he is looking for information on his uncle, who disappeared — "

"Dammit, do you think I don't already know that? I pay you to tell me things I *don't* know!"

Fackson passed Barrington a typed list of the people Tapscott had met in La Rochelle: De Lattry, the French lawyer, the unknown man in the working-class suburb, and, at the moment, his visit to 23 Rue des Cygnes.

"Somebody's using young Tapscott to yank our chain," Barrington said. "We need to find out who. And how much they really know. And put a stop to it, ASAP, before they cause any real damage."

18

"Then Paul really *was* here in La Rochelle," I said, more to myself than to Lili, as if somehow putting it into words would make it more believable. The photo was dated June 9th, two days after the American military had claimed he died at Normandy. "That photo —"

"Ah, but you must take that photo to your father. It will be good for him to see how happy his brother was with my aunt. That shows in the faces, yes?"

I nodded. They did look like happy young lovers, and I wondered, *Were* they lovers?

Then Lili frowned. "But there is something else you should know. The fact is, they betrayed your uncle."

"Betrayed him? Who?"

"His commanders, of course. They sent him to France intending, yes *intending*, for him to be captured. *Tante* — Aunt — Cecile pieced together the story over the years. His superiors lied to him about his mission, and sent him to work with a Resistance unit they knew, *everyone* here knew, had been turned by the Germans."

Which accorded with what Farentoise, the old radio operator, had just said.

I played along, as if this were new to me. "What would be the point?"

"My Aunt Cecile, she spent years trying to understand that. She concluded it was to distract the Germans' SS tank division in their advance north to reinforce at Normandy."

"How did your Aunt Cecile come into it? How did she and my uncle meet?"

"Your uncle, he parachuted into the farmland east of La Rochelle. As I said, the Resistance unit that was to meet him at the landing site had already fallen under German control. That is why we were sure that those who sent him expected him to be captured immediately. But he evaded the Germans – or perhaps he just had the good fortune of landing in the wrong place – and moved to the back-up meeting point, at the St. Sepulchre church here in the city. Another Maquis unit, of which my grandfather was a member, heard what had happened, and sent Aunt Cecile to intercept him before he got to the church. It was clear that his mission had been betrayed, so he had no other choice than to trust her."

That also accorded with what Farentoise had said: Agent Perceval didn't make contact with the Resistance unit to which he'd been sent, but instead found his way to another, through a woman.

I still found it hard to believe that Paul's own people would double-cross him like that, deliberately sending him into a trap. But suppose, just suppose, it were true? That would explain the cover-up ever since. The OSS, the U.S. Government, his commanders — none of them would want to admit that they had tricked one of their own into going on a suicide mission.

"He – one person – was to delay a tank division? How?"

"Aunt Cecile spent years reading, talking to people, trying to understand. There were many other diversions those few days, all over France, some by the French Resistance units, others by special units parachuted in. But those were *military* actions. Paul's mission, she concluded, was unique as a *psychological* diversion."

"Psychological diversion?"

"Apparently the people behind this plan expected that if they held out bait, Hitler would take it, and divert reinforcements away from Normandy to search here for it. The bait, of course, was the promise of the Spear."

"What spear?"

"The Holy Lance, the spear that the Roman soldier used to pierce the side of Jesus on the Cross? You know of that, of the Spear of Longinus, the Holy Lance?"

I wondered, for that first moment, if I'd heard correctly. "The Spear of Longinus was here in La Rochelle?"

She shook her head. "Of course not, no. That was only a cover story, a lie that the Americans made up. The true Spear — the one generally accepted as the true Spear — is, *was*, in Vienna. I say 'was,' because Hitler captured it and took it to Germany when he invaded Austria. *Tante* Cecile researched all this. The fact was, Hitler already *had* the true Spear even before the start of the War."

That stopped me. Finally I managed, "Hitler was that interested in the Spear? I'd never pictured him as religious."

"No, no, not religious, not at all. He was an occultist. He believed that the Spear carried powers he could tap for his own ends."

I found that hard to believe, then. Later, I'd learn just how obsessed Hitler and some of the others were with tapping powers from other dimensions.

"So it was really all a diversion? My uncle was dropped into France as part of . . . part of a lie? But it was crazy, one man to stop a tank division."

"Perhaps it doesn't make sense to us now, but you must understand the times — the desperate need for the Normandy invasion to succeed. And you have to understand the mind of Hitler, and those closest to him."

I took a sip of wine to slow myself down and think. "But if Hitler already had the Spear . . . I don't understand. What would be the point?"

"There is a term . . . " She wagged her finger, as if summoning the word. "Disinformation, that's it. Are you familiar with it? Providing information to deceive or distract?"

I nodded.

"As Aunt Cecile finally came to understand it, the OSS sent Paul here as an unwitting source of disinformation. The object was to make Hitler believe that the Spear he held was only a copy, and that the real Spear was somewhere in La Rochelle. If Hitler could be made to believe that, then perhaps he would divert the *Das Reich* Division to search for it here. Even if the diversion worked for only a day or two, then it would be worthwhile. With the invasion in the balance, every hour that the *Das Reich* was delayed would increase the chances that the invasion would succeed."

The memory of some old photos of Uncle Paul came to mind. They'd been on the old piano at home for as long as I'd been on earth. In one, he wore a priest's cassock, in the other his flying helmet and goggles. Young, idealistic, full of life. Soon to be double-crossed by his own commanders.

But was it really a betrayal? They hadn't told him the whole truth about the mission, it seems. But he had been sent on a real mission, an extremely important mission — one man to divert a German division. That was worthwhile, even if it cost his life.

Around 1943, the British had dressed a corpse in an officer's uniform and planted it so the body would wash ashore carrying fake plans about the invasion of Italy.

It wouldn't have been that much of a stretch to send in a live agent believing his own false story. "Disinformation." "Psy-ops" — psychological operations. It made sense — at least if you focused only on the big picture, and tried not to think about the poor sucker who got stuck with the job.

If it was a psy-op, then maybe that explained the secrecy.

Still, why would it need to remain secret for 60 years after the war ended?

Lili stood and walked over to look down the street toward the port. Finally, she turned back to me and said, "But then something very unexpected happened."

She paused and took a deep breath. "By divine coincidence, when your Uncle Paul came to La Rochelle, he found not the Spear of Longinus, but instead what is perhaps the Holy Grail."

19

I stared at Lili. She *couldn't* have said what I heard. Or was this all just another set-up, another bizarre joke? "My uncle found the Holy Grail? But I thought the Grail was just a legend, not real."

Before she answered, the husband appeared at the door, tapping his wrist-watch.

"Henri reminds me that we must leave soon. We are meeting another couple for dinner. We have only a few minutes more to talk now. I am sorry."

"My Uncle Paul discovered the Holy Grail?"

She smiled and shook her head. "Ah, but I did not say it *was* the Grail. I said only that it was *perhaps* the Grail. Or perhaps it was something very different, not the Grail at all. All we know is that it was in a chest left here by the Templars, a thousand years ago."

"A *Templar* chest?" *La Rochelle and the Mysterious Treasure of the Knights Templar* — that little book that someone had left for me at the bookstore today.

"Any idea what was in that chest?" According to the radio operator, Paul had found "the most powerful weapon." Had the chest held that "weapon," whatever it was?

"No one knows for certain. But some people claimed the Templars were alchemists. Others said the Templars were the true Guardians of the Grail. But of course those are only old legends."

Alchemy, Grail, secret mystical organizations, and other assorted hocus-pocus. What the hell did this nonsense have to do with my uncle? Was I being jerked around here, just as we'd been jerked around for six decades?

Yet Lili seemed sincere enough. And that *was* Paul in the

photo, I was sure of that much.

"So my uncle came to La Rochelle supposedly looking for the Spear of Longinus, which was never here, but instead found a Templar chest, and — "

"No, that is not correct. He did not *find* the chest of the Templars. No, the fact is, it was *passed* to him, for safekeeping. You must understand the times. Your uncle was sent on a false lead, but that false information was really intended to mislead the Germans, and it did that. When they heard that the Holy Spear was hidden here in La Rochelle, that became a priority. Despite the invasion already underway, they sent soldiers, the SS and the Gestapo, here to La Rochelle, to search for that Spear, which of course was not ever here."

She shrugged. As the Eskimos have a hundred words for the different varieties of snow, so the French have a hundred ways of shrugging, each conveying nuances that are indecipherable for the non-French.

"In any case, the Germans were here in La Rochelle, searching house to house for the Spear, and it seemed only a matter of time before they would find the Templar Chest. At the time, it looked like the perfect solution when your uncle appeared looking for something important. Since a plane was coming to take him out, it was a way to get the Templar Chest away from the Nazis. Let your uncle take it away, so at least it would be safe in England."

"I talked to someone else here who told me that Paul found what he called 'the most powerful weapon.'" I threw that out to see how she would react.

Another of those Gallic shrugs. "Perhaps that is so, who can say? Did this person tell you of the Templar Chest?"

I shook my head. "Only that Paul radioed London that he had found something that he termed the most powerful weapon."

"*Most powerful weapon.*" Then I wondered: did Paul really send that, or was that how Farentoise translated it? Or was that the way he remembered it after all these years?

The more I learned the less I really knew.

Still, a weapon of some sort was the only reasonable explanation. The Templars were alleged alchemists and, by legend, guardians of the Grail. But alchemy was medieval nonsense, and the Holy Grail, the cup of the Last Supper, was just a legend. No one in a time of war would be interested in that, would they?

But what kind of thousand year old weapon could have been of any interest back in 1944, when atomic weaponry was already on the horizon?

"Maybe the story got a little mixed up," I suggested, groping to find a scenario that made sense. "Maybe there was some research into atomic energy being conducted here, and — "

"Yes, the Germans were conducting research into their own version of the atomic bomb, we know that now. But they would not do that here, not in France. Never. They would *never* trust us, for good reason."

❏

She walked out of the room, and I wondered if somehow I'd offended her. She returned with the bottle of wine. She refilled my glass, then poured the last of it for herself.

"There are many possibilities, yes. But I think what I have told you is the truth. Your uncle was given the chest of the Templars for safe-keeping. Alas, neither he nor that chest has been seen since."

"How did that chest get here? Why La Rochelle?"

"La Rochelle was the main Atlantic naval base for the Templars. Beyond that, it has long been an important seaport, and it was also a major base for the German submarines, especially early in the war. The allies sent bombers to damage the German submarine effort. Inevitably, some of the bombs went astray and hit in the town. One destroyed a building in the center of La Rochelle, in the area of the Templar Commanderie."

"I stopped for coffee at a café near the Commanderie today."

"Men searched the ruins of the building the night the bomb struck, looking for bodies. Fortunately, no one was seriously injured. But they found an ancient metal chest that had been hidden in the walls. They saw the Templar Cross on the chest, and covered it over again with debris so it would not fall into the hands of the Germans. Later, when the Germans were not around, they brought the chest to an educated man who was also a member of the Resistance, a professor before the war, Professor Dosois. It was his idea to hide it from the Nazis, and I think it was also his decision to pass it to your uncle."

"Is this professor still alive?"

"Alas, no, he's been dead many years."

Henri appeared. Now he was wearing his suit coat, and held a wrap for Lili. "We must go." He turned to me. "Perhaps you can come to talk another time, Monsieur." I didn't pick up any enthusiasm behind the suggstion.

"Do you know what happened to my uncle?," I asked Lili.

She shook her head. "It seems that both he and the chest disappeared the day after that photograph was taken. I think *Tante Cecile* never heard from him again."

20

I was already outside on the street when Lili threw open a window and called me back. "I remembered something that might help you."

It was a small tattered book. "I said that Aunt Cecile did much research to find the truth about your uncle and what happened to him. This was her book, one that she ordered from England. I think you should have it. Perhaps it will help you in your search."

British and American Covert Operations in Southern and South-Eastern France, 1942-1944. The author was a Professor G.B.W. Tabersley, a military historian at Oxford University.

I flipped through the book as I walked the quiet streets back to the hotel. No mention in the Index of Paul Tapscott (no surprise), nor of Operation Perceval (again no surprise), nor of any Templar chest found in La Rochelle (I'd have been surprised if there were).

There had been a number of reconnaissance operations in the La Rochelle area, scouting out the Nazi sub base there, but those all took place long before Paul's 1944 arrival here.

What did interest me was a footnote, referring to,

> . . . *the short visit to La Rochelle on 10 June 1944 by Col. Gniessbach of the Nazi Ahnenerbe, a branch of the SS. While some writers have speculated that Gniessbach's visit linked with the vicious German reprisal at Oradour, that is incorrect. In the first instance, the German records show that Gneissbach was on the ground not more than two hours, certainly not time enough to have made the journey to Oradour and back.*
>
> *Gniessbach, it should be remembered, led the German archaeological excavations at the Cathar*

fortress of Montsegur in the summer of 1943. That was clearly not a military operation. While nominally part of the SS, the Ahnenerbe or 'Ancestral Heritage Organization', popularly known as the Occult Bureau, consisted of what might be termed "scholars in uniform."

Oradour was a small town near Limoges where more than 600 French civilians were rounded up and killed on Saturday afternoon June 10, 1944, in retaliation for *Resistance* operations that killed a German officer and several soldiers.

The Cathars, the book explained, were a sect, nominally Christian, that flourished in southern France at the end of the previous millennium. Also known as the Albigensians (as they were centered around the city of Albi), they were condemned as heretics and stamped out in a campaign culminating in the fall of the last Cathar fortress of Montsegur in 1208.

Supposedly, on the night before Montsegur fell, four Cathars escaped from the mountain fortress carrying some kind of treasure. According to some of the legends, that treasure consisted of gold.

Other legends claimed that the "treasure" was the supposed Cathar secret of "creating unlimited wealth."

By still other accounts, that treasure was the Holy Grail.

Whatever it was, the treasure was never found, though there are some indications that it may have been passed to the Templars.

The story-line of the Cathars and their downfall seemed almost a pre-echo of the Templars' demise, less than a century later. Their wealth and alleged ability to tap occult secrets made them a target of those who were threatened by them, or envious, or both.

As had the Cathars, the Templars also spirited their treasure out just before the end. And, as with the Cathars, there are still no solid answers to the question of what that treasure consisted of.

Certainly some of the Templar treasure was made up of wagon-loads of gold and precious objects.

But what else? Did the Templars hide the occult secrets of creating unlimited wealth? Or other occult secrets of antiquity? Or was it the Holy Grail?

❏

No messages waited for me at the hotel. I was hungry, but intrigued enough to want to follow up on Professor Tabersley. I went online and pulled up a phone directory for Oxford, England, where there was only one G.W.B. Tabersley.

I called. A woman answered, and told me that the Professor was "indisposed," but that he was free to meet tomorrow lunchtime, and that his "usual honorarium" was £250. I said I'd be back in touch.

I checked my answering machine at home. Nothing further from Shelly Sherman. That was surprising, as she'd been so eager to talk about Cal yesterday. Maybe she was feeling better now. Or maybe she was at his memorial service.

I went online to see about a flight to England, then called back Tabersley's number in Oxford. She took my hotel's fax number and promised to send a confirmation and directions by morning.

21

The old port was ringed with restaurants, and ocean scents blended with the aromas of garlic and broiling fish.

It was low season, and I managed one of the prime tables on the sidewalk terrace overlooking the stone towers that had guarded the harbor entrance for centuries. Radiant heaters kept us warm despite the cool, salty air. Yachts and ocean-going sailboats now filled the old harbor of the Templars.

Maybe Uncle Paul walked past this spot sixty-some years ago.

Uncle Paul, Agent Perceval, who may have found what was "perhaps the Holy Grail," supposedly left by the Templars 900 years ago.

Past this spot, seven or eight centuries earlier, also walked the knights of the Templar order.

The Templars, supposed Guardians of the Holy Grail. But also supposed alchemists and heretics.

Cal Katz, killed within minutes of sending me that Butterfly warning. That was definitely not a drill.

❏

Even paranoids sometimes have real enemies.

A cold wind had come in off the Atlantic, rattling cans and leaves. The streets were dark and empty now, and I was on edge as I walked back to the hotel. I told myself it was just paranoia, that sense that I was being watched..

But I made it back safely to the hotel.

Where no messages were waiting for me.

❏

I called Dad to tell him about meeting Lili.

What I was going to tell him sounded bizarre — even to me, and I'd heard it all first-hand. Paul had been sent by the OSS to find the legendary Spear of Longinus. That, however, was only a cover story: the reality is that Paul's own people sent him to France intending for him to be captured, then tortured until he gave up a secret — a secret that was a lie from the start.

But Paul fooled them, and turned up, not the Holy Spear of Longinus, but something even more legendary: the Holy Grail. Yes, Dad, your brother found the Holy Grail. How 'bout that!

Or maybe not really the Holy Grail, after all, but some kind of atomic weapon that the Knights Templar had stored away in a chest seven hundred years earlier.

Either he'll be so sedated by the drugs he's taking that he'll say "good job," or he'll ask what kind of drugs *I* was sniffing to come up with that kind of scenario.

But I didn't get to tell him any of it. "Your father cannot come to the phone," Mrs. Fox told me, sounding almost pleased.

"Can't come? Why not?"

"Didn't I tell you that his healthy spell was too good to last? He tired himself out. Now he needs to rest. Maybe he'll have a little strength tomorrow, though I doubt it. He's failing fast. You should stop this running around the world and spend these final days here with him."

❏

The phone rang again, moments after I hung up. "*Monsieur*, a fax has arrived for you."

A man's thick scrawl:

Noon
Turf Bar, Oxford
Duck or grouse
Morse with a moustache

Whatever that meant.

Day Three

"You say you're shaking my faith in reality to prepare me for what you call the Knowledge? What's your point?"

"To the contrary, I am only shaking your faith in apparent reality, to open your mind to the possibilities that open in the deeper reality. The discoveries of modern science are confirming the intuitive insights of the ancient wisdom. The findings of modern science and modern thinkers help us understand how physical reality — that is, reality as we believe we know it — is largely a construction of our minds. Today's technology demonstrates that we live in a flexible world that is mostly energy."

He paused, then added, "Once we grasp the implications that flow from that — that the world in which we live is largely energy, and that our minds can be transformers of energy — then a totally different view of reality opens up. Then you can begin applying the Knowledge in your life."

"But what is the Knowledge?" I blurted in frustration, immediately wishing I had just let it pass. Don't ask a question of a lonely old monk if you don't have hours to listen to his answer.

From
JOINING MIRACLES:
Navigating the Seas of Latent Possibility
by "P"

22

I woke early and stood by the open window, watching dawn come to La Rochelle, hearing the morning's stillness broken only by the cries of sea-birds and the low throbbing of a fishing boat headed out to sea.

Massive cumulus clouds over the Atlantic gleamed like soft pink marble pillars in the rays of a sun that hadn't yet touched land; the water in the channel shimmered, reflecting the rosy glow of the sky.

The tang of salt hung in the air, blending with the scents of fish and mud flats, and the aromas of rich coffee and hot croissants drifting up from the hotel kitchen.

La Rochelle was a fairy-tale town. It would have been a nice place to explore. Maybe another time, but not now, not with Dad's time running out.

❏

Change of planes at Paris-De Gaulle. I grabbed the *International Herald-Tribune,* hoping for more news on Cal Katz.

Nothing. Probably it was just what it seemed: Cal's bad luck to come home and find a violent addict going through the apartment.

Still, it seemed more than coincidence, coming minutes after he'd sent that fax: *You are the Butterfly. Sending very important info regarding our most recent conversation. THIS IS NOT A DRILL!*

❏

It was tempting to forget about going to London, and just catch the first plane to Boston. I could be in Burlington by mid-afternoon.

But that wasn't what Dad wanted.

I found an internet café at the airport, scanned in the photo Lili had given me of Paul with Cecile, and e-mailed it to him so it would be waiting when he flicked on his computer in the morning. That would give him a lift.

Then — was it really another coincidence? — I spotted a pink backpack in line at the boarding gate for the flight to London. Carried by a chestnut-haired woman wearing white shoes with pink laces. The woman I'd seen in La Rochelle yesterday, taking pictures of the Templar area. That was 300 miles back, and now she was making the same two flight connections to the same place.

❏

I made it through British customs and immigration, and caught the shuttle bus from Heathrow to Oxford.

No sign now of the woman with the pink backpack. Too bad, in a way; it might have been interesting to meet. But the good news was it meant that she wasn't following me.

I left my bag at the railway station and caught a cab to the Turf Bar.

I'd never been to Oxford and envisioned it as a quaint medieval university town of turrets and spires clustered around a quiet little village filled with quaint pubs and shops. The turrets and spires were there, but I had the proportions wrong: today's Oxford is a commercial city, and the colleges are the adjunct.

The cab driver threaded through the tight streets, providing glimpses of grassy quadrangles nearly hidden behind the stone walls of the colleges before pulling up at the entrance to a narrow alleyway.

The light mist and cool fresh air felt good on my face as I walked the warren of passageways between the high stone walls of the college buildings.

I came around a corner and saw the little white pub that was the Turf Bar, and had an image of the way things used to be back in the days when those twisting alleyways had been footpaths between sheep-meadows.

A turf fire burned in an outdoor fireplace; the smoke triggered memories of charcoal grills and wood-fires at the beach.

It was dark and cozy inside, and a couple of framed photos commemorated the times the Turf Bar had been used in the *Inspector Morse* mystery series on PBS.

Then it clicked. "Morse with a moustache," Tabersley had faxed. A Morse look-alike?

But what was "Duck or grouse?"

I got a half-pint of the thick local beer, and wandered through the hodge-podge of rooms that had been grafted on over the centuries.

The second room was larger and more open, with dark wooden rafters lacing through stone walls. The aromas of burning turf and hot food mingled, and I realized I was hungry.

Of the dozen tables, only a couple were occupied now. At one, a couple of guys were speaking German; three young women huddled over glasses of wine at another. One popped a pill and washed it down with her Chablis, and I heard a snatch of a phrase: "a good little pick-me-up to get through the day."

I spotted an outdoor area enclosed by plastic walls, a sheltered garden for bad weather. Someone had painted the words "Duck or Grouse" on the low rafter that hung over the entrance. Duck your head, or grouse over the consequences.

I ducked my head and peered in: one man, sixtyish, ruddy-faced, a thatch of unruly white hair. A reasonable look-alike for Inspector Morse, but he sported the kind of bushy white Guards' moustache that the prickly Morse would scorn.

"Professor Tabersley?"

"Dr. Livingston, I presume?"

"No, I'm Greg —"

"A joke, my young friend, merely a joke." Tabersley stood to shake hands, then brought his empty glass to the side window that accessed the bar. I gulped the last of my half-pint, and ordered another. Tabersley let me pay for both.

In his rumpled tweed jacket and knit tie, he projected an air of academic seediness, though he bore the blotchy nose and cheeks of a dedicated drinker.

❏

"We'll be left alone out here in the garden," he said after inhaling the first third of his pint. "We can talk without being overheard."

A couple, mid-30's, stepped through the opening and settled at a table on the far side. Both wore gray business suits. Even their faces looked gray — too many hours in offices and pubs. The man went to the bar for drinks while the woman fumbled in the large canvas bag she used as a purse. Probably lovers out for a covert drink.

"So, my young friend, tell me: why are you really here? Why this interest in my all-but-forgotten book?"

I figured there was nothing to lose by leveling with him, so told him about Uncle Paul, and the family's long quest to find the truth.

He took his time lighting his pipe, then said, "All that was a long time ago, so why are you here? Why now?"

I didn't want to say more than necessary, but at this point I felt I didn't have much choice. "Earlier this week, a couple of men, supposedly from the CIA, appeared at my father's door, asking about Paul, asking when the family had last heard from him."

"Which I presume was 60-some years ago?"

I nodded and handed him the letter Willoughby sent to Dad, pointing out that it arrived by messenger minutes after the CIA men left.

"You're certain they really were CIA?"

I'd asked Dad that question, and immediately regretted it when I saw embarrassment flash across his eyes. He'd neglected to look closely at their credentials. He'd slipped up — an old ball-player who'd lost a step and knew it.

Tabersley shrugged. "No matter, the larger question is what possible link a man of 1944 could have with a terrorist group active today. Did they say what group it was?"

"They told Dad they couldn't answer that, as it was a matter of national security."

"I'm not surprised. Intelligence organizations take information in and give nothing back — unless it's a way of collecting more information."

He studied the letter, then asked, "Looking at the date, I presume you've already been to La Rochelle. Turn up anything there?"

Instead of replying, I set the context by telling him about that other letter from Cecile Du Fresne that indicated that Paul may have been alive in La Rochelle as late as the ninth or tenth of June, 1944, two days after the U.S. Government claimed he'd been killed in Normandy.

"I presume you passed that information on to the authorities?"

"My family did, at the time. The reply came back that there had been an error, along with revised official word that Paul had died trying to blow a bridge near La Rochelle on June 11. They sent us a photo of a plaque commemorating an unknown American soldier, and told us that Paul was that soldier."

"Utter bloody nonsense, of course. If the soldier was indeed unknown, then how could they then claim it was your uncle? I see that sort of thing time and again as I do my research. So arrogant, so damned arrogant, they are – forever taking us for such fools. Well, perhaps you and I shall at last open this up."

23

I gave him the materials Dad had prepared for me, copies of files the family had accumulated over the years.

First, copies of that pair of photos that had rested in matching frames on the piano at the old family home in Burlington since long before I'd been born. The first showed Paul in a long black cassock, standard garb in the Jesuit seminary.

The second photo, taken a couple of years later in the summer of 1943, when he finished basic flight school, showed a romantic figure in a canvas flight helmet and goggles, his new silver wings prominent on his chest. He looked very pleased with himself.

"It was a proud day for Paul, the day he won his wings," Dad had said so often, then he would usually add, "But something happened, and I think that's the key to this whole damned thing."

Paul Tapscott, strange combination of warrior and would-be priest. Uncle Paul, pilot and spy. He'd been about 23 when this picture was taken, and the resemblance between us was striking. I'm a dozen years older now than Paul had been in the photo, a couple of inches taller, and 15 or 20 pounds heavier, but we still look enough alike to be brothers, almost twins, sharing the same wavy dark hair, the long nose, the strong eyebrows, the same smile.

Paul graduated from Georgetown University just before the start of the war, a history major, and spent some time traveling around Europe, managing to sell some free-lance articles on what he saw in the shadow of the looming war. Then, apparently to no one's surprise, he announced that he planned to enter the Jesuit order and study for the priesthood.

The Jesuits are the elite among the orders of the Catholic

Church — the best educated, with advanced degrees the norm. His parents were delighted and honored.

Founded in the 1500's by Ignatius Loyola, a former soldier, the Jesuit structure and discipline were intentionally modeled on that of military organizations. Education is the order's top priority now, and Paul's *alma mater*, Georgetown University in Washington, is the oldest and most prominent of those they founded in this country.

But the Jesuits had played different roles in earlier centuries. By some accounts, they functioned as the Pope's intelligence-gathering unit. Some claimed that Jesuits had set up and formed the core of secret societies operating within the government of certain countries.

Their legendary spiritual disciplines — some claimed the exercises bordered on the occult — further heightened the image.

A quasi-military clandestine spiritual order – that was the mystique of the Jesuits, and very likely part of what drew Paul to the order.

Intriguingly, that was also the mystique of the Knights Templar . . . as I'd discovered yesterday in La Rochelle — where Paul was last seen.

24

Tabersley finished the file, looked out into the garden for a moment, then said, "My specialty is military history, particularly clandestine operations of World War II. What you have laid before me touches, coincidentally, on some still some unanswered questions about activities in those days before and after D-Day."

"Unanswered? Relevant to my uncle?"

Tabersley shrugged again. "Too soon to know." He stood, swayed, and steadied himself on a chair for balance. "I propose we eat, while we can still navigate our way to the buffet. Then we can talk at leisure."

❑

He led the way with careful steps to the doorway, ducked under the Duck or Grouse overhang, then headed down a kind of alleyway to the food, located in a small annex.

He touched the walls for balance every few steps, reminding me of those videos of astronauts ricocheting off the corridors of the space shuttle.

The aromas of hot meats and spices coming from the buffet room at the back were heavy, greasy, and tantalizing. I tried the Shepherd's Pie; Tabersley had lasagna. Once on the plate, it was hard to tell the dishes apart.

He worked through half his plate, then said: "What does not seem to fit the OSS pattern for that stage of the war is the fact that your uncle was operating alone, not as part of a Jedburgh or Sussex unit. Further, that he was in La Rochelle, significantly away from Normandy."

He dug another couple of fork-fulls off the plate, then said,

"However, let us suppose that your uncle was indeed in La Rochelle at the date in question. Why would the powers-that-be deny it? Why would they still try to hide the truth? What intrigues me is the cover-up, the reluctance after all these years to come clean with the family."

"So you do think there was a cover-up, that it's not just our paranoia, not just a foul-up?"

"If it walks like a duck and smells like a duck, then it's probably a cover-up. But why would it continue for some 60 years?"

❏

Time to give him another piece of the puzzle. Maybe he could make sense of it. "In La Rochelle yesterday, I heard from a couple of sources that my uncle was sent to a Resistance unit that the OSS already knew had fallen under German control."

"Why would they do that?"

I told him what Lili had said, that Agent Perceval had been sent in with the cover story of retrieving the Holy Spear, as a way of distracting Hitler and that tank division on its race up to reinforce at Normandy. I didn't add that Perceval had found what was "perhaps" the Holy Grail.

He shrugged. "No doubt you find that shocking, that your uncle may have been misled and indeed sacrificed by his own people. In normal times, yes. But this was war, and the stakes were immense. He was a soldier, and sometimes soldiers must be sent to die. That's what war is."

He lifted his empty glass, then knocked it back onto the table. I let the hint pass. Despite the food, Tabersley's eyes were getting blurry, and I needed to get solid answers before he faded.

"But do you understand the significance of the so-called Holy Spear?," he asked.

"I know what it was, the Roman centurion's lance. Longinus used it in giving the *coup de grace* to Jesus on the cross."

"Yes, but why would that have been of significance during World War II?"

This was Oxford, and I had the feeling I'd be the dumbest guy in one of his tutorials. "I have no idea," I responded, really wanting to say, That's why the hell I'm here, to have you tell me.

"Because Hitler and Himmler and some of the others were bloody obsessed with the occult. The Spear has been an artifact of spiritual power for the past two thousand years. The legends have it that whoever possessed the Spear in effect controlled great spiritual power. It was a talisman bringing the power of the so-called 'other side' — spiritual forces — to bear in this world. Charlemagne had it, Napoleon possessed it for a time, and so quite naturally Hitler wanted it. Indeed, one of the first things he did after taking over Austria was to send his people to grab the Spear and move it to Germany, and it's said he gained immense confidence by having possession of it. It seems he really did believe that it enhanced his powers."

He paused to light his pipe again before going on. "It would have been quite a clever ploy indeeed, convincing Hitler that what he had was not the true Spear, particularly at D-Day. It might have been enough to shatter his confidence, enough to cause him to divert all resources to grabbing this supposed true spear."

Another try at lighting the pipe. "*Now* what you say makes sense. *Now* I understand why your uncle — if, indeed, it was he — would have been sent on a bogus mission. The cover story was bogus, but the mission, of diverting the *Das Reich* SS tank division, was very real."

He puffed the pipe. Aromatic clouds enveloped me, suggesting forests and berries, and making my eyes burn.

Then he said, "When you mentioned the Spear of Longinus, a name came to mind, though it is a long shot, a very long shot. There is someone who might just have some answers for you."

He lumbered to his feet. "I need to make a few phone calls. Wait for me, have another pint." As if an afterthought, he added, "Might as well order me another while you're up."
❏
He returned after ten minutes or so, his face even more flushed. "I managed to turn up a couple of very interesting leads. One of them agreed to meet with you today. As for the other, I'm still in the process of making contact, hoping for a call-back any moment."

"I was planning to fly back to the States tomorrow."

"I'm offering to put you in contact with perhaps the last two people walking the face of the earth who might know the truth about your uncle. Are you interested, or are you not?"

It didn't require much thought. I nodded. "Maybe I can catch a later flight tomorrow."

"If the second one agrees, then it means a trip to Germany. But I suspect it will be well worth your while if you make the journey. Are you interested? Yes? No?"

"Germany," I hesitated. Then said, "Yes, on your recommendation." Would he still make the same recommendation if he hadn't downed all those pints of beer?

"I've also arranged for you the rare privilege of meeting with Larkwood, reported to be principal author of the legendary Larkwood Report. You're doubtless familiar with it?"

"Larkwood Report? Never heard of it," I said, but he didn't hear, as he broke off to cough.

He gave me the details of how and when to get to Larkwood's home, then said, "The other contact, presuming he's not already residing in the deepest regions of hell, could be even more valuable to you. I'll be in touch when and if I hear from him."

25

It was still drizzling when I left the Turf Bar. I wandered back to the main part of town, not sure what I had gotten into.

It did sound as though — maybe — I was finally breaking through to people who might know the truth. But was it the real thing, or just another in that long string of false leads?

I phoned Dad, hoping for his input. Mrs. Fox answered. "Your father and I are about to leave for a doctor's appointment. He does not have time to talk now. However, he does seem to be having a good day, so far. Good, of course, given his condition."

❏

There was plenty of time before the meeting Tabersley had arranged, so I stopped in a bookshop and asked one of the clerks if they had anything on the Larkwood Report.

Her look suggested I'd asked for something particularly kinky, then led me to a section that seemed to be on the cusp between modern history and the paranormal. A peculiar spot for it, but as I quickly found out, the so-called Larkwood Report was a very peculiar subject.

The first mentions were in books by professional debunkers, and they treated Larkwood as a joke on the True Believers and Conspiracy Freaks who took it seriously.

From those books and others, I pieced together that the Larkwood Report was a legend, but *only* a legend: there was no proof that there ever had been such a report, no official confirmation, nor even official denial.

Legendary or not, a cult following had sprung up around the Larkwood Report, people convinced that the same forces within the

U.S. Government that refused to release the bodies of the aliens who supposedly crashed in the desert at Roswell, New Mexico, in 1947 were also covering up the truth of what Larkwood had found in the ruins of Nazi Germany

The Roswell incident in 1947, the Larkwood Report of 1946, and the disappearance of Paul Tapscott and whatever he found around 1944. All three in roughly the same mid-1940's time-frame. Coincidence or conspiracy?

The Report that supposedly didn't exist got its unofficial name from Dr. Horace Larkwood, a psychology professor who had served as a civilian employee of the U.S. Government during World War II, doing unknown research.

❏

Larkwood lived in a converted carriage house, on a mews behind a larger house at the edge of the town. The drizzle had ended, and a pale sun was peeking through the clouds.

A tall woman in a blue cotton uniform answered the door. "You are Mr. Tapscott," she said, no welcome in her voice, then led me to an enclosed porch at the back, what the Brits call the "conservatory."

A skeletal old man sat hunched in a wheelchair, a wool blanket over his legs despite the sun's warmth. Professor Larkwood held out a hand. It was bony, the skin dry and cool. His eyes, sunken back into the skull, glittered Wedgewood blue, welcoming but shrewd.

"Find yourself a chair, make yourself comfortable. Elsie tells me she's only going to let me have half an hour with you before she drags me away for my nappy-time."

He turned to the woman. "Now Elsie, why don't you bring our young visitor a nice cup of tea?"

Larkwood maneuvered his electric wheelchair around to face a green grassy slope that led down to a small river.

Then he shook his head. "I rarely receive visitors, particularly those interested in the report. However, Tabersley vouches for you, and that's in your favor. But I'll tell you at the start, if you've come here hoping to read the Larkwood Report, then yours has been a fruitless journey. I don't have a copy, none of us on the team were allowed to keep a copy of our own work. Once we finished writing it, they took it away from us, classified it too top-secret for the likes of us to be trusted with. Officially, our work never happened. As you perhaps know, the report isn't merely classified, it's as if it never *did* exist."

Larkwood shook his head. "Should have known even then that the government was slipping out of control."

I suddenly realized that his accent was not exactly British, and then I understood: he was born American but had lived here for much of his life. Why was that?

"Who classified your report? Why?"

"The question is not who *classified* it, the real question is who's *still afraid* to let it see the light of day? And why? Questions for which I don't have answers."

❑

He let that hang in the air, part query, part warning.

I said, "I didn't come here to see your Report. The fact is, I'd never heard of it until an hour or so ago, when Professor Tabersley arranged for us to meet. What I want, *all* I want, is to find what happened to my uncle."

I told him about the family's 60-year quest for the truth of what happened to Paul, along with most of what I'd turned up in La Rochelle: that he'd been sent in on Operation Perceval, a bogus mission, supposedly to find the real Spear of Longinus. I didn't mention that he had turned up the Templar Chest, nor that it might have held the Holy Grail, or some kind of thousand-year old weapon.

He listened, then said, "When Tabersley mentioned there might be a link with Operation Perceval I decided then and there that we needed to talk . . . even if I had to wheel myself to London in this damned chair."

Elsie returned with a china pot of tea, and two cups. She filled both cups, then said, "If you're *sure*, professor, that you'll be all right?"

"Been all right for 96 years, odds are I'll make it through the next hour. Better you go take a nap, you're looking a bit peaked yourself."

Larkwood took a few sips of his tea before saying, "I'm not supposed to talk to anyone about my report, not even acknowledge that the report ever existed."

He took another sip. "They threatened me, back when I had Mavis and young children. The old carrot and stick: keep your mouth shut and good things will happen to you. But if you ever talk, you can count on facing IRS audits every year for the rest of your life — and they will be the *least* of your problems."

He looked directly at me. "You can understand that when the opportunity came to live and work over here, I took it. It seemed prudent. I had a family to think about."

He chuckled. "But things like that don't scare me any longer. *Nothing* scares me. What can they do to an old geezer like me? Give me the death penalty? Hell's Bells, I'm already living under a death sentence, and execution day is coming up any time now."

He shimmied himself up in the wheelchair. "Whether silencing me was bureaucratic idiocy or something more, I don't know. But no matter: I remember every word in that report, every footnote, every source, every odd little detail. Might not be able to recall what I had for breakfast this morning, but I do remember what went into that report. I remember some other things, odd little details, that *didn't* make it into the final draft."

I waited, letting the silence hang in the air.

Finally, Larkwood said, "I've been thinking things over since Tabersley called, and I decided I'm going to do all I can to help solve your puzzle. It's time I talked to somebody about it. While I still can. It's time the truth came out."

26

Larkwood began by putting his report in context. It was 1945. The war with Germany was drawing to a close, but the threat loomed of a new conflict with Stalin. The Americans, the British, and the French all set up teams to sweep through Germany to grab the Nazi technology before the Russians could cart it away. As much as the Nazis were hated, the German technological advances were respected, even to the point of awe.

Most of the interest centered on weaponry: rocketry, aircraft design, the German atomic program.

But there were indications that the Germans had been doing some work on another kind of science. "For want of a better term, we referred to that as 'intangible science.' That intangible science was the focus of what's come to be known as the Larkwood Report."

"Intangible science? I haven't heard that term."

"Ever hear of the Foo Fighters?"

"Foo Fighters? The rock group?" The Foo Fighters came along in the mid-1990's, definitely not Uncle Paul's era, and I wondered if this trip was a waste of time. Maybe Larkwood was terminally confused.

"No, no, I'm referring to the *real* Foo Fighters. Around the end of '44, American bomber pilots flying over Germany began coming back with stories of little balls of light that suddenly began appearing around their planes. Some described them as energy balls, others as flying crystal balls. Somebody dubbed them Foo Fighters, and the name stuck."

"They sound like UFO's."

"That term came along only years later. Officially, the powers-that-be within the military pooh-poohed the idea of Foo Fighters. But that was just for public consumption, the usual show of bravado to calm the troops. In private, the brass wanted to know what the hell was going on. Were these balls of energy bouncing around in the skies some kind of Nazi secret weapon? Maybe some sort of a death ray that hadn't quite been perfected? In short, what in blazes had the Krauts come up with?"

Larkwood shook his head, took a breath, and continued. "But there were other crazy things the Nazis had been exploring. `Crazy,' that is, if you operate only from a conventional world view. But *were* they really so crazy, after all? That's what some folks in the government sent me to find out."

"Did you turn up anything about my uncle — about Operation Perceval — in your report?"

Larkwood shrugged. "I stumbled on Operation Perceval — that is, what I *believe* was Perceval — only by chance. Or maybe by synchronicity, one of those cosmic jokes that make life so interesting. I had a hunch that Perceval, whatever it was, just might be relevant to the work we were doing, so I asked for a briefing. That briefing never happened. Nobody ever said 'No,' nobody ever said 'Perceval is off-limits.' They just didn't cooperate, didn't respond at all. Nowadays they call it stone-walling. So I made it my business to find out on my own."

He rested, letting the breath come back, and I realized that the energy in his eyes and manner were deceptive.

"Operation Perceval, as I explored it, seemed to have two phases. First was the apparent decoy operation to France in early June of '44. After that, nothing from Agent Perceval for nearly a year, just silence. Naturally, the assumption arose that Agent Perceval had been captured, probably killed. But then things changed. It seems that after being dormant for a year, Agent Perceval 'awakened,' and made radio contact some time during the month of April, 1945, a few days before the end."

"Awakened?," I echoed, jolted by the possibility. "But — but how could they know it was really him?"

Larkwood shrugged his bony shoulders. "That I don't know, though I did raise the same question at the time. There were backup codes, memorized by the agent for just such a possibility. Of course, the Germans could have forced that kind of information out of him, then used it. But it seems that his people, the OSS, took it to be an authentic communication."

I tried to keep my expression neutral, tried to hold back the burst of elation I was suddenly feeling. At last, I was finally getting somewhere.

Still, though, there remained the question: suppose Paul *did* survive to the end of the war, *then* what happened to him?

For the first time, I noticed a grandfather clock ticking loudly somewhere behind me. I might be getting to the truth at last, but Dad's final days were ticking by.

Then Larkwood went on: "The interesting thing was that when he 'woke,' Agent Perceval was positioned in the Austrian Alps, in the area south of Munich, the Alpine Fortress the Nazis had been developing for a final stand. No idea what his message said, but, given the context of the times, odds were it related to a German looking to barter in exchange for saving his skin. There was a lot of that going on, just about then. In any case, Perceval's message lit a fire at OSS HQ, by then in Paris, and it seems a team jumped on a plane and got there *tout de suite.*"

I hesitated, almost afraid to ask the question: "Did they find any trace of Perceval?"

Larkwood shrugged, his bony shoulders evident even through the thick sweater. "All records were lost — so they said. Or, according to another alibi, burned up in a mysterious warehouse file. We tried to interview certain people. Couldn't get to them — to one in particular. Supposedly he was engaged in some super hush-hush work, so we never were able to finish that story. Then the word came from upstairs, this time really strong: Move on, forget you ever heard about Perceval."

Larkwood shook his head. "But I wasn't about to give up, because I'd become convinced by that point that Operation Perceval, and whatever it led to, was the key to the whole Nazi program for tapping these higher powers I'd been sent to explore."

"Higher powers?"

"Agent Perceval – whoever he was – apparently stumbled on what the Nazis had been looking for all along."

"What was that? What had they been looking for?"

"Whether there was a power within the human mind – or at least within certain trained minds – that can direct and focus energies from other dimensions."

27

I took a sip of tea, stalling for time to absorb what he'd said, and what it implied. "A power within the mind that can direct and focus energies from other dimensions? Are you suggesting that Perceval uncovered some kind of occult power?"

Should I level with him? Should I tell him what Lili said? That Paul may have found the Templar Chest, which contained what was "perhaps" the Holy Grail. Or was "perhaps" the most dangerous weapon the world has ever known.

Larkwood continued before I could speak. "Occult power? Or was it an artifact of some kind? I never found that out. But whatever he turned up became of extreme interest to his American control officers back in England, and to the Germans, which —"

The door opened and Elsie walked in. "Time for you to rest, Professor."

"A couple of minutes, Elsie. My young friend and I need a bit more time to finish our chat."

She hesitated, then backed away. "You do need your rest, Professor."

He turned back to me. "As to the question behind all of this — whether I can tell you what happened to the agent who was Perceval." He let it hang in the air, then shook his head sadly, "That I do not know for certain, but I've always been of the opinion that Perceval, whoever he was, slipped away from both the Germans and the Americans."

I felt as if I'd been spun in the chair. "Slipped away from both? He wasn't killed by the Germans? Why would he run from his own people?"

"Perhaps because he grasped the real significance of what he'd turned up, and concluded it was too dangerous to allow it to fall into the wrong hands."

"What 'wrong hands?'"

He shook his head. "If only I knew. It is curious that I was later blocked from investigating this Operation Perceval."

Something came to mind, something said by De Lattry, the canny old lawyer in La Rochelle: *Governments take on lives of their own. Bureaucracies grow within them, power bases develop, and subtly, over the span of years, things change. All it takes is a few determined men working silently within.*

"He slipped away, you think. But then what? Did he survive?"

"Who can say. I never came on any indication, one way or the other. But of course there was the cover-up that blocked me from exploring the whole Perceval issue."

"Why would they keep that cover-up going for 60 years, even against his family?"

"Perhaps sheer bureaucratic inertia. Perhaps something more sinister. I have no idea."

"Why? Who would care enough for so long?"

"If you find the answer to that, I hope you will tell me."

❑

Time for me to give some back. I told him the story as Lili had told me in La Rochelle, of the old Templar Chest that had been uncovered in the bombing raid, and Paul's blunder in radioing back to OSS London on a code that the Germans had already broken.

He nodded, as if he'd been expecting to hear something like that for the past sixty-odd years.

❑

The door opened. Elsie strode in, grasped the handles of the Professor's wheelchair, and pulled it back out the door. "My public calls," Larkwood said as he was zipped back into the hallway. He looked embarrassed. "Leave me your phone number in case anything else comes to mind."

"That power you think Paul found in the Templar Chest: any

idea what it might have been?"

Larkwood reached down and hit the handbrakes on the wheelchair. Elsie stumbled over it, then backed away, glaring at me.

"First, we need to be precise," Larkwood said. "I think he did *not* find any *thing* in the chest. That's to say, there was not a magic amulet or a wand or a cup or a spear or any other nonsense like that. I think what was important in the chest was not any particular artifact, but rather the *knowledge* — the practical how-to — it may have contained."

I waited for Larkwood to go on, wondering how long Elsie would allow before she moved again.

"But what that knowledge actually was?" Larkwood shook his head. "Unfortunately, that I was never able to ascertain." He looked at me, his watery eyes sad. "Just as I was never able to determine what happened to Agent Perceval."

"One more thing, if you have the time," I said.

"Take as much time as the Good Lord, and of course Elsie, allow me to have."

I quickly told him about the visit of the CIA men to Dad that started this renewed search for Paul, and their claim that Paul's name had come up several times in the chatter of some unnamed terrorist organization. "Any ideas what group that might be, or why they'd have interest in Paul and what he found way back then?"

He shook his head, barely more than a slight nod in each direction, so frail he was. "I have no real idea how this could link with any terrorist group. Did they mention which one? There are hundreds of them, perhaps thousands."

"They told my father that the name of the group was classified."

"They're still playing that game, pump the source, but never prime the pump." He cleared his throat. "This is pure speculation, what I'm about to say, an old man's nightmares. But now that you raise the issue, something *has* indeed been troubling me. This so-called concert that's coming up, Twisted Messiah. That's no concert, not to an old man's eyes. That's Nuremberg again, done up in modern style. Do you understand the allusion?"

I nodded, taking a moment to put it together. I knew of Twisted Messiah, of course, you couldn't be alive these days without hearing more than you wanted about the group and the event. In my mind, they were a garbage group, but master media exploiters.

What surprised me was that their fame — or *infamy* — had even reached somebody like Larkwood.

"Nuremberg — you're referring to Hitler's Nuremberg rallies?" I'd seen the old movies of masses of marchers, spotlights tracing virtual cathedral walls into the summer night sky, then Hitler mesmerizing the masses with his rhetoric.

"Precisely so. But this Jesse Cripes is a mere singer, so they say. Nonsense. This old man sees chilling similarities to what the Nazis did, stirring up the deeper, darker emotions, harnessing the energies of the unthinking, aimless, ungrounded rabble. They are after the same effects, translated to today's idiom and today's media."

I wondered what this old man, brought up in a more genteel time, had thought of Twisted Messiah's toilet video.

"Are you suggesting that Twisted Messiah could have some interest in Paul and what he found? Even so, how could they have turned up more than his own family after all these years?"

"I have no answers."

❑

Elsie came in then and without another word pushed his chair out the door and down the corridor. I followed, despite the look she threw over her shoulder.

He hit the brakes again, and Elsie stopped short with a grunt. "I failed to make my point. Let us assume, for the sake of the argument, that it *was* in fact the Twisted Messiah crowd who have been following your uncle's career."

"I'd never . . . never thought about that." It seemed far-fetched. Then.

"But suppose it is the case. What would that mean? Does it mean that they also are pursuing what the Nazis pursued: a power within the mind that can direct and focus energies from other dimensions."

"Direct and focus energies from other dimensions — I don't really understand what that means."

"What they were exploring, groping for in the darkness of that time of limited knowledge, is what the scientists of today are also groping for. The mind is a real force. Everything is mind-stuff — I'm quoting Sir James Jeans on that, of course. What I think we're finally beginning to realize is that our world is far different, and far more wonderful and mysterious, than we realize. And I suspect that whatever your uncle turned up may have been, potentially, a crucial tool for our understanding just what our human capabilities are in this wider, more wondrous world."

❑

I was finally at the door, escorted by Elsie with a hand firmly on my elbow, when Larkwood said, "What your uncle turned up is a crucial tool for our understanding of just what our human capabilities are in this wider, more wondrous world. No, not just for *understanding*. It seems that what he found was *practical knowledge,* how to apply those greater capabilities. That knowledge must not get into the wrong hands. It *must* not. You must see that it does not."

"I'm trying."

"It's an awesome responsibility, but one that seems to be the destiny of your family to bear."

28

Our world is far different, more wonderful and mysterious, than we realize. . . . And I suspect that whatever your uncle turned up is a crucial tool for our understanding just what our human capabilities are in this wider, more wondrous world.

Larkwood's final words echoed in my mind as the choir sang vespers. I'd walked back across Oxford after leaving his home, and had been drawn by the music coming from the massive yet somehow delicate sandstone cathedral, with its ceiling soaring toward the heavens.

Now I was finding myself moved in a way that no church had moved me since childhood, recharging me with that old sense that there was a meaning and depth of reality that we could never grasp.

Our world is far different, more wonderful and mysterious, than we realize.

My father and mother had always been religious — scrupulous about Mass on Sundays, faithful in keeping the rules, even insisting on our getting together to say the rosary during lent. But I'd wondered, even as a teenager, how much of that was spiritual zeal, and how much just playing by the rules. Mom and Dad belonged to that generation where you followed the rules in everything — the rules set by the corporation, by the community, by the dress codes of the country club and the restaurant.

But for me church-going had come to feel too much like just going through the motions, paying dues, getting the ticket stamped, punching the religious time-clock, and I'd drifted away when I went away to college. Too many repetitions of what seemed the same old sterile rituals had left me numb.

Naturally, that had been a point of major contention with Dad; now not only was I failing to play by the rules of church-going, but was failing as well to get my career ticket stamped with a steady job and clear career-progression.

But all those differences faded as I let the music fill me and recharge my spirit as I sat in the back of the cathedral, one of a hundred or so souls.

The mind is a real force. Everything is mind-stuff. Sir James Jeans.

That was from the new world-view of quantum physics, but not so very different from a lot of the old messages they'd taught back in my Catholic-school days:

Prayer works. The spiritual is real. What we experience on the material plane is only a shadow of all there is.

Nor so very far from what Larkwood was saying about the new discoveries, and about how all of that tied in with what Paul may have found: *Our world is far different, and far more wonderful and mysterious, than we realize. Whatever your uncle turned up may have been, potentially, a crucial tool for our understanding just what our human capabilities are in this wider, more wondrous world.*

And: *A power within the mind that can direct and focus energies from other dimensions.*

The mind is a real force. Everything is mind-stuff.

29

I dozed through most of the train ride back to London, feeling the after-blast of too many beers with Tabersley. I paused at a news-kiosk at Euston Station, wondering if, by any chance, today's *Washington Post* had made it this far. Any developments on the murder of Cal Katz?

No *Post*, but something even more intriguing: that gray man in the gray suit walked past, the man who had shared the garden room at the Turf Bar with Tabersley and I, and his lady-friend. Another coincidence? Had he just popped up from London to visit an old flame?

I let him pass, then tried to follow, but I was bogged down with my carry-on and quickly lost him in the crowd.

❏

My time in London was short, and I didn't feel up to fighting the Circle Line all the way round to South Kensington, so caught a cab from the stand in front.

A man jumped in with me. That was surprising, as I'd always found the British good about not jumping lines. I started to protest, but he smiled and said, "My treat, we're headed the same place."

He passed the driver a £5 note. "Let's hear some music."

"What kind of music, gov?"

"*Loud* music. My friend and I want to have a private chat."

He flipped a wallet open and showed me a photo ID. I looked at it closely. It did seem to be genuine CIA identification, and he was the guy in the photo: mid-30's, prematurely white hair.

But an infectious smile.

"How do I know your ID is real? What do you want from me?"

"That's exactly how your Dad reacted when we visited him the day before yesterday."

"It was you who saw him?"

"That was me, along with a friend from another three-letter agency, to make us legit."

"That still doesn't mean you're who you say you are. Anybody can fake IDs these days."

"You'll just have to take it on faith, then. Just so long as you understand that I'm from the government and I'm here to help you."

Even he laughed. "What is it you want to help me with?," I asked.

"We want to help you do the right thing."

"Which means?"

"Which means you don't have a clue what you're getting into. You're in over your head. The smart thing, for you and for us, is to go home and spend these last weeks with your Dad."

"If you — your agency — had told the truth 60 years ago, I wouldn't need to be here."

"That's true. But you're a smart guy, a consultant no less, you've worked inside enough government agencies to know that they're not perfect, that they don't always know what they do know and don't know."

"What exactly is it you're saying — apart from making the point that you think you know all about me?"

"I'm telling you that I'm authorized to offer you a deal. Go home tomorrow, don't make any more waves, and one of our people will bring you and your father the agency's entire file to look at."

"Why didn't you make that deal 60 years ago?"

He shrugged. "Can't say, wasn't there. I know how you must feel. One of my uncles is a MIA from Vietnam. A thing like that tears the family up, for sure."

"I don't understand this sudden burst of interest in my uncle now, after sweeping him under the rug for 60 years."

"I don't know that, the decision was made way above my pay-grade. But I can tell you this much Your uncle's name has come up several times recently in the chatter — communications intercepts —

we've been picking up from a certain NGPF, and we —"

"What's an NGPF?"

"Non-governmental Political Force."

"Which means?"

"NGO's are Non-governmental Organizations, like the UN or the World Bank — organizations that have a world-wide reach, even though they're not governments.   That's supranational, not supernatural.   Now the Big-Thinkers have come up with a related term, NGPF — Non-governmental Political Forces. Meaning they're not governments, they don't control territory or a country or anything like that. But they have political impact on a scale wider than any one country or region. Again, supranational."

"I'm still not clear what you're talking about? Like a terrorist organization?"

He nodded. "Yeah, like that. Not all NGPF's are necessarily terrorist in nature, but they have that potential. We need to keep an eye on them, just in case. We can't risk another 9-11."

We were passing Hyde Park now, the traffic moving surprisingly quickly. It seemed surreal to be here in a cab, having this conversation. "You're telling me that the name, Tapscott, links with some potential terrorist group? I don't believe it — any more than we believe anything else you people have ever told us."

He smiled disarmingly. "I can understand why you feel that way. But this no BS, this is fact. On a number of occasions — I'm not permitted to be more specific than that — on a number of occasions we've picked up chatter that refers not just to 'Tapscott,' but more specifically to 'Paul Tapscott.'"

"It's a big world. There are probably a hundred people with that name around the world."

"Again, I can't be more specific, but the context of this chatter tells us it's your uncle. You do know what we mean by 'chatter?' Intercepts of various types, could be e-mail, phone, whatever."

"And you want me to just take your word, pack it in, go home, and leave it to the professionals like you? No deal. Your agency has been playing games with us all these years. I'll *share* with you, maybe. But I won't back off."

"It doesn't bother you to be interfering in a matter of national security?"

"What's the group?"

"It'd probably surprise the hell out of you if I told you, but I'm not authorized to do that at this point in time. What I can tell you is this much, and even this'll probably surprise the hell out of you. The group in question is not from the Middle-east, not at all. Even so, it has world-wide connections. Bottom line, this is potentially very serious stuff, and we can't afford to have you get in the way, complicating things. That's why we're offering the deal. Go home, stay out of this, and we'll tell you what we can."

"Uncle Paul has been dead for 60 years, so what could a terrorist group possibly find of interest about him?," I responded, wondering whether that group had heard of something that is "perhaps" the most powerful weapon ever known, or "perhaps" the Holy Grail. For that matter, did the CIA know about that? Did anyone other than Lili and I?

"I'm being absolutely straight with you, Greg, we don't know *what* the hell about Paul interests them. That's not coming through in the chatter, just his name. We're hoping maybe you can help us."

"I can't help you if I'm back in Burlington."

"You might, if you and your Dad will open up to our interviewers. Besides, you can't help anybody if you're dead."

"'If I'm dead?' Is that supposed to be a threat?"

"Of course not, for God's sake! What doesn't seem to be getting through to you is that now it's *not just* your uncle they're interested in. You're an amateur, and you don't have a clue. You're being followed — you didn't know that, did you?"

"Of course I did. You followed me and caught up with me at the cab stand." Would he take the bait and tell me more?

"I'm not talking about *us*, I'm talking about *them*. Yeah, we followed you to your Dad's, then across to France. But so did somebody else. Correct that. It's 'somebodies' — plural. The fact is, it's not just the NGPF in question that's following you, but also another team, from another group, as well."

"Two groups following me? I don't believe that."

"If you're *smart* you'll believe me. You're the swimmer, and you don't even see there's a school of sharks circling around you. Better get out of the water while you can. The last thing your family needs is for another member to disappear . . . like your Uncle Paul."

❑

As I was climbing out at the hotel, he said, "By the way, planning to watch the concert tonight?"

"What concert?"

"Twisted Messiah — it's a really big deal, they're blasting it around the world live, you don't want to miss that."

"It's not my kind of music." Another strange coincidence, that both Professor Larkwood and this CIA guy were both interested in Twisted Messiah. Or *was* it a coincidence?

"Not mine either. But I wouldn't miss it, if I were you. Word is, they're setting it up as a kind of coming-out party."

"Coming out? Out of what — the closet?"

"That remains to be seen. But you should watch it, take my advice. You just might pick up a very important clue."

"Clue to what?"

"To what we've been talking about . . . to what the hell this is all about."

30

The Devlin House Hotel, arranged by the airline, turned out to be a great square Victorian relic near the Gloucester Road tube stop. The exterior seemed grim, something left over from Dickens, but the interior was charming with a bright, cheery lobby, and a gleaming rose-marble floor and curving staircase that provided a touch of restored elegance. A mural caught the lobby as it had been on the night of a grand ball, back around 1890, the men in tuxes, the ladies in elegant hoop skirts.

My room lay at the end of a labyrinth of corridors, big and airy, with a view of the hotel's small English garden, still flower-strewn even in October. A nice change from the cookie-cutter rooms of the big chains in the States.

No electronic door-locks here — that was 21st Century; this place was still back in the 19th Century, and liked it that way. Instead of a smart card, a solid metal key hooked to a big brass star heavy enough to ensure it was left at the front desk for safe-keeping.

I dropped my bags, washed up quickly, and headed downstairs. Camilla at the front desk pointed out Carston Gardens on the map, only a short walk from the hotel, a chance to stretch my legs, get some air, and maybe catch P. Willoughby where he least expected me.
❏
This part of the Gloucester Road, around the hotel and tube stop, was cluttered with American junk-food shops: Burger King, McDonald's, a couple of pizza outlets, a 7-11 that doubled as a Dunkin' Donuts. Welcome to London.

I'd forgotten just how noisy London could be, with the rattle of diesel busses and taxis, the steady roar of the traffic on the main streets, the low rumble of the trains rolling in and out under the tube station. I'd forgotten, too, the way the oily diesel exhaust hangs in the air, mingling with the dust from construction sites, and the aromas of rich, dark beer emanating from the pubs, and the pungent spices from the Indian restaurants along the way.

Carston Gardens, just off the busy Gloucester Road, was quiet, a haven of faded gentility around the narrow strip of green that provided the name. The "gardens" were a fenced-in private park, fifty feet wide and a couple of blocks long, kept up by the residents of the rows of Victorian-era apartment blocks that lined the sides.

Carston Mansion stood astride the garden at the far end, a great brooding presence that overwhelmed the neighborhood. It was five stories, brick, ornately decorated with a half-dozen gables and too many Mary Poppins chimney-pots to bother counting. Dozens of small windows, each outlined by a white frame, dotted the walls. Despite them, the old building still seemed like something out of Stephen King.

I rang the bell for flat 12. After a couple of minutes, the front door finally opened a crack, and a woman looked me over through the opening before unlatching the chain.

She held the door in one hand, a cigarette in the other. She was about 60, and weaved a little on high-heeled slippers. I picked up a whiff of sherry mixed with the smoke. Streaks of faded copper ran through hair now mostly white. She wore a lavender sweater over an aqua satin tufted housecoat. A pair of glasses hung on a diagonal across her face.

Had I wakened her, or was she winding down after a hard morning at the office? Or the pub?

"I'm Greg Tapscott. Mr. Willoughby is expecting me," I fibbed, holding up a copy of the letter he'd sent to Dad, supposedly sent from Carston Mansions, #12, Carston Gardens, London, SW7.

"Is this some kind of prank?" She puffed on her cigarette, her eyes squinting against the smoke. "That's my flat number, but I didn't send it."

"It was supposedly sent by P. Willoughby. Do you know him?"

"I can tell you this: if it's Mr. Willoughby you want, then you've come too late."

"Too late? We were to meet today, actually yesterday, but it got put off. When do you expect him back?"

"He won't be back. He's dead."

I caught hold of the railing. "Dead? When? How?"

"Had to be at least two years ago. That's when I took over flat 12, two years this month."

"But we just got his letter, only a couple of days ago."

"Well, there's the postal service for you these days."

"Are you Mrs. Willoughby?"

She shook her head. "No, he was a young fellow, so they tell me. I'm Mrs. Caradee, Grace Caradee. I don't think there *was* a Mrs. Willoughby, he wasn't inclined that way, so I've heard."

"How did he die?"

"Auto crash, so I was told."

"There has to be some misunderstanding. I mean, that letter was dated only a few days ago. He wrote us to say he had information."

"Then you'll have to find yourself a good medium who talks to the spirits, won't you? The building manager, she's new here, couldn't tell you a thing, even if she was inclined to."

31

I pounded the streets of South Kensington, baffled. And angry. It wasn't enough that my family had been lied to for 60 years — now it turned out that this most recent jerking-around had happened at the hands of Willoughby, a man dead for two years.

Why? Who could hate us enough to keep the wound open for 60 years? To what end? Malice? Or to hide something else?

I emerged onto Kensington High Street by the big Waterstone's bookshop.

Waterstone's didn't have what I was looking for, but a clerk reminded me of Foyle's, a tube-ride away in central London.

❑

Something else was happening then, something that wouldn't ripen — very bad pun intended — wouldn't ripen into trouble for some time:

These old locks were so damned easy to slip. But that was bloody old England, for you, always a decade or three behind the times.

Edison made it into Room 119 in 22 seconds, eased the door shut, and stood in place for a few seconds, pulling on surgical gloves and scanning the room into his memory. He wasn't nervous, this was what he did for a living, and risk-taking was always a high.

But something about this room didn't feel right, nothing he could pin down, but he had learned to trust his instincts.

The laptop was on the desk, the screen lit, but he wasn't interested in what was on the computer, he was here for the Katz papers. If they were here.

The carry-on lay on the rack, unzipped. He started to go through it, but the feeling of danger kept nagging at him. He checked the bathroom. Nothing.

He pulled open the closet door and a blond woman sprang at him, a long silver blade at arm's length. An amateur, he knew, as he pulled back. But the blade was serious, nothing to fool with.

He spun, catching her off balance, and used her momentum to leverage her into the wall. The knife would hit first, she'd drop it, her wrist would be broken, and he could deal with her, find out who the hell she was.

But she stumbled over her own feet, and hit the wall head-first. She dropped hard, her head bent back like on a rag-doll. Broken neck. The blond wig had fallen away in the impact, revealing a shaved skull.

"Shit!," he muttered, realizing instantly how much worse the situation had become.

He checked the eyes: no reflex in the pupils.

He scooped the body up and laid it into the bathtub before the fluids began to flow.

He went through her things quickly. A small camera, a tape recorder, some computer disks, a blank notepad. Cash, but no purse, no wallet, no identification.

He lifted her long skirt, yanked down the soiled panties and pulled back in shock, finding something he had not expected. She was a he.

He probed the pubic hair until he found what he *had* expected, then took some photos of the face with her own camera, wondering if the sore on her mouth would show up as ugly on the photo has it had been in life.

He slipped the camera and cash into his pocket, and finished the job he had come for.

❏

It wasn't until later, after he was out of the hotel and safely on the Tube, that he realized he'd overlooked something.

What in hell had become of that knife?

32

Foyle's, it's said, is the largest bookshop in the world, spread out across a handful of rickety old buildings on the edge of Soho. I had no real idea what I should be looking for, but if it existed it was probably buried in the stacks at Foyle's.

I started with the Mind/Body/Spirit section on the second floor, and dug out a half-dozen books on the Grail quest. There were no chairs, but at least there was a niche where I could lean against one of the few areas of wall not covered by shelves.

According to Lili, Paul had stumbled on the Templar chest, which contained what was "perhaps" the Holy Grail.

Which raised the question: exactly what *is* the Grail? It's become a figure of speech — the Holy Grail of computing, the Grail of new medicine, diplomacy's Holy Grail.

Was what Paul found — something that was "perhaps" the Grail — another figure of speech? Maybe not.

So what IS the Grail? Everybody knows it's the cup that Jesus used at the Last Supper.

But sometimes what everybody knows is wrong. Or only part of the answer.

Start fresh.

The Grail meant different things to different people, but most commonly the cup used by Jesus at the Last Supper. In some versions, that same cup had also been used to collect Jesus' blood after His side was pierced by the spear of the Roman Centurion Longinus.

Interesting connection: the spear of Longinus — the Holy Spear that, according to Lili, Paul had been sent to La Rochelle to retrieve. But that Spear was not and never had been La Rochelle, something that everybody other than Paul knew.

As a result of that contact with the divine, that cup, or Grail, supposedly became imbued with a variety of mystical powers from another dimension. Precisely what those powers consisted of varied with the legend, but among them were the power to heal, and the power to work miracles.

Further, the Grail was supposedly invisible, and could only be seen by the pure in heart, and only when the time was right for the Grail to reveal itself.

Which, in my case, turned out to be true. What I was seeking was right there in Foyle's, but invisible to me because I didn't know what I was looking for.

❑

The Grail as the cup from the Last Supper — that was the Grail story I was used to. But — something I hadn't understood earlier — that was by no means the only version of the Grail story.

Not only were there a variety of alternate Grail legends that differed significantly from the traditional Christian version, but some of those other Grail accounts even predated Christianity.

Holy Blood, Holy Grail, a big seller in the 1980's postulated that the Grail legend was a cover story conveying a different possibility altogether: that the "grail" was code for the womb of Mary Magdalene, who came to France bearing the unborn son of Jesus, who then supposedly initiated the bloodline of much of European royalty. That had been part of the plot of a thriller, *The Da Vinci Code*, a best-seller a few years back.

Maybe there was something to that interpretation. Then again, maybe not.

In any case, I figured, that account probably was irrelevant, as Paul, back in 1944, would have been focused on the mainstream version.

I stuck to that version, and came on something that made sense: the legend of the quest for the Grail formed the core of German Richard Wagner's opera *Parzival* and other elements of his ring cycle . . . operas that were particular favorites of Hitler.

Parzival. Perceval. Paul's code-name, so I'd been told.

Lili back in La Rochelle: the point of the OSS sending Paul on that fool's errand, supposedly to search for the Spear of Longinus, was disinformation — planting false information to deceive and distract.

So maybe even the mission's name was disinformation: Operation Perceval. Perceval, *Parzival,* to hammer the disinformation home.

❑

I nearly missed the clue when it came: that word disinformation again, but in a different context.

What if, the author suggested, all those legends of the search for the physical Grail – the actual cup of Jesus – were in fact *deliberate disinformation?*

What if, as another book put it, the Grail stories were "*decoys to distract the uninitiated or unworthy onto a search for something physical, when in fact the core of the true Grail was a coded reference to the hidden potentials of the human mind.*"

I reread that line — *a coded reference to the hidden potentials of the human mind* — not realizing then that I'd soon be hearing something very like it from a very different source, in a different country.

Had Paul found the true Grail, the ultimate truth hidden beneath the disinformation spread by the Grail myths?

Was Larkwood's guess correct? Had Paul/Perceval stumbled on a power within the human mind that could direct and focus energies from other dimensions?

Had Paul found the secret of tapping those hidden potentials of the human mind?

33

I was hungry, but needed to check one more strand. The Templars were not only the supposed Guardians of the Grail, but also, allegedly, alchemists. That's what Lili, back in La Rochelle had said, and what I'd seen mentioned in a couple of books since.

Could alchemy — as improbable as it seemed — be the lead I was looking for?

The alchemy section was in a little cubby-hole around the corner, a hot airless place that seemed just right for reading about a dead science — if you wanted to grace alchemy with the word science.

Reading up on alchemy seemed a waste of time. Still, Dad wanted every stone turned, so I stuck it out . . . and, as things turned out, it was very good that I did.

Granted, alchemy was the starting point from which modern chemistry had originated, but supposedly alchemy had been discarded from real science the way a snake sheds its skin as it matures.

Still, as I read, I began to wonder: was it possible that there was more to alchemy than we thought we knew nowadays? After all, some of the most outstanding minds of past centuries had taken it seriously — Albertus Magnus, mentor to Thomas Aquinas, Roger Bacon of Oxford, Paracelsus. More recently, Carl Jung, who made a major study of alchemy. Could they all have been misled?

Could there, just possibly, be *some* truth to it? Maybe enough truth — or seeming truth — to have caught Paul's attention . . . and the attention of all the others who came after him?

By one interpretation, alchemy focused on literally transmuting lesser substances into gold. In this view, alchemy could be considered, as one writer put it, "a kind of science of energy transformation."

I reread that: *A science of energy transformation.*

Energy is transformed in an atomic explosion. So couldn't it be said that modern nuclear physicists were practicing a kind of alchemy?

It seemed far-fetched that there could be any link between the alchemists' "science of energy transformation" and what happened at Hiroshima. Yet Paul had turned up something at La Rochelle, something that people were still interested in. Particularly the CIA and, so they claimed, one terrorist group.

I read on, and came on this: "The secret of alchemy is this: there is a way of manipulating matter and energy so as to produce what modern scientists call a *field of force.*"

Now I was suddenly very interested. Field of Force. Manipulating matter and energy. Terminology that echoes atomic physics.

Then I found something even more intriguing: In Colin Wilson's *Great Mysteries,* something said by a modern-day alchemist, a Monsieur Fulcanelli, circa 1937, to a French atomic physicist: "The liberation of atomic energy is easier than you think . . . I am telling you this for a fact: the alchemists have known it for a very long time."

Alchemy, a science of energy transformation.

Alchemists have known for a very long time the secrets of liberating atomic energy.

Paul *did* stumble on a very old and very dangerous secret.

Lili, back in La Rochelle: *Your uncle found what is perhaps the Holy Grail, or perhaps something quite different altogether.*

Farentoise: *I was only the radio operator, it was better not to know. But I did understand what your uncle's message said, most of it. He said that he had located the most powerful weapon, and was ready to bring it back according to the original plan.*

The most powerful weapon! What *else could it be* other than atomic energy?

But the secrets of atomic energy in a Templar chest misplaced for 700 years? How could that be possible?

"So maybe Paul didn't find the Holy Grail, after all. Instead he came on secrets of atomic energy discovered nearly a thousand years ago!"

I was tired and hungry, and the words came out in frustration.

But I'd mumbled them aloud, and a woman was looking strangely at me.

"Sorry," I said, "just thinking aloud." Attractive, large luminous eyes, flowing chestnut hair. For some reason, she looked familiar.

"Alchemy does that to you, to us all, makes us a little — well, different."

I went back to the book. Tend to business on this trip, no time for chatting her up, too bad. A minute later, I realized she had an American accent.

I was about to shut that book and move on when I read that in August, 1945, the American intelligence services attempted to contact this Monsieur Fulcanelli, the alchemist who'd claimed knowledge of how to use his science to liberate atomic energy. But they couldn't find him.

The American intelligence services. Meaning the OSS. Had they come looking for a lead to whatever Paul turned up in that old Templar chest, a year earlier?

If the OSS was still looking the summer after the war ended, didn't that indicate that they had failed to get what Paul turned up?

Which probably meant that Paul had failed to make the planned pick-up, so likely didn't make it out of La Rochelle.

Which probably meant that the Germans got him.

Which in turn meant that I had come to the end of the trail. If the Germans captured Paul, a spy operating behind their lines, there were two options: either they shot him on the spot, or they took him off to one of the camps and worked him to death.

It caught me then, the sadness that had hung there all these years, the regret that I never got to know my uncle, the soldier-spy. Sadness even more for the terrible waste — not just of his life, but that the end to have come just when it did, just when he had stumbled on something so literally earth-shaking.

I had a sudden intuitive flash of what he must have felt, facing a firing squad, knowing that he'd uncovered knowledge lost for a thousand years, knowledge that could change the course of the war, and even the course of history. But it would never be, because he was about to die a grubby death in some dark alley or death camp, one of tens of millions of wasted, twisted lives.

"Are you all right?"

It was that woman, her eyes wide.   I realized my eyes were running with tears.

"I'm all right," I managed. "I'm just —" Just what? Just sad to face the truth we've all avoided these years: that Paul died a long, long time ago, and we'll never know the truth of where or when. "I'm just tired, too much bad air in here. Yawning too much."

Real men don't cry — that had been Dad's message, one that I had actually taken to heart. But now, just in past couple of days, since I'd heard the news that he wasn't going to be around forever, all the old barriers had broken. But I wasn't about to admit it, not here, not to her.

"It does get to you — the stale air, reading all this old stuff. You can only take so much, then it gets to you."

I was done here, there was nothing more I needed to read on alchemy or the Grail or any of it. I had the answer now: Paul really was gone. But I didn't want to go back to the hotel and sit alone, and I wasn't ready to call Dad with the news — that could wait till I was back home and could tell him face-to-face.

I blurted, "Tell me, is there a coffee shop here?"

She laughed softly. "Yes . . . but it's somewhat austere. After all, this is *Foyle's* — a British tradition, and Foyle's is primarily about *books*, not that peripheral nonsense."

Then she smiled. "Besides, it's already jammed. If you really want coffee, I can show you a place, if you like. I was about to take a break, myself."

"Sounds good."

She peered at me for a long moment, then said, "But I do have a question for you. It may seem like a very odd question, but when I saw you a few minutes ago, I was wondering — were you by any chance in La Rochelle yesterday — at a café by the old Templar Commanderie?"

34

She held out her hand. "I'm Katje de Vriess — pronounced Katie, but spelled with a J instead of an I."

Her accent was almost American, but with an undertone of something European. As if reading my mind, she added, "My parents were European."

Her hand was silky soft. She was maybe early 30's, if that. The light tortoise-shell glasses gave her a scholarly air. She was taller than I'd realized when I'd seen her in La Rochelle, with a face that was more attractive than beautiful, framed by that magnificent strand of flowing chestnut hair. Her smile was warm and genuine, though tinged by what seemed sadness in the eyes. She wore a neat plaid blouse with tan slacks. Again the pink backpack, but tonight no white shoes with pink laces.

"You were in La Rochelle yesterday?," I said. "I think — I'm sure — I saw you there, taking photos in the Templar area. *Amazing* coincidence."

As I said the word, it struck me: maybe too *much* of a coincidence.

Another amazing coincidence that she, pink backpack and all, had been in the same line at the airport in Paris to take the same flight to London.

"I'm here — and was there — doing some research for my thesis. *Trying* to take pictures, rather. For some reason, my camera kept giving me problems each time I set foot in the confines of what had been the old Templar Commanderie. When I shot from the outside, everything was fine, but once I went into what had been their area, the camera just wouldn't work. I think that's when you saw me, when I was at the next café, trying to figure what was wrong."

"Your thesis," I said, fumbling for something to keep the

conversation going. "What's the topic?"

"I'm in the middle of a career change. My life changed, I was tired of doing what I did, so decided this time round to get a degree in something that truly did interest me."

That opened doors to many questions. What were you doing before? Why change careers so soon? What's the new direction?

But no need to ask any of them. She said, "My thesis covers a certain aspect of medieval history."

"I'm listening."

She looked away, as if embarrassed. "Most people think it's kind of flaky. But you were in La Rochelle."

What the hell does La Rochelle have to do with anything?, I wondered. "Try me."

"The working title is 'Searchers for the 'Latent Miracle Power:' The Knights Templar and the Alchemists.'"

I stumbled backward and caught my foot on a low shelf. "Say that again?"

She seemed to shrink back. "Look, I know, well, I realize it *is* a strange— "

"You're really researching the Knights Templar?"

"Of course the Templars. The Cathars, too. And the whole alchemical tradition, because they were questors for, maybe even the guardians, of what I term the 'Latent Miracle Power.'"

She twisted her fingers to set off Latent Miracle Power in visual quote marks.

"La Rochelle was the main Atlantic port of the Templars, and I felt I needed to see it, to walk the streets, to try to envision the way it used to be. That's when I saw you at the café, reading something very intently."

"Not so intently that I didn't notice you, too," I said. "You were taking pictures of the old Templar Commanderie."

"I'm flattered that you noticed me."

"I'm flattered, as well," I said. Flattered but wary.

She stared at me for a moment, her face blank, before breaking into a smile. "Of course it's *not* a coincidence, not *just* coincidence that we cross paths in two countries in two days. It *has* to be synchronicity."

She broke off. "Synchronicity? You *are* familiar with the

term?"

I nodded. "A bit. It comes from Jung. A kind of special coincidence."

"More than that, a *meaningful* coincidence, an event that shows there's a deeper harmony in the universe."

Meaningful coincidences. I still didn't realize it at the time, but those links were now beginning to come together.

She went on: "Jung was very interested in the real meaning of the Grail and alchemy — sorry, you probably already know that. My friends tell me I sound like a professor, and they don't mean it as a compliment."

Bumping into her *was* a meaningful coincidence. Or a set-up. Worth checking out.

Besides, she seemed interesting. And single. And I still wasn't ready to be alone with my thoughts. "Maybe we can find a pub. It seems we have areas of mutual interest. It's too late for coffee, anyway."

The hint of a smile. "That sounds intriguing."

❑

The pubs were crowded, smoky, and noisy, so we found an Indian restaurant on a side street.

"Feeling better?," she asked after the waiter brought beer.

"I'm fine."

"You weren't just yawning back there in the bookstore, you were crying. I don't want to intrude, but — can I help?"

"It's a long story, a lot of things," I said, trying to recall just when I first saw her at Foyle's. I was pretty sure she'd been there when I arrived, which meant she probably hadn't been following me.

"How long will you be in London?," I asked.

She shrugged. "Two or three days. It depends."

What I really wanted to ask is why she happened to be writing a paper on the Templars and alchemy. But I didn't ask, because I didn't want her asking what I'd been doing in La Rochelle.

"How about you, Greg? How long will you be in London?"

Did I detect more than casual interest in her tone? Just wishful thinking? Or healthy paranoia?

If interest is there, it's in vain. "The day after tomorrow, probably." Unfortunately.

She asked, and I told her that I'm a consultant in Washington.

That seemed to surprise her for a moment.

Then she laughed. "Not only will we always have La Rochelle . . . but we have Washington, as well. Don't get paranoid, don't think I'm following you, but it so happens that I live in the Virginia 'burbs. In McLean. I'm sure you know the joke that a consultant is somebody who used to have a steady job. That fits me, too. And I like it that way. I'm — I was — an investment banker. But that was all-consuming, and it was taking my life where I didn't want it to go. Now my interests have changed — witness my flaky new field of study."

"So your degree is what? An MBA? Or a diploma in witchcraft?"

She laughed. "Zing! You nailed me! I do have an MBA, as a matter of fact, and now I'm going for a master's in psychology, focusing on . . . " She shrugged. "I suppose you'd call it the paranormal. So you weren't so far off, after all. I'm here, La Rochelle as well, doing some research."

"Tell me again about your thesis. I remember something about the Templars and — "

"'Searchers for the Latent Miracle Power: The Knights Templar and the Alchemists.'" She shook her head. "But don't get me started on that, because I can be extremely boring."

"It's an unusual topic for a banker. How did you happen to choose that area?," I asked, hoping she would take the cue and run with it.

"I was very unhappy, working around the clock, my marriage . . . had ended, and I saw not much ahead but tons of money coming my way and just more of the same. So I set out to do something different."

She smiled. "Bad habit of mine, I got ahead of your question. Why this degree, this thesis? Things evolved, as things tend to do once you've made a change. I did more reading, some synchronicities came to be, I got interested in Jung, and some of his work had to do with alchemy."

She sipped some beer, before going on. "Once I started reading more about alchemy — the true alchemy, the hidden reality of alchemy — everything fell into place. The Templars were alchemists. They were also the first investment bankers, another coincidence, given my

own background in banking. I saw you were reading up on alchemy at
the bookstore. How much do you know about it, the *true* alchemy?"

Now it was my turn to shrug enigmatically. Was she just
making conversation, or was she probing me? Still, it's a chance to test
some information. "A bit. I know now that alchemy wasn't just weird
old men in funny hats doing kinky things with beakers. It seems there
was a lot more to it that, even more than trying to turn lead into gold."

She nodded, approvingly. "Of *course* there was more to it.
Changing lead to gold — that was just disinformation to throw the
unworthy off the track."

Disinformation — that word again. Paul's Operation Perceval
was disinformation, to distract the Germans. And maybe the legends
of the quest for the physical Grail, the cup — maybe they also were
part of a medieval disinformation campaign.

I threw out some bait to see how she'd respond. "Something
I read suggested that the alchemists spread those rumors about trying
to transform lead into gold in order to hide what they were really up
to — hiding secrets they'd uncovered for transforming energy and
matter."

Her eyes told me I was on the right track, so I added,
"Supposedly the alchemists had long ago discovered the secrets of
liberating atomic energy. Think there's anything to that?"

The waiter arrived at that moment with fragrant platters of
chicken tandoori, curry, rice, chutney. Bad timing. It gave her time to
think — in case she wasn't who she claimed to be.

We shared the food and she ate a couple of bites, then looked
up. "Do you seriously believe that, that somebody discovered atomic
energy hundreds of years ago? True, Fulcanelli supposedly claimed
that. But does it make sense to you, any sense at all?"

If it didn't make sense, then my whole new hypothesis on what
Uncle Paul found and what happened to him pops like a soap bubble.
"Supposedly the American OSS took it seriously."

"I know, I know, I read that story, too, about the OSS showing
up in Paris that summer after the war, looking for Mr. Fulcanelli.
Maybe I'm cynical, but I think the truth is more like somebody wanted
an expense-paid junket to Paris, and figured alchemy and atomic
energy would be enough to get his boss to sign off on his travel
orders."

❏

We focused on the food for a while. Even then, so soon after first meeting, I was already falling a little in love with her. She was quick, she was smart, she was interesting. And there was an energy between us that she seemed to be feeling as much as I.

Already I was thinking that this was a woman I could end up marrying. And maybe even living with happily ever after.

But was it for real, or had she been sent to snoop on me? If the CIA cared enough about Paul to interview Dad, then I was the next logical source. A romantic thought.

So maybe I'd snoop back on her. "I'd definitely be interested in hearing about your thesis — even at the risk of you slipping into a professorial mode."

She leaned back in her chair and smiled. "I'm hypothesizing that the *true* quest for the alchemists was the same as the true Grail quest."

She broke off and shook her head. "I'll rephrase that. What I'm proposing is that the *true*, deeper Grail quest was for the same thing as the true quest of the Alchemists: to find the secrets of tapping the higher potentials of the human mind."

35

Lili had suggested that Paul turned up what was "perhaps the Holy Grail." I'd pretty much written that off at the time, because everyone knew the Grail legend was just that — a legend, a fantasy, an old story with no truth behind it.

Yet Larkwood seemed convinced that Paul had stumbled on, as he put it, "a power within the human mind — or at least certain trained minds — that can direct and focus energies from other dimensions."

I'd just been reading about the Grail, back at Foyle's, intrigued by the alternate interpretation, that the Grail was *perhaps a coded reference to the hidden powers of the human mind.*

Now here was Katje, coming up with the same stuff.

Coincidence?

Synchronicity?

Or a set-up? No matter how much I was falling for her.

"It sounds as though you're describing something like a . . . like a technology of magic," I probed.

She considered that a moment. "A technology of magic? Interesting concept . . . though I don't like the word 'magic' because it connotes carnival side-shows and stage magicians and sham. I'd rather call it the latent miracle power. It's a power, a capability that is latent, dormant within all of us, just waiting to be activated."

"Why *miracle* power? What's the miracle?"

"If you go back to the source of most of the myths and legends, back, indeed, to the *source* of most religions, you find there's a common thread: the concept that we humans have a latent miracle power within us, a power that links us to God, to the Ultimate — to whatever term you care to use. The miracle is that we are capable of things way beyond what we'd normally consider humanly possible."

She paused to see how I was taking this. I nodded, saying nothing, wanting her to continue.

"That may be the *source*, but it's been obscured, even hidden. Sad but true, awareness of that latent miracle power has been one of the best-kept secrets over the centuries."

"Why hidden?"

"The elites — typically priesthoods — were determined to keep the knowledge to themselves, as a way of monopolizing power and control. In other places and other eras, it was dangerous to speak of these things, because they conflicted with the settled approaches of other elites. That, as you know, is why the alchemists and others coded their knowledge, to avoid persecution."

"Coded? How?"

"Language itself can be coded — messages can be written in a different alphabet, or in numerical equivalents, or in an unknown language. It can be by means of symbols, with the Christian cross being a common example, which — "

She began again: "We associate the cross with the religion and the death of Jesus on the Cross. But there's a further code within the symbol: the cross itself is an ancient symbol for the concept of spirit entering into matter — the vertical, the spirit, intersecting into the horizontal, material plane."

"I never heard that before."

"Knowledge can also be encoded in the form of stories that operate on multiple levels. The Parables of Jesus are one instance. On one level, they're stories about shepherds and birds and ordinary people of a certain time and place. But they carry universal messages on a deeper level. The Grail legend is of course another example of a story carrying a deeper message."

I listened, part enchanted by her personality, part enthralled by the excitement in her eyes as she talked about these things. Enthusiasm is infectious — and magnetizing.

She paused for a sip of beer before going on. "Beyond stories or legends, the knowledge can be encoded in rituals, which act out the deeper reality. Both the Catholic Mass and the rituals of the Masons come to mind in that regard — rituals which operate on the deeper levels of the mind as the participants act out the roles. Knowledge can even be encoded in structures, as in the case of the pyramids and the Gothic cathedrals."

That triggered something I'd read from that pamphlet on the Templars, the one I'd been given back in La Rochelle: "I read that perhaps the Knights Templar had financed the wave of cathedral construction that swept across Europe around the 1200's, and that those Gothic cathedrals were encoded knowledge. What do you think? Any truth to that?"

Something clicked behind her eyes, and she pulled back in the chair. "Why did you ask me that?"

"It seemed apropos," I tried.

She shook her head. "You're not just being polite, not just being a good listener. You're *pumping* me. Why?"

That surprised me. I thought I was the wary one, the one being pumped. I hesitated, not sure how much I wanted to say. "It's a long story. I'm trying to find out what happened to my uncle."

"Your uncle? Are you telling me your uncle got lost in the occult section at Foyle's bookshop?"

36

Barely an hour had passed since we'd started talking in the book-stacks at Foyle's, and already Katje was beginning to seem like an old friend. Maybe even more than that.

Maybe it *was* more than just random chance that we'd met. Maybe it was synchronicity that we'd happened to be in the right place, talking about the right subject.

It seemed safe to tell her some of it: how Uncle Paul, an OSS agent, had disappeared at the time of D-Day, and how the family had never really been satisfied with the answers. I told her, too, about Dad's cancer, and his wish to find out the truth about his brother before he died.

"It turns out," I added, "that my uncle disappeared from La Rochelle after *perhaps* turning up some artifacts left by the Templars." It seemed safe enough to leave it at "artifacts," and not get into what that Templar Chest contained.

"You think your uncle was killed at La Rochelle?"

"We *did* think that, for many years. Until just a few days ago, in fact."

She nodded. "And you just want to come up with some solid answers before your father passes away? I can understand that."

She shook her head. "But aren't you leaving out a step?"

"What step is that?"

"Why you're asking me questions about coded knowledge and the Templars and the alchemists and the Holy Grail. You aren't going to find your uncle in a bookstore in London, and you're definitely not going to find him in my research notes. So what is it you're *really* looking for?"

I took a deep breath, not sure how to play it. Then I figured, Why not tell the truth? "The fact is, I'm floundering. What I am sure of — *reasonably* sure of — is that my uncle was in La Rochelle, and that he turned up some artifacts hidden by the Templars back in the

1300's, when the king's men were closing in. I'm thinking that if I can figure out what he found, then maybe I'd have a better chance of finding out the rest of the story."

Her expression softened. "Do you know what kind of artifacts he found?"

"Not really, just conflicting guesses," I fudged.

"As you probably know, there are many accounts about the supposed lost treasures of the Templars — just as there were stories about the lost treasure of the Cathars. The Cathars were another group operating in Southern France in that same general time period as the Templars. Like the Templars, the Cathars — or Albigensians as they were also known — were eradicated as supposed heretics. What was so heretical? We don't really know, because the victors get to write the histories. But, basically, the Cathars were Gnostics — they were open to *gnosis*, direct knowing of the divine, without the intervention of intermediaries who would tell them who God was and what God wanted. That, of course, made them anathema to the Vatican."

She broke off. "Ah! But there I go, lecturing you. I warned you about me."

I shrugged. "That's fine, you've done my research for me."

Another sip of beer. "I understand why you went to La Rochelle, Greg, but what brought you to London? Why here? Or am I being too snoopy?"

Truth could carry me only so far: "It seemed that if I could get a better sense of what my uncle turned up, that might provide some clues on what happened to him. I was hoping Foyle's might have the perfect book."

That skipped over why I'd come to London in the first place — to track Willoughby to his lair. But Willoughby was dead, so there was no point in taking her down that track.

She said nothing for a bit; it took willpower to resist filling the silence by blurting out more.

Finally she said, "If the various legends of the Templars are true, their ultimate *raison d'etre* was accumulating and safeguarding the spiritual and occult wisdom they'd accumulated over two centuries. And you're suggesting that your uncle found it?"

"*May* have found it."

"But does it really make sense that the Templars would run from La Rochelle and leave behind their spiritual core, the occult wisdom they'd spent two centuries amassing? It seems to me that's absolutely the *last* thing they'd leave behind."

"Unless they felt it was so irreplaceable it couldn't be risked in a sea journey."

She nodded. "Good point."

❑

After a moment she asked, "You said your uncle turned up some artifacts in La Rochelle. Do you have any idea what they might have been?"

Normal curiosity, or serious snooping? I shook my head. "I'm floundering."

"The reason I ask is — well, the Templars were a very interesting order. Do you know much about them?"

"Not a lot," I said, wanting to get her take.

"That's the point, nobody really knows that much about them. In part, that's because they were suppressed by the Catholic Church, and the winners get to write the history. But in part also because they were a secretive bunch — actually the prototype for secret groups that came later, like the Freemasons, the supposed Illuminati, and others. They were dedicated men, who took vows of silence, and kept their vows."

Most of this I'd read in that pamphlet. Then she said, "But the biggest secret of all is what they were really about. Supposedly, the order was formed to protect pilgrims on their journeys to the Holy Land. But it seems they didn't really do much protecting. Instead, the first dozen members got to Jerusalem and then spent years tunneling under the old Jewish Temple. Why? What were they looking for? Did they find it? If so, what happened to it?"

"The Grail, the cup Jesus used at the Last Supper, could very well have been hidden under the Temple. After all — "

"That's possible," she said, "provided you take the legend of Grail as cup at face value. Which I don't. I think that was another instance of long-ago disinformation — to send everyone off looking for a cup so they'd miss the point of the real Grail. The real question is, What IS the Grail? I think it's one-and-the-same as what I've been calling the LMP — oops! LMP is my personal jargon, my mental shorthand for what I term the 'Latent Miracle Power.'"

"Where do the Templars come into it?"

"According to the rumors of the time, they spent years excavating under the Temple — and I think there is truth to that. There are other stories, very likely true, that they sent expeditions out over the known world of the time, the rest of the middle-east, even the Far East, so some claim. Were they on a quest for the ancient wisdom of other traditions? I'd love to say yes, but the fact is we just don't know. It was a very long time ago, and the Templars were very secretive."

If she was there to pick my brain, she was doing a good job of letting me pick hers first.

"It's even possible that — well, keep in mind that the Christians controlled the Holy Land for a couple of centuries during the peak of the Templar power and influence. Think of the Dead Sea Scrolls in Jordan, think of the Nag Hammadi Scrolls found in Egypt — they've only been turned up in the past half-century or so, since the end of World War II. Manuscripts that no one had any idea ever existed. But think of it, the Templars had the virtually unfettered run of the Holy Land for decades, a band of rugged warriors who could go where they wanted, and had the stamina to dig down and to climb up and explore caves. It's quite possible that they turned up *other* ancient manuscripts, ones we've never heard of, containing knowledge that we can't even begin to conceive of."

I kept my mouth shut, let her go where she wanted without signaling my special interest.

"The short answer is, yes, I think the Templars were formed not to protect pilgrims — that was just disinformation, a cover story."

She paused, then added, "That was the cover story. But the truth, I've become convinced, is that the real mission of the Templars, at least at the start, was to search for lost wisdom, particularly what we'd call occult knowledge — the secrets of tapping the higher human potentials."

That sounded very close to what Larkwood had said was what the Nazis had been looking for: *Whether there was a power within the human mind – or at least within certain trained minds – that can direct and focus energies from other dimensions.*

37

Our hands seemed to come together naturally as we left the restaurant, and we walked closely, our bodies touching. It seemed almost too good to be true.

That was when we heard sounds echoing down the streets — amplified music and voices. We headed toward them and saw a cluster of flashing blue lights coming slowly along the Tottenham Court Road. Police cars.

The night remained clear, though a chilly wind had come up. No sirens, but the wind carried the blurred amplified sounds. A crowd was building, people spilling out of the pubs and restaurants despite the October chill.

A peculiar time of the night for a parade, going on nine on a mid-week evening. We huddled in a doorway out of the wind, our bodies drawn together, not just for warmth.

Another couple joined us, then another.

"Should have bloody well known," one of the guys said once the little parade moved closer and the sounds became less distorted. Behind the lead police car, a flatbed truck carried three giant TV screens.

"What's going on?" I asked.

"You don't know? It's another damned Twisted Messiah rally. Holding them every night now, their way of building hype for that big concert tonight. In bloody Germany, it is, at that. Germany — that's the proper place for that lot."

A lot more police had quietly filtered into the area, not interfering, just standing by.

"The media, for once, are showing some sense, keeping the

reports low-key. The last thing this country needs is for this nonsense to take off. From what I've been hearing, this isn't just about rock, this has suddenly broken out, become a full-fledged world-wide political movement, so I hear."

I'd heard about that concert — the first worldwide concert via internet. But Twisted Messiah wasn't my type of music, and I hadn't really focused on it.

Not until Larkwood this afternoon: *Twisted Messiah, that's no concert, not to an old man's eyes. That's Nuremberg again, done up in modern style . . . chilling similarities to what the Nazis did, stirring up the deeper, darker emotions . . . translated to today's idiom and today's media."*

Followed up by that CIA guy in the cab today: *Your uncle's name has come up several times recently in the chatter we've been picking up from a certain NGPF, Non-governmental Political Force. Not all NGPFs are necessarily terrorist in nature, but they have that potential.*

And then: *You should watch the Twisted Messiah concert tonight. You just might pick up a very important clue to what the hell this is all about.*

❏

Twisted Messiah had burst onto the scene a couple of years back with a music video that got the world buzzing — the infamous "Toilet Video."

It ran in shadowy black-and-white. A couple in long hair and black leather, sexes unclear at the start, writhed against each other. The camera moved like a voyeur, catching the dirty tile and open stalls of a grungy public toilet. Their bodies pounded to climax as the singer screamed,

> *The best sex*
> *Isn't what turns you on.*
> *The best sex*
> *Is what turns your stomach!*

When they were done, the girl bent over one of the sinks and vomited. The boy laughed.

It wrapped with a shot of the group, zooming in on the lead

singer, Jesse Cripes, in his trademark shoulder-length hair, beard, and floor-length robe — a replica of the Jesus of countless holy pictures. Backlighting gave the effect of a scarlet halo around his head.

Twisted Messiah's first album, "Masses" had captured the wave of outrage. For the jacket cover, Jesse Cripes and the rest of the group had dressed in robes, positioning themselves to simulate Leonardo's Last Supper, but with one difference: instead of a table, they sat around the body of a naked woman, echoing the symbolism of a Black Mass.

The controversy made their reputation. Shock was their marketing ploy, and they worked, week after week, to provoke. The more the outrage, the better the sales, and the more the cult-following built.

"Sacrilege is in the eye of the beholder," Jesse had said on the *Today* show, defending that first cover. "If you choose to see sacrilege, that's your problem, not ours."

"A playful spoof," one columnist wrote. A piece in the art section of the *New York Times* described Twisted Messiah's product as "a creative extrapolation of multiple genres, breaking through to a musical orgasm of body and mind."

Sales of the "Masses" album surpassed those of the peak albums of Michael Jackson, Madonna, and the Beatles. From that point, the group dominated the entertainment industry.

The hype billed it as "Twisted Messiah's Birthday Gift to the World," supposedly celebrating Jesse's 30th birthday. It promised "to bring the family of Twisted Messiah fans together in the universe's first worldwide simultaneous musical come."

Fans from all over the world had been gathering at the concert site, an abandoned air base in the former East Germany, not far from Berlin. Most had been camping on the base despite the October chill. A half-million were expected to be present for the live concert, which would be beamed by satellite to stadiums and sports arenas around the world.

The live broadcast on conventional television was being funded by the media conglomerate that published the group's music and videos, as the PR hype put it, "to foster a spirit of global cooperation."

38

"I'm enjoying this, very much," Katje said after the Twisted Messiah rally had passed. "But I'd like to make it an early night. This may sound awful, but I want to watch that Twisted Messiah concert."

"You're a Twisted Messiah fan? But you don't fit the profile — you're not grungy and angry."

She smiled. "Not to worry, I'm not a fan, far from it. But I *am* fascinated by the potential a NGPF like that could have, putting together —"

"NGPF?," I interrupted, surprised to hear her using the term. The CIA guy today: *We've been picking up the name Paul Tapscott in some of the chatter of a certain NGPF.*

"It's a new buzz-word, meaning — "

"I know: Non-Governmental Political Force. It's just that I hadn't thought of Twisted Messiah as a political force. They're just a rock group."

"They most definitely *are* a political force. Very dangerous, combining the power of celebrity and rock music with a viciously nihilistic political message as a kind of sub-text. That mix could shift on very short notice — so the political comes to the fore, and the music recedes to be only the medium."

Larkwood, at the end. *This is pure speculation, an old man's nightmares, but it's obvious to me that this so-called Twisted Messiah concert is not a concert at all, it's the Nuremberg rallies again, done up in modern style.*

"Someone I know, Fr. Pat McDufferin, a Jesuit priest in Washington, at Georgetown University, claims that Twisted Messiah is not so much a Non-governmental *Political* Force as an **NGRF** —

Non-governmental **Religious** Force. That's chilling, to think that maybe these kids are getting a kind of spiritual input from this. The music, the imagery — it's so dark. Destructive. Negative."

Larkwood: *I see chilling similarities to what the Nazis did, stirring up the deeper, darker emotions, harnessing the energies of the unthinking, ungrounded, aimless, rabble.*

"You're a deeper thinker than I am, seeing religious and political aspects in that awful music," I probed, wanting to know more without seeming too interested. A Jesuit at Georgetown — the Jesuit link again, and at Paul's *alma mater.*

"Have you seen any of the other Twisted Messiah concerts? Have you taken a look at the fans? They're the losers of the world, the kids who aren't going anyplace in life, and they *know* it, and even *revel* in it. 'Those who choose to lose' — that's what I call them, the Twisted Messiah fan-base, and they're all around the world. They choose to lose . . . and they're too dumb to realize that they're being used by others. We think of the group's name as just another innocuous brand name, but these kids know that name was no accident. They're waiting for their messiah, as twisted as it may be. For some of them, the more twisted the better, because the one thing they're good at is hating and destroying. They're waiting for a direction, for a purpose, for a leader, for a transcendent purpose for their aimless lives. Give them that, and God help the rest of us!"

The CIA guy: *Not all NGPFs are necessarily terrorist in nature, but they have that potential. They have a political impact on a scale wider than any one country or region. We need to keep an eye on them, just in case. We can't risk another 9-11.*

And: *It would probably surprise the hell out of you if I told you what group had the chatter about your uncle. We just don't know what the hell about Paul interests them.*

And: *What I can tell you is this much . . . the group in question is not from the Middle-east. Even so, it has world-wide connections. Bottom line, this is potentially very serious stuff.*
❏

"At the risk of sounding pompous," Katje said, snapping me out of that train of thought, maybe just as well. "The title of the thesis I'm writing — 'Searchers for the 'Latent Miracle Power:' the Knights Templar and the Alchemists' — encapsulates the problem. Whoever is behind

Twisted Messiah, whoever is pulling the strings — *they* are aware of the LMP, though perhaps not under that name. And they want to tap it for their own ends."

Something went ping! in the back of my mind. "Why *miracle* power? What's the miracle?" I'd asked her that earlier, but wanted a fresh take on it now.

"Trace back to the source of many, even most, religions and spiritual traditions, you find there's a common theme, that we humans have, latent within us, a power that links us to God, to the Ultimate — to whatever term you use. In part, it's a recognition that there is something beyond, and in part it's awareness that at least some of us are capable of tapping extraordinary human capabilities. In some cultures, it's only the shamans who seem to have these miracle powers, but they show the way. In other traditions, it's certain holy people or miracle workers who exhibit special powers. But they illustrate what capabilities are latent within us, or at least some of us."

Larkwood: *Agent Perceval apparently stumbled on what the Nazis had been looking for all along: a power within the human mind, or at least within certain trained minds, that can direct and focus energies from other dimensions.*

She paused to see how I was taking this. I nodded, saying nothing, wanting her to continue.

"That may be the *source*, but it's been obscured, even hidden. Sad but true, awareness of that latent miracle power has been one of the best-kept secrets over the centuries."

Larkwood: *Let us assume, for the sake of the argument, that it was indeed the Twisted Messiah crowd who have been following your uncle's career. What would that mean? That they also are pursuing what the Nazis pursued: that power within the mind that can direct and focus energies from other dimensions.*

"What makes you think the Twisted Messiah leadership is even aware of what you call the Latent Miracle Power?," I asked, hoping she didn't have a plausible answer. "If they're like most, they're just out to rake in money."

"I wish that were all there is to it. But there are a lot of other small signals, certain symbols they use, the whole thrust of the performances. Granted, I'm much more attuned to these codes than most other people simply because of the research I'm doing, but, trust me, they're there. And not by accident."

"What is it you think they — the Twisted Messiah leadership — is ultimately after?"

A rueful smile: "Isn't it obvious? To learn to tap these powers from the other dimensions."

"I'm not exactly sure what you mean by that — powers from other dimensions," I probed.

"Suppose, just suppose, that it was true about the Cathars and Templars, that they *had* found a way of tapping so-called 'unlimited wealth.' That wealth would be a war-chest, so to speak. They already have a world-wide army in the mindless masses of kids who're ready to follow their Twisted Messiah. It's my impression that these kids have been brainwashed into believing that their lives are futile, that they have nothing to contribute, nothing to accomplish, and hence nothing to lose if they get into crime or drugs or whatever. In that sense, they're a lot like the Islamic martyrs of the middle-east, willing to die for the cause."

She shook her head, then continued. "But there's a difference, a crucial difference. The Islamic terrorists at least have a cause, a belief system, that motivates them. These kids *have* no cause, other than destruction for its own sake. Worse, they're among us, every race and nationality, not just identifiable men with middle-eastern features."

The CIA guy, on Twisted Messiah: *We don't know what the hell about Paul interests them.*

Larkwood's parting words: *What your uncle turned up is a crucial tool for our understanding of just what our human capabilities are in this wider, more wondrous world. No, not just for understanding. What he found was practical knowledge, how to apply those greater capabilities. That knowledge must not get into the wrong hands. It **must not**.*

39

Another odd turn of events: Katje's hotel happened to be not far from mine, also in South Kensington. But I could accept that as just a coincidence now, as I'd moved beyond suspecting that she was a member of one of those schools of sharks supposedly circling me.

Taking the tube across town gave us a little more time together. I hadn't told her that I was heading back to the U.S. tomorrow. Now that I'd met her, I really didn't want to leave for home, but neither did I want to waste any of the time that Dad and I could spend together.

My cell-phone chirped as we came up out of the Gloucester Road tube stop. "Sorry, do you mind if I take this? My father is — has been quite sick."

"Take it, by all means," she said, moving away. I took her hand and pulled her back, signaling her to stay.

But it turned out to be Professor Tabersley, not Mrs. Fox. "Did you meet Larkwood? Did he tell you anything useful? He didn't by any chance give you a copy of his report, did he?"

"He said he was never allowed to keep a copy of his report," I replied. "He did have some useful input, though — as background, though no specific leads. Frankly, I'd never heard of the Larkwood Report before this. I had no idea it was so . . ." I groped for a word, surprised at the expression on Katje's face.

"I suspect 'controversial' is the word you were seeking," Tabersley said.

"Exactly." Why was Katje so interested?

"I'm calling to say that, as promised, I have managed to arrange someone else for you to meet who is at least as controversial, though in a very different way. I said today that you might have to look for him in the deepest regions of hell. I was wrong. The name is Dr. Gniessbach, pronounce 'knees-bach.' Get some paper, and I'll spell it out for you, as it's one of those German names."

"Gniessbach?," I echoed, groping fumbling for a pen and something to write on. Katje stuck some index cards in front of me, her expression even more unreadable.

"Not only is Dr. Gniessbach still among the living, but it seems he's eager to talk to you. He claims he recalls your uncle and what happened with perfect clarity, and would like nothing better than to clear his conscience by telling you the truth. It seems he even has some kind of a gift for you. He wouldn't be specific, but I got the sense that it might be something that belonged to your uncle."

"That's incredible. I can't thank you enough."

"Perhaps, when this is all over and settled, you might thank me by coming around to see me again. Perhaps we'll write a book out of it, if you're game."

"It's a promise, I will keep you informed. And this Dr. Gniessbach — when do I see him?"

"Technically, it's Herr Doctor Colonel Gniessbach, if you want to be fussy with titles, as the Germans are — they like to list each and every one of their titles. But I think he's content with just Doctor these days. The details are being faxed to your hotel."

"Where is he located?"

"Germany."

"But that's — that would take at least another day to go there. Is this tomorrow?" Another day away from getting back to Dad.

"I think it will be very much worth your time. Whether it is to be tomorrow or another day — they will tell you that in the fax. Ah, before you go, there is one other matter we need to talk about."

Money, I suspected.

But I was wrong: "You showed me a letter of condolence sent by your uncle's OSS commander. As you no doubt recall, it was signed not with a name, but with the designator, B/F-12. That intrigued me, and I am looking into who B/F-12 might have been. If I learn anything, you can be sure that I will pass it on."

❏

"I detest people who snoop," Katje said when I clicked off, "but you *did* tell me not to leave while you took the call, and then you dropped a couple of very intriguing names: Larkwood and Gniessbach. Are they who I think they are?"

"That's one of the people I met with today, Professor Larkwood in Oxford."

She stared at me. "You met *Larkwood?* I can't *believe* it. I'm envious! He's always been notoriously reclusive, I suppose because of all the nut-cases from Area 51 who'd love to get their hands on his report. And you actually got to *meet* him!"

"There was a chance my uncle's name had come up in the course of his research."

"Had it? Did you get any leads?"

"No mention of Paul," I said. That was true. Agent Perceval was another matter, but she hadn't asked about that. But then I hadn't told her Paul was Perceval.

"And *your* day — was it productive?," I asked, deftly changing the subject.

She poked me in the ribs. "I know what you're up to, trying to confuse me. You also mentioned the name Gniessbach, Dr. Gniessbach. Did I understand that you're going to meet him? You'll need a translator, and I speak German like a native."

"You do?"

"My mother was German, my father Dutch. A strange combination, for people of that vintage, given the events of the war. The Dutch of that age hated the Germans, as you can imagine. But they met overseas, in Africa, they were economists with the World Bank, so that didn't matter so much."

"But you're American?"

"I was born there, while they were stationed in Washington. That gave me U.S. citizenship by birth. Plus, of course, Dutch and German citizenship. You name a passport, I've got it. But getting back to Dr. Gniessbach . . ."

"I'm surprised you've heard his name."

"You shouldn't be, not if you recall the title of my thesis, 'Searchers for the Latent Miracle Power: the Knights Templar and the Alchemists.' It was Dr. Gniessbach, then a colonel in a branch of the Nazi SS, who led the 1943 dig at Montsegur, the last Cathar fortress. Of *course* I know his name. I wrote him twice, asking to meet, and never got a response. I even wrote in German, so he'd be sure to understand what I was asking. So how did you manage a pair of coups like that?"

"I met with somebody else in Oxford, and he opened the doors. Professor Tabersley, you probably know that name, too."

"What's his specialty?"

"Military history, particularly covert operations."

She shook her head. "Are you going to Germany to see Dr. Gniessbach? If you are, I'll pay my own way if you let me come with you. Heck, I'd even pay *your* way to see him."

"Why so interested?" I still didn't really know very much about her.

"Because Gniessbach led the dig at Montsegur. I want to know what he turned up. The Cathars were, by legend, Guardians of the Grail, as were the Templars. Also, like the Templars, they were reputed holders of secret knowledge from antiquity. Being able to cite him in a personal meeting would be an incredible coup for my thesis."

"What was the Cathars' secret knowledge?"

"If I told you the secret, then I'd have to kill you to keep it a secret, wouldn't I?" She shook her head. "Sorry. That was a very lame — an absolutely *terrible* attempt at a joke, wasn't it?"

"It would be even worse if you weren't joking."

"The fact is, I have no idea, nor does anyone else, what those secrets might have been. By one account, the Cathars had the secret of generating supposedly 'unlimited wealth,' as supposedly did the Templars, as well. More likely, they just happened to be prosperous at a time when most people were struggling to survive. So the real secret is that other people created rumors because they were envious."

"But there's just a chance Dr. Gniessbach might know that secret?"

"I hope so."

❑

Edison had gotten a couple of good shots of Katje at the restaurant and sent them to Fackson's office. They ran them through the facial-recognition programs, but no matches came up.

"So apparently it is just what it seems — a casual pick-up," Fackson said.

"My nose tells me it's more than that," Edison said. "Don't know why." He'd ducked into a doorway to make the call. He hadn't told Fackson about the woman — the woman/man — he'd accidentally killed in Tapscott's hotel room. This wasn't the time, out here on an open line.   "That other team — they still following Tapscott?"

"Yeah, a bunch of amateurs. I'm surprised Tapscott hasn't spotted them by now. Next question you're going to ask, Do we know yet who they are? Answer is no."

40

Katje seemed as reluctant as I to end the evening. We stopped at a pub near her hotel and took our half-pints outside on the terrace. It was cool there, but at least quiet, and free of the smoke that filled the pub.

"You're serious? You're really interested in flying off to Germany just to see this Dr. Gniessbach?"

"I am *very* serious. If you're going, then I really want to go with you. And I meant what I said about paying my own way, definitely that. I even meant it when I said I'd pay your way, if that's an issue."

"It's up to Gniessbach to say when. He's sending a fax. It could mean catching a flight out of here early tomorrow, very early."

"I'm used to early flights. Whatever it takes."

"I'm not 100% certain that I'm going. Tabersley says he's set up the meeting, but I haven't gotten confirmation yet."

"You're very reluctant to let me tag along, aren't you? I won't be in the way, I won't make a scene, I promise."

The CIA guy: *You're the swimmer, and you don't even see the school of sharks circling around you. Better get out of the water while you can.*

Katje: One of those sharks, or another swimmer?

She set her beer on the table and turned to look at me straight-on. "I wasn't totally honest with you before."

My breath stopped. *The fact is, it's not just the NGPF in question that's following you, but another team from another group as well.* Not Katje!

"I made a point of saying I wanted an early night because I want to watch the Twisted Messiah concert. That's true, I really do feel the need to see that, though I don't really want to. What was a little dishonest was what I *didn't* say. I didn't want — Darn, this is hard to say. What — what I'm getting at is that I need to be alone tonight. I just wanted to short-circuit any — "

"Whatever," I replied, ever gallant.

"I'm still not making my point, not really. Maybe I sounded very forward earlier, inviting myself on the trip to Germany. I want to go with you, but didn't want . . . didn't mean . . . "

"You want to keep it 'just friends,'" I volunteered.

An expression flashed across her face, almost as if she was about to cry. "Thank you," she said softly. "It's not you, it's me — "

She forced a smile. "That's an old cliche. But I don't mean it that way. Something happened. A relationship I was in — it ended, and I'm not . . . not comfortable yet . . . in getting involved." She shook her head. "I'm really making a mess of what I'm trying to say."

"I understand. Understand as much as I need to understand. And you're right, I probably do need a reliable translator."

"You're wonderful. And I won't always be — won't always be so confused."

41

I turned the corner and spotted a half dozen white police cars, blue lights flashing, parked down the street surrounding the Devlin House. A fire?, I wondered, but there were no fire trucks, just police cars.

A uniformed officer stopped me as I tried to cross the police lines in front. I told him my name, he checked a clipboard, then let me through.

A pair of men in suits intercepted me when I stepped inside, discreetly showed police badges, and asked me to step into the lounge "for a few brief questions."

They seated me at the end of a couch. One sat next to me, crowding to the end. The other sat across, so close I smelled his smoky breath.

"You checked in to the hotel today? At what time?"

They already knew that: the computer had time-stamped my registration. Probably just a throw-away question to size me up. "I'd have to check my receipt to be sure, but it was this afternoon, I think it was about half-past four."

"And how long did you stay in your room?"

"Not long, just long enough to wash up. What's this about?"

"And then where did you go?"

"Downtown — central London. Foyle's bookshop." After I said it, I realized I'd left out my visit to Carston Gardens trying to find Willoughby.

"Did you buy anything there — any evidence that would establish the time you were away from the hotel?"

"What's this about?"

"A crime has been committed. We are seeking to give you an

opportunity to clear yourself."

"Am I suspected of something?"

"We are asking these questions of all guests, sir. We want to establish a time-line, simply that."

I dug out my receipts for the evening — a couple of books I'd bought at Foyle's, time-stamped with time of purchase. The credit-charge slip for the restaurant, also time-stamped.

"I see that the dinner charge was for two people. Who was the other person?"

"A woman I met. She's not staying at this hotel."

They exchanged a glance. The older detective nodded and handed me back the receipts. "That will be all. Thank you for your cooperation."

❏

Other hotel guests, milling around the lobby, filled me in on what had happened. The body of a woman had been found by cleaning staff, stuffed into a laundry chute, her neck broken. Obviously not an accident.

I checked at the front desk: a message waited in my in-box: a fax I'd just as soon not have received:

> *Elderresidenz Seeblick*
> *Bad Kronsee, Germany*
>
> *Dear Mr. Tapscott:*
>
> *Herr Dr. Gniessbach has asked me to respond on his behalf to your request made through Professor Tabersley of Oxford. As you know, Dr. Gniessbach is elderly, and has been in poor health for some time. His energy is limited, and he does not often agree to meet with strangers.*
>
> *Therefore, you should be pleased to learn that he invites you to "Seeblick" to discuss "Perceval," and your uncle, Paul Tapscott. As you requested, he will expect you here tomorrow at 13:00 hours.*
>
> *For Herr Dr. Gniessbach, I am,*
> *Elfriede Schwarnhof*
> *Assistant Director, Guest Services*

The second page was a map, placing Bad Kronsee, south of Munich, in the foothills of the Alps.

Was it even possible to get from London to Munich to the village of Bad Kronsee by one o'clock tomorrow afternoon?

I went up to the room, intending to check airline schedules when my cell-phone rang. I clicked on, figuring it was probably Katje pushing me to let her come along to see Gniessbach. Either that, or bad news about Dad.

Neither: it was Dad himself, his voice hearty, telling me that the doctor had found him in "pretty good shape, under the circumstances. Looks like I'm going to have a few more good days, so I want you to go on to Germany and see that Doctor Greaseback."

"Dr. Gniessbach?"

"If that's how you pronounce it, yeah. See him, see what he can tell us."

"But how did you know about him?"

"Somebody in Germany forwarded his fax to me."

I hadn't given Tabersley Dad's fax number, I was sure I hadn't. So how could he have passed the number on to Germany?

"I have a feeling about this, Greg, a really good feeling that this is going to pay off. I'm doing just fine, so I'd like you to go and see this German, see what he has to say. I think that just might give us the information we need. A really good feeling."

"I hope you're right, Dad."

42

I went on-line and checked airline schedules. Provided I left well before dawn, and provided there were no air-traffic delays, I could make it to Munich and on to Bad Kronsee in time for the meeting with Dr. Gniessbach.

I reserved a seat, along with a car from Munich airport, then went back and reserved a second seat for Katje, just in case.

It would be good to bring my own translator, I lied to myself, knowing what I really wanted was more time with her. But for her sake — for her safety — I was hoping she'd changed her mind.

I phoned her hotel to tell her that I might leave to see Gniessbach at the crack of dawn tomorrow, and that she probably didn't want to even think of getting up that early.

"Absolutely I want to go, and my offer still stands, to pay my own way. It's not just an offer, I insist, *absolutely insist*, on paying my full share. Call me when you get up. I'll tell the front desk to put you through. I'll be ready, I promise, and you can swing by for me on the way to the airport."

"I may change my mind and not go."

"You won't change your mind, Greg, and I won't change my mind. I'm still going to pay my own way, okay? Now take a nap until midnight, then flick on the Twisted Messiah concert."

❏

I went back online to check for e-mails. Nothing that couldn't wait.

I ran the name Katje de Vriess through Google and a couple of other search engines.

Everything checked out; she did seem to be the person she said she was. There were even a couple of photos from an article on a banking deal she'd been part of a couple of years back. Her hair had been shorter then. That was Katje, no question about it.

Beyond that, there was a record of her going back nearly four years, which meant she wasn't just a fake persona invented last week to be a cover story. Maybe there were ways of doctoring the record, but this seemed good enough for me. For now, at least.

Before logging off, I ran "Cal Katz" through Google News and pulled up some news stories on his murder, but no new details. No arrests yet. I wasn't expecting there ever would be.

Cal had said he was sending something, so I put in a quick call to the reception desk at my apartment back in Washington, and asked Doreen to check my mailbox. There were no thick envelopes waiting, and nothing from Cal Katz.

I started to shut down the laptop for tomorrow's journey. By chance, I happened to hit the CD eject, and the tray slid open.

A Fuji disk.

Nothing remarkable about that, Fuji had a big presence in the CD market.

Nothing remarkable, except that I had never used a Fuji disk, not in this laptop, not in any computer I'd ever owned.

I slid the disk back into the tray: it was blank.

Then I mentally backed up and reran the past few minutes. I'd been tired, I'd been strung out from the police contact, and I hadn't really noticed anything unusual about coming in and seeing my laptop open on the desk. That was normal, to have the laptop ready in hotel rooms.

But, now that I thought about it, I hadn't opened up the laptop today. I hadn't even taken it out of the carry-on bag.

So what was it doing out on the table, already plugged into power and phone lines?

For that matter — now that I looked around — why was my carry-on open? I had opened it earlier to get out my toothbrush, but then I'd closed and locked it. I never leave a bag unlocked in a hotel room.

Something even more chilling: in the bag, centered perfectly atop my last clean shirt, was a very large switch-blade knife, open.

I pulled up the directory to see if any files had been altered in the past few hours. The laptop was new, and I hadn't had it long enough to put much onto the hard drive. Now every folder in My Documents had been tagged to copy to drive D, where that Fuji disk had been.

A chill moved up my spine. Somebody had been in the room, messing with my computer. Somebody who carried a very large knife.

Somebody who had planned to copy my files.

But why didn't they finish the job, and take the disk with them?

I panicked then, and jumped out of the chair to check under the bed, in the closet, behind the shower curtain. Nobody.

But why? Why make a copy and then leave the copy behind?

Now what that CIA guy had said didn't seem so bizarre: *What doesn't seem to be getting through to you is that now it's not just your uncle they're interested in. You're an amateur, and you don't have a clue. You're the swimmer, and you don't even see the school of sharks circling around you. Better get out of the water while you can. The last thing your family needs is for another member to disappear like your Uncle Paul.*

Three loud knocks on the door. "Police. Open please."

43

I checked the peek-hole: two men, one holding police credentials up to the lens.

What the hell do I do? The knife! Hide the knife!

No, don't hide it, don't touch it, just cover it!

I pulled the top back over my carry-on to cover the knife. I wanted to zip it shut, but figured they'd hear the sound.

"Mr. Tapscott? Police. We need to ask you a few questions."

I opened. Two men in suits, one gray, one brown. Not the same men who had interviewed me in the lobby. They showed me ID, but I didn't pick up the names. The one in the gray suit was older, maybe mid-40's. His cheeks were ruddy — too much standing around in the elements in his early days on the force, or too much time standing around pubs these days?

I stood at the door, not inviting them in. "I've already been interviewed, downstairs in the lobby."

"Yes, yes, of course. Just a few more questions. Do you recall what time you checked into the hotel?"

"As I told the other officers, it was around half-past four, maybe five this evening. The time was stamped on my registration card. I can check it if — "

"No need for that, sir. And where were you from five onward? Did you stay in the room?"

"I went to Foyle's and bought a couple of books. I showed them the sales receipts, time-stamped. Then I had dinner, and they saw the time-stamped on the charge slip."

"I see, yes, yes," the older one said. "Do you mind if we come in, have a look around?"

"Why? Am I — You don't consider me a suspect, do you?" A dumb thing to say. Calm down.

"Tell me, Mr. ah — Tapscott: did you find anything amiss in your room?," the younger one asked, barely looking at me as he spoke, his eyes constantly roaming.

The older guy made no secret of his curiosity, roaming around, peeking behind the door, opening the closet, looking in the bathroom, even behind the door.

"Amiss? I'm not clear what you mean? It's just a hotel room."

"Of course, of course. And your things — anything disturbed?"

"Not that I noticed." A true lie, sort of. I didn't notice anything disturbed . . . at first.

"You do know what this is about, sir?," Mr. Gray-suit asked. "It's about the woman, sir." Then he paused, and they both studied me.

"I heard a rumor downstairs that a woman had been killed. Is that what it's about?"

"Exactly. The woman who was found dead in the hotel this evening," the young one said.

The older guy cut in. "How did you know it happened while you were out?"

Good question. "Because I assume I'd have heard some kind of ruckus if I'd been here at the time. Or heard the sirens, or whatever. As it is, I came back to the hotel to find the police here."

They doled out a little more information. The body of a woman — actually a man dressed as a woman — had been found stuffed into the laundry chute earlier this evening. The death apparently occurred between four o'clock, when the shift changed, and seven-thirty, when the body was found. She/he had died of a broken neck, apparently suffered in a scuffle.

I nodded. They didn't say anything more, waiting for me to fill the silence — an interrogation trick that I use sometimes when I'm interviewing people who aren't likely to level with me. The silence does hang heavy, and you're tempted to say something, *anything*, just to break it. I resisted the temptation to blurt out a confession.

Instead I said something almost as dumb: "How did she, I mean he, get into the laundry chute?"

"We were hoping that you might be able to help us answer that question."

I was about to say, How would I know, I wasn't here when it happened.

But I bit my tongue. They hadn't said exactly when it happened, so how would I know whether I was here or not? Tricky guys. "Sorry, I don't know. I don't even know where the laundry chutes are here, or even what they look like."

They both nodded in unison. Then Gray-suit said, "It does seem, from what you've shown us, that you were in central London at the probable time of the occurrence. So perhaps we can cross you off the list."

They moved toward the door. "We do appreciate your cooperation. Anything else that might be of assistance?"

"I can't think of anything," I said. There was the matter of finding that Fuji CD in my laptop here tonight, a brand I'd never used, and finding that it contained a backup of files from my hard-drive. But I didn't want to open that door. I hoped my expression hadn't changed.

"Oh yes, one more matter," the junior one said, just before he made it to the door. The old Columbo technique: save the tricky question for last, after the suspect has relaxed.

"There is the matter of the photo." He reached into his pocket and pulled out a color photo for me to look at. I could have done without it — the face was blackened and bloated from hours head-down in the chute, with blood sinking to the lowest point.

I handed it back. "If you're asking me if this is someone I recognize, the answer is no. I don't think even her — his — mother would recognize that face."

"True, sir, very true," the senior man said, then was silent again. Both stared at me as if expecting me to speak.

"Look," I finally said. "I don't understand. Somebody died, but there —"

"Not just died, sir, but died a violent death."

"But there are probably hundreds of guests here in the hotel, so why are you asking me these questions? Why me?" It wasn't easy getting that pitch of righteous indignation when I knew that somebody had been messing with my laptop — and there was a good chance that it was the deceased.

"We are not necessarily singling you out, sir. We have talked to others. But naturally we wanted to get your inputs ... particularly since the deceased was found in the laundry chute on this floor, only a few steps from the door to your room."

That stopped me, and the silence hung heavy in the air.

If this interrogation were being judged, this would be the Triple Columbo with double Axel. These guys were Olympic-class in the use of the Pregnant Silence technique.

"It occurs to me, maybe you've already pursued it, but it seems the victim was a man dressed as a woman. Maybe he was a transvestite hooker. Maybe he was working the hotel and upset his client."

Brown-suit started to say something, but Grey-suit cut in. "Interesting idea."

"And tell me, Mr. Tapscott, what made you think of that, ah, interesting scenario?"

"I read the newspapers. That sort of thing happens in Washington, and I expect here, too."

More silence, just two pairs of eyes staring unblinking at me.

Finally I said, "You asked me how I spent my time in London, and I showed you my receipts, and you seemed satisfied that I wasn't here at the right time to have killed this person. What more can I do to help you?"

"You've been most helpful," the senior man said. "But we will need to keep these receipts and other notes."

"No, you can't keep them," I said, though I had no idea what I'd ever need them for. So far as I knew, there was no client on this trip who'd be scrutinizing my expenses.

"If you wish, we can arrange to have them copied downstairs. The hotel will oblige us, I'm sure."

I went downstairs with them to make sure that I got all my originals back. Just in case a third team came asking questions.

As he handed them to me, the senior man said, "What connection do you have with Twisted Messiah and the New Cross movement?"

Then I knew what it was about him: he wasn't just a cop, he was a national security type, a spook-chaser. This wasn't just a routine hotel robbery or something like that.

"No connection at all," I responded. "Do I look like the sort who'd be a Twisted Messiah fan?"

"So you will not be watching tonight's concert?"

"If I do, it'll only be from morbid curiosity." That, and the urging of the CIA guy: *Take my advice, watch it. You just might pick up a very important clue to what the hell this is all about.*

He stared at me for a moment, his eyes as expressionless as a fish on a tray of ice. Then he nodded and they left.

What the hell IS this about? A long-dead uncle. The CIA. British intelligence. Something that may be the Holy Grail — or something else altogether. A dead cross-dresser. And me.

44

The room phone dragged me out of sleep. Five to midnight. I picked up, dreading a call from Burlington. "Just a friendly reminder of the Twisted Messiah concert. Enjoy . . . or whatever." Katje's voice.

This is crazy, I need sleep, not this garbage, I thought, flicking on the TV, still oblivious to the strands that were coming together around me.

A shot from a helicopter taken hours earlier, just before sunset, caught the size of the crowd massed at the abandoned air base outside Berlin for the live performance. It reminded me of photos of the 1963 Civil Rights march on Washington, when the sea of faces listening to Martin Luther King filled the Mall from the Lincoln Memorial back through the Reflecting Pond toward the Capitol, bodies packed together as densely as blades of grass.

The director cut to shots of the other audiences in Munich, Paris, Sydney, Miami, all sitting as quietly as church-goers, and it was as if the same young faces had been cloned in cities around the world, a rag-tag army in dirty clothes, unkempt hair, rings in noses, lips, cheeks, ears, and assorted tattoos. Skinheads coexisted alongside kids whose long hair was streaked day-glo purple and chartreuse.

All in all, they were the kind of lost kids seen on the streets of any city, messy kids with angry, unhappy faces, hanging out together to pass empty days.

The cameras zoomed in on individuals here and there, and I began to realize what was different about these faces. These kids weren't here just for music. There was a quiet intensity tonight: these had come with a deeper agenda than just partying. Had they come here, as one of the news articles suggested, in search of "a way to put some kind of meaning into their chaotic, aimless lives?"

The silence in the stadiums was chilling: tens of thousands sat immobile, as if waiting for the Rapture.

These weren't just fans, these were cultists.

At last the lights dimmed. The crowd stood in a wave that rolled a half-mile along the runways. A single spotlight found Jesse Cripes. He raised both hands, as if giving a blessing, then walked slowly up the aisle to the stage. The other members of the group followed a dozen paces behind. A drum beat out a march rhythm. The spectators stood in reverent silence.

Jesse wore his trademark beard and shoulder-length blond hair. Coupled with his usual ankle-length loose robe and sandals, he was a look-alike for the Jesus of the holy pictures — though the image was jarred by his fluorescent orange and hot purple robes.

He arrived at center stage and turned to the audience. The hush continued as he reached into his robe and pulled out a pack of cigarettes and lit one. The brand happened to be one of the corporate underwriters of the world-wide telecast.

The opener, the group's early hit, "The Best Sex," began as a soft ballad, as sweet as the bubble-gum music of the early '60's. But the tone shifted in the second piece, a harsher, harder beat building, concluding with Jesse screaming, the massed voices of the audience joining in:

The best sex
Isn't what turns you on.
The best sex
Is what turns your stomach!

I caught a shadow passing across the screen behind the stage, then another: part of the show was an array of lightning-fast visuals flashing across the sub-conscious, synchronized with the beat of the music.

Each lasted only an instant, not long enough for the eye to focus, just long enough for the image to register somewhere back in the mind, triggering intriguing dark impulses.

Scary, horrifying images balancing arousal and disgust. Yet magnetizing. That scene from the old video of the couple copulating in the grungy public toilet.

A pair of naked girls, wispy blonds with pre-pubescent breasts, straddling a black — no, not a man, it was a decaying corpse.

"Do it! Taste it! Fuck it!" the audiences around the world roared along with Jesse to wrap up the piece.

❏

The Vril Song came next, controversial from the group's second album, *"VRIL!"*

The sound built until it seemed to reverberate in my chest, drawing my heart-beat into its pounding rhythm. The audiences around the world rose, as if hypnotized, to sway with the rising beat, their fists pounding out the music: *"The Vril is high! The Vril is high!"*

The camera drew back from Twisted Messiah on the stage in Berlin to cut to arenas in Paris, Amsterdam, Moscow, London, Atlanta, Tokyo, Los Angeles. Audiences around the world joined in the mantra: *"The Vril is high! The Vril is high!"*

Jesse led the chant; as his tempo and volume built, the music rose to match it, a peculiar mix of rock in a march tempo. His gestures were jerky, almost mechanical, so he seemed like a strange puppet dancing in synch with the music and words.

The camera moved in for a close-up as he finished. His eyes were blank, rolled back in his head, and the words shrieked out of lips covered with a fine foam. His face gleamed with a weird intensity, the sweat casting a sheen across his porcelain-white skin.

When he came to his climax, the music abruptly stopped, and there was only the sound of his voice, shrieking across the Berlin airdrome and echoing around the world:

The Vril is high!
We move with a Different Power!
We follow a New Cross!

Jesse raised both arms and crossed his hands over his head, forming the asymmetrical X of the New Cross — the proportions of the Christian cross, twisted onto its side as if broken off at the base.

The camera cut to the audience, and tens of thousands duplicated the gesture, chanting, "We follow a New Cross!"

Now the director shifted to another camera, and the flaming

red X — the New Cross — appeared in the night sky over Berlin, a holographic image beamed up, a gyrating apparition in the dark night.

We move with a Different Power!
We follow a New Cross!

The red New Cross in the sky began to turn. The music built, a rough, crashing heavy-metal rock-march, and the New Cross in the night sky turned faster and faster, spinning until it was like a flaming red wheel. Jesse resumed his chant, and the crowd chanted with him, a single massed voice, the low rumble of an earthquake:

We move with a Different Power!
We follow a New Cross,
We follow the Twisted Messiah!

❏
Washington

Fackson called Barrington on the secure line. "Young Tapscott is watching the Twisted Messiah concert now. It's well after midnight where he is."

"Why are you telling me that?," Barrington growled.

"Because we still don't understand why the hell Katz was researching Twisted Messiah. He wasn't into their music, there wasn't a single one of their CDs in his apartment — or on his computers, either."

"There's none of that crap in my place either, I can tell you that."

"But Katz, remember, had some files going on TM. It's turning out that Katz' interest in Twisted Messiah intersected with his interest in the Tapscott family, and—"

"Hold it! What's this about intersecting? You mean that Tapscott and Twisted Messiah weren't separate projects for him? They were parts of the same thing?"

"That's what we're finding."

"Shit! That *is* bizarre!"

Barrington was silent for a while, letting Fackson sit and wait. Then he said, "You told me there was another bunch on young

Tapscott's tail — they still there?"

Fackson had hoped that wouldn't come up. "We have reason to believe it's Twisted Messiah types."

"Shit, why them? What the hell's going on?"

"We're working on it."

"Then work goddam harder. We can't let this get out of control."

Fackson hadn't told Barrington about the man/woman Edison had killed in London. Maybe it would work out.

With luck.

Day Four

"The core of the knowledge is simple: by taking control of our expectations, we can to a very significant extent, change the flow of what we experience in life."

"Change the flow of experience? What does that mean? Change the way things work out? But how can that —"

The Knowledge tells us that if we consciously select and join a track in reality — that is, if we develop and hold a clear, focused intention of an outcome, then we greatly increase the probability of that version of reality being the one we experience."

"Increase the probability? How? Magically, or just because we work harder when there's a clear goal in mind?"

He nodded. "Yes."

"Yes? Yes which?"

"Yes both. Effort is important, to translate into the physical world. But there is also — to use your term — a 'magical' side, which means using the powers of the mind to shape the ways in which reality as we know it emerges from the sea of undifferentiated possibilities."

"The sea of undifferentiated possibilities? What's undifferentiated?"

"Everything is, until the reality that we experience becomes actual. Our friends in the new physics — quantum physics, as some call it — came up with the term 'undifferentiated' to express that at the level of the quantum, which are the building blocks of our physical reality, there are no fixed certainties, only probabilities. Nothing is fixed or 'real,' they tell us. The core of physical reality is nothing more than an indeterminate maze of probabilities. Or, if you prefer, a sea of latent possibilities."

I had an image of sailing across that sea of latent possibilities into a beautiful sunset — someplace warmer than here.

"Life is the process of navigating this sea of undifferentiated, or latent, possibilities. We start each day, even each moment, facing an array of possibilities, all of which winnow down to the one reality we actually experience. In a way that scientists can't totally explain yet, it seems that our mind, by its selections and expectations, in some way brings about the reality that actualizes from the array of mere possibilities."

"Actualizes? What does that mean?"

"Becomes actual. Becomes the reality that we experience."

I shook my head. "How? How could that possibly be? After all, reality is reality. It's what's real in the world. How can what's going on in my head impact what's going to happen out there in the real world?"

"By joining the track, and not just wishing but actually expecting it, we play a key role in determining which of the potential realities becomes the actuality which we in fact experience."

From
JOINING MIRACLES:
Navigating the Seas of Latent Possibility
by "P"

45

I hadn't gotten much sleep, and not much of what I got was good; nonetheless I was glad for wake-up call that signaled the end of this night.

I wondered how much of the rest of the world had churned with nightmares of naked young girls and bloating, blackening corpses.

After the 9/11 attacks, one of the themes Dad harped on was how, in at least one area, he agreed with the Islamic fundamentalists: so much of the output of Hollywood and its wicked sister, the Music Industry, was garbage polluting the minds and imaginations of the whole world.

After what I'd seen last night, I was thinking that my Old Man and the Ayatollahs might just have a point.

❑

There was still the matter of that switchblade to deal with. Obviously, I couldn't leave it behind in the room. I wrapped it in toilet paper, careful to avoid getting my prints on it, then slid it into a sanitary napkin bag, and tucked it in the side flap on my carry-on.

Now if only I could find someplace to dump it before going through airport security. *And* remember to do it . . . a big if, as groggy as I was feeling.

I phoned Katje. "Do I still want to go? Absolutely! I'll be downstairs in front of the hotel in fifteen minutes," she said, sounding a lot more energetic than I.

The lobby was back to normal, it seemed — no more police.

Until I started to check out. Then a man in a rumpled suit

materialized to flash a badge and ask my name and room number. I was carrying the knife — worse than that, I'd wrapped it up, concealed it, tampered with evidence in a murder case. All he needed to do was ask to look in my bag and I was in deep trouble. I had trouble getting enough breath to say my name.

But he only nodded and checked off my name on a clipboard.

Crisis averted.

❏

The hotel had arranged a car to the airport, and we swung by to pick up Katje. As promised, she was waiting out front.

We got her bags stowed and she climbed in the back seat with me and took my hand. "I really do appreciate your letting me come along, Greg. And what I said stands, I pay my own way, every penny. I insist, starting with the car."

"But what's your fee for translating?," I joked. Jokes never seem to come off well before dawn.

"Depends on how interesting the material is," she smiled.

❏

We checked in at the airline kiosk and were about to go through security when I thought of that damned switchblade.

"I need to make a pit-stop," I said.

"Can't it wait till we're through security? You never know, a line could form quickly."

"Can't wait, sorry," I said, looking around for a men's.

"At least leave your bag with me," she called as I scurried away.

"No, I need it."

"Do you think I'm going to steal it?"

A couple minutes of washing and rewashing my hands before the area cleared and I felt safe in stuffing the knife into a refuse bin, hoping there wasn't a hidden security camera recording me.

"You are a strange man," she said when I got back.

❏

We picked up armfuls of newspapers at the gate.

No mention of a dead woman found at the Devlin House Hotel. Maybe word got out too late to make the deadlines.

The big news of the day, naturally, was the Twisted Messiah concert. It was the lead story even in the staid *London Times*. The *Times* took the phenomenon seriously, seeing Twisted Messiah and the movement that had suddenly sprung up from it, as a "very dangerous and disruptive force." As the editorial put it,

> The threat posed is clear, though difficult to fit into the traditional categories. In one sense, Twisted Messiah can be seen as Neo-Nazi in direction, yet the attraction extends equally across the spectrum from hard-right to hard-left. The message, at its core, is a nihilistic embracing of political chaos — the destruction of all existing political and moral systems and institutions.
>
> That message seems to resonate with today's disgruntled youth, particularly in a Europe where unemployment especially among the young is as high as it is. Social and welfare benefits are generous — unduly generous, some say — but still many see no future for themselves. That anger broods over the continent and the world, a force waiting to be tapped by the kind of nihilism that Twisted Messiah advocates on a subconscious if not conscious level.
>
> For those, bored and dissatisfied with the present and despairing of the future, the message of "pre-emptive destruction" offered by Twisted Messiah and their "New Cross" movement is all too appealing.

Eloquent but overblown, I thought.

Then I thought again. There did seem to be a sickness afflicting the developed countries. Most people, even most politicians, agreed that something was wrong, though the differences lay in the diagnosis of the cause.

Some blamed high levels of unemployment, while others said the cause was overwork among those who did have jobs. Welfare was too generous, some claimed, while others said it was too limited. Some said the cause was a spiritual emptiness, others that it was a normal readjustment as people moved away from the "verities" of the established religions and conventional belief systems.

One thing was clear, though: Jessie's "Birthday Gift to the World Concert" had, literally overnight, achieved worldwide impact.

After the music ended, the fans had come together in cities around the world for supposedly spontaneous rallies and marches. The police had handled them well in some places, but in others the rallies had blossomed into nasty confrontations.

Twisted Messiah seemed to have reached world-wide critical mass through this one concert. Until a few weeks ago, it had been just another group — bigger than the Beatles or Michael Jackson at their peaks, more confrontational than Madonna, more political than most of the other major groups put together.

Now, it seemed, Twisted Messiah was creating a new style of politics conveyed by music and celebrity.

Augmented by terrorism?

And determined to grab — could it be possible? — whatever Paul found?

❑

I dozed, and woke when the plane began its descent.

Katje had flicked on the in-flight TV news. More on the rallies the Twisted Messiah fans had held in several cities around the world. Most were peaceful, though in Mexico City the police had used teargas, and in Los Angeles a sniper had fired into the group, killing one, injuring a half-dozen.

The next story was relevant in a way I wouldn't understand until nearly a day later. It was a report that Jesse Cripes, Twisted Messiah lead singer, had flown from the Berlin concert to his "private refuge" in the German Alps for a few days of rest and "consultations" with advisors.

An aerial photo showed the layout: four long buildings enclosing a grassy inner courtyard. It seemed a strange place for a rock-star, and even stranger when I read the story: it had been built seven hundred years ago as the Cloister of St. Ursula.

Jesse had renamed it "The Cloister of the Sensuous Virgins."

Jesse kept one of his private helicopters in the courtyard so he could get in and out without encountering the fans who camped around the area when he was in residence.

As events played out, that helicopter would be like me: a butterfly whose flapping wings helped to set off the storm that was poised to sweep around the world.

46

The snow-capped Alps gleamed in the morning sunshine as the Airbus banked for final approach to Munich. If only Dad weren't dying, this journey would be an adventure, not a distraction.

Hertz gave us a sporty green Audi. It was a perfect day, with clear sun and the crispness of autumn in the air. I rolled the sunroof back, wound my way out of the airport complex onto the Autobahn, and pointed it toward the mountains that filled the horizon to the south.

Bad Kronsee turned out to be a small resort town on the shore of a royal blue mountain lake. "Bad" literally translated to "bath," though it had more the meaning of "spa," and the town centered around the hot springs that had been drawing people there since the time of the Romans.

We arrived in time for a quick lunch on the terrace of the Post Hotel. Sunbeams danced atop the rich blue water, and gleamed from snow-capped mountains beyond.

It was a scene from a postcard, yet Katje seemed to be feeling the same as I: depressed by what we'd seen of the concert last night, and drained by lack of sleep.

Instead of the local beer I craved, I settled for a pot of rich German coffee to compensate for the sleep I'd sacrificed watching Twisted Messiah.

❏

While we waited for the food, Katje filled me in on her earlier research on Dr. Gniessbach and his background.

He had been in his mid-30's at the end of the war, which meant he was well along into his 90's now. He held two doctorates, one in anthropology, the other in psychology. He had been a professor until he entered government service in the *Ahnenerbe.*

The *Ahnenerbe* — officially the "Ancestral Heritage Organization," but popularly known as The Occult Bureau — had been set up by Heinrich Himmler, a member of the Nazi inner circle, who shared with Hitler a deep fascination with the occult.

That aspect had never been publicized at the time, nor even after the war, because Churchill and others were concerned how the public might react to learn of a serious occult aspect within Nazism.

Initially, the *Ahnenerbe* had been an independent organization, but shortly before the start of the war it was absorbed into the SS, a better-known and more sinister organization also set up under Himmler's direction. At the time of that merger, Gniessbach had been required to give up his civilian status and be sworn as an officer in the SS, later rising to the rank of Colonel.

The work of the *Ahnenerbe* focused on two main areas: first was the occult, which included following up on legends of supernatural powers and ways of tapping Vril, or earth energies. The second involved racial research, attempting to prove the superiority of the alleged Aryan race.

Dr. Gniessbach's work had focused on the occult side, and he apparently had no involvement in the racial work — a fact that saved him at the end of the war.

Col. Dr. Gniessbach had directed the Occult Bureau's excavation at the Cathar fortress of Montsegur in 1943. The Cathars — or Albigensians as I'd learned of them back in Catholic schools — had been declared heretics in 1208, about a century before that same fate struck the Templars.

After nearly 40 years of fighting, the Cathars had been driven to their final fortress, Montsegur, perched atop a craggy mountain in the Pyrenees. According to the legends, on the night before Montsegur fell, four *Parfaits* — the Cathar equivalent of clergy — had lowered themselves down an unguarded rocky face, carrying the Cathar treasure.

To this day, that treasure has never been found, nor does anyone know for certain what it was. Gold? Jewelry? Manuscripts containing archives of the group, or even the alleged occult secrets they supposedly possessed? Or the Holy Grail?

❏

Though distinct groups, there were surprising commonalities between the Templars and the earlier Cathars.

Both groups were, by legend, guardians of the Holy Grail.

Both supposedly possessed mystical secrets of antiquity, including the ability to create "unlimited wealth."

And both were destroyed by the combined powers of the Vatican and the French kings of the time. The Church because it wanted to suppress growing spiritual rivals; the Kings because they wanted to grab the physical wealth as well as those rumored secrets of accessing "unlimited wealth," supposedly held by both groups.

In any case, the Nazis sent Dr. Gniessbach and a team to excavate that mountain fortress of Montsegur in the Pyrenees in the summer of 1943. What, if anything, they found, is unknown.

❏

Gniessbach had surrendered to the Americans not far from here, just across the border in Austria.

Some SS officers served years in prison, a few went away for life. Gniessbach got off with two years in an American prison, as there was no evidence that he had been involved in any of the atrocities. It seemed that he had been nothing more than an academic in uniform — though that uniform was the black death's head uniform of the SS.

❏

The waitress brought the bill, and Katje leaned forward. "How are you at remembering faces?"

"I usually recognize mine in the mirror — though I had a hard time with what I saw there this morning."

"Be serious. I am good at faces, and I'm quite sure the man at the corner table behind you was at that pub in London last night. Mid 40's, brown jacket, sunglasses and a Tyrolean hat that looks very silly on him. The way he sits tells me he's American."

"You can tell Americans by the way they sit? I recognize them by their baseball hats."

She smiled. "You're being silly. Americans do tend to sit and walk and stand differently than Europeans. Americans tend to be more expansive in how they occupy space."

"I'll try to hold myself into a smaller space. Sorry, that's another bad joke."

"It's more than synchronicity when we see the same stranger several hundred miles later."

I glanced at him as we walked out. I didn't feel I'd ever seen him before.

But I'd see him again before long, on an occasion I'd never forget.

❏

Only later, when we were in the parking lot, something else registered: his feet, tucked under the table, were mammoth.

The book-seller in La Rochelle: *The man who came asking questions about you, he had — how do you say in English? — he had les pieds plus grande. . . . the largest feet I have ever seen on a man.*

47

Elderresidenz Seeblick — roughly, "Lake View Retirement Home" — was situated on a hillside south of the town. With its white stucco walls, gabled roofs, and wooden balconies festooned with flower boxes, it had the feel of an Alpine ski lodge.

But the interior was darker and more claustrophobic than the exterior suggested, and hospital scents blended with the cloying residue of institution-cooked food.

Elfriede Schwarnhof — who'd signed herself in the fax as Assistant Director, Guest Services — met us in the reception area. She was younger than I'd expected, probably not yet 30.

At first glance, she was the Nordic ideal, blond and blue-eyed with fair skin and a healthy bone structure.

But it didn't come together for her. String-straight hair hung shapelessly over forehead and ears, framing a puffy, chalk-white face. Wire-framed granny glasses did nothing to bring life to her features, and the mustard-yellow pant-suit with lumpy, thick-soled Doc Martens shoes made her even more graceless. The edge of a tattoo peeked out from her sleeve; her fingernails were painted black.

I wondered how she was received by the residents here, who had come of age three or four generations back.

There was no welcome, not even vitality in her eyes. Her expression conveyed anger — at us, at the world, at herself.

She left us in an enclosed sunroom at the back of the building, one of several arrayed along a long glass-fronted balcony. The view was south, toward the snow-capped Alps gleaming in the midday sun.

Then it struck: I was about to meet an SS officer, one of those terrifying men in black uniforms.

More than that, the SS officer who had captured Paul. Captured him, and then what? Perhaps tortured him to make him talk, then maybe put him up against a wall and shot him. Or sent him to one of the camps to be worked to death.

The war was a long time past. But would he tell the truth? Would he admit what he had done?

And if he said, "Yes, I killed your uncle, but I was only following orders" — what then? Could I accept that? *Should* I?

The door swung open and I saw a shriveled old man in a wheelchair, his legs covered by a blanket, his face withered to an expressionless mask of wrinkled leather. A pair of fierce eye-brows, still black, slashed across his pale skin. His eyes, though pale blue and watery, were alert, and still crafty.

I had a sense of *deja vu*. Yesterday it had been Larkwood in a wheelchair, now it was Gniessbach, equally wizened and withered, looking astonishingly like the other old man.

Elfriede rolled the wheelchair next to me, and Gniessbach held out his hand. It felt as bony and cold as a cadaver's.

"You're here to talk about your uncle. I remember him as if it were yesterday." He broke off and peered at me. "You do resemble him a great deal, resemble him so much it is uncanny."

He turned to Katje, and I saw the glint in his eye that said, *Ach! If only I were a half-century younger!* Oddly, that humanized him in my eyes as I saw the personality residing within this crumbled exterior.

"Zis is your vife?," he asked in accented English, holding his hand out to her.

"No, we're just friends," Katje responded in German, holding his hand.

"Zen he is a foolish young man zat he has not already married you," he said, again in English, his eyes twinkling mischievously.

Exactly what I had been thinking myself — based on knowing her all of about 20 hours. I had the sense I was going to like this old cuss, despite myself.

Katje smiled, but kept her eyes from meeting mine.

He spoke English well enough, and Katje was there to help out. I thanked Elfriede and said we wouldn't need a translator. She ignored me and settled in a chair by the door.

"I knew your uncle for nearly a year," Gniessbach said, "from June of '44 until the end. He changed my life. What he did at the end, in the spring of '45, cost me the good life I could have had with the Americans. But it saved my soul."

He let that hang in the air. Even Elfriede was visibly surprised.

"And that, I see now as I come to the end of my term on this earth, was much more important than the chance to eat a little better back in those hard years after the war. So whatever it is you want to know, ask, and I'll tell you. For your uncle's sake."

He turned to Elfriede. "I thank you for watching out for me, but I'll be safe with this young man."

"But I must —"

"No, tell me none of your regulations. The only must is that you must now leave us alone."

She froze in the chair, the pouty expression of an angry child on her face.

"*Raus!*," he barked.

She jumped to her feet. "*Jawohl, Herr Doctor*," she said, then spun on her heel and walked out, her shoulders stiff with anger.

Something like a smile split his desiccated face. "So, sometimes I can still command respect, even here."

❏

He paused a moment, perhaps resting. Then he cleared his throat and continued. "I have talked to no one about this, understand that. Not since the Americans back in that spring the war ended. They pumped me, then threw me on the trash pile, let me go to prison. But I survived, did all right in the end."

"How much time do we have to talk?"

"Time? We have as much time as you care to listen, or until the Almighty takes me — whichever comes first. That cannot be too soon for me, though I hope to be spared long enough for you to hear my confession."

Until the Almighty takes me — echoing Dr. Larkwood yesterday in Oxford.

"I'm not a priest —" I began, then realized he hadn't meant it that way.

I explained why I had come: my father was dying and wanted to know what had happened to his brother.

Gniessbach shook his head. "Ach, but you have come to ask the one question I cannot answer: I do not know what finally happened to your uncle. No one does. There is only conjecture."

He cleared his throat every few sentences; water ran from the corner of one of his eyes.

❑

He confirmed the story I'd already heard from Lili and the old Resistance radio operator in La Rochelle. Paul Tapscott had apparently been used as a decoy by his OSS commanders, who had knowingly sent him to a partisan unit that had already been turned by the Germans. So it *was* true. Paul's own people, safely back in England, *had* intended for him to be caught and interrogated.

Paul's mission had been a sham from the start. He'd been sent to La Rochelle, supposedly to find the true Spear of Longinus — but the cover story that the Spear was in La Rochelle was a total OSS fabrication, set up to draw the *Das Reich* SS tank division away from its race north to reinforce at Normandy.

Still, as Lili had said, Paul managed to pull off the unexpected. First, he avoided capture when he landed. Second, he came up with, as Gniessbach put it, "something even more priceless than the Spear."

My impulse was to ask what that was, but I've finally learned that it's usually best to let people tell their stories in their own way. The story might just go in an unexpected direction if you let it run.

Gniessbach also echoed what the old French radio operator had said: Paul blundered by sending a message back to England, using a code that the Germans had already broken. That message — that he had found "what was potentially the most powerful force the world had ever known" — was picked up by a German signals unit.

Because it had come out of La Rochelle — a key site of the Knights Templar — a copy of the message was routed to the Occult Bureau. Even though resources were desperately needed to repel the invasion in Normandy, Heinrich Himmler personally authorized an immediate flight from Berlin to La Rochelle to follow up on the possibility. Dr. Gniessbach headed the team on that plane.

The Germans, still controlling La Rochelle, knew where Paul would be waiting for the American plane to land — an open field on the outskirts of town. A squad captured him when he arrived there with the Templar Chest. That American plane never arrived, which left open the question of whether the pilots were warned off before getting close, or whether the plane was not sent at all.

Gniessbach sighed. "By that point, I knew that the war was surely lost. The invasion, under way a few hundred kilometers to the north, was clearly the beginning of the end. I had long since lost what little faith I had in the Nazi cause. I knew the end was inevitable, and I thought perhaps Paul might be helpful to me later, so I took him and the Templar Chest to an *Ahnenerbe* facility near Hitler's Alpine retreat at Berchtesgaden, here in southern Germany."

Was I really hearing this? "You brought Paul to Germany? He didn't die at La Rochelle?"

Gniessbach nodded, and told the rest of it. He interrogated Paul, using Scopolamine, a truth drug, and it soon became obvious that Paul had been misled by his OSS superiors. But Gniessbach quickly realized that it was in his own best interests to continue the deception. He sent a report to Berlin, saying that Paul had died during interrogation.

In fact, he took Paul to a small monastery across the border in Austria, near the village of St. Johann am Fleckensee, and arranged for the monks there to hold him until the war ended.

"Your uncle, of course, had studied to be a Jesuit priest before the war, so I think he may have been relatively content with the monks. In any case, he had no choice. Escape would have been impossible. And I think even then he was already making his plans. He would not leave without what was in that Chest."

"What happened to him then? And what happened to the Templar Chest?"

"Ah, the chest, yes. As I said, I was disillusioned with the war, even more disillusioned with the Nazi leadership. I had to account for the chest, since Himmler himself had authorized my flight to La Rochelle. But that was not difficult, I simply left certain items off the inventory that I sent on to Berlin. I did report some daggers and some chalices. It was those chalices that drew Himmler's attention, and he sent a plane to fetch them, hoping that one of them might be the Holy Grail."

Gniessbach chuckled, then cleared his throat again, and went on. "With the invasion under way then, in June, followed in July by the attempt on Hitler's life, they were too distracted to catch my lies.

Once I sent the chalices, Berlin forgot about the chest and left me alone."

He paused and looked out at the Alps before continuing. "I arranged my duties so I passed through the area frequently, and each time I made a point of stopping at the monastery to visit your uncle. We had many long talks. He was young, and innocent in a way, yet very intelligent."

Gniessbach shook his head, a strange sad expression in his eyes. "I thought, because he was innocent, that he was someone I could trust."

He shifted in the chair. "As it turned out, I was very wrong. Your uncle betrayed me, just as he betrayed his OSS commanders. He tricked us all."

48

"Paul betrayed you? Betrayed his American commanders?" That *couldn't* be true. Paul was the straightest of straight arrows. He would never betray his own people. Nor his country, of course.

Gniessbach nodded. "He double-crossed me. And yet now I thank him for it. As I said, it was through Paul that my soul was saved — if, that is, my wretched soul *is* saved, after all."

He looked at me, his watery eyes laughing, yet sad at the same time. "Perhaps if I tell how it happened it will make better sense?"

He cleared his throat, then cleared it again before beginning. "In that final week of war, I gave Paul access to a radio so he could contact his people in England and act as – how do you say in English? – as an intermediary, a broker."

He snorted, a kind of laugh, but his eyes stayed serious. "Of course I did not know then what was in his mind."

So Larkwood had been right: Agent Perceval did awaken from dormancy to send a message after a year of silence. "But if Paul sent a radio signal, then his commanders must have known that he'd survived the war."

"Of course they knew. There were recognition codes that only he knew, as well as the radio frequency at which they would be listening each night."

His commanders knew that Paul had been alive as late as the spring of 1945, but didn't tell his family. Why not? Snafu? Lost paperwork? Or something else?

He rested again, then added, "I directed what he was to tell to them — that the materials from La Rochelle would be turned over to the OSS, provided a suitable arrangement was made for a certain individual. The OSS was very interested, because they were hoping to grab German secrets before the Russians could, and they had convinced themselves that the Templar Chest contained the secrets of atomic energy."

"Atomic energy?," I echoed, to draw him out. "Did Paul tell them it held atomic secrets?"

"No, he did not tell them that, not at all. But that is what they convinced themselves he meant."

"I don't understand," I probed, wondering how much Gniessbach really knew of the contents of that Templar chest.

He paused for a sip of water, then added, "They believed what they wanted to believe, and one of them came at once, ready to negotiate. He had been Paul's commander, the one who sent him on the fool's errand to La Rochelle. At the time of the invasion, your uncle had been expendable. Now the same man saw in Paul the opportunity for a great success to cap his OSS career, and had convinced himself that I was offering to trade him the German atomic secrets. He arrived just behind the first wave of troops. There was no resistance, of course, so it was perfectly safe for him to come then."

Gniessbach rolled his head back, and a crackling sound came out. For an instant, I wondered if that was his death rattle. Then I realized he was laughing.

"But by the time his OSS contact arrived, it was already too late. Your uncle and the contents of the Templar chest had disappeared. Your uncle stole a plane and flew away with the chest."

"How could he steal an airplane during wartime?"

Gniessbach shrugged. "For all practical purposes the war had ended. Security and discipline had broken down. After all, what was the point of fighting on?"

It made some sense. Paul had taken pilot training before he was washed out, supposedly because of that heart problem. But how real could that heart problem have been if the OSS then immediately took him? "Do you know where he went in that plane?"

Gniessbach paused, savoring the moment. "As I said, no one knows for certain. There was only conjecture at the time. But I *think* I know where he went in that little plane. I am quite certain. But it does no one any good, I think."

"Will you tell me?"

"Of course. Better than that, I will give you photos and a map. But I doubt if they will help you." He reached under the blanket that covered his legs and slipped me a battered envelope.

I opened it and pulled out a map, along with some grainy black-and-white snapshots. In the first, Paul smiled for the camera, the same carefree youthful smile as in those pictures on the living room piano in Burlington.

In the second, a man in civilian clothes and a monk stood on the shore of a small lake. A strange, ugly castle loomed behind them, as graceless as a cement block standing on end. I wondered why Gniessbach was showing me this picture. Then he passed me a magnifying glass: the monk was Paul, the man in the suit was Gniessbach, 60 years ago.

He nodded, his rheumy blue eyes twinkling. "I took Paul away from the monastery for a day now and then. We had some interesting talks, he and I."

"Had he become a monk?"

"Only a monk for a day — the robe was borrowed so he could pass in the outside world without attracting notice. For the same reason, I wore civilian clothes, not that ghastly black uniform."

He made a gesture. "Please, the photos are yours to keep. The map as well. Bring them to your father."

"Where were they taken?"

"At the village where I hid Paul for that final year of the war, *St. Johann am Fleckensee* in Austria. In English, you would say St. Johann on Lake Flecken."

He cleared some phlegm from his throat, then continued. "The castle you see in the background is the *Schloss* Flecken, which, as doubtless you already know, would later develop a certain infamy, once the Americans arrived. Ironically, it was only two or three kilometers from the monastery where I had installed Paul for that final year of the war, my personal prisoner."

The third photo showed a small airplane that resembled a vintage Piper Cub, though it was painted in military camouflage and bore the Nazi Swastika.

"That was the *Fieseler Storch*, the very plane that your uncle stole to make his escape, along with the Templar Chest."

"You said you'd tell me where Paul went in that plane."

Gniessbach nodded. "Unfortunately, it will not help you, not at all. Open that map and you will see why."

It was a pilot's map. Someone had plotted a course, penciling in a line that stretched from the village of St. Johann am Fleckensee south-west to a hand-printed X.

"The spot you see marked on that map?" He handed me the last photo, larger and obviously newer than the others, and I saw the shadowy outline of an airplane beneath a layer of gray ice.

"That is where I believe your uncle is today — buried these past six decades, along with the plane and the Templar Chest, under the ice of the Hochweisse Glacier."

49

"I have some questions," Katje said, then quickly told him of the thesis she was writing.

The old man smiled, a rictus softened by the glint in his eyes. "Any questions from a fellow scholar will be answered to the best of my ability."

"I've read that you led the *Ahnenerbe* excavations at the Cathar fortress of Montsegur in the summer of 1943. Is that true?"

He nodded. "Of course. It was much better duty than fighting the Russian front."

"Will you tell me what you found?"

One shoulder dropped in a kind of shrug. "Of course, but the answer is nothing. Nothing, that is, of any significance. Many Cathar artifacts, broken dishes, tools, that kind of thing. Some charred human bones, of course. When Montsegur surrendered, the victors burned alive the last Cathars. 'Kill them all,' the commander said, 'and let God sort out the innocent.'"

He shook his head. "Brutal times, yes? I ordered that those bones be reburied out of respect. That was my idea, I must tell you. Some of the others, they thought that was a waste of time."

"The Cathars were, by some legends, guardians of the Holy Grail. Did you find any evidence one way or the other?"

Again that one-shoulder shrug, an old man's energy-saving gesture. "There were caves under the mountain, and other tunnels in the area. My men explored them all, and found nothing significant. The Grail, if it was ever there, had been taken away 900 years earlier. You are familiar with the account that four Cathar *Parfaits* carried the Cathar treasure down the sheer cliff face on that final night? I think that is a true story. But what that treasure consisted of, I have no more idea than you do."

"I see," Katje said, tiredness and disappointment in her voice.

Then he smiled. "But I will tell you what I *think* to be true, and that is that the Cathar treasure, whatever it was, was passed to the Knights Templar. I know there are those who say the Cathars and the Templars were enemies, but I discount that. There were family links between the Cathars and leading families with sons who became Templar knights. Besides, there is the saying, 'The enemy of my enemy is my friend.' Without question, the Cathars and Templars shared common enemies: the secular authorities, the Kings, primarily of France, who coveted the holdings of both groups. And of course the Vatican, which feared both the Cathars and Templars as competing spiritual forces. The Cathars knew their time was finished, so where other than to the Templars would they have passed their treasure?"

Katje paused before asking the next question, and Gniessbach added, "It is ironic that within less than a century, the Templars themselves would suffer the same fate as the Cathars — imprisoned, tortured, declared heretics, the order disbanded, their holdings distributed among those who attacked them."

"There is another legend," Katje said, "that the Templars had advance warning of the attack that was to come, and so had time to spirit their movable treasures out of France."

"Yes, I have heard that also. What is your question?"

"By some accounts, most of those holdings passed through La Rochelle, the main Templar port on the Atlantic coast. First, did the *Ahnenerbe* ever confirm the truth of that story? Second, any information on whether the Cathar treasure, whatever it was, might have been among those things?"

"You do know, I am sure, that Hitler and Himmler were obsessed not only with the Cathars but with the Templars, as well. Hitler even commissioned a portrait of himself in the armor of a Templar knight. So in answer to your first question, of course the *Ahnenerbe* investigated that issue of what Templar treasures passed through La Rochelle. But with no certain answers. It is the second question that is most interesting. Was the Cathar treasure taken to La Rochelle? If so, what happened to it?"

Katje nodded. "What *did* happen to it? Do you know?"

"I think the question you are really asking is the same question as in the mind of your gentleman friend: was that mysterious treasure that the Cathars tried to smuggle out of Montsegur what we know of as the Holy Grail? Did the Templars take it to La Rochelle? And then what happened to it?"

He wagged one index finger. "I do not know the answer to any of these questions. But of course the thought was in our minds when we read that intercepted radio message your uncle sent: 'potentially the most powerful force the world had ever known.' One hears what one is listening for. To the Americans that meant atomic weaponry. To us in the *Ahnenerbe*, it meant something quite different. It suggested the Holy Grail, which in turn perhaps was a metaphor for accessing energies from other dimensions."

Larkwood yesterday: *Agent Perceval apparently stumbled on what the Nazis had been looking for all along. A technology for tapping a power within the human mind – or at least within certain trained minds – that can direct and focus energies from other dimensions.*

"Is that what Paul found?," I asked. "Did he find a way of tapping energies from other dimensions?"

"I think yes. And then he took it with him when he flew that plane onto the glacier."

"Do you think he intended that — to die on the glacier?"

"I think not. But who knows for certain? Perhaps he decided it was best to ensure that the Templar Chest and what it contained was placed someplace where it would be out of reach of . . . out of reach of the wrong people."

❑

We sat in silence for a few moments. Then I asked something I should have earlier: "Was what he found in that Templar chest what we think of as the true Holy Grail?"

Gniessbach nodded slowly. "I think so, yes. I think it was indeed the Grail. But not the Grail that legends would have us believe."

❑

Dr. Gniessbach pushed a button. Elfriede appeared and wheeled him to the front door so he could bid farewell to his visitors.

That gave her a chance to alert the men waiting in an old white

Mercedes in the parking lot.

　　She returned Dr. Gniessbach to his room, then returned to the sunroom where he had met with his visitors, to retrieve the tape-recorder she had hidden under the table. The conversation came through clearly.

　　At the end of her shift, she brought the old man his usual drink, today with an extra ingredient.

50

We sat in the parking lot of *Elderresidenz Seeblick* for a while, absorbing the implications of what he'd said, and figuring out what to do from here. Katje seemed drained, her face pale. Before long, she cranked the seat back and napped.

It was too late to catch a plane back to the States today, but I could spend the night at Munich airport, hop the first flight tomorrow for Boston, connect to Burlington, and be there by dinner-time. I wouldn't be wasting any more of the final days before the drugs turned Dad comatose.

That's what I wanted to do, and what common sense indicated was the intelligent move.

But now there was another option: follow the lead Gniessbach had given, go to St. Johann on the Fleckensee and try to find that old plane buried somewhere in a glacier.

Dad's perennial advice: Take it one step at a time. According to the map, St. Johann wasn't far. I could drive there, find out what I could about Paul's plane, and make it back to Munich in time for tomorrow's flight home.

❏

The road south from Bad Kronsee led through a stretch of southern Bavaria with prosperous villages marked by the colorful paintings on the building walls and onion-domed churches. It was a land ideal for coffee-table photo-books and travel calendars, and I was glad for the chance to see it.

The character of the area changed after I entered Austria. Now it was no longer a touristy area of cheery villages and flower-decked hotels; now we were in a primitive, deserted land of forests, rocks, and roaring brooks. There wasn't much traffic, just some heavy logging trucks and very few cars.

A couple of those cars hung behind, but they were in no hurry, and neither was I, for the moment.

The sun had dropped near the tops of the row of great jagged peaks that filled the horizon to the south, most of them already snow-covered in October.

Somewhere up in those mountains was the Hochweisse Glacier, and somewhere in that river of ice, two miles wide and hundreds of feet thick, rested a tiny, World War II airplane containing – if Dr. Gniessbach was telling the truth – Uncle Paul's body and the contents of the Templar Chest.

Gniessbach had told how security had broken down on that last night of the war, giving Paul the opening to break into Gniessbach's room and gather up the manuscripts from the Templar chest, along with the microfilmed copies Gniessbach had made.

The *Fieseler Storch*, a small spotter plane like a Piper Cub, lay hidden in a clump of trees near the small grass field that doubled as a runway. To fly it in daylight, with the American air forces in total command of the skies, would be suicide.

At night, though, it would be different. At night a plane with German markings might have a chance.

Paul had taken basic and advanced flight training before that alleged heart murmur had washed him out, so the slow, light *Storch* would have been easy to manage. He took off around three in the morning, well before first light.

But with the Americans advancing from the west, and the Russians racing in from the east to grab as much of Austria as possible before the end, his options were limited. There was no telling where he had intended to go. Perhaps to Switzerland. Perhaps to southern France. Possibly Italy.

But wherever he was headed, he didn't make it across the Alps. He may have been shot down by a fighter plane. Maybe the weather closed in as he was trying to make it over the crest of the mountain range. Perhaps he ran out of fuel, or got lost, or the carburetor iced up.

In any case, Paul and the Templar materials were gone by the time the OSS team rolled into the village of St. Johann on the

Fleckensee that morning.

The OSS officer didn't believe Gniessbach when he said that Paul had escaped, assuming at first Gniessbach was holding out for a better deal. Days passed before he finally put out an alert for Paul, accusing him of a range of crimes. But the Americans found no trace of either Paul or the plane.

Gniessbach served a couple of years in prison, then was released and got on with his life.

But he never lost his interest in the Templar Chest.

His first lead came around 1959, when he heard rumors of a downed *Storch* spotted by an airline crew flying from Munich to Milan. The angle of the sunlight happened to be just right, and the shadow of the plane stood out against the blue-white ice below.

Eventually, he hired a pilot to fly him over the spot, and took these photos of the plane.

But he told no one, ever. And neither the OSS, nor later the CIA, ever came back to follow up with him.

Paul Tapscott had been forgotten by the OSS, perhaps. But somebody remembered.

❏

The road wound through a series of hairpins, and a couple of times I had to pause for logging trucks to squeeze around the tight corners. Then minutes would pass without encountering other vehicles.

I came on a small lake at the summit, and pulled into the parking area where there was a *Schnell Imbiss* — a little roadside stand selling hot wursts and cold drinks.

It seemed like the loneliest restaurant in Europe. Usually places like this had a rack of wursts grilling. Here the fire was going, but nothing cooking: we might be today's only customers.

Katje woke and walked over to the stand with me. "I'm sorry, I'm not very good company, I'm just not feeling up to par. Maybe a coke or something will perk me up."

I looked back when I heard the crunch of tires on the gravel parking lot, and turned to see a battered white Mercedes pull up directly next to ours. I wondered whether I'd locked the car doors, then figured it made no difference: we were carrying our passports, and the luggage was locked in the trunk. The only thing in view was the envelope Gniessbach had given me — not likely to be something thieves would go after.

Better to play it safe. I asked Katje to order me a coke, and turned back to the car. The Mercedes was a clunker that looked as if it had lived hard . . . as did the pair inside: the driver was a thickset guy with curly dark hair, three days beard, and a grimy, once-white cable-knit sweater. The passenger was smaller, with a black leather jacket and a ponytail.

They stared at me as I took Gniessbach's envelope and the car phone, and pretended to make a call while walking back to the wurst hut. I heard the Mercedes fire up and leave, headed the way I was going.

Cal Katz: *Sometimes even paranoids have real enemies.*

51

The village of St. Johann am Fleckensee – St. Johann on Lake Flecken – lay at the end of a bypass from the main highway. I drove slowly down the quiet main street, feeling a sense of awe that I had finally made it to the place where Paul lived the final year of his life.

Back then, St. Johann had been just a simple village of farmers and wood-cutters. Today it was a resort town, catering to skiers in the winter, hikers in the summer. Now, in the off-season, the sport-shops and cafes were closed, and it seemed deserted, even desolate . . . as quiet as it must have been here during the war.

A church bell rang out the hour. I rolled down the car window, and a wash of fresh air brought the scent of newly-cut wet pine lumber, wood-smoke from the chimneys, a hint of manure from the fields.

❑

I hadn't anticipated that the roads would be so winding or narrow, and it had taken longer to get here than I'd planned. The sun had long since slipped behind the high mountains. The sky was still light, and the glacier glistened in sunshine, but it was shadowy down here, and the air was cooling quickly.

I found the airport about a mile from the center of the village in a flat area beside a small river. The slopes of green mountains loomed to the side, the tops hidden in clouds. It would be an interesting experience to take off or land here in bad weather. Ancient Chinese curse: May you fly from interesting airports.

If Gniessbach was right, Paul had come to this airport that final night of the war, pushing the Templar Chest in an old wooden wheelbarrow from the monastery.

The place didn't appear to have changed much over the years
— a small stucco building with the boxy, utilitarian look that said
Military, along with three small hangars, also of World War II vintage.
A couple of single-engine planes, and a helicopter.

Katje was still dozing off and on, and stayed with the car while
I tried the main building. It was like airport ops centers everywhere:
maps tacked on the walls, a bulletin-board with air advisories, an air-
to-ground radio crackling in the background, an ill-matched
assortment of battered chairs and tables, overflowing ashtrays,
chipped cups with coffee streaks baked on the sides.

On the wall, a half-dozen photos tracked the development of
the airport. I'd called it right: this building had been here from the
start, a Nazi flag flying from the roof. In that first photo, a collection
of fighter planes, all bearing the Swastika, were lined up in front of
these same hangars.

I followed voices until I found two men in leather flying jackets
hunched over a map in a back room. One of them, 40-ish, barrel-
chested, with a thick black beard, looked at me and grunted a sort of
greeting. The second man was tall, with flowing blond hair and a ring
in one ear. He ignored me until I said I had come to see about
chartering a helicopter.

"Why?"

"I'm told there's an old plane frozen into the Hochweisse
Glacier. I'd like to fly up and see it."

A look passed between the men; I caught the blond man
winking to the other. The barrel-chested man responded, "Fly over
the glacier? *Ja*, sure. But it's not cheap, you understand that?"

"I'd want to touch down beside the plane."

"Touch down? On the Hochweisse? But that is impossible, yes?
It is not permitted to land on the glacier there, it is very unstable. The
ice could break apart and set off an avalanche. Not even St. Nicholas
in his sleigh would be allowed to land on the Hochweisse. But which
plane is it we are talking about?"

"Which plane? There's more than one?"

His laugh was deep and throaty, but there wasn't much humor
in it. "*Ja*, a few."

Not so sure this was a good idea, but seeing no better option,
I spread out the map Gniessbach had given me. The men bent over it,

studying the point on the glacier that Gniessbach had marked as the site.

Another glance passed between them before the one with the beard shrugged and said, "*Ja*, if you have the money we will take you there to that spot. But not to land. Definitely not to touch down, as the ice there is unstable, very dangerous. Even the noise of a copter, if it is too low, could fracture the ice, causing an avalanche to develop."

"When? Now?"

"Not now, not today. Already it is too late. Perhaps tomorrow, if the weather is good."

"Has anybody —" I broke off, fumbling for the right way of putting it — "has anyone ever been up to the plane? Was the pilot's body ever retrieved?"

The bigger man shrugged. "I cannot be sure, but I think no. As I say, the glacier there is very unstable. I think no one would have tried."

52

I drove back to the center of the village, not sure whether to feel a sense of accomplishment or of relief. I was relieved, in a way, that landing on the glacier was out of the question: that saved me from facing the next problem – whether to see if Paul's body could be retrieved. Now I had no choice: I had to let him rest in peace where he was.

But at least I could fly over the glacier, then go home and tell Dad I'd seen Paul's final resting place. I could take some photos, even toss out a wreath.

The main street ended at the Grunz Family Sporthotel, a big alpine lodge on the shore of the lake. It seemed open for business, though there were only a half-dozen cars in the parking lot.

"Yes, I think we can find a room for you," Frau Grunz said, after making a show of studying the contents of a file-folder.

She wore a colorful Austrian *dirndl*, but the gaiety of the dress seemed out of place on this dour, unhealthy woman. She was somewhere around 50, or maybe 60, and pale. She looked deeply tired, and dark rings of grey circled the eyes, the kind of grey that would be etched into the skin until death.

"*Nein, wir mochte **zwei** zimmern, bitte,*" Katje said.

Frau Grunz shrugged, her eyes calculating, *So much the better, two rooms, twice the profit.*

❏

Katje managed a wan smile as we were going up the stairs. "I'm really feeling crummy, Greg. I think I'll just sack out for a while and maybe I'll become human again. Is that okay? Just tell them your translator is having female problems."

My room was compact, though clean and comfortable. A fluffy down puff covered the bed, and I almost succumbed to the temptation it offered after a short night of troubled sleep.

A flower-decked balcony overlooked the lake. As still and pale as a mirror, the Fleckensee was a couple of miles long, maybe a half-mile wide.

Schloss Flecken — Flecken Castle — commanded the far shore.

Not at all like the castles of fairy-tales and travel posters, this was a graceless, boxy structure, with the charm of a medieval prison. It reminded me of a concrete block turned on its end.

I dug out the black-and-white snapshots Dr. Gniessbach had given me, the close-up of Paul, and the shot of Paul in a monk's robe, standing with Gniessbach in a business suit. No question of it: the photos had been taken here, with Flecken Castle in the background.

Something Gniessbach said came to mind: *Schloss Flecken would later develop a certain infamy, once the Americans arrived.*

What kind of infamy? I should have asked him then, and whether that infamy related to Paul in any way. But the conversation had moved on, and it slipped my mind.

No matter, I had Gniessbach's phone number, I'd call him later and ask about that "certain infamy."

Ask as well another obvious question I'd overlooked: Did he know the name of the American OSS officer who came in response to Paul's message.

A tourist brochure told a bit more: Flecken Castle, built in stages from around the years 1000 to 1400, had passed through many hands as the tides of conflict ebbed and flowed. Now it was a luxury hotel. There was no mention of what "certain infamy" it might have gained at the end of the War.

❑

I locked the materials Gniessbach had given me in the room's wall safe, and headed out to see what I could learn from the little town. I slipped the photos of Paul in my pocket — those from home, from Lili, from Gniessbach — in case I ran across someone whose memory stretched back to 1945.

Katje had loaned me her camera, and I snapped scenes as I walked, something to give Dad a sense of the place.

The bells of the onion-domed church tolled as I walked the

shops on the main street: a one-room grocery store; the Karl
Forstinger *Fleischerei*, with slabs of meat visible in the window; the
Schwanz *Bäckerei-Konditorei* that tempted with aromas of cakes and
breads; the drab *Volksbank*; the Eduscho coffee-shop; Klamm's sport-
shop, filled with gear for climbing and skiing; the Geiger shop with
costly replicas of traditional Austrian peasant clothing.
❏

The tourist office occupied part of the ground floor of the village hall.
The thin woman behind the counter was maybe 30, blond, a study in
lines and angles. Her nose was long and straight; her blond hair was
shiny and straight; dark-framed metal glasses cut across her face,
adding to the sense of angularity. Even her fingers were long and
bony.

    But her blue eyes were warm, and she became friendly when
I mentioned the old monastery.

    "Ah, but it is not a monastery any longer, not a real monastery,
though some of the old monks remain. Now it is — how do you say in
English? — an executive retreat, a training center, yes? But you are
free to visit, you can walk there on the path by the lake, the monks
who are still there welcome visitors. I can arrange that for tomorrow,
if you like."

    "It's not a monastery, but there are monks?"

    She shrugged. "That is the arrangement the order made when
they left. Some of the old monks stayed behind, as they had lived most
of their lives there."

    I was at the door before I thought to ask about Dr.
Gniessbach's comment. "Someone mentioned that the castle gained
what he termed 'a certain infamy' when the Americans came at the end
of the war."

    "Who told you that?"

    "An old German, he'd been a soldier here."

    She shrugged, her eyes suddenly distant. "I have no idea what
he meant. Schloss Flecken was built more than 900 years ago, and
many things have happened there over the years."

53

Washington. 9:45 A.M.

"Gniessbach!" Barrington blurted. "How in hell did he stumble on that old bastard!" He and Fackson were in the secure conference room.

"Now he's driven on to a small village in Austria —"

"St. Johann on the Fleckensee."

Fackson nodded, wondering how the Lizard knew. "His first stop was the local airport, trying to arrange a helicopter ride up to the Hochweisse Glacier. The pilots told him it was impossible to land, for safety reasons."

"He wanted to *land* on the glacier? Why? It makes no damned sense. His goddam uncle's not on that glacier."

"He talked to the pilots about an old plane frozen into the glacier."

Barrington shook his head. He was almost laughing. "Somebody's given him a bum steer. Gniessbach, probably. I wonder why. What's *he* got to gain?"

"There's something else. From the time he left Gniessbach, Tapscott has been followed by others. Difficult to say at this point just who they are. Two men, twenties, appear to be local punks. The car they're driving, an old white Mercedes, is registered to a local thug, probably the driver, but we haven't yet found who he and his partner might be working for. They made a try for him along the road but he got away, perhaps never realized what had almost happened."

"You have no idea at all who these punks are?"

"It's not certain, no solid evidence, but my people over there have the sense these are Twisted Messiah types."

"Twisted Messiah again, Jesus! First via Katz, now this. What the hell is it all about? Your people are still checking Tapscott's mailbox here in DC?"

"Of course. Mail arrives there by ten most mornings. I'll tell you the minute Katz' papers arrive."

"The orders stand: as soon as we have that set of the Katz memos in hand, then Tapscott is to — to be taken care of."

Fackson nodded. He had still not told Barrington about the woman/man Edison had killed in London. He was still hoping that nothing would come of it and Barrington would never know.

Still, it was puzzling: the tattoo in the pubic area is a marker for the Twisted Messiah security cadre, so what had she — rather, *he* — been after in Tapscott's room? Why would those Twisted Messiah bastards be interested in the same thing as Barrington and his sons?

54

A strange kind of dusk had fallen on the village by the time I left the tourist office, the kind of semi-evening that happens in the valleys of high mountains, where the sky is still bright though the sun has long since dipped behind the peaks. The last sunlight glistened on the Hochweisse glacier.

It was too late in the day to hike to the monastery, yet if I put it off till morning, then I'd miss tomorrow's flight back, and lose one more of these final days with Dad.

What were the chances that any of the monks would remember Paul after six decades? Still, Dad would want me to try, just in case. If nothing more, I could take some pictures, so he could see where Paul had lived at the end.

I made a decision: to decide in the morning.

Back in the room, I took a bottle of Gosser beer from the mini-fridge to sip on the balcony. The evening air was cool, with a hint of rain, or maybe even snow, on the way. Not looking promising for the chances of a helicopter flight up to the glacier tomorrow.

Schloss Flecken, at the head of the lake, was bathed now in floodlights, and the light and the mist rising from the water softened the crude shape of the place, making it easier to accept the functionality of its graceless design. It had been built nearly a millennium ago for protection, not to fit the Disney image of a castle.

Gniessbach's strange comment again came to mind: *Schloss Flecken gained a certain infamy when the Americans arrived at the end of the war.* Maybe that was something I could check on-line.

A door rattled and Katje stepped out onto the balcony of her own room. "I thought I heard you. Now *that* is a good idea," she said, and disappeared back inside long enough to get her own bottle of Gosser. "I'm feeling better, and after some of this Austrian folk-medicine I'll be better still, no doubt. Productive afternoon?"

"Productive but still puzzling. I'll tell you at dinner. I'm going to phone my father now with an update."

She looked across at me. "Am I part of the update you're going to give him?"

I couldn't help laughing. "Maybe. I'll see how he's feeling. But I think he'd like you. He hasn't liked many of my girlfriends lately, but you're different."

"So I've been promoted from translator to girlfriend?" Her eyebrows did a little dance that was hard to read in the shadows. "I'll see you at dinner."

❑

I couldn't pick up a dial tone on the cell-phone, so went to a phone booth off the lobby and put it through the hotel's line — a good thing, as it turned out, as it meant that Mrs. Fox had that phone number later, when the crisis hit.

It turned out to be a very good conversation. Dad, usually edgy and impatient on the phone, today was warm and relaxed, and we chatted on about things from my childhood, about Mom, about memories of camping trips with Uncle Paul in the days before the War.

In the end, I held back and didn't tell him what Gniessbach had told us — that Paul had been frozen into a glacier for 60 years. It seemed better to wait until I had actually flown up there. Something he'd taught me a long time ago: Don't make promises that you're not sure you can keep.

Nor did I tell him that I was here with Katje. She didn't quite qualify as a girl-friend, at least not yet. Nor was she just a translator.

The fact is, I still wasn't sure just how much I could trust her. The CIA guy had said there were two teams following me. That seemed crazy, but suppose it were true. Was she on team 1, or team 2 — or just an interesting new friend? No point in confusing Dad with something that was confusing me.

As he was about to hang up, Mrs. Fox, cheerless as ever, grabbed the phone to insist on taking the number of the hotel and the number of the cell-phone, which she already had. "Just in case anything happens, as it must, sooner or later."

I thought again of what she had said in Burlington: *Sometimes, just before the end, they have one final good spell, and they seem to be coming out of it. But it's only a reprieve, one last gift of time. Then they go.*

Mrs. Fox, the eager evangelist of pessimism.

But this time her pessimism would prove justified: this turned out to be the last time I talked to Dad before he died.

55

But it turned out that conversation hadn't quite ended: Dad took back the phone.

"Where are you, Greg?"

I thought he already knew. "In a little town in Austria."

"No, I mean, where are you at this moment?"

"In a phone booth in a hotel lobby."

"Are you standing or sitting?"

What was he getting at? Or were the pain-killers getting to him? "I'm sitting on a little wooden bench inside the booth."

"Is the wood solid?"

"Sure, of course. Solid enough to hold me."

"What's the floor like?"

I looked down. Better to go along with him than to dwell on what had become of his mind. "It's tile, and it's solid."

"But it's *not* solid, not solid at all," he said. "Nor is that wooden bench solid. Didn't you take physics in college? These things *seem* solid, but the deeper reality is that they're all made up of atoms, and atoms are something like 99.99 percent empty space. So that solid floor is an illusion. A *useful* illusion, to be sure, but still an illusion."

Where do you go from something like that? "Yeah, I took physics. They got into that."

"But if things are 99.99 percent empty space, then why do we see them and feel them as solid? Because something in the nature of our consciousness and our physical apparatus, brain, eyes, senses, work together to create this useful fiction, that all is fixed and solid. Given who we are, we humans, we couldn't function if we didn't have that illusion to help us make sense of things."

He paused, apparently waiting for my response. "I suppose not."

"We couldn't function without that illusion. Trouble is, we tend to forget that it *is* just fiction, and we get caught up in that fiction and come to believe that it *is* the reality, and not just an illusion of solidity that our minds have constructed. We forget it's only the *reality as we perceive it,* not the *true* reality."

I didn't know what to say. He was talking what seemed to be quantum physics — not an area that had ever been one of his topics of conversation before.

"Once we grasp that the true reality is different than what we've come to accept in that useful illusion, then a whole new paradigm opens up to us. A new paradigm, and with it some incredible opportunities."

"Paradigm?," I echoed. That wasn't a word I'd ever heard my father use.

"Paradigm, or 'perception,' if that's more comfortable. Basically a new way of looking at things, a new framework for making sense of reality. But don't get hung up on the words. My point is that once we break out and look at reality via this new paradigm, then everything becomes different. We have a new vantage point, and hence incredible new opportunities in how we can shape our lives."

I was flummoxed. I had no idea what he was getting at. Was this a reaction to the drugs they were giving him? But what drug infuses the patient with a passion for quantum physics?

After a pause, he said, "Maybe that's what happens when we die. Our physical apparatus just drops away, and then we can look past the illusion of fixedness and solidity and grasp things as they really are. Then we function in the true reality, working with things as they really are."

"Interesting point."

"I guess I'm rambling. I've been reading a lot. Not much else I can do in this state. I've come on a very interesting little book, *Joining Miracles.* Somebody sent it to me. I'd like you to read when you get back here. I'm eager to get your take on it."

"Who sent it?"

"I don't know, it just arrived, there was no return address."

❏
I put in a call to my answering machine back in Washington.

Not good news.

First a call from the Devlin House Hotel in London, asking me to call. Puzzling. Why would a London hotel call me in Washington? Had I left something behind? Not that I could think of. For sure I had not left that switchblade behind, that was buried in the piles of trash at Heathrow.

Next a call from a Detective Inspector Gardener of the London Metropolitan police, asking me to call back at my "earliest convenience." Not good.

I went back up for my laptop, and plugged it into one of the outlets in the lobby. I ran Google for London + evening papers, and came up with the link to the Evening Standard.

Murder Suspected in South Kensington Hotel

The body of an individual, as yet unidentified, was found in the laundry chutes of the Devlin House Hotel in South Kensington yesterday evening. While final results await an autopsy, it appeared that the person had died of a broken neck, apparently suffered in a scuffle.

Metropolitan Police were reported to be seeking to question an American who checked out of the hotel early this morning. According to one unofficial source, the hotel chambermaid found a shoe under the bed he occupied, which appeared to match a shoe on the deceased individual's body.

I'd never thought to look under the bed.

And suppose I had found that shoe, what would I have done with it? Stuffed it into the trash bin at Heathrow, along with the knife?

56

A couple of tables in the Sporthotel's main dining room were occupied by local men drinking beer, and a family celebration filled the big round table in the middle of the room.

No sign of the CIA spook from London. No sign of the man Katje saw in the pub back in South Kensington last night, and at noon today in Bad Kronsee, that American with the big feet hiding behind a Tyrolean hat . . . unless he'd changed hats and buried himself in that family party.

The waitress, a lean, dark-haired girl, probably not over 18, but, like Frau Grunz, already looking permanently tired, brought us tall glasses of the local beer, cloudy with herbs. Local melodies, heavy on the clarinet and accordion, played through the PA system: Austria's version of Muzak. Kitschy, maybe, but we were in the Alps.

When in Austria, eat *Wiener Schnitzel* — that made ordering easy.

I'd brought down the pictures of Paul from home, as well as the others I'd picked up along the way: from Lili in La Rochelle, showing Paul standing with Celine, the two looking like happy young lovers; and the new ones of Paul and Dr. Gniessbach taken not far from here with the castle in the background, the same castle now floodlit at the end of the lake.

I borrowed a magnifying glass from Frau Grunz, and Katje moved around the table to sit beside me to look at them. That felt nice.

"It's uncanny, how much you resemble him," she said after looking through them. "He was such a good–looking young guy. What a shame that he died so young."

"He was a mythical figure to me when I was a child. I had elaborate fantasies that he was really on a secret mission and would show up some day."

I hadn't thought about that in years, nor about the imaginary conversations I'd had, envisioning his suddenly returning one day, and he and I becoming buddies. In my mind back then, Uncle Paul had frozen in time, forever the age when he left — action-hero and favorite uncle rolled into one.

Now, as it turned out, he *had* frozen in time, literally: frozen into a glacier not so many miles from here.

57

"There's something important that I haven't told you about myself," Katje said, mid-way through her second glass of the local beer. She reached over and took my hand and held it. She was still sitting on my side of the table.

I waited, wondering. A jealous husband who was ready to kill me? A gay lover who would drop poison in my beer?

"I died, last year. It changed my life."

That was a conversation stopper. Finally I blurted, "Dying does tend to change one's life," not sure whether this was a joke.

"My parents were atheists, totally convinced there was no God, no higher powers, nothing beyond this material life. That was the way they raised me, and I'd never thought any differently, never had any interest in exploring any of that side. They were killed in a plane crash a couple of years before, in Africa. I missed them, very much, but as far as I was concerned, that was that, they were dead, nothing was left but the memories."

I had no idea where she was going with this, but I nodded. We were still holding hands, and I felt her energy.

"Then I died, and that totally turned my world upside down. That made me understand that everything I thought I knew was wrong, everything I'd always dismissed as ridiculous just might be right."

She stopped, and I felt her body throb. "I think I'm not really making sense. I'd better start over. Jeff — my husband — and I went to Wisconsin for a long weekend. It was early winter, and we'd planned to ski, but a thaw hit and the skiing wasn't very good. We could have just sat around the fireplace, but that wasn't for Jeff. He was ten years older, extremely competitive, a real risk-taker. He loved living on the edge — he was a go-go investment manager who thrived on pushing the envelope, both on the job and in the rest of his life. I was a very driven person back then, but nothing like him."

What does this have to do with dying?, I wondered. She had paused now, and the redness around the eyes told me she was fighting back tears.

"Jeff rented a ski-doo, supposedly to do some back-country touring on the trails. He drove, I rode on the back, scared out of my wits when he veered off the trail and cut across a small lake. They'd warned us to stay off the ice, as the ice wasn't thick enough to be really safe. But tell Jeff something was risky, and he was drawn to it like a magnet. Coming back to shore, we hit slush under the snow-cover, and the slush gave way and we were in icy water, so cold it felt like fire. He let go of the ski-doo, but it was too late, we were in the water, wearing heavy coveralls that soaked through and dragged us down. I tried to swim, but it was too cold, and the clothes too heavy, and it was no use and I couldn't keep my head above the water.

"The water was crystal clear, and I saw bubbles coming up from the ski-doo on the lake bed, and felt myself sinking down to it. And then I wasn't sinking any more, then I was rising up, and I thought 'I'm saved,' but it wasn't what I thought it was. I saw my body sinking down, but I was floating up from it. I couldn't understand, how could my body be going one direction when I was going the other? About then I felt myself slipping into what seemed like a tunnel."

She broke off for a sip of beer, just enough to wet her mouth. "I didn't understand what was happening then, but later learned that I'd had a classic Near Death Experience, the tunnel, the light, the people standing up there in the light at the end of the tunnel. I'd paid no attention to the literature on Near Death Experiences, wrote that off as just earnest nonsense. But there I was, zipping up through the tunnel toward the light, the brightest light you could ever imagine. I knew that Jeff wasn't going to make it, and I knew I wasn't going to, either, and I didn't mind, I was content. My life was over, I was dead, and that was fine. It was an incredibly peaceful feeling, especially for somebody as driven as I was then."

She looked away for a moment, then went on. "That's when I saw my parents. They'd been dead about two years at that point. But it *was* them, no question in my mind, and they were waving to me, and it was as if I heard them saying, 'Go back, Katje, go back. We were wrong, go back and learn the truth.'"

She took another sip of beer. "Something happened then, and it was as if I was being pushed sucked backward the way I'd come, like being ejected back down the tube of a vacuum cleaner, and I found myself back in that icy-cold body again, fighting for breath. People had seen us go through the ice, and they managed to snag my body with a long pole, and the rescue crew got there in time to get me going again."

She paused, blinking away tears, and said, "From then onward, everything has been different. The experience jolted me into a different paradigm — a totally different framework for viewing the world."

Paradigm.

I raised my hand and she paused while I tried to formulate the question. It's funny how sometimes you hear a certain word, a word that comes along maybe once a year, and then it seems to pop up everywhere. Is it just that your ear gets attuned, or is it coincidence? Or is it beyond mere chance?

"It's strange," I said, "that you happened to use the word 'paradigm.' It's not an everyday word, yet within the past few minutes I've heard it from both you and my father."

"Paradigm — it's a model, a way of looking at things, trying to make sense of reality. My old paradigm, my old view of reality, was that this is it, there's nothing beyond. But that near-death experience jolted me, it made me understand that my old way of looking at the world was totally . . . inadequate, *incomplete.* I quit my job and started reading, and that's why I'm now writing a thesis on the Latent Miracle Power instead of wasting my life shifting money from one set of pockets to another."

I waited, then finally asked. "And your husband — Jeff?"

She shook her head. "Jeff didn't make it. By the time they pulled him up it was too late."

"I'm sorry," I said. The polite response, but so inadequate.

"It's . . ." Her voice quavered, and she paused before saying, "It's strange to say, but I've come to understand that's what he really wanted. He was a risk-taker, always living on the edge. But I think

that was just a kind of cover-story, even from himself. He was very
smart, very talented, but as I realized too late, also not really a happy
person. He almost took me with him — not that he intended it, he just
didn't think."

"I'm glad that didn't happen to you."

She managed a wan smile. "At first I was devastated, but now
I can see it in a kind of perspective. Jeff got what he really wanted,
deep down. And I got to live another life."

❏

She started to say something more, then broke off and looked away.
Finally she said, her eyes still not meeting mine, "I have no idea how
you feel, but I think it really was synchronicity that you and I met.
That was the track I wanted to join, to meet somebody really
interesting. Which you are, and I hope —"

She broke off when the waitress arrived with our schnitzels —
golden brown, still steaming from the pan.

I dug in, unaware that her experience was about to intersect
with events poised to occur in my life, demonstrating again how there
is no such thing as coincidence, not when it comes to important
matters.

She looked up after a minute or so, and said, "Now I think you
understand — why I said last night that it wasn't you, it was me. Why
I said I wasn't feeling ready for a relationship. Since Jeff. It's taken
me time to come to terms with . . . with everything, not just losing Jeff,
but discovering what I really wanted to be doing with my life."

58

We were both hungry, and continued to eat without saying much. We seemed comfortable together in the silence — something my mother used to say was a very good sign.

That image of Mom made me think of Dad, and I realized I'd left my cell-phone up in the room. It's not essential, I told myself. If anything happens to Dad, Mrs. Fox has the phone number of the hotel.

But that didn't satisfy me. I wanted the security of having that cell-phone beside me.

"Forgot something," I told Katje. "Back in a minute."

❑

The Sporthotel had looked new from the outside, but as I hurried up to the room I passed old photos showing how it had expanded over the years. New wings and additions had been tacked on here and there, some blending in better than others. Today's dining room had been the original lodge in the first photo, taken in the mid-1950's.

To get to my room I left the original part, crossed into the hotel lobby, then up a half-flight of stairs, down a short corridor into another wing, probably added in the 1960's, then up more stairs into the newest part, dating probably from the '90's.

But even here in the newest part, the hall lights were on timers that shut off before I'd quite made it to the next switch. As charming and quaint as it had seemed earlier, now it was dark and spooky, as if the place were infused with ghosts of long-dead holidays.

I stepped into my room, groping for the light switch. My legs went out from under me, and I hit the floor hard, and something rammed into the base of my skull.

"Do not move, you understand?," a man's voice said, speaking

English with a strong German accent. The voice was raspy, the air filled with smoky breath and rotted teeth. "You give us what we want, we won't hurt you, yes?"

This couldn't be happening, Austria was a safe place. "What do you want? Money?"

The metal thing pushed harder into my neck: a gun barrel. "Don't play no fucking games with us, yes? What old Gniessbach gave you, we want that."

"I . . . I left it downstairs, in the hotel safe."

He slammed my head onto the bare wooden floor. "We know it's in the wall safe here, and you got the key. Either you give it to us, or we beat the shit out of you and take the key, and then maybe kill you just for the fun of it."

"Who are you?"

"We could tell you that, but then we'd have to kill you." He laughed, a nervous giggle. I still didn't find it very funny as a joke.

"If you don't give us that fucking key fast," another voice said, another man standing in the darkness by the door, "we kill you anyway. Stand up slow, and put your hands up on the wall, way up above your head."

I did, and he pulled something over my head and around my neck then yanked hard and it cut off my air. I clawed at it, and he pulled it tighter, and the world slowed down as my oxygen cut off and I felt hands going through my pockets and then the tinkling of a key into the safe and the walls of my vision closed in and it was like I'd fallen into a sudden dream and I was hearing Katje telling her story . . . *I saw my body sinking down, but I was floating up from it and I felt myself pulled into a tunnel. My life was over, I was dead, and that was fine. It was an incredibly peaceful feeling.*

Then I was back, lungs burning and my head pounding, and I threw myself backward and I jerked my head back suddenly and felt the satisfying impact of hard head against soft nose tissue, and he grunted and let loose of the garotte around my neck and I got some air.

Lights flashed. A woman screamed. I recognized the guy who'd been choking me — one of the thuggy-looking guys in that old white Mercedes at the *Schnell Imbiss* along the road today, the one in the black jacket. He had a hand up, trying to slow the blood that gushed from his nose.

The other, the one in the white sweater, threw the balcony door open and ran out onto the porch that ran the length of the building. Black Jacket followed him.

Frau Grunz sat on the floor of the hallway, her eyes wide. "That other man, the third man, he knocked me down he was running so fast."

"Are you all right?," I asked, pulling myself up. My legs were weak, as I understood just how close I'd come to dying.

Then it struck: "A third man? I only saw two."

"I came to tell you — your friend told me you were here. I came to tell you that you have a phone call from America. Something about your father, something I could not understand."

59

I raced downstairs to the small phone booth by the reception desk, then took a couple of deep breaths before picking up, dreading what was coming.

"This is Mrs. Fox, Mrs. Geraldine Fox, your father's principal health care aide. We met when you were in Burlington last week."

"Yes, yes, I know who you are. Is everything — why are you calling? Has something happened to Dad?"

"As I have been telling you, your father was very ill, and even though I gave him the very best in care, he was not as strong —"

"Is he . . ."

"If you will please let me continue. A little while ago, at one-fifteen, to be precise, your father had a bad coughing spell — never a good sign for someone in his condition. I was in the other room, and when I came into the living room I found him slumped over in his chair, still trying to breathe. I of course called the rescue squad, using the 911 number and —"

"You're telling me he's . . . dead?"

"No, not dead. If you'd just listen, stop interrupting with all these questions. I tried the number of your cell-phone. There was no answer."

"If not dead, then what? Why are you calling?"

"To tell you that your father is in the hospital."

"How is he? Is he going to live?"

"I am not his doctor, that is not for me to say."

Finally a doctor from the emergency room came on the line to say that Dad had a choking spell, and some material, apparently part phlegm, part gastric contents, blocked his airflow. The rescue squad arrived quickly, but they found that his heart had stopped. They managed to pull him back using defibrillation paddles to jolt the heart, but it took three jolts before he showed signs of life. He was in the ER being assessed now, but it was too early to determine whether brain damage had occurred.

"Was it a heart attack?"

"We're running tests to confirm, but my guess is that there was no heart attack, just interference with his airflow. That interference, the materials in the air passage, could have been precipitated by effects of the underlying situation."

"You mean the cancer?"

"Exactly."

"Will he survive?"

"He seems out of danger, for the moment."

"I'm in Austria. I'll try to catch a flight home tomorrow."

"That would be wise."

❑

Katje was standing by the phone booth when I emerged. She hugged me. "I couldn't help hearing. Not good news, is it?"

I told her about Dad, and told her about the men in the room.

"Two men went out via the balcony? You're sure?," she said. "Then that's who the third man was chasing. He's the one we saw in London, then again at Bad Kronsee when we were having lunch — that American in the Tyrolean hat."

"Did he have big feet, unusually big?"

She looked at me a moment, puzzled. "I don't know. I didn't notice his feet. Anyway, he almost knocked me down, running out to the parking area, then jumped into his car. I ran out to see what he was up to. He took off in pursuit of an old white car, a smelly old clunker that really burned oil."

Frau Grunz appeared, and Katje spoke with her in German, then turned to me. "I told her about the men who broke into your room. She said that is impossible. This is Austria, and such things do not happen here. But if it did happen, then it must have been foreigners who did it because now there are too many foreigners in Austria." She winked as she spoke.

"It was the same pair who pulled up alongside us at that *Schnell Imbiss*," I said. "The men in that old white Mercedes.

Obviously it had nothing to do with the hotel, they were after us, so tell her I understand."

But Gniessbach's papers, the maps and photos he'd hoarded for all these years, were gone, and there was no getting them back.

Katje translated again. "I told Frau Grunz about your father, and she says she is very sorry to hear that, and want us to have a schnapps as her guest." She nodded. "Seems you might as well, as we can't very well drive to Munich tonight."

I went back up to the room for a moment, just to make sure nothing else had been taken. Good news: neither my laptop nor Katje's camera had been touched.

Two men after Gniessbach's papers, and another man after them. What the hell was it all about?

Day Five

"BUT HOW CAN I TELL THE DIFFERENCE between — " I groped for words — "between something that's part of the different Reality Track that I've supposedly joined, and something that's a mere coincidence?"

"A mere coincidence?" Brother Freddie shook his head. "I'm not sure that there is such a thing as 'a mere coincidence,' the universe being, as it is, all of a piece."

He didn't seem to have grasped the point of my question. "I mean, how can I be sure that what seems to result from a coincidence is actually the result of my selecting a Reality Track, and not just something that would have happened anyway?"

He laughed, but I didn't see the joke.

"You're asking how you can prove whether or not the outcome in fact resulted from your selecting a certain Reality Track. What kind of evidence were you anticipating? A thunderclap ? Or perhaps the sound of trumpets?"

Even I had to laugh. "Nothing like that, obviously. But

. . ." I couldn't finish the sentence, because I didn't have any idea of what kind of evidence could convince me that people could learn to bring about coincidences.

He shook his head. "That's good, because in all my years, I've never heard trumpets announce anything. A few thunderclaps, yes, but those only to announce that my expectation of a storm was being fulfilled."

"Then how can I be sure it's actually anything more than a coincidence?"

"What happened with you is typical of the way things come about when you select a Reality Track. Things don't materialize out of thin air, and they rarely announce that something special is happening. Instead, it's usually more subtle. What seem to be coincidences occur . . . but in fact they are significant coincidences that come in the guise of apparently normal happenings. And they are normal, once you have stepped into the Reality Track in which they are meant to occur."

From
JOINING MIRACLES:
Navigating the Seas of Latent Possibility
by "P"

60

Pounding at the door. I snapped awake and checked the clock: a little after one in the morning.

"*Herr Tapscott! Kommen-Sie!* You must come now! Another telephone call for you from America!"

I threw on some clothes and ran down to the little phone-booth where I had taken the call before, took a deep breath, then picked up. "Mr. Gregory Tapscott?," an American voice said. "Hold please."

At first it sounded like static on the line. Then I seemed to hear a voice. "Greg, you there?" Dad's voice, a raspy whisper.

"Dad?," I said, not sure what I'd really heard.

"I died, Greg."

I tried to process that. Was I still dreaming?

"Greg? Are you there?"

"I'm — yes, I'm here."

"I died tonight. I just wanted you to . . ."

I stood holding the phone, bewildered. Katje appeared out in the hallway, her hair tousled, wearing a jogging suit and rubber thongs on her feet..

". . . wanted you to know that I pulled through. I came back," he continued.

The voice was like Dad's, but coarser and weaker, like something from a movie seance.

"But I was dead, dead for I don't know how long, before they pulled me back. Your mother sends her love." His voice broke and I sensed he was crying. "She told me I needed to come back and help you and Paul finish this."

"You're okay?," I managed.

"They tell me I choked on something and the EMS team got there in time and pulled me back. That's what they tell me. But I know it was your mother sending me back."

"I'll catch a plane tomorrow out of Munich. I can be there in plenty of time — "

"No! Don't come now. I'm fine. I simply choked on something, it wasn't the cancer. You're needed there. Find out the truth about Paul. You told me earlier that you're going to that monastery where Paul was held. Go there. See what you can turn up. I want to know the truth."

Katje was outside the phone booth. I opened it long enough to say, "It's Dad. He's okay."

"Greg," Dad said, "is somebody there with you?"

"It's Katje, somebody who's helping me. A friend."

"Katie? A female friend? Well good for you. Will I like her? Are you going to bring her home to meet me?"

"I hope so, Dad," I said.

61

I woke next at dawn, and saw big snowflakes drifting past the window. An inch or so of fluffy white snow lay like a decoration on the red geraniums in the flower-boxes on the balcony.

I dressed quickly and stepped onto the balcony. The air was fragrant with the scent of fresh snow and balsam, but visibility was close to zero; I could barely see down to the shoreline through the snow, and a fog rose from the water. There would be no helicopters going up to the glacier — not until this burned off.

I called the hospital in Burlington; Dad had been moved from the ER to a room on one of the wards. I was put through to the floor nurse. "Your father is resting — that's about all we can tell you at this time. What happened last night — it seems it was just a choking spell, though it was a very close call for him."

❏

The snow had stopped by the time I finished a quick breakfast. The edge of the sun burst through a gap in the mountains. The still lake gradually shifted from gray to pale blue, and the mountains, dusted with a fresh coat of snow, glistened as if it were the first day of creation.

The tops of the higher mountains behind were still shrouded in clouds, as was the Hochweisse Glacier. It would be hours before I could hope to fly up to see Paul's plane. Monks were early risers. Maybe I could make a quick run up to the monastery now and still be back in plenty of time to take a copter flight up to the glacier, or just drive back to Munich.

Katje hadn't come down to breakfast, so I slipped a note under her door and set out on the hiking trail that circled the lake. It was still shadowed here in the valley, but the bright autumn sun gleamed off the snowy mountain tops. The snow was already melting.

The path ran along a lake-side promenade for the first hundred yards or so. In the village shops, I'd seen postcards of this promenade as it was in summer, shaded by luxuriant plane trees. Now the branches had been cut back to stumps for the winter, leaving the trees oddly misshapen. The small guest-houses, cottages, and boat-rental stands along the shore seemed equally forlorn.

I checked behind; no one was following me.

I was edgy, naturally enough, after last night. But I told myself I was safe enough, now that they had what they'd come for — Dr. Gniessbach's papers and maps.

But what could be so interesting about those old papers? I had no idea, but now it was no longer my problem. Too bad I'd lost the map to Paul's plane, but that meant one less problem, one less thing to keep me from going back to be with Dad in his final days.

❏

The village ended, and the trail skirted the shore for a few hundred yards, before cutting through patches of forest that angled up from the water to wind alongside soft green meadows. Sheep and cows looked up from their grazing to regard me, then went back to grass-processing.

The lake remained mirror-still and fog-shrouded, and I walked the path at waters' edge, sniffing wood-smoke, damp leaves, hearty food simmering somewhere.

As I walked on, the castle emerged from the fog, ghost-like, mysterious, ethereal.

A weathered carved-wood sign pointed the side-trail to the monastery, a narrow path that curled up into the forest. I climbed, the scent of balsam blending with the dusky aromas of leaves, mud, and fresh manure. After ten minutes, the scent of wood-smoke became stronger, and I emerged into a small clearing.

A tiny stone chapel stood in a bower of pines. The door was unlocked, and I stepped in. The interior was simple, a small altar surrounded by a few rows of wooden benches.

I sat for a moment, absorbing the peacefulness.

Then I sensed a presence, and a figure appeared from the shadows. At first I thought it was a man in combat fatigues. But it wasn't a soldier, it was a monk in a dark green robe. I'd seen monks in brown and black habits, and nursing nuns in white, but never one in forest green.

He held out his hand. "Welcome. I'm Brother Jack." He was as tall as I, though built like a fullback — wide and strong — and looked as though he spent more time working out than praying. His eyes twinkled as if at some private joke. "We've been expecting you, Greg. Brother Augustus is eager to meet you."

"*Expecting* me? How did you know I was coming? How did you know my name?"

"I didn't say we *knew* you were coming, I said we were *expecting* you. There is a difference. In any case, Fraulein Hilda at the tourist office phoned." He laughed. "Why? Did you think we're psychic?"

Then I realized: Brother Jack was speaking in English, in perfect English. In *American* English. What was an American monk doing in an obscure little monastery in Austria?

He led the way back through the curtain, through a small anteroom, then along a covered arcade to another old stone building, all but invisible behind a cluster of pines.

It was more austere inside than I expected. Simple wooden furniture, walls bare except for a cross here and there, and some other religious symbols I didn't recognize. It smelled of apples and baking bread, soups and spices, and I wondered if this place was as peaceful as it seemed.

62

Brother Jack knocked on a battered oak door at the top of a flight of worn wooden stairs.

Inside, an old monk sat in a soft leather chair. Two others sat beside him, as if waiting for me. The old man wore a brown habit; the other two wore green habits like Brother Jack's, and it struck me again how much those green habits resembled military uniforms.

The old monk looked up and smiled, "Come and sit beside me, Greg. I am Brother Augustus."

I shook the hand he extended; it was calloused and hard. He looked fit for his age, and apparently still helped out with the physical labor around the place.

He introduced Brother Theo. Mid-50's, tall and lean. British accent. He wore what seemed to be a wedding ring. As, I noticed a moment later, did Brother Jack.

"I'm looking for news of my uncle, Paul Tapscott, missing since World War II. I was told that he was held here as a prisoner in 1944-45." I passed him one of the pictures of Paul.

"Who told you that?"

"Dr. Gniessbach."

Augustus said something in German; moments later, Brother Jack produced a battered leather photo album. He flipped through the pages, then pulled out two photos and handed them to me.

They grainy black-and-white, obviously old. One showed a group of monks lined up in front of the chapel I had just entered. Paul, unmistakable, was on the end, though dressed in civilian clothes. The other was a close-up: Paul, smiling, next to a young monk.

I recognized that young monk: Brother Augustus, many years younger.

I felt a surge of elation, again feeling it really was finally coming together. Now I had three concrete bits of evidence. Photos of Paul in La Rochelle, Gniessbach's photos of Paul, now these pictures of Paul with the monks.

But after these photos were taken, then what? "Dr. Gniessbach told me that Paul stole a plane in the final days of the war, then crashed on the glacier," I prompted.

"Dr. Gniessbach told you that?," Brother Augustus said. "Then he is mistaken. Or is misleading you. Your uncle was not on that plane."

He wagged his index finger, his eyes twinkling. "No, I must correct myself. Brother Paul *was* on that plane, but then he was forced off at gunpoint by a German pilot who wanted the plane for his own escape. It is that unfortunate fellow who is entombed on the glacier, may God rest his soul."

"*Brother* Paul? Are you saying he became a monk here?"

"Not exactly, no."

"Not exactly? I don't understand."

"When Gniessbach left him here, Paul chose to follow our rule, living our life, praying as we do, eating with us. But of course he had his own work to do, which he did in private."

"What work?"

"Attempting to decode the Knowledge from the Templar Chest."

"Was he successful?," I asked, realizing as the words came out that I had skipped over a question. I should have played dumb and asked, What Templar Chest?, to get his fresh take.

"He made a start before Gniessbach came back for him in those final days of the war."

"You said that Paul was forced off the plane by another pilot. Then what happened to him?"

Brother Augustus shrugged. "After that, I cannot say."

"The work he did while he was here, decoding the Templar material — is that still here? His notes? Anything?"

"He took it with him when he left the second time."

"*Second* time? Paul was here twice?"

"Of course. First in '44-45, and again in '55."

He pulled out several more photos from the album and gave them to me. Paul was in each, though now this was Paul a decade older than in the others. Some of the pictures had been taken in the village, and in the background were some of those early post-war Volkswagen Beetles, along with classic '50's-era Mercedes with the big chrome grills.

❏

"But if Paul returned here to the monastery in 1955, then he must have still been alive that late."

Brother Augustus chuckled. "He certainly *seemed* to be alive."

"This is — I'm finding it hard to grasp that Paul survived ten years after the war and never contacted his family. After he returned to the monastery, in 1955— what then? Did he stay, or leave?"

"He stayed with us a few weeks, then left again."

"Where did he go? Is he *still* alive?"

Augustus shook his head. "After that I cannot say."

"Why would Paul have stayed in hiding all those years and not gone home?"

"Is it not obvious? Because the American authorities considered him dangerous. If they had found him, they would either have shot him on the spot or locked him away for decades in a prison or a mental hospital."

"Criminal? Insane? Was he . . .?"

"No more than I," Augustus said, chuckling, and glancing at the younger monks, a mischievous glint in his eyes. "Though some of the brothers here might consider that an indictment."

"You say the military would have shot him or locked him away for decades. Why? What did he do that was so wrong?"

"Not so *wrong*, rather so *threatening*," Brother Theo interjected. "Paul did two things that were threatening to those in positions of power. He snatched the Templar secrets from those he considered unfit to possess them. And then there was the other matter of — "

"The other matter is irrelevant," Brother Augustus said, slapping his hand on the arm of the chair. "Irrelevant at this time. That would only confuse the issue."

Brother Theo nodded. "What Brother Augustus is saying is that the Americans hurried here in response to Paul's radio message because they believed he had access to the Nazis' secrets of *atomic* power. Naturally enough, when they arrived and found that he had gone with those secrets, then they were very troubled. They put out a bulletin accusing him of theft — though of course for security reasons they couldn't say that they believed he had stolen atomic secrets. In those days, few had ever heard the term 'atomic.'"

"*Were* there atomic secrets in that old chest?"

"They caught Dr. Gniessbach at once, but Gniessbach *wanted* that. Like the other Germans, he preferred to be captured by the Americans rather than the Russians. It took a few days before the Americans accepted what Gniessbach was telling them — that Paul was gone, along with the contents of the chest. But then things got complicated. They needed a culprit."

"A culprit?"

"It seems that the OSS officer in charge had raced across Europe in response to Paul's message, thinking he would make a name for himself by securing the atomic secrets of the Nazis. Once he got here, of course, he found that there were in fact no atomic secrets, but he needed to justify his trip, to cover up something else. For that he needed a culprit, a scapegoat, a villain. That is why he accused Paul Tapscott of stealing secrets. That took the pressure off himself."

"Do you know the name of this OSS officer?"

Brother Augustus shook his head. "It was a very long time ago."

❏

I should have followed that up by asking, "You said that OSS officer 'needed to justify his trip, to cover up something else.' What was it he needed to cover up?"

But I failed to ask, and that would come back to haunt me later.

63

Washington, 4:33 A.M.

Fackson grabbed it midway through the first ring, hoping to get it before it woke Elynis, the third Mrs. Fackson. He was used to middle-of-the-night crises, and had long ago developed the ability to deal with problems and then go back to sleep. Elynis was new to this life, had not developed that knack, and made it clear that she did not intend to.

"All hell is breaking loose here." Despite the scrambler, Fackson knew Edison's voice. "They broke into Tapscott's room last night and stole some papers out of his room safe. I chased them, got a license number, but they slipped away."

"What papers? Not Katz' papers? He didn't have the Katz papers, did he?"

"No way of knowing what they got. But my feeling, there's no way he could have gotten anything from Katz before he left Washington. My gut feel, this was something he got from that old German, Gniessbach."

"Any idea who did it?"

"Reasonably sure it was Twisted Messiah's bunch. Same old white Mercedes that tried something yesterday. I'm having our locals run a trace. It's only ten in the morning here, they haven't gotten back to me yet."

"The Lizard is gonna have a stroke when he hears that. Suppose it was Katz' papers they were after. Question is, what the hell would the Twisted Messiah gang want with Katz' stuff?"

"Maybe that goes back to why Katz was interested in *them*. Why did he have all those files on Twisted Messiah? Did that somehow link up with his other investigations? Maybe if we answer one of those questions, we'll have solved the other."
❏

"I still don't understand," I asked Brother Augustus. "Why would Paul run away from his own people? The war was over, and they were coming to rescue him."

"Is it not obvious?" Brother Augustus said. "Because by then Paul was beginning to understand the importance of the knowledge in the Templars' Chest. He knew it was too important, too dangerous, to allow into the hands of any government."

De Lattry, the old lawyer in La Rochelle: *Governments take on lives of their own. Bureaucracies grow within them, power bases develop, and subtly, over the span of years, things change. All it takes is a few determined men working silently within.*

Brother Theo said, "Why did Paul run? Because from the moment he stumbled on the Templar Chest, his life changed forever. As perhaps you know, that chest had been hidden in La Rochelle in 1307, when the Templars learned they were about to be attacked by the forces of the king and the pope."

"What was in that chest? What could have made Paul willing to sacrifice the life he could have had at home, after the war?" If it was the Grail, I wanted them to say it without prompting.

Augustus answered, "The deeper question is why the establishments of the time attacked the Templars. Why do you think that was?"

The Templars had been wiped out a thousand years ago. Why was he asking me this? "Because they'd been declared heretics."

"But those same Templars had long been the primary protectors of the Vatican. Now, rather suddenly, they were considered heretics. Why? What caused the change?," Theo asked.

I shrugged. If there was something I was missing, then let them tell me.

"In truth, the charge of heresy was only a cover. First the Cathars, and later the Templars were attacked through a combination of greed for their material wealth, as well as fear of a mysterious power they had supposedly learned to tap."

Mysterious power. Was that, I wondered, that rumored ability to create unlimited wealth?

"There is nothing *mysterious* about the power," Augustus broke in. "It's nothing more than a basic human potential that we all have, but one that most of us have been conditioned to overlook. The Templars learned to tap this power, and that, of course, was *extremely* threatening to the establishment, just as it would be – as it *is* – today."

The old man paused to sip coffee, then continued: "The

established powers couldn't afford to let that knowledge leak out into the general population."

"Why?"

"Because if it were widely spread, that would destroy the basis of their own power."

"What is that power? Do you have any idea?," I asked.

"The established powers of the day, of *whatever* day, find that the more we ordinary people believe in our own limitations, the more their control is enhanced," Brother Theo said. "Why? Because if we *believe* we are limited, if we believe that our problems are beyond our control, then our own sense of limitations bestows power on them."

Brother Augustus cut in: "*That* is the great secret that the establishments of every age don't want us to know: that we are *not dependent* on them, that we have *within ourselves* the power to change the flow of events, even – *especially* – those outside our direct physical control."

The room went silent as the old monk spoke. From the glances that passed between Theo and Jack, I got the sense that Brother Augustus had said something that outsiders weren't supposed to hear.

"And that's what Paul found – the secret to tapping the power discovered by the Templars?"

Brother Augustus nodded. "Exactly so. And of course Paul was determined — indeed, he was convinced that he *had the duty* — to keep it out of the wrong hands."

I was leaving, when a question came to mind, one I'd already asked and hadn't really been answered: "Did Paul ever say anything about what it was he found in the Templar Chest? Did he explain what that power was?"

"Yes, of course we talked," Brother Augustus said. "As he expressed it, what he turned up was an intuitive prefiguring of the findings of modern science."

I waited for him to amplify, then asked, "But what does that mean?"

The old monk shrugged. "I cannot say. For that, you must ask him."

"*Ask* him? How can I — " I broke off. "Are you telling me that Paul is alive?"

He shook his head. "As I said, he was here last in 1955."

64

A brilliant clear sun had climbed over the mountain tops by the time I left the monastery. The pale blue lake was mirror-still, with only wisps remaining of the morning's fog. The air was cool and moist, redolent of damp leaves, soil, pine trees, and, as I came down the hillside, the freshness of the glacier-fed lake.

But I was lost, bewildered.

Paul died on the glacier, according to Dr. Gniessbach.

Not so, said the monks: Paul and the chest were thrown off that plane before it took off. And they had photos that almost certainly were of Paul in 1955.

But if Paul survived, why didn't he come home to his family when the war ended? According to the monks, because he was determined to keep the contents of the Templar Chest from even his own government.

Why keep it from his own people? Supposedly because "*that chest held the secret to tapping an innate human power we all have, but most of us have been trained and conditioned to overlook.*"

And because that secret was "*too important, even too dangerous, to allow into the hands of any government.*"

Which again brought to mind something else De Lattry had said: *Governments sometimes are formed by the people, but then they take on lives of their own — taken over by groups of determined men working silently within.*

Next question: what IS that innate human power, the secret too dangerous to allow into the hands of any government?

According to the monks, that power was not the secret of

eternal life, nor even of creating unlimited wealth. The power was more prosaic, yet more potent: as old Brother Augustus put it, *The Great Secret is that we have within us the power to change the flow of events, even those outside our direct control.*

Whatever that meant.

Was that what Lili had referred to as "perhaps the Holy Grail, perhaps the most powerful force the world has ever known?"

Perhaps. Probably. It might even be what Katje had been calling the Latent Miracle Power.

But my mission wasn't really to uncover what Paul may have turned up. It wasn't even to uncover Great Secrets, no matter how intriguing.

I was here, at Dad's request, to find out what really happened to Paul. That was my core objective, to find when and why Paul died. Everything else was just nice to know. Nice but not necessary.

If the monks were to be believed, Paul didn't dare go home because his own people would have killed him, or locked him away. Maybe because he knew too much. Or because they needed a scapegoat.

Scapegoat for what?

Would the OSS, would the Army, would any branch of the U.S. government have cared enough about some old chest to go after Paul? After all, the war was over and done.

But then why would the American military have set Larkwood and his team to study whether the Nazis had uncovered, as he put it, 'some kind of power within the mind that could direct and focus energies from other dimensions?'

And then why did they — whoever "they" were — deny Larkwood access to information on Operation Perceval?

Strange.

Next question: after Paul returned to the monastery in 1955, what then?

Brother Augustus "couldn't say." Because he didn't know? Or because he was covering up something?

And one final question: if Brother Augustus was right, that it was someone else, not Uncle Paul, buried in the plane in the glacier, then why were those thugs last night so interested in grabbing Dr. Gniessbach's maps?

65

A note from Katje told me she was taking a walk around the village, so I drove out to the airport to see whether the pilots were in the mood to visit the glacier today.

But even as I headed there, a trip up to the glacier seemed a futile exercise. Now I'd lost the maps Gniessbach had given me. Finding the plane would depend on whether those pilots could remember the location on that map I'd shown them.

And if they could find the plane? Then what? I could take some pictures for Dad, maybe toss a wreath.

Yesterday that had seemed like a good idea, the best I could do under the circumstances.

But that was before I'd talked to the monks, before they'd told me that Paul had been forced off the plane, along with the chest, by some poor drunken pilot.

Who was right? Was it Paul up there in the ice, or was it some forever nameless German?

I was relieved to find that there was no sign of the pilots, the Ops Center was locked, and there was no one around to ask when they'd be back.

❑

My cell-phone still wasn't getting a dial-tone up here in the mountains, so I used the hotel's line to call the hospital again. No real change in Dad's condition.

❑

Katje was back from her walk, visibly much better than yesterday. We had a quick lunch at the hotel, and I passed on what I'd learned from the monks: that supposedly Gniessbach was wrong, that Paul had not been in the plane that crashed. Then I showed her the new pictures the monks had given me, of Paul's return to the monastery in 1955.

"Why didn't he go home at the end of the war like all the other soldiers?"

"According to the monks, because he was made a scapegoat by his OSS commanders, who claimed he had stolen atomic secrets or something. That was nonsense, just something they came up with to cover themselves. He did take some of the contents of the Templar chest, and that only because he wanted to keep it out of the hands of those same commanders. He didn't trust them with it. He didn't trust any government or any bureaucracy with it."

She nodded, and watched a couple in a paddle-boat split the glassy lake water. "Does that sound plausible to you?"

"I don't know what to think."

I repeated what the monks had said about the Great Secret, that it was "*a basic human potential that we all have, but most of us have been trained and conditioned to overlook,*" and that it was, as Brother Augustus put it, "*the great secret that the establishments of every age don't want us to know, that we are not dependent on them, that we have within ourselves the power to change the flow of events, even – especially – those outside our physical control.*"

I saw the excitement in her eyes. "It certainly sounds like what I've been referring to as the LMP — the Latent Miracle Power."

"That's just about what the monks finally said, that Paul had found the secret to tapping the power discovered by the Templars, and that he ran with it because he felt he had the duty to keep it out of the wrong hands."

"But does it really make sense to you that the government would chase him for more than 60 years for something like that?"

"None of it has ever made any sense."

66

Frau Grunz, so dour when we arrived, actually hugged me as we left, and said she'd be praying for Dad. I promised to send her the news. "A picture, that would be good," she said. "You send me a new picture of you with father, then I will know our prayers were answered, yes?"
❏
The way seemed shorter going back than it had coming — it always does — and we left the high mountain area and were approaching Bad Kronsee sooner than I expected. I tried the cell-phone; it was picking up a dial tone now, so I pulled off the highway at the entrance to a logging road.

A small brook passed by the road here, and I listened to the gurgling water as I punched in the number of the *Elderresidenz Seeblick* in Bad Kronsee. We weren't far from there now, and there were some follow-ups I wanted to ask Dr. Gniessbach.

You said those maps showed Paul's plane frozen into the glacier. Some pilots said the plane you marked was much too recent to be Paul's. Any further thoughts?

You said Paul stole the plane, but the monks just told me that Paul had been forced off the plane, along with the contents of the chest. Who is right?

Some men broke into my room last night, nearly killed me, then stole all the materials you gave me. Any idea who they were? Who else would care about Paul, after all these years?

A man answered. "*Sprechen-sie Englisch?*," I asked. "Do you speak English?"

"Yes, a little. What is it you want?"

"I visited Dr. Gniessbach yesterday. Is it possible to return today to speak with him for a few more minutes?"

"No, that is impossible."

"It's extremely important."

"I tell you, it is impossible. You see, Dr. Gniessbach, he is dead. He died last night."

I don't know how long I was speechless. The man said, "Hello? Yes? Are you still there?"

"Dr. Gniessbach — what did he die of?"

"Who can say? He was very old, you must know that."

"Then let me speak to Elfriede Schwarnhof."

"No, that is impossible as well. Fraulein Schwarnhof did not come to work this day. We do not know where she is. She did not call in sick, she has not even come to collect the pay she is owed."
❑

I clicked off. Gniessbach was old and frail. As he'd put it, *We have as much time as you care to listen, or until the Almighty takes me.*

Had the Almighty taken him so conveniently after our visit? Or had Elfriede hurried things —

"Greg! Come! Hurry!," Katje shouted. She unsnapped the door-locks and signaled for me to jump behind the wheel and get going. I didn't ask questions, just fired it up and pulled out of the side road.

"A truck, a black van, went by. It slowed down, and then passed by a second time, really looking us over. I got a bad feeling."

This was a remote stretch of road; there had been very little traffic, and I hadn't thought of how isolated and vulnerable we were.

I hit the gas and we were moving. A few kilometers and we'd be at the autobahn.

A black van rounded a bend, and headed at us, way over onto our side of the narrow road.

"That's the truck, Greg! The one I was telling you about!"

The van stopped, blocking the road. I threw our Audi into reverse, checked the rear-view mirror, and said, "Oh shit!" A dirty white Mercedes a was yard off my tail, blocking the exit. The same two guys, one in the greasy white sweater, and the little guy in black leather, jumped out and ran toward us.

I clicked it back into drive, looking for enough room to squeeze past the van. The driver blocked me, and the passenger jumped out onto the pavement, holding a gun at us, a squat little thing, probably an Uzi.   Now the two guys from the Mercedes were upon us, hammering on the side windows. One had a pistol, the other an Uzi.

"They've got us, Greg."

We stepped out, hands up. They dragged us to the van and shoved us onto the hard metal floor of the van, then scrambled in and slammed the door. The driver hit the gas.

Close-up, White Sweater seemed a slob in the mold of the characters John Belushi used to play. But he spoke some English, and handed us each a bottle of beer. "You drink," he said, forcing a rictus of a smile.

"We're not thirsty," I said.

"You drink, or we pour it down you, understand?"

"Why? Why are you doing this?"

"Just drink the goddam beer, yes?"

The van was moving now, throwing us around in the back. Two of the other thugs grabbed me, and White Sweater came over and poured the beer into my mouth until I choked. "Okay, I'll drink," I said. They eased off, and I swallowed some. It tasted okay.

"More. You drink all, now," he said.

"It could be rohypnol, the date-rape drug," Katje said.

"It could be poisoned Kool-Aid," White Sweater said. "That would be worse, yes? Now you drink it!"

67

"Bad news," Edison said when Fackson came on the line. It was the end of the work day in Washington. Tapscott and the woman have disappeared. Most likely grabbed along the road."

"The hell you mean, 'most likely?' We're supposed to have a team watching them, so why the mystery? Who the hell would have wanted them?"

"Tapscott checked out of that hotel in Austria after lunchtime. Our guys tried to follow, and found all four tires had been cut."

"Shit! I can't believe it! I thought you had two cars."

"We did, but I'd left early in the second car, tracking the plates on that grungy old Mercedes that — "

"Hold on! If that was lunchtime there, then we're talking nine, ten hours ago. And they just told you now?"

"Their cell-phones didn't work in the mountains, and they were in a hurry to rent another car and get under way. They traced the route back to Munich. No signs of them. Then they checked with the car rental place at the airport, and it turns out Tapscott's Audi had been turned in hours ago. When they showed the rental guy a picture, he said it wasn't Tapscott who turned it in, it was a couple of greasy scuzzbags, from what he says. Which makes me think they were grabbed along the road."

Fackson rubbed his temples, a stress reaction he'd had all his life. He still didn't understand why: to relieve pressure, or to stimulate the brain. "You've got to find where they took them. *Who* took them, for that matter. Then, somehow, get Tapscott back so we can get him up to London and retrieve Katz' papers from the hotel."

"Hold on, we're not sure it's the Katz materials up in London. All I heard is that he left something in the safe. It could be any damned thing."

"Suppose it was Twisted Messiah that grabbed Tapscott — where would they take them?"

"Beats me, but I'll ask the local talent."

Day Six

"LIFE IS THE PROCESS OF NAVIGATING THIS SEA of undifferentiated, still latent, possibilities. We start each day, even each moment, facing an array of possibilities of how things might flow from this point. That array finally winnows down to the one reality which we actually experience."

"Why? What does that winnowing-down?"

"It seems that we do it."

"I know I don't, that's for sure."

"I wouldn't be so sure, my young friend. In a way that scientists can't totally explain, our mind, by its selections and expectations, in some way shapes the reality that actualizes from the array of mere possibilities. Contrary to what we've been led to believe, we're not just passive spectators waiting for reality to come to us. Rather, we can select the version of reality that we prefer to experience."

"Actualizes? What does that mean?"

"Becomes actual. Becomes the reality that we

experience."

"How? Reality is reality, and I don't see that what's going on in my head can shape what's going to happen out there in the big world."

"By joining the track, and not just wishing but actually expecting it, we play a key role in determining which of the potential realities becomes the actuality which we in fact experience."

"How?"

"By making a conscious effort to select an outcome — and by expecting it to come about — we vastly increase the probability of it coming to be."

From
JOINING MIRACLES:
Navigating the Seas of Latent Possibility
by "P"

68

A scream, a long, wailing cry of terror, pulled me out of a nightmare. It was dark, and I didn't know where I was. My heart thundered fast in my chest, my head throbbed, my body stank of cold sweat, my mouth was sandpaper dry.

Then another scream, a woman's voice, that broke into staccato "No! No! No!" Then silence.

"Greg!," a voice whispered in the darkness. Katje's voice. I was lying on a floor, and felt her beside me. I tried to move my hands. They were taped in front of me, the tape covering my wrist-watch, but my feet were free. I shimmied up, bracing against the wall, until I was standing. We were in some kind of storage room.

I was remembering events now: the highjacking, the van, the beer they made us drink. Then it got jumbled, just images, dream-like snatches of questions that made no sense, of being dragged up some stairs, of dirty, scary people, nightmare people.

"You heard the screams? There were others, before you came to," Katje said. I offered my hand, and she leveraged herself to her feet.

The only window was about 10 feet up, and we could see only the sky. It was dark outside, night, and only a sliver of pale artificial light shone onto the top of the wall.

Another scream. Then silence.

My eyelids were heavy, my legs tired. I slid back onto the floor, this time with my back braced against a wall so I could sit.

More of it came back now: Dr. Gniessbach was dead. The trap along the road. The van and the grungy old white Mercedes and the beer that knocked us out. The men who had jumped me in the room at the hotel. Dad's choking spell..

The two grungy guys who had jumped me in the hotel to steal Gniessbach's papers were also among the ones who held us up on the road. Why go after us twice? Why get the stuff out of the safe, then high-jack us along the road?

The CIA guy on the train back from Oxford: *We've been picking up the name Paul Tapscott in some of the chatter of a certain NGPF, a Non-Governmental Political Force that may have terrorist potential. It would probably surprise the hell out of you if I told you what group had the chatter about your uncle. We just don't know what the hell about Paul interests them.*

It was obvious now: that NGPF was Twisted Messiah.

Somehow, a rock group had made the leap from rock stardom to Non-Governmental Political Force.

❑

I woke again to a roar. I was disoriented at first, then remembered where I was, and recognized the sound: a helicopter spooling up, and the whop-whop as it took off. Very close by, as if just outside the room.

I heard the sound fade, then nothing more.

69

The door crashed open, jolting me awake. My head still ached. The sudden bright light burned my eyes. I was desperately thirsty.

Four men, White Sweater and Black Jacket, plus two others even grungier, stood over us, their expressions showing how it pleased them to have us helpless.

Black Jacket's nose was swollen, and both eyes had blackened. That pleased me. I'd done that, broken his nose when I'd lashed back with my head to stop him choking me.

"You got us in a lot of trouble, you piece of shit!," one of the new men said. British accent, a mop of greasy, shoulder-length hair, a week's growth of beard on a thick, broad heavy-featured face. He was missing an eye where a scar slashed from forehead to the side of his mouth.

"Answer me!," he screamed, kicking my leg. If he'd been wearing boots, not dirty running shoes, or if he'd been sober enough to aim the kick, he might have broken the ankle.

"What's the question?"

"That map, it wasn't no damned good, it was a bloody fake." Another kick, but this time he lost his balance and it went high, not connecting at all.

"The papers you took from me — that's what I got from Dr. Gniessbach, exactly what he gave me. Why did you want them?"

"You know bloody damned well why. We know all about your uncle and what he found, and now we want it. You set us up, you let us fall into the goddam trap, but it's not going to happen again, I tell you that. This time you're going to take us there."

This time I was ready for his kick. Now he aimed higher, at my groin, but he was slow. I rolled and he missed. He lost balance, stumbled back, and fell hard onto the floor.

White Sweater said something in German, probably saying he could do better, but mop-head growled and he backed off. Two more, just as scruffy, came into the room. Mop-head said something I didn't understand, and they grabbed me from behind and slammed me into a chair and wrapped a rope around me, then one of them knelt and pulled my shoes off.

"You're going to wish you'd talked sooner," Mop-head said.

The door opened again and a thick, muscle-bound guy with a shaved head hustled in and whispered something to Mop-head. He jumped up and followed him out, his face betraying fear.

The others, White Sweater and the two new ones glared at us. White Sweater said, "You better to tell me, now. Then it makes it not so hard for you, understand? Where is the stuff we need?"

"I don't know what you're after. You got the map and things. That's all I have."

"It won't just be you he hurts. Your girlfriend, too, and he'll make you watch. He's mean, the worst guy here. He gets off on it, yes?"

"Tell me what you want."

"You don't believe me? You hear those girls screaming last night? They're dead now, and there's plenty of room to bury you two."

The door crashed open again, and Mop-head stuck his head in and muttered something I missed. There was no doubt of it now, he was in panic mode. I knew enough German to understand some of it: "It's a disaster! The police will be coming! The media! We must get them away! We must clear things up!"

Katje spoke softly. "Did you understand all that? Something has happened, something gone wrong, something about a helicopter."

"I heard a copter taking off earlier. It seemed very close by, almost just outside the door. What was that —"

The muscle-bound guy stuck his head in and grunted an order.

White Sweater sliced the ropes that held me in the chair, then kicked my shoes to me. "Put them on, fast."

They shoved us out the door and into a courtyard. The courtyard was surprisingly big, an atrium surrounded on four sides by white stucco buildings. One of the buildings had the look of a church.

To me, still half-drugged, it seemed like part of a dream.

The night sky was still dark, the air cool and damp, with snow still falling on top of the couple inches that already covered the ground.

A van pulled up and again they shoved us into the back. We pulled ourselves along the floor to brace our backs against the heavy wire barrier blocking off the driver's compartment. White Sweater and Leather Jacket climbed in back with us.

The driver hit the gas, and we passed through gates. I got a glimpse through the small rear window. My first impression had been right: the place did look like a monastery. Or a convent. And now we were on the outside again.

Convent. Something about a convent. In the news yesterday.

Then I remembered that TV segment on the plane yesterday. After the Twisted Messiah concert in Berlin, Jesse Cripes had flown by private jet to his compound in the German Alps, a former convent, renamed The Convent of the Sensuous Virgins.

Those bone-chilling screams that split the night. What in hell had been going on? Some convent this was.

We bounced around on the hard floor as the van clattered along a bumpy road. We hadn't gone far, only a few hundred yards, when the driver rounded a bend and slammed on the brakes. We slid against the divider to the passenger section. Leather Jacket wasn't braced and stumbled the length of the van and hit the wire barrier face first.

"*Schiesse! Das Polizei!*," somebody shouted

White Sweater pulled a knife out of his pocket and came at us. I got my legs up and kicked, connecting solidly with his crotch. He dropped the knife and doubled up, groaning.

Leather Jacket pulled himself to his feet. His face was latticed by impact with the wire, and blood spurted from his nose and the broken stumps of teeth. He grabbed the knife and sliced the tapes that bound our hands. "You make no trouble with police, yes? Or I kill you both. You understand?"

The beam of a light cut through the back window and somebody yanked the side door open. I was blinded by a pair of bright lights. "*Raus!*," a voice commanded.

70

The German police bundled Katje and I into one of the cars, then left us alone while they frisked and handcuffed the men from the van and hustled them into another car.

A pair of officers climbed in our car, nodded to us, and started the engine.

"Where are we going?," Katje asked in German.

"You must first answer some questions, yes? Then another man, he wants to speak to you."

They had set up a command post in the town hall of the next village, and uniformed officers questioned us for fifteen minutes or so. They told us that we had been in the convent of Jesse Cripes, and were very lucky to make it out alive.

"They kidnaped us," I said. "We definitely weren't there by choice, I hope you understand that."

The lead officer nodded, saying nothing.

They separated us, and grilled me on what I had seen and heard. Which wasn't much: the sound of a helicopter taking off, those blood-curdling screams. Then they had me draw a map, as best I could, of where we had been kept within the monastery walls.

When that was done, they brought Katje and I together again for another interrogation, this time comparing our accounts, particularly our impressions of where we had been kept in the convent, and what else had happened.

But the questions I expected they didn't ask: What were you two doing in Jesse's convent? Why was Twisted Messiah so interested in a pair of American tourists?

71

The lead officers left the room, and a junior guy appeared with our luggage. "You will be free to go soon, but first you must speak with a certain man, yes?"

Yes? As if we had a choice.

There was a trace of light in the sky now. If it was true that we'd soon be free to leave, then there was a chance of making it to Munich in time to catch a flight back to the U.S.

But how would we get from here to Munich? Would the cops provide a chauffeur?

I went through my luggage. Nothing seemed to have been taken, but my cell-phone was gone from the side-flap.

The door opened again, and a woman in civilian clothes wheeled in a cart with sandwiches and an urn of coffee. I realized we hadn't eaten since yesterday noon.

I was on my third cup and second sandwich when the door opened again, and the man who'd caught me on the train back from Oxford appeared. Again he showed his CIA credentials. This time, I took a very close look. Jason Sjodin.

"Pronounce it 'showdown,' if you like," he said. "I hope we are coming up to the showdown."

"Is Sjodin-Showdown your real name?"

"It is. For today." He poured himself a coffee and sat across from me. He looked tired. "I warned you about swimming with the sharks, and doggone if they didn't almost get you."

"How did you know we'd be here?"

"Because we tracked you."

"Because of my uncle?"

"Because your uncle is of such interest to a certain NGPF." He turned to Katje and said, "Sorry, that's an acronym for —"

"I'm familiar with the term: Non-governmental Political Force. And that NGPF is TM — Twisted Messiah."

He flicked his head. "You said that, not I. Whether you realize it or not, you set a trap for them, sending them up to the glacier. It's a mess, but you got them to crawl out from under the rock, and that gave the Germans a pretext to move."

I wasn't sure how to respond. Was he fishing for information, or was he actually sharing info? "What's the pretext? To rescue us?"

He was silent a moment. "They didn't tell you? The dumb shits tried to land one of Jesse's copters on the glacier in the middle of the night. That set off a hell of an avalanche. That's when the Germans got their clearance to move in. The avalanche was in Austria, but the copter had German registry."

"What happened to the copter? Any damage from the avalanche?"

"Appears that everybody on board was killed. The copter was ground up by the flow of the ice, but the avalanche didn't do any damage down in the valley."

"We heard a copter take off sometime in the night. Then there was panic later. But they just threw us into the van, didn't tell us anything."

"Did you hear anything in there to indicate whether Jesse Cripes might have been on that chopper?"

"I speak German," Katje said. "I was able to overhear a lot of what they said. There was no mention of Jesse, but they were concerned about the media they knew would be coming."

"There were screams in the night, a couple of times," I said. "It sounded as if —"

"My advice, better not say anything about screams, any of that, once you get out of there. Fact is, I'm surprised the Germans were willing to let you go after you told them that."

"We were *victims*, we're not any part of the Twisted Messiah entourage!," Katje said. "What possible grounds could they hold us on?"

"I don't know the German term, but in the American system we'd call it a material witness. They'd lock you up for your own protection, to keep you safe so you could testify to what you witnessed. They've got a cordon around the convent, but there's still a hell of a lot of Twisted Messiah's army of creeps out in the rest of the world. *All over* the world. I'd watch my tail, if I were you."

"Back in London, you told me there were two groups following me," I said. "You said one of them was an NGPF. That was Twisted Messiah? What was the other?"

I felt Katje tense up as I spoke. I hadn't told her about this CIA contact, and hadn't mentioned his warning that I was being followed by two separate groups.

"No need to tell you that Twisted Messiah has a lot more going than just a fan club. It's got the functional equivalent of a covert army with terrorist potential, and they're scattered in cells all over the world — that's not news to you now. You've seen them in action. They're thugs, dumb bastards. But there are a hell of a lot of them, and they're everywhere. You're not cleared to know just what they're capable of, but let your imagination run wild — then realize they can do worse, *much* worse than that. They've got an army of dead-end kids around the world, all willing to drink the Kool-Aid, and they've got tons of money and contacts to buy any kind of damned weapons, even WMD. Play with those possibilities when you wake up in the middle of some dark night."

"What's the second group? Why all this interest in me?"

"Their interest is not in you, it's in your uncle. If we knew what really happened to him, or when we do find out, you'll be the first to know . . . and that's a promise. But right now, we — your country, and the whole doggone world — needs your help."

"You're avoiding my question. Who's in the second group?"

"I'll get to that. Just hear me out. This is serious stuff, given the capabilities of Twisted Messiah's crazy army. I know they grabbed something from you, and that's what got them into the mess up on the glacier. We need to know what that was, and why was it so important to them."

I didn't know what to say. For the sake of my country, tell the truth. But I'd be telling the successor agency to the OSS, which lied to Paul and intentionally sent him into a trap. And then stonewalled the family for six decades.

Besides, I'd be passing on leads to what Paul had sacrificed his life to keep out of the hands of the CIA's predecessor agency.

❏

Katje spoke then, giving me thinking time. "I don't know if you're aware of it, but two men jumped Greg in his room and stole something from his safe."

He nodded. "Yeah, we know that."

"But there was another man, someone we'd seen both in London and in Bad Kronsee wearing a Tyrolean hat. He chased the two who'd attacked Greg. Was he one of your people?"

He shook his head. "Hey, give us credit. If our guys were there in disguise, they'd be in better disguise. Maybe something like a Groucho Marx glasses and moustache, not a Tyrolean hat."

"That's not a serious answer."

"Point taken. No, he was not one of us, he was from that second group. Which we'll talk about later."

He was right: this is serious stuff. I hadn't thought of it that way before, but Twisted Messiah did have the makings of an army — tens of thousands, maybe hundreds of thousands, of loser kids around the world, dead-ended by choice, angry, destructive. At least some of them, maybe a lot of them, would be willing to drink the Kool-Aid and kill themselves for the kick of destroying the people and society that they hate.

"Let me prompt you," he said. "We do know that you got some aerial maps from Dr. Gniessbach, and that's what they stole. But what we don't know is what the hell they expected to find up on the glacier."

I wasn't surprised that he knew about Gniessbach. So I gave him a little more help. "Dr. Gniessbach's maps showed where a plane, supposedly piloted by my uncle, crashed on the glacier in 1945."

He shook his head. "I don't know whether you believe that or not, but that's wrong. That was *not* your uncle in the *Storch*, it was a German. We've known that since the start, since days after it happened, back in '45."

That was in accord with what the monks had told me, but no need to share that with him.

"But that's what Gniessbach told me, and I had the sense he honestly believed it. Those maps are what the Twisted Messiah scumbags wanted, and that's what they got."

"Then they're even dumber than we thought. They caught themselves in a trap of their own making. So what did they think your uncle had up there with him in the glacier?"

Now we were getting close to the secret Paul wanted to keep. "Why don't you tell me?"

"I'll tell you what we think. You confirm or deny, okay? What we've picked up is that they think your uncle had some kind of ancient artifact that he turned up in La Rochelle. The Nazis wanted it, and Paul managed to keep it out of their hands, with Gniessbach's connivance. Confirm or deny."

It was *not* an artifact; it was knowledge — according to Larkwood. But artifact was close enough for government work. For now. Until I was sure I could trust him. "Basically correct," I said, hoping I hadn't put too much emphasis on 'basically.'

"Something you may or may not know is that the high Nazi leadership, particularly Hitler and Himmler, were occultists. They were believers in far-out stuff like magic, earth energies, things like that. Some who've studied them think they were also into black magic — and that the death camps were a kind of ritual killing to appease the gods and enhance their powers. We have evidence that the Twisted Messiah leadership has that same belief system."

I felt a chill then, hearing again those blood-curdling screams in the night. "I've heard some of that, heard that both Hitler and Himmler were occultists. The black magic and ritual killing aspect is news to me."

"There is some evidence, but not enough to act on, indicating that Twisted Messiah may be acting out fantasies like that — killing for sport, killing as offerings to whatever dark gods they follow. Which probably explains the screams you heard last night. A lot of kids, Twisted Messiah groupies, have gone missing around the world."

72

One of the German police came to the door, and our Mr. Showdown
— Sjodin — left us for a few minutes.

When he came back, I tried to grab the initiative. "Now it's
your turn. That second group you say has been following me — who
are they? What are they after?"

"Ask me another question. I can't tell you that."

"Dammit, you said you'd tell me more."

"What I said was that we'd get to that later. We just did. And
I told you I can't tell you much about them."

"Can't tell me? Because you don't know, or because you don't
want to?"

"Because I'm not authorized to tell you. You're not cleared to
hear any of that stuff."

"So we're authorized to be the bait, but not authorized to know
who's coming after us?"

"Look, I just work here, I don't make up the rules. Besides, this
second group, they haven't tried to kill you, that's not what they want."

"Then at least give us a heads-up on what they do want from
me."

"I don't think we know *what* they want from you, and that's the
truth. Maybe somebody at Langley knows, but they haven't told me."

That was hard to believe, yet something in his expression and
non-verbals told me he was telling the truth.

So I gave him a little more, to see how he'd react. "Cal Katz —
does that name register with you?"

Tired as I was, it gave a jolt of pleasure to see the genuine shock
on his face. "Of course I do. Are you aware that Katz was killed in

Washington a few days ago?"

I told him about that fax Cal had sent that first morning: I was the Butterfly about to set off a storm that starts ITB — Inside the Washington Beltway — and was to spread around the world, and that he was sending supposedly important information relating to that final conversation I'd had with Cal.

He tried very hard not to let it show, but I picked up the burst of excitement in his eyes. "What was that recent conversation about?"

"He'd asked whether I'd ever had a relative serving in the OSS. I mentioned my Uncle Paul. He said he'd get back to me. That was about a week before that fax."

"And that fax came the morning you left Washington?"

I nodded.

"Did you get what Katz sent?"

"No, I left the same day that fax came, within the hour."

"Have you gotten it since — maybe it came to your apartment?"

So he knew I lived in an apartment. What else did he know — rather, what did he and the CIA *not* know about me? "I've called. Nothing. According to the article in the *Washington Post*, it seems he was killed within a short time, maybe just minutes, from the time he sent the fax."

"So maybe he never got to send it. Damn! Any idea at all what he was sending?"

I told him what I recalled of the fax, the warning that I was to be the butterfly who sets off the storm. "Beyond that, no idea, though he did hint there was a link to a family member who'd been in the OSS — apparently Paul."

Katje broke in: "I heard you say that there were two groups following Greg, At least tell us whether they link through this Cal Katz. That might spur some ideas, help Greg to help you."

He shook his head and looked at me. "That was news to me, what you said, that Cal Katz had sent you that fax. We hadn't looked into his murder, figured it was just a random homicide, the sort of thing that happens. You can bet I'll phone home with that news. But, offhand, I can't figure any link to Twisted Messiah. Nor to the other group that's been interested in you, either."

"If you tell me who that second group is, that might ring some bells for me."

"Look," he said, doing that open-palms sweep that's supposed to convey nothing to hide but usually means the opposite. "I've leveled with you, told you all that I know, the truth as I know it. But I can't go there. I'm not authorized to tell you who that second group is. All I can say — and don't ever let on that I told you even this much — is this second group is a matter of politics, and that's outside the purview of my agency."

"Domestic? You mean American domestic politics?"

"I can't comment."

"But what would an American political party have to do with my uncle? Or with Twisted Messiah?"

"I didn't *say* it was a political party, and that's all I am going to say. Maybe we'll talk later, after I've conferred with Langley."

Why didn't I level with him then? Because I was wary. And aware of the way his agency's predecessor had sent Paul into France on a lie. Profoundly aware as well that Paul had sacrificed the life he could have had to keep something out of that agency's hands.

❏

He left us for a few minutes, then came back. "Okay, you've been helpful. Somewhat helpful. So I've done you a favor in return, arranged for the German police to drive you up to Munich so you can catch a flight home today."

He paused long enough for that to register, then added, "That *is* what you want? To fly back to see your father?"

"Of course." It was what I wanted, then. I didn't know the twist that would be coming along shortly.

"Just keep this in mind," he said. "You know you had a close call this time. If we hadn't been here, if there hadn't been that police roadblock, those bastards would have killed you by now. So watch yourself. Just keep in mind what happened to Cal Katz. Same thing could happen to both you and Katje. It's not something you want to play around with."

73

Munich airport shone in a haze of snowflakes as we approached —
massive and modern, a gauzy apparition out of the 22nd Century.

It was a miracle: we were alive, we were free, we had our
luggage and passports and money and credit cards, and we'd be able
to catch a plane out of here.

The green-and-white police car dropped us off out front.
Convenient. Fun, too, watching the faces of the people who were
checking us out, and wondering why the fuzz was releasing us here.

Katje went to check on flights while I found a public phone.
My hand shook as I punched in the numbers for the hospital in
Burlington. It had been almost 24 hours since I'd last checked on Dad.

The hospital receptionist put me on hold while she checked to
see if I was authorized to be told whether my father was dead or alive.
Thank you, federal bureaucrats, for complicating life.

"He is on the fifth floor. I will put you through," she came back
to say, speaking as if she had learned English by listening to robot
messages.

"Fifth floor? Then he's alive?"

"My records do not show otherwise."

A floor nurse picked up. "Your father is doing well, surprisingly
well. He waited all day for you to call. It's too late now, of course, for
him to be disturbed." I sensed disapproval in her tone.

"Something happened. I was tied up most of the day." Tied up, literally. But it was still the middle of the night in Burlington, no point in trying to explain that.

"He left a message for you. He said to tell you he's coming out of it, and above all — those were his words, 'above all' — above all to carry on. He was very determined about that. He does not want you to come here, not until you have finished your 'mission' — mission was the term he used. He said you'd understand."

She cleared her throat. "However, I feel duty bound to tell you that he has been coughing a lot and seems to be raising a great deal of . . . of material."

"Is that a good thing?"

"The doctors are somewhat puzzled."

❏

I hung up, still not sure where things stood. At least Dad was still alive. And still determined for me to push on.

But it couldn't be good that was coughing up a lot of junk.

Katje hurried up, her face looking as puzzled as I felt. She had gone down to tell the car-rental agency that the Audi had been car-jacked from us.

"They laughed at me. They already *have* the Audi. It was returned to them yesterday."

"Funny, I don't recall doing that."

"I'm serious, Greg. Not only that, but look what they found in the car, under the seat." She held up my cell-phone. Not that I'd use it again, now that I knew it was being tapped. But it would be an interesting souvenir for the mantlepiece.

❏

Good news. The early flight to Washington still had space in business class, and they let me trade my return stub from the flight to La Rochelle.

We made it through security and still had time to spare.

Business class tickets entitled us to the airline's club lounge. I grabbed a coffee and pastry and used one of the phones to call my answering machine in Washington. I couldn't remember when I'd last checked messages.

Nothing from Shelly Sherman, nothing more on Cal Katz' death.

A bunch of junk calls.

Then a call from Professor Tabersley in Oxford that had come in just minutes ago: "I have been trying and trying your cell number with no one picking up. Modern technology does not always deliver on its promise. If you get this call, you may wish to contact me as soon as possible, as I have come upon something that may be of extreme interest in your search. Indeed, it may answer a great many of your questions."

Katje hurried up, pointing to a TV in the corner. An aerial shot of an oily smudge on ice. The camera, in another helicopter pulled back, and that smudge turned out to be one small dot on the Hochweisse Glacier.

A close-up of the ice flow that had stopped short of a village.

Another close up of that smudge, closer-in to show the tangle of metal and rotor blades and debris.

"There are no signs of life," she translated. "The authorities are not sure when if ever they'll be able to get in and retrieve the bodies, because that could set off a further avalanche."

"So Jesse Cripes may or may not be buried up there?" Not far from where Uncle Paul may or may not be buried.

"So it seems," Katje said.

❏

I punched in the number Tabersley had left on my answering machine.

"Ah, good, good," he said, sounding sober. "I have news for you. Care to meet me for lunch? The sooner I tell you the better, for you, and for me."

"What do you mean?"

"I think you may be at greater risk than you realize, and that risk redounds to those who come in contact with you. The sooner I share the information with you, then the sooner I am, as the saying goes, off the hook."

I may be at greater risk than I realize. How much greater risk than being kidnaped by Twisted Messiah's thugs?

"I'm actually in Germany as we speak, at Munich airport. I'm ticketed back to Washington. Is this something you can tell me over the phone?"

A pause. "Reluctantly, very reluctantly. The walls have ears, and all that, you know. In any case, I'll take the risk. But first, let me ask: you flew down to see Dr. Gniessbach. Was he was able to help you?"

I told him how Gniessbach had captured Paul in La Rochelle, then saved his life by keeping him as a private prisoner for the final year of the war.

"Did he answer all your questions? Are you satisfied?"

"I was. Until I heard the opposite story." I told him the conflicting accounts: according to Gniessbach, Paul had been frozen into a glacier these past decades, while the monks contradicted that.

"Was that by any chance on the Hochweisse Glacier?"

So he had seen the news. I nodded. I wanted to hear what he had to say first, before we got into any of that.

When I told him that Dr. Gniessbach had died overnight after my visit, he seemed only a little surprised. "This is a dangerous business in which you've become enmeshed."

Katje hurried up again and handed me a note: "There are showers available to us here in the lounge, and there's just enough time before boarding, if you're quick."

Nothing sounded more appealing, after what we'd been through in Jesse's convent.

Then Tabersley said, "You showed me some documents when you were here the other day. One of those was the letter from your uncle's superior officer sending condolences to the family. Do you happen to recall who signed it?"

I tried to picture that letter it in my mind. "There wasn't a signature, just some code, B/ F and a number, I think 12."

"Indeed yes, B/F-12 A bit of obfuscation typical of the OSS. That intrigued me, and I've done a bit of research in the days since we last talked. It appears that B/F-12 was the designator used by a Mr. Hadley Barrington. Your uncle would have reported to him in 1944."

It took me a second or so to place the name. Rather, I knew the name, as anybody who lived in Washington would, but it took the time to fit that name into this context.

"*The* Hadley Barrington? The power-broker? They call him the Grand Old Man of Inside-the-Beltway Washington."

You are the Butterfly, and you're about to set off a storm Inside-the-Beltway.

"The very one. Though now he seems to be in the process of passing on the mantle to his sons."

Something else clicked. Barrington. Elections. Two brothers running for office. One for governor, the other for U.S. Senate. From Louisiana. Talk of a political dynasty. Hadley Barrington's sons.

Then I remembered something the CIA guy had said this morning: *I'm not authorized, to tell you who that second group is. All I can say is — and don't ever let on I told you even this much — is that this second group is a matter of domestic politics, and that's outside the purview of my agency."*

"Domestic? You mean American domestic politics?"

"I can't comment."

"But what would an American political party have to do with my uncle? Or with Twisted Messiah?"

*"I didn't **say** it was a political party, and that's all I am going to say."*

74

"Tell me, how much do you actually know about the OSS?," Tabersley asked.

I was getting a sense of his style in conducting his tutorials: start by putting the student on the defensive with a question from outer space. "The OSS was the predecessor of the CIA — that's about the extent of what I know."

"Then a brief tutorial. Until the start of the Second World War, the United States had virtually no intelligence capability. In the years between the wars, one of your American Secretaries of State scorned the idea of developing an intelligence capability. 'Gentlemen don't read other gentlemen's mail,' he said. That was Henry Stimson, the de facto chairman of the old-line, East-coast Establishment, but a naive twit, in certain ways. In time, someone grasped the reality that the Nazis were not in fact gentlemen, nor were the Japanese. Thus it came to be that the Office of Strategic Services, the OSS, was formed at the start of the war, under General William Donovan — another Wall Street lawyer, often called, with some justification, 'Wild Bill.'"

I was craving a shower, and wishing he'd get to the point.

"The OSS attracted bright people, no question of that, many of them Eastern Establishment. It attracted others with special skills and a love for their country. But it also attracted young men on the make — people who weren't classic WASP, weren't true Ivy, weren't old-line Wall Street, weren't old money. People, in short, who were drawn to the OSS for the contacts they could make. A good many saw the OSS as their ticket inside the Establishment when the war was done. In today's parlance, that element within the OSS might be called 'Establishment wannabe's.'"

It seemed odd to hear "Wannabes" from this Oxford don. Wannabes — kids who wannabe a rock star and will do anything at all pursuing that dream.

Even more surprising was the thought that once upon a time the Grand Old Man of ITB Washington was an Establishment wannabe. Interesting.

"If you're suggesting that my uncle . . ." I began, then rephrased it. "He was an idealist, not someone on the make. He left a Jesuit seminary to help out in the war."

"Aha! So the crafty Jesuits have a hand in this, do they?"

"My uncle never became a full-fledged Jesuit. He left the novitiate after a couple of years."

"Perhaps not your uncle, but a good many others did very well for themselves from the war. For some, the war was the best thing that ever happened to them and their careers. Hadley Barrington epitomizes the type: the 'Establishment wannabe' who used the war as his stepping-stone into the inner circle."

"Barrington has been around so long that I assumed he was Establishment from the start."

"Not at all. The war was his ticket inside, and that gave him entree to the revolving door — a stint in government to make contacts, back to the private sector, then a rotation back to government at a higher level for a while, then back into the private sector to capitalize on those new contacts. Barrington, as you may know, was one of those who created such a mess in Vietnam. Washington, as is often the case, rewarded him for failure. From there, it's been ever onward and upward: advisor to Presidents, Secretary of Commerce, an ambassadorship. Now he's regarded as a figure of awe."

"I'm surprised that you know so much about Barrington," I said, curious why a British professor would have any interest in Barrington.

"My specialty is military history, particularly clandestine operations of World War II. There are still some unanswered questions about Barrington's activities in those years, you see."

"Unanswered? Relevant to my uncle?"

"I have no idea, so let me tell you what I do know, and you can

go from there." I heard him lighting his pipe. I was in for a lecture.
So much for squeezing in a shower before take-off. But this was
worth it.

    "By the end of the war, Hadley Barrington had carved himself
a mysterious little fiefdom within the OSS, in what was then called
Morale Operations. In today's parlance, that would be Psy-Ops —
Psychological Operations."

    He paused, and I heard him scratching another match, then
sucking the pipe to life.

    Finally he said, "At the end of April, 1945, the final week of the
War in Europe. Barrington, then enjoying the pleasures of Paris,
suddenly commandeered an OSS plane to fly him to the Austrian Alps.
But why he went, and what if anything he accomplished, the record
does not show. I've tried at various times to access the files of
Barrington's final operation, with no success. Parties unknown
cleaned the files — a long time ago."

    This matched what Dr. Gniessbach had told me.

    "In short, there is no way of knowing what Barrington was up
to on that mysterious run south. There is no paperwork evidencing
where he went after climbing off the plane at a little field just south of
Munich. But we do know that in those final days of the war many of
the top Germans were scrambling to work out their own private
arrangements with the victors. The allies were making a concerted
effort to grab German technology fast, in part to learn from it, in part
to keep it out of the hands of the Russians. Barrington no doubt
realized that if he could pull off a coup of any magnitude, such as
securing the services of a team of rocket or atomic weapons scientists,
that would secure his post-war reputation."

    I'd heard this from both Larkwood and Gniessbach. "Was
Barrington successful?"

    Tabersley nodded. "No one knows. What, if anything, he
turned up was lost in a dark hole of government secrecy and
conveniently missing files."

    Now I shared something I hadn't earlier. "Dr. Gniessbach
claimed that he gave my uncle access to a radio and had him offer to
work out a deal."

    "Did he, by any chance, tell you where he hid your uncle?"

    "In a monastery in Austria. At St. Johann on the Fleckensee."

"On the Fleckensee! I'll be damned! Next to *Schloss* Flecken. You *do* know that story, do you not?"

"Dr. Gniessbach said the castle, as he put it, 'gained a certain infamy once the Americans arrived.' I didn't get to ask him what he meant by that."

"Good Lord, man! *You don't know?* You were right there, in the shadow of Flecken Castle, and you didn't *know*?"

I was having trouble keeping my eyes focused after two nights without any real sleep. "I asked there in the village, at St. Johann, the tourist office and a restaurant just down the lake. They didn't know, either."

"They *said* they didn't know. Don't you understand by now, the Germans and their Austrian cousins have selective memories? Or perhaps they knew you were American and did not wish to hurt your feelings."

"I don't know what you're talking about. Was there an atrocity there?"

He shook his head. "Not an atrocity — the *gold*. The Fleckensee gold!"

75

Tabersley told the story:

In the final months of the war, the Nazi high command emptied the Reichsbank in Berlin, moving trainload after trainload of gold, cash, and jewelry to various hiding spots around the Alps, in anticipation of making a final stand there.

Eight tons of that Nazi gold had been stored for a few weeks in *Schloss* Flecken, that ugly concrete block of a castle that filled the far end of Lake Flecken. The castle that Dr. Gniessbach had said "would later develop a certain infamy, once the Americans arrived."

Parties still unknown to this day stole that eight-ton stash of Nazi gold sometime in those first confused days at the end of the war. Eight tons of gold, 16,000 pounds of it, enough to fill several trucks, worth then – at the artificially low official rate of $35 per ounce – about $9 million, though much more on the open market. But, given inflation, $9 million 1945 dollars would be equivalent to maybe ten times that in today's dollars, and much, much more if it had been wisely invested.

Who engineered that theft, one of the largest in history? According to the rumors of the time, "a team of American Army officers and OSS agents." The perpetrators were never caught.

Castle Flecken was barely a mile down the lake from the monastery where Uncle Paul — an OSS agent — had spent most of the year before that great theft.

❏

I sat there, holding the phone, stunned, unseeing, the image of that graceless castle searing into my mind, wanting it not to be so.

But it made too much sense. Paul had been in the perfect spot to pull it off. He'd spent most of a year in the area. Even in the monastery he would have picked up bits of news and gossip. He might have heard of the arrival of eight tons of gold in a convoy of trucks, guarded by a bunch of soldiers. Other soldiers would have been left behind to guard it. That would not have gone unnoticed in little St. Johann.

Paul had been through a war. He might have changed. He might have felt he'd done his duty, now the war was over, and here was the opportunity of a lifetime. After all, it was Nazi gold, and they certainly didn't deserve it, so why not grab it and live happily ever after?

It could have happened that way.

But, suppose, even if he had been part of the team that grabbed the gold, there still remained that question: What happened to the Templar chest and its secrets?

Find what your uncle found, and very possibly that will lead you to him.

Would Uncle Paul have been willing to walk away from his family and the life he could have had for a share of eight tons of gold?

Or was that whole scenario of the Templar chest a cover story, to fool Gniessbach, and to fool the monks?

Still, what was that old Brother Augustus had said? *The other matter is irrelevant at this time. That would only confuse the issue.*

That "other matter" — was that the stolen gold?

❑

"Are you suggesting that Uncle Paul was part of this theft?," I finally asked Tabersley.

"Suggesting? No, I have no evidence, one way or the other. But one must face the fact that it is a possibility. It seems he was present at the time and place in question. It would explain why he never came back at the end of the war. Perhaps he *could not* because he knew he'd be caught and prosecuted. Or perhaps — remember the times, people had become habituated to killing, to killing as a matter of course, all through the war — perhaps his partners were greedy, and decided to kill him to make a bigger share for themselves."

"What about Barrington? Are you suggesting that Barrington may also have been involved in the gold theft?"

"I would not *dare* to suggest such a thing! With good reason.

The possibility was raised, a long time ago, and it went nowhere. All records were lost in a fire, supposedly. Then Barrington and some of the others managed to resurrect documents — travel orders and that sort of thing — that proved that they had been nowhere near the gold. They followed up with a flurry of lawsuits alleging slander, and all voices were hushed."

I nodded, not sure where any of this was leading.

"Now some might have claimed that these various travel orders and other documents were forgeries, produced to fit the need, but, since the supposed originals were destroyed in that alleged fire, it didn't go anywhere. Besides, life was cheap in Germany in those days after the war. Contradictory witnesses tended to have short lives."

"Suppose my uncle had been part of this theft, and suppose that Hadley Barrington, his Commanding Officer, had been —"

"A reasonable assumption, I would say. A share of that gold would have given Barrington a very nice head start in building his fortune."

"But now he's an old man, probably into his late 80's."

"Don't you follow your own politics? Barrington has two sons running for office in this election. One is an incumbent U.S. Senator, the other is running for governor of some state, I forget which."

"But my interest is not in Barrington. That's peripheral. My focus is on Paul. Is there any evidence that Paul was part of the gold theft?"

Tabersley shrugged. "No more and no less evidence than there is linking Barrington to it. All evidence has been lost, or obscured, in the mists of time."

❑

There didn't seem to be much else to cover.

"Remember what I said before," Tabersley said. "I would like to be kept informed on how this all turns out. Indeed, we might even get together and do a book, if you're so inclined."

"A good book has a beginning, a middle, and an end," I responded, "and it remains to be seen if I'll ever find the end of this story."

"One more thing," I said. "Earlier, at the start of this call, you said I may be at risk, and I might be putting you at risk."

"If I may turn Von Clausewitz around, Politics is war by

another means. People die in wars. I don't want to be one of them."

I figured I knew what he was getting at, but played dumb just to see. "You're serious that you think there's that level of risk?"

"Don't you see? Barrington, the old spy, the old bastard, would be determined to keep the story of his involvement in the gold from ever coming out . . . particularly now, when his sons are facing an election. He's seeking to found a dynasty, and I expect will let nothing stand in his way. And *that*, my young friend, is why I wanted to get this information to you as soon as possible. For your sake. But also to get it off my shoulders. I expect you're being watched by his people. So be careful. Be *very* careful. Particularly until the votes are counted."

76

I hung up, drained — not just from the stress and lack of sleep, but exhausted in spirit. I didn't have it in me to face the implications of what Tabersley had just suggested — that, Uncle Paul may have been part of, maybe even the instigator of, that massive gold theft.

What was I going to say when I talked to Dad? Continue the fiction that Paul was a hero? Or tell him the sad truth, that he had spent his life wondering about a brother who had chosen to turn his back on his family?

Katje came again, looking scrubbed and refreshed. "You are a chatty one. But there's good news and bad news. The bad news is the plane is delayed a few minutes, which means you'll have time to get in your shower, after all. Provided you're quick about it."

"That doesn't sound like bad news to me. What's the good news?"

"The good news is that now I won't have to spend the flight sitting next to a smelly guy."

❑

There was more bad news when I came out of the shower, this on the television.

Fresh aerial shots of the helicopter crash on the Hochweisse Glacier, taken just before the weather closed in, blocking any further rescue efforts today. There had still been no signs of life around the crash, and it was becoming increasingly doubtful whether rescue personnel would ever get to the site. The ice had been made even more fragile by the crash and fire that resulted. Now the authorities were facing the question of whether to risk lives on a lost cause.

*In what is believed to be a related incident, German
police have been refused entry to the former
monastery, now owned by Twisted Messiah lead
singer, Jesse Cripes.*

An on-site reporter appeared against a backdrop of Jesse's
restored monastery. Something in the camera angle gave the old place
the creepy appearance of a haunted castle.

*The police continue to tighten the cordon established
earlier today around the converted monastery,
renamed The Convent of the Sensuous Virgins by
owner Jesse Cripes, lead singer of the group Twisted
Messiah. The inhabitants refuse to allow the police to
enter, and what had earlier seemed only a minor
incident has now grown to a major police presence,
involving an undisclosed number of officers, some in
camouflage uniforms. Is Jesse inside? No one knows
— or, if the police do know, they are not saying.*

The anchor took over:

*Although the German police have not confirmed it, it
is believed that they initially came to the converted
monastery with questions about possible involvement
in the crash of the helicopter on the Hochweisse
Glacier in Austria overnight, resulting the loss of an
unknown number of lives. As of the present time,
Austrian rescue personnel have been unable to get to
the wreckage of the helicopter because of the risk of
triggering an additional avalanche. It is not known
whether Twisted Messiah lead singer Jesse Cripes, or
any other members of the group, were aboard the
crashed helicopter.*

The screen switched to a string of traffic, filling all lanes of the
German Autobahn, blocking the flow for miles behind.

Meanwhile, as the situation intensifies at Jesse's convent-residence, a rag-tag convoy of Twisted Messiah fans in old campers and trucks is heading south along the Autobahn toward Munich. These fans, who had camped out after the Twisted Messiah concert earlier this week at an abandoned air base in the former East Germany, now seem determined to bring support to their beleaguered music idol. What they plan to do, no one knows. For the moment, at least, German police are monitoring the movement, but have made no attempt to stop or divert them.

This was the first I'd heard that the German government had quietly allowed nearly 100,000 Twisted Messiah fans to stay on at the abandoned East German airfield after the concert ended. Apparently the hope had been to avoid a confrontation with that many angry fans, figuring that the onset of winter would force them to disperse.

A mistake, because now the fans were still together, easily led, and angry at what one of their leaders was calling the "persecution" of Jesse.

Already, demonstrations by groups of Twisted Messiah fans had begun in other cities around the world; so far, more than a dozen police and protestors had been injured.

77

It was a relief to settle into the wide leather seats in Business Class and look forward to eight hours in the air without problems. The flight crew welcomed us with complimentary champagne — particularly tasty while the poor slobs were still crowding into tourist class . . . my usual domain.

The pilot came on to say that jet stream was cooperating and we'd make up the time we'd lost and then some. If that held, we'd be on the ground in Washington just before 2:30 in the afternoon, local time.

The champagne was working its magic, and I felt ready to dig into the copy of the *Washington Post* that I'd grabbed before boarding.

All election stuff — but what else do you expect from the company paper in a company town where the company's business is government and politics?

One reference to the Barrington Boys on A-17, along with a photo of the two of them standing with Barrington *pere*.

I'd seen old Barrington's picture dozens of times, sometimes in the *Post* with politicians, other times in business magazines or a snippet on the TV news, distinguished by his trademark heavy-lidded eyes and the wrinkled parchment skin of a heavy smoker. The sons had the same lidded eyes, but somewhere along the way had learned to smile for the camera, and that softened the effect. Maybe that was why they were the ones running for votes, and the old man was running the money for their campaigns. Both of the sons were way ahead in their races.

Was this old man really the person who had sent Uncle Paul into a trap?

More riots set off by Twisted Messiah fans in various cities around the world, though no real damages or injuries. I wondered if these had been staged as demonstrations of what they could do. Nothing like a little blackmail to soften the stances of politicians.
❏

Then this in the *Crime and Justice* segment of *Metro*:

Consultant Found Mugged, Murdered in Rockville Parking Lot

The victim's name didn't register at first: Darren Mann. Then it clicked. Darren Mann was Danny Mann, and we'd worked together on a team effort at HUD a year or so ago.

I remembered him as a geeky guy, a true propeller-head, with a shy, sly smile, tall and awkward, with a shock of brown hair forever falling across his glasses. He had a doctorate in political science, and would have made a good professor — if only all the tenured university slots weren't filled for the next couple of decades. So, like the rest of us, he'd stumbled into consulting and developed a specialty, combining poli-sci and statistical analysis in a way that the bureaucrats liked when they went up to the Hill to talk budgets.

He'd come back to his apartment in Rockville late Monday night. Whether someone had been waiting for him specifically, or he'd happened to be the unlucky target of opportunity, was unknown. He'd been strangled, and the killer took his keys, slid the body under the car, and ransacked the apartment at leisure.

The body was not found until yesterday morning.

I stopped breathing for an instant.

How many times on that project had I seen Danny Mann and Cal Katz chatting together? Dozens, at least. Neither was into exercise, so while the rest of us would take a walk on the mall or amble down to see the Cherry Blossoms, the two of them would sit in the HUD cafeteria, talking politics and conspiracy theories.

I closed my eyes, savoring that image of my two friends. Not close friends, not people who I'd ever hung out with, apart from some lunches when we were all working in the same agency. Cal, nearly as wide as he was tall, surrounded by clouds of stinky cigar smoke, wasn't into the things I was — he wasn't into biking, or hiking, or anything physical. Nor was Danny. So we didn't get together on weekends to go jogging out along the C and O Canal, nor to bike along the old railroad trail on the Virginia side.

But we were all companions in that army of over-educated migrant brain-workers. We all shared the outsider's perspective on the inside world of Beltway Washington, and the outsider's sense of humor. Cal once put it, "If you aren't part of the establishment, then it's your patriotic duty to laugh at the pretensions of those who are."

But this was not a joke, this was not the high-school in-crowd lashing back. This was definitely not a drill. This was real.

And permanent. A lot of years of life had been taken from them.

I didn't know who had done it to them, nor did I know for sure why.

But I lay back in the soft leather seat, seven miles over the Atlantic, and felt a kind of energy surge through me. Energy fueled by anger. Not just anger, fury. I'd never been one for revenge. Two wrongs don't make a right, only more stress and commotion.

But this was not going to pass. I was going to find who and why, and then I was going to — going to do what?

No idea.

Not yet.

But I'd do something. For Cal. For Shelly. For Danny.

But not just for Cal and Danny, but for myself too. And for Katje. Cal had put himself at risk by stirring up hornet nests. He was paranoid for good reason. But Danny hadn't volunteered to hold backups for Cal. Nor had I volunteered. Nor had Katje volunteered for the way things had turned out.

We were at risk, we could feel ourselves in their sights now.

78

A final snack as we came down the Atlantic coast, a slow descent, the mass of Chesapeake Bay, the Bay Bridge, Baltimore in the distance, the Washington Beltway and its never-ending river of cars, the quasi-Aztec ruins of the Xerox Training Center along the Potomac, the developments and shopping malls flashing past faster and faster as we drop altitude before the big 747 touches down as soft as a balloon.

Our luggage made it with us, and the drug-scouting dogs passed us without a second sniff.

Once past customs, my first task was to call the hospital and see how Dad was faring. I found a public phone and dug out some American change I'd tucked in a flap in my carry-on.

"He's resting now," the floor nurse said. "He did show some improvement today, but doctor thought it best to keep him in for another day of observation. Perhaps he'll be released tomorrow."

❏

We rode the shuttle-bus out to the long-term lot where Katje had left her car. There were just the two of us, and a couple of businessmen.

"Not supposed to do this, drop you at your car," the bus-driver said when we got to the lot, "supposed to leave you at the pick-up, but somethin' don't feel right to me, there's a car followed us out, slow-like. Don't hurt to play it safe."

"Sometimes even paranoids have real enemies," I said.

"Ain't *that* the truth! 'Round these parts for sure."

❏

An odd turn of events: Katje's car was a BMW, the twin of mine. Hers was silver, mine was red. A bizarre coincidence, I thought for an instant, then remembered something she'd said back in St. Johann: *There is no such as coincidence, not when it comes to important things.*

Was having the same car an important thing? Maybe only in the context of how in tune two people are. Who knows?

The afternoon was warm for late October, and she cranked open the sun-roof to get some fresh air: even in Business Class the airlines are stingy with air.

She came off the Dulles toll-road at Route 123, Chain Bridge Road, then asked if it would be okay to stop by her place for a minute before dropping me home. It was only a couple of blocks out of the way.

She'd already made it clear just how much she was looking forward to getting back to her own place. Alone.

To tell the truth, for once that was just fine with me. Despite dozing on the plane, I didn't think I'd ever been quite as sleep-deprived. A solid 12 hours in my own bed, alone, called seductively.

She lived in a townhouse cluster in McLean, brick Federalist style. A bit dowdy for her, I was thinking, until she explained it had been her parents'.

I got her bags out of the trunk and followed her. She unlocked the door, and punched the security code into the system.

Then I heard a sound come out of her, as if she'd been hit in the solar plexus.

The place was a mess, books pulled off the shelves, drawers emptied on the floor, cushions from the sofa and chairs tossed in piles.

She sagged, and I caught and held her.

"It was *them*, it *had* to be — to have disarmed my security alarm, and then reset it. The Twisted Messiah creeps. They had time to copy my keys, and I was stupid: I'd written the security code on an index card, along with other things. Somehow they figured it out. It had to be them, that's the only explanation."

"But that was just this morning. They moved fast to get the keys all the way back to the U.S. even sooner than we did."

She wandered through the rooms, shaking her head.

I tried to figure out how the Twisted Messiah creeps could have moved fast enough to get her key from Germany to here ahead of us. Maybe by private jet. Or is there a way to digitize the information on a key and send it electronically to a locksmith here?

❏

"The real issue," she said after a bit, "what I find chilling, is that they would care enough about *me* to bother. I can understand their interest in you. But I'm just a passer-by. I didn't have any knowledge about your uncle, just what I picked up from being with you."

"They don't know who you are. They saw us together, and it probably seemed we were working together."

"In any case, I can't spend the night here, not if they have the key. I'm going to a hotel. Just stay with me long enough so I can grab some clean clothes, okay?"

"Lingering is not a good idea — they could be hiding here."

That stopped her. For a moment. "I'm not going to deal with the police tonight. I'll be quick."

I grabbed a wrench from under the sink and walked through with her. Nobody popped out from the closets, no boogeymen under the bed.

I started putting the books back on the shelves while she packed. Hers weren't the Crichtons and De Milles and Hydes and Ambroses that fill my shelves. Hers were heavy stuff on geo-politics and international economics.

Plus one whole wall on spirituality.

❑

We were crossing the Potomac on Chain Bridge when I said, "There's no need to go to a hotel. There's plenty of room at my place."

"That's a lovely offer, but I really can't."

"Anybody following us? Have you been checking the mirror?"

"No, I haven't. Why? You don't think . . . "

"I just wouldn't want to think they followed you to a hotel. I'd worry about you there, all alone."

She laughed. "You *are* manipulative, aren't you?" Suitable pause before adding, "Okay, you talked me into it. Provided there's a second bedroom. Or a comfortable sofa. And provided I get to control the lock on my door."

"Whatever turns you on."

A thought came to mind as we pulled into my building. If Twisted Messiah's people got hold of her house key while we were held in the convent, and flew trans-Atlantic to poke through her things, they'd probably do the same thing to my place. They had the same access to my house-key when they got hers. Was it such a good idea to come here?

Then I told myself: Not to worry, this place is secure. The front desk is staffed around the clock.

79

Nkwame was on-duty at the front desk, and beeped me in — a small stroke of very good luck, as I wasn't in the mood to deal with Mrs. Poulson, the sourpuss building manager.

Like some of the other part-timers, Nkwame was a student at American University, a few blocks up Massachusetts Avenue. I think he was from Nigeria. When I first moved to the building, another tenant had cautioned me not to ask many questions because these foreign students were "sensitive." Maybe they didn't have the right visa to work part-time, or maybe they were political refugees and didn't want to talk.

No matter, he gave me a look that said he approved of my taste in women.

He filled out a visitor parking pass for Katje's car. She brought it out to put on the dashboard while he went into the back office to pick up the mail they'd been holding for me.

He returned, shaking his head. "There's nothing being held back there for you. Did you check your box?"

"It's empty. I'd left word to hold everything while I was away."

So where did it go?

And what happened to that "very important info" Cal Katz had planned to send?

❏

It felt good to turn the key and be back: a rental apartment, but still home. It had been an interesting trip — "interesting" as in the Chinese curse, May you live in interesting times.

I went in first, just in case. And slipped on the accumulation

of mail and newspapers that had piled up inside the door — way inside
the door, too far to have just been slipped under.

That was odd, as I'd asked for my mail to be held downstairs.
But instead of holding it, somebody had taken the trouble to bring it
up. Beyond that, had unlocked my door to put it inside.

I brought Katje's overnight bag into the second bedroom,
normally my office.

While she settled in, I thumbed through the pile of mail,
looking for anything from Cal Katz. Nothing. Bad news, in one way —
that meant they'd gotten to Cal before he could pass it on. But good
news for me: one less problem to worry about.

The place was stuffy. I paused for a long drink of water, then
unlocked the sliding glass doors to the balcony and stepped out to get
some fresh air after all those hours locked in the plane.

It was the usual bizarre, where-am-I?, my body-clock's all
screwed up feeling. It was still daylight, a half-hour before an October
sunset, but my body was telling me, Never mind the daylight, it's
midnight here inside you. I was hungry, too. Despite the meals on the
plane, the body knew it was still short one feeding.

I took the portable phone out onto the balcony and dialed the
hospital to check on Dad. This is where it all began, I realized — phone
calls on the balcony.

But this time there wouldn't be a fax arriving from Cal Katz.

It had rained earlier in the day, and a haze still hung in the air.
Was I glad to be back? Not really. I was tired, but the traveling had
been fun. Seeing new things, putting together the pieces of the Paul
puzzle.

Meeting Katje.

Unfortunate that it had all been under the pressure of Dad's
impending end.

The floor nurse picked up. "Your father insists that he needs to
talk to you. I'll put you through to his room."

"Before you do, how's he doing?"

A long pause. "It's hard to say. Why don't you talk to him and
draw your own conclusions?"

"Greg!," his voice was strong and upbeat, not that whispering
croak the last time we'd spoken. "I'm cured, *healed*. It's a miracle."

"Cured?"

"The cancer's gone. Now it's just a matter of purging the junk out of my system. Then I'll be good as new – *better* than new."

"That would be great, Dad," I said, hoping he didn't hear the skepticism in my voice.

"*Would* be great? It *is* great! You don't understand, do you? Paul came here last night and healed me."

"Paul who?"

"Paul *who*? Paul-who-do-you-think? Your *Uncle* Paul, who else?"

"Uncle Paul? But —"

His voice dropped to a whisper. "Paul *was* here last night, in the middle of the night when it was quiet, right here in this room, big as life. We had a good talk, caught up on a lot of things."

Mrs. Fox's rule: *Sometimes, just before the end, they have one final good spell, and they seem to be coming out of it. But it's only a reprieve, one last gift of time. Then they go.*

"I'm glad you're feeling well, Dad."

He laughed again. "I'm not just *feeling* well, I'm *doing* well. I know you think I'm delirious. You think all the drugs they pumped into the Old Man have sent him over the edge, made him hallucinate." He chuckled. "It's all right what you think. That's okay, I can understand why you'd feel that way."

"You have been taking a lot of medications, Dad. They can have mind-altering effects."

"Booze can have mind-altering effects, too. The fact is, I saw *Paul*, not a pink elephant. Think what you want, but I know what I saw."

80

I called the hospital back and got the same floor nurse. "My father is convinced that his brother came to visit him in the middle of the night. His only brother is dead, so did somebody visit him, or was it a — some kind of dream?"

"That's why I wanted you to talk to him directly. He's been telling us the same thing all day, about supposedly seeing his brother for the first time in many years."

"Would it have been possible for a visitor to have slipped in during the night?"

"Visitors aren't allowed in the rooms after hours, and we look in on all our patients through the night. I wasn't on duty then, but there's no way a visitor wouldn't have been noticed."

"What if he were dressed as a clergyman?"

"Clergy always check in at the desk before going into the rooms."

"Dad claims he's feeling better. What do you — "

"He's been telling us the same thing, that his brother healed him. At least his spirits have been good all day, I can say that."

Often, just before the end, they have one final good spell and seem to be coming out of it. But it's only one last gift of time, then they go.

"Greg? Hold on a moment, will you? Your father is buzzing. There's something he wants." She was back in a moment. "Well, that's a coincidence. What he wanted was to talk to you again. He wanted to know how to call you back. I'll connect you."

"Haven't heard from you in a long while, son, just wanted to see whether you'd forgotten the old man."

What could I say? That we'd talked not five minutes ago and now I was sure he was out of it?

"Hah! I knew it! I said that just to test you. Admit it, you believed me, you thought I'd forgotten already, you thought I'd lost the last of my marbles."

"It's good you still have the old sense of humor, Dad."

"There's this shepherd out in the desert. He sees a plume of dust coming, and a car stops and a young guy steps out, dressed to the nines, pointy-toed city-slicker shoes, hand-tooled briefcase, every electronic gadget you can imagine hanging off his belt.

"He says to the shepherd, 'Yo! Shepherd. If I can give you an exact count of how many sheep you have, will you give me one of them?' The shepherd already has more sheep than he has food to give them, so he agrees. The young man fires up his laptop computer and his Blackberry and his GPS system and a couple of other toys, and pretty soon prints out a 150-page report. He says, 'You have exactly 1586 sheep.' 'That is correct,' says the shepherd. 'You may take one of the sheep.' The yuppie selects the sheep of his choice and fits it into his car.

"The yuppie is about to drive off when the shepherd says, 'If I can tell you exactly what your profession is, will you give me back my sheep?' 'Sure, why not?,' replies the yuppie. 'Clearly, you are a consultant,' says the shepherd. 'Correct,' says the yuppie, stunned out of his Guccis. 'How did you guess?' 'No guessing required,' replies the shepherd. 'You turned up here although nobody called you. You expect to get paid for an answer I already know, to a question I never asked, and you don't know anything about my business. Now give me back my dog.'"

I found myself laughing and crying at the same time. How many times had I bristled at his consultant jokes, how many times had I taken them personally? This might be the last I'd ever hear him tell.

"You know the story of when Moses went up to Mount Sinai and came back with the stone tablets, the Ten Commandments? Remember what else happened?"

"I'm not sure, tell me," I said, expecting I was walking into another joke.

"Moses' people didn't believe at first that he'd been talking to

God, and demanded proof. Remember what came next? God told him
to throw his staff on the ground, and he did, and the staff turned into
a snake."

I waited for the punch-line.

"Was that a miracle? We don't know how it could have
happened. Imagine, a stick changing into a snake. Sounds like a
miracle to me. But there are a lot of folks who would say, 'We can't
explain it, so therefore it could not really have happened.'"

I supposed he figured I was one of those people, and he was
probably right. At that time.

"We think of the concept of parallel universes as just some
nonsense from science fiction. But it's not. It's actually the most up-
to-date thinking in the field of quantum physics, the idea that the
universe is constantly branching into multiple copies, one for each
possible outcome. The scientists who know about these things tell us
that supposedly every possible alternative already exists, though we
only experience one of them."

He paused, then went on before I could respond. As if I had
any idea how to respond to that.

"You see, Greg, that's what we were talking about the other
day, that 'useful illusion.' The illusion stems from the way our human
physical apparatus shields us from the reality that's out there — the
reality that what seems to be solid matter is actually 99.99% empty
space. Nor do we realize there's a cloud of as-yet unsettled
possibilities out there, and that none of them becomes fixed and
settled until we observe it."

I couldn't figure where he was going with this.

As I was soon to learn, though, I'd have been well advised to
listen more closely, as it was about to become very relevant in ways I
could never have imagined.

"This sounds like pretty far-out stuff, I know," he continued,
"but it's actually mainstream science — or about to become
mainstream. Have you heard about the quantum computers that IBM
and other labs are working on? They'll perform complex
computations at a speed way, way beyond any of today's computers.
And you know how they're going to do that? By performing
calculations simultaneously in several different universes. The answer
you get will depend on which universe you're in. How about that!

Stodgy old IBM exploring multiple universes!"

"I'm not sure where you're going with this, Dad."

"The point is that all alternative tracks already exist. We're beginning to grasp the implications of that, hence the serious work on the potential of quantum computers."

"And Moses and the rod that turned into a snake — how did Moses come into this?," I asked. I was intrigued by what he was getting at, and had to recognize that there might not be another chance to talk again.

He laughed. "Oops! You got me there, I was rambling, drifted off the point. The skeptics say that since it doesn't seem possible *to them* for Moses' stick to have turned into a snake, well, then *it just couldn't be*. Narrow-minded dim-bulbs, no matter how many degrees they have."

He broke off into a coughing spell. Then he said, "*You* understand, don't you?"

"Can't say I do, Dad."

The explanation is as plain as the nose on their faces. All alternative tracks exist, so maybe in the blink of an eye Moses side-slipped from a universe where he was throwing a *stick,* into a different version of the universe, where, in that version of reality, it happened to be a *snake*."

"That is . . . uh . . . an interesting explanation."

"It follows on what we were talking about yesterday — the different paradigm. We take for granted that there's only one way of viewing things, the way we've always viewed them. Then something happens to force us to look in a different way, and from that different vantage point we see things in a completely different way — reframe things in a totally different context."

"Umm," I replied.

"There's a saying among the folks who're working in this field, 'Shut up and compute.' Meaning, nobody understands *why* these things work. But they *do* work, they *do* yield useful results. So it's best to shut up, to quit asking *why* they work, and just *use* them. Maybe someday we'll understand why, but in the meantime, we need to make use of them. If it weren't for quantum physics and these kinds of discoveries we wouldn't have transistors, or computer chips, or lasers, or CAT scans or MRIs or a lot of the other stuff we use every day without asking why it works. Like other things, it's best to just take it on faith. Try it, see if it works for you."

"Is this — " I hesitated, not sure how to phrase the question so it didn't offend him. "Is this something you read?"

"Read? Yeah, in the book. But it was also what Paul was talking about last night."

"What book was that?"

I thought I told you: *Joining Miracles*."

"I'll try to find it. Who's the author?"

"P."

"'P?' That's all? No other name?"

"Get yourself a copy, then we can talk about it. I'll be interested in hearing your thoughts on it."

81

I hung up, puzzled. Dad had never been one for abstract theories, yet now he had a sudden passion for quantum physics. Why? Was it something in the water he was drinking? Or in the drugs they were pumping into him?

Katje was still in the shower, so I logged onto Amazon to see if that book he talked about really existed.

It did: *Joining Miracles: Navigating the Seas of Latent Possibility*, and the author was indeed P. I didn't recognize the publisher, so it was apparently a small house, or maybe even self-published. It was ranked 12,986. Definitely respectable.

Even then, I hadn't begun to guess the truth.

I ran "*Joining Miracles* + P" through Google. At the top of the first page was a review of *Joining Miracles* by Patrick McDufferin, S.J., a Jesuit priest and psychologist on the faculty at Georgetown University.

Even then it seemed more than coincidence. Georgetown again. The Jesuits again.

I read it quickly. This was the money quote:

> *One might ask what thread binds these disparate strands — the Templars, the Grail, alchemy, even the blood-curdling occult obsessions of the Nazis.*
>
> *Without expressly stating it, this little book suggests an answer: They all touch upon the question of whether we humans are merely of the material world, or whether we are something more . . . perhaps even something in the nature of transformers between the worlds of matter and spirit.*

I looked again at the review, now intrigued. I pulled up a sidebar that had accompanied the original article: "Who is 'P?'"
❏
Katje emerged at last, now wearing a sky-blue jogging suit, and looking less frazzled.

I told her about my strange conversation with Dad, and showed her Fr. McDufferin's review.

"I can't believe it! This is no coincidence, this *has* to be synchronicity. I *know* this Fr. McDufferin."

I don't know how I responded. Maybe I just stared at her, not sure I could have heard right.

"He's been an unofficial advisor on that paper I'm working on."

"Your thesis? On the Templars and the other searchers for the Latent Miracle Power?"

She nodded. "Now that I think of it, I actually mentioned him to you, back in London, when we were first talking about Twisted Messiah. You've heard the new buzz-word, NGPF — Non-governmental Political Force? Well, he has a twist on that. He posits that Twisted Messiah and groups like that are what he calls NGRFs — Non-governmental *Religious* Forces because they cross the line between musical groups and quasi-religious cults."

I remembered that, the first day we'd met, after the CIA guy had warned me to give up and go home because of the various groups on my tail, one of them a NG**R**F — presumably Twisted Messiah.

"Father McDufferin has doctorates in both literature and psychology, and teaches in both the English department and the medical school." She hesitated. "I could probably arrange for us all to meet, if you'd like."

"When?" I wasn't sure about this, but I was intrigued by Dad's sudden interest in a book that also seemed to overlap with, as Fr. McDufferin's book review put it, "the Templars, the Grail, alchemy, even the blood-curdling occult obsessions of the Nazis." And with the latent miracle power that both Katje and my father had spoken of.

She shrugged. "I've heard him say that he's taken vows of poverty, chastity and obedience, but not of passing up a decent meal. I could give him a call, see when would be a good time."

"I'm hungry, too. Maybe a dinner would tempt him."

❏

The phone rang just before she picked up. It was Mrs. Poulson, the building manager, complaining that I had failed to collect and pay for that postage-due mail.

"I've been away. I didn't know I had any postage due."

"The management advances the postage as a service to our residents, but that must not be taken advantage of. We do expect to be repaid, it is essential that you understand that."

"I'll pick it up in the morning and pay you then. Do you have it in front of you? Who's the sender?"

"You will learn that when you pay. You need to pick it up now. And pay what is due."

More than once I'd ridden an elevator with another resident after an encounter with Mrs. Poulson, sharing a mutual sense of gratitude that they were not Mr. Poulson.

She clicked off before I could ask why my mail had not been held, as I'd asked, but had instead been put in my apartment. I hadn't authorized anyone to come in, and there was no notice that the staff had come in for repairs.

Katje, while I was on the call, had used her cell-phone. "I just talked to Father McDufferin. He's chaplain on call at the hospital tonight, but we could have a quick bite someplace close by. He never got to have lunch, and so he's ready for an early dinner."

❏

"Dammit! There was postage due! How the *hell* did you miss that!," Fackson snapped when he heard the replay of the conversation.

"It wasn't our fault, it was the front desk at his place that screwed-up," Larson said. "They forgot to put a notice for him, that's why we didn't know. But not to worry. He's going to pick it up now, we'll get it off him, one way or another."

82

Fr. Pat McDufferin was not what I'd expected. Instead of the traditional black robe of a Jesuit, he wore a grey Harris tweed blazer over a midnight blue turtleneck. He seemed to be around 50, a fraction under six feet, broad-shouldered, with an ample belly and a twinkle in his eye. The remains of sandy hair circled a very large dome.

He held out his hand, and his grip was firm. "Call me Father, call me Pat — or Tom or Dick or Harry — call me anything you please . . . just don't call me late to dinner." He patted his tummy. "An old joke, but ah!, all too true."

Again I wondered if this was such a good idea, bringing this to a Jesuit— a member of one of the secret organizations modeled on the Knights Templar.

❑

We were able to get a booth — good, so we could talk more freely. A fireplace blazed across the room. The waitress brought us frosted mugs of beer — refreshing, but not up to what I'd been tasting in Austria and England.

"I'm chaplain on call for the hospital tonight," he said, "so perhaps we'd be best to get to business first thing." He turned to me. "Katje briefed me a bit when we talked earlier. It seems my review of *Joining Miracles* caught your interest. Perhaps it would help if I began by free-associating some ideas?"

I wondered just how much she had already told him. I wondered, too, whether she had engineered this so he could pump me.

"I believe one of your areas of interest is in coded knowledge, particularly as it relates to the alchemists and the Knights Templar?"

He went on, now echoing some of what I had already turned up, though adding new twists. The legends of the quest for the Holy Grail, and the stories of the alchemists' quest to turn base metals into gold, were probably both intended as coded descriptions of an inner, mystical or spiritual process that referred to developing the hidden powers of the human mind.

"The so-called `Great Work' of Alchemy was a secret ritual, preceded by fasting and meditation, that supposedly enabled the alchemist to bring about that change from lead to gold. In today's terminology, we'd say that the fasting and meditation and ritual steps were a program designed to bring about a certain kind of altered state of consciousness in which one could transcend the usual assumed limitations. Put bluntly, it seems that the Great Work of Alchemy was a kind of `technology' for getting beyond the usual human boundaries in order to access the higher powers."

"A technology for achieving alternate states of consciousness?," Katje echoed, as if hearing the phrase for the first time.

"Both of these quests," he continued, "Alchemy and the Grail, were expressed as stories — to encode the deeper realities behind the narratives. Why encoded? First, because they wanted to pass on the great secret — that we humans *are* able to tap higher powers, that there *is* meaning and design, that we *can* take greater control of the flow of physical reality. The initiates wanted to keep that knowledge alive, yet had to encode it to protect themselves. After all, they and the knowledge they possessed were dangerous to the status quo. This was the era in which alchemists were burned at the stake, alongside witches and other supposed heretics."

It almost seemed that he'd been listening in on what Brother Augustus had said back in the monastery.

He sipped his beer, then went on: "Second, and no less important, they coded the knowledge in order to ensure that their secrets didn't fall into the hands of those who would corrupt and misuse the knowledge."

❑

The waitress brought our burgers. Fr. McDufferin made quick work of the first half of his before going on.

"There is, of course, another common thread between the legends of the Grail quest and the work of the Alchemists, which is a point I raised in my review of *Joining Miracles*. Both schools touch in a somewhat unique way on the ultimate question of whether we humans are just bits of moving flesh, or whether we are creatures with the unique ability to act as living bridges between this world of matter, and another dimension that we can only dimly perceive."

I was about to ask him to rephrase that when he added, "In today's technological parlance, one might suggest that we humans are like 'transformers' between the worlds of matter and spirit. That's Ouspensky's term, 'transformers:' I can't claim credit. But the point is, because we have one foot — so to speak — in the material world and another foot in the ineffable world, we may have a unique ability to translate and transform energies from one to the other — and back again."

He ate a bit more, then said, "I'm suggesting that we begin to tap that latent miracle power when we recognize this inherent capability we have, to be human, yet to play a role in the working-out of the larger, unseen world."

He paused, then added, "As I read that small book, I found myself wondering . . . It's a stretch, but I did find myself wondering whether the author found the secret how-to, the recipe, the operations manual for accomplishing that."

❑

Then I asked the question I'd been holding: "The author of *Joining Miracles* — what do you know about him?"

He shook his head. "Nothing at all, nothing beyond what you can find on his web-site."

"So you have no idea who the author, 'P', is?"

He shook his head. "No one does. That's part of the mystique."

83

Fr. McDufferin finished his burger without another word. Whether he'd said all he had to say, or was just intent on his food wasn't clear.

Eventually, he pushed his empty plate away, and said, "Apropos Twisted Messiah and company, there is a certain theme that carries through most of the versions of the Grail legends: the Wounded Land, a land that is barren, the people dispirited and demoralized. Why is that aspect of the Grail story relevant even today? Because, I suggest to you, we are still living in the Waste Lands of modern times, where people are demoralized despite prosperity. Again why? Because their minds have been clogged with negativity, hopelessness, defeatism. I think, even more to the point, that they are feeling trapped in the here-and-now, and have lost any real sense of meaning and personal potential. That, of course, is where my interest in Twisted Messiah and its cultist followers comes in."

"They *want* the followers to be demoralized?," I blurted.

He nodded. "Demoralized, imbued with the sense that they are worthless, indeed that all of human society and life itself is worthless. The leadership wants to stoke anger, bitterness, hatred — because it seems they have plans to use the negative emotional energies that are generated."

His eyes probed Katje's and mine. Then he said, "To be more blunt, I am convinced that the people behind Twisted Messiah deliberately set out to engender that demoralization, that sense of ultimate futility, in the followers."

He finished the last of his beer, then added, "In short, I think those pathetic young people have lost touch with the possibility of the higher potentials. And I think that is no accident."

"No accident? I'm not sure what you mean."

"I think it's not by chance that so many of us today have lost touch with the higher potentials latent within us all. Just as the establishments of the past were terrified of the supposed occult knowledge allegedly possessed by the Templars and the alchemists and the others, so also are many of today's establishments equally terrified that the populace would begin to recognize the existence of these higher powers . . . and perhaps even begin accessing them."

He paused while the waitress cleared the table, and I remembered what old Brother Augustus had said, back at the monastery in St. Johann:

> *There is nothing mysterious about the power that Paul discovered. It's nothing more than a basic human potential that we all have, but one that most of us have been conditioned to overlook. The Templars learned to tap this power, and that, of course, was extremely threatening to the establishment, just as it would be — indeed, as it is — today.*
>
> *The established powers couldn't afford to let that knowledge leak out into the general population, because if it were widely spread, that would destroy the basis of their own power.*
>
> *The established powers of the day, of whatever day, find that the more we ordinary people believe in our own limitations, the more their control is enhanced, because if we believe we are limited, then our own sense of limitations bestows power on them.*
>
> **That** *is the great secret that the establishments of every age don't want us to know: that we are not dependent on them, that we have within ourselves the power to change the flow of events, even – especially – those outside our direct physical control.*

The waitress finished, and Fr. McDufferin continued. "The establishments today are more subtle. They don't try to suppress knowledge, nor do they burn dissenters at the stake. They couldn't get away with that now— not in the era of television and the internet.

Some reality TV program would be right there, filming the spectacle. So how do today's powers-that-be operate to keep this dangerous awareness of higher potentials from the populace?"

He paused, as if waiting for a reply, then went on: "Mockery is one weapon: when did you last hear anyone in the mainstream media talking about higher spiritual potentials, other than to set up the rebuttal? Outside of certain churches, outside of small groups, probably never. Expressing a belief in anything higher than oneself, even making a serious attempt to explore the possibility, opens one to ridicule."

He paused, then went on, "Mockery is one method, the churn is another. The churn— keeping us so distracted with the excitement of the here-and-now that we don't have time or inclination to draw back and ask, Why all this?"

"And Twisted Messiah?," Katje asked.

"A very cleverly programmed agenda to fill that void. But not out of benevolence. The leaders seek the power that the followers can give them. They want to use those rootless young as the batteries to power their secret agendas."

❑

I wondered whether to tell him that — was it only this morning? — we'd been in Jesse's convent. I decided to leave that up to Katje, to tell if she wanted to.

But would he believe it, if she did tell him?

Would any rational person believe it?

In the end, we didn't have to decide: his cell-phone rang. A bad accident on I-66. He was needed to perform the Last Rites.

Before leaving, he added this: "It seems that Jesse and the lot of them are caught in that dreadful convent of his, or perhaps dead. But I don't think it's over yet. I fear there will be at least one final spasm — perhaps several. Evil does not give up easily."

"Final spasm? Some kind of an attack?"

"Something of that sort. Something destructive."

There was still one question I wanted to ask. But I hesitated because I wasn't sure how much I could trust him. It was not for nothing that the term "Jesuitical" had come into the language: Jesuitical — crafty, devious.

Katje asked the question in my mind: "Suppose somehow

Twisted Messiah, or a group like them, got their hands on this knowledge, the how-to for tapping these higher potentials, what I've been calling the Latent Miracle Power?"

He shook his head. "The power is neutral. It can be used constructively or destructively. But I think it would be disastrous if Twisted Messiah, or others like them, learned to tap that power, because they could turn it to their purposes, unfolding their version of reality."

❑

We were out on the street, the rain having given way now to a light mist. The air was fresh and bracing.

Fr. McDufferin paused to peer at me over his glasses. "There is another aspect. Twisted Messiah's various spokespersons and apologists have disavowed any link with the Nazis, when it was obvious to even the most historically illiterate viewer that the whole spectacle of that concert the other night was a deliberate *hommage* to the massive rallies the Nazis staged at Nuremberg before the war."

Then he shook his head. "Whoever choreographed that show understood the real appeal of Twisted Messiah. It's not the music. What's ultimately drawing these millions of young people is the devilishly clever way Twisted Messiah taps *their unconscious craving for meaning*, for a kind of spirituality, for a yearning to ally with something larger than themselves. They don't know what it is they're looking for, but they do sense that there *is* something. The Twisted Messiah leadership, as did Hitler and others before, are attempting to capture that drive and twist it to their own ends, turning the young followers into a kind of human batteries."

"Batteries? Literal batteries, somehow tapping this latent miracle power?"

McDufferin nodded. "In one sense literal — witness the way we saw Jesse come to life on stage, just as Hitler drew on the energies of the crowds to become more and more animated."

Again he paused before adding, "But there's another aspect to it that I fear even more. The impressionable young fans, still searching for a way to bring meaning to their aimless lives, still searching for something greater than what they see in themselves, can easily be manipulated to translate the energies of that quest into dark ends."

"Dark ends? What are you saying?"

"I'm suggesting that it would not be difficult for Jesse Cripes and the others to convert those energies to a political force, even a subversive force."

"That sounds like a cult. The first worldwide cult, a media-driven cult."

"Alas, that is precisely what I see. And I don't like the implications, not at all. The cult at Jonestown ended badly — group suicide by Kool-Aid. David Koresh and his cult ended fatally. The members of the Heaven's Gate cult saw suicide as their ticket to the great spaceship in the sky. Members of the Solar Temple coordinated group suicides in both Quebec and Switzerland. I could go on."

The impressionable, searching for a way to bring meaning to their aimless lives, searching for something greater than what they see in themselves, can easily be manipulated to translate the energies of that quest into dark ends.

84

We stopped at Borders and each bought a copy of *Joining Miracles* from a stack on one of the tables.

That was odd: according to the clerk, *Joining Miracles: Navigating the Seas of Latent Possibility* had been featured on that display table for months, yet I'd never noticed it — and that at a Borders I usually browse at least once a week.

It had probably also been on display on the tables at Foyles, yet invisible to me.

The Grail: invisible, can only be seen when the time is right for it to reveal itself.

Maybe we were getting close.

"The sub-title, '*Navigating the Seas of Latent Possibility*' — could that relate to the Latent Miracle Power you're writing about?," I asked Katje on the drive home.

"I've been wondering that myself," she answered.

❑

I'd forgotten to pick up that postage due mail on the way out, so stopped at the front desk when we got back. Mrs. Poulson had left for the day, but Nkwame found it waiting on her desk in the back office.

A thick manila envelope bearing the inimitable stubby printing of Cal Katz.

For the lack of a postage stamp or two, I was still alive.

❑

Katje had gone upstairs ahead of me. The TV was on, and she stood transfixed.

Breaking news. The anchor's voice-over said, "What you are about to see is a taped replay, as it happened approximately two hours ago in Germany. This is not – repeat not – live."

Jesse Cripes' "Convent of the Sensuous Virgins" gleamed in police floodlights, as if part of a sound-and-light show. The on-site reporter narrated, pausing for the sound of helicopter engines spooling up inside the convent walls.

The police floodlights cut off abruptly and the screen went dark for an instant before a night-vision camera cut in, the images now ghostly green and black.

The dark shadows of a SWAT team began scaling the walls. The engine spooled up in a shrill whine, then the bulbous shape of the small copter lifted over the wall. It cleared the rooftops, then shot out over the valley.

What happened at that point was not clear. Some observers claim they heard gunshots as the copter passed overhead. By other accounts, the pilot miscalculated and hit tree branches. The camera followed as the dark chopper tumbled, then exploded into a fireball on the hillside.

The reporter came on to do a stand-up with the copter still burning in the background.

Within moments, the commando team was over the wall. Shots were heard, the crackle of automatic weapons. A second team, whether police or military we don't know at this time, crashed through the main gate in an armored vehicle. More shots were heard. But since then, silence, so we have no way of knowing what is happening inside the former convent.

Now the screen filled with the ball of orange flames churning on the hillside.

Fire-fighters struggled through the densely-wooded slope to the spot where the remains of the copter still blaze, red-orange flames guttering like a scene from the Apocalypse. But whether the fire crews were able to save lives remains to be seen. The whereabouts of Twisted Messiah lead singer Jessie Cripes are unknown at this time, though as of midnight local time, about four hours before the crash, Jesse was

*confirmed to be inside the convent. Jesse may — and
I stress may — have been on the helicopter, or he may
still be in the castle. We just don't know, and perhaps
the authorities don't yet know, either.*

Katje turned to me. "Something else came on just before this
— that convoy of Twisted Messiah fans that was driving down from
Berlin to protest? It seems that at least a couple thousand of them are
already in Munich. And not just in Munich, either. They're forming
up in Washington, too. Hordes of angry Twisted Messiah fans have
quietly converged on the downtown areas of several cities around the
world, forming flash-mobs that hit, do some damage, then move on."

"Was this planned?"

"The police don't know – or aren't saying. The same
convergence of fans is hitting other cities, around the world. So far
there's been no real violence. But there's no telling how long that will
last. Especially if it turns out that Jesse Cripes is in fact dead."

*You are the Butterfly who sets off the storm that begins inside
the Washington Beltway and spreads around the world.*

Perhaps the Butterfly set off not just one, but *two* storms, and
now the storms were converging.

The German police had now taken control of Jesse's former
convent, and all who had been inside were being held for questioning.

A press conference was expected later in the day.

"That sounds very ominous. If Jesse were alive, don't you
think the authorities would announce that, and ease the pressure?"

"Makes sense."

"But Jesse and this whole Twisted Messiah thing is so central
for some of these kids. It's all they have, like their religion and politics
and folk-heros all rolled into one. It's a cult. If Jesse is dead . . ."

"Then he becomes their martyr."

The CIA guy yesterday on Twisted Messiah's army: *Let your
imagination run wild — then realize they can do far, far worse than
that. Look at it, they've got an army of dead-end kids around the
world, all willing to drink the Kool-Aid, and they've got money and
contacts to buy any kind of damned weapons, even WMD. Play with
those possibilities when you wake up in the middle of some dark
night.*

85

I dug out Cal's first message, the one that started things off that first day:

WARNING! YOU ARE THE BUTTERFLY!
You're about to set off a storm that starts ITB and spreads around the world!

Sending very important info regarding our recent conversation.

Pass it on if anything happens to me.

Do not call me. I'll call you when/if it's safe.

THIS IS NOT A DRILL!

Now I had that envelope containing Cal's "very important info."

So he really had sent it, after all.

But pass it on to whom? How?

An even more basic question: what the hell was in this envelope? What could he have turned up that cost his own life, and probably that of Shelly Sherman and Danny Mann as well?

I wanted to chuck this whole package, pretend it had never arrived. I had problems enough of my own — Dad, Uncle Paul, all the rest of it. I didn't need another complication — a lethal complication, at that.

I slit the envelope open and was bathed in the fumes of the awful cigars that were Cal's olfactory trademark. Something broke in me then, as I sniffed that scent of the cigars I'd always tried to stay upwind from, and my eyes filled with tears for the little guy.

He was a one-off, definitely not at all one of the boys. People tended to laugh at him behind his back; he knew that, and neither cared nor had any desire to be anything other than the person he was. Whether he'd been happy I have no idea, but he was fulfilled in his work, of that there was no doubt.

Somebody had stolen decades of life from him. I couldn't do anything about that; I couldn't give him back those years. But I *could* do what he'd asked.

The first item was Cal's note, in his inimitably hard-to-read, stubby handwriting, made even thicker by the Sharpie pen he used. Why hadn't he just typed it and made things easier?

Then I understood, and was impressed at how cagy he'd been. His handwriting *was* inimitable, and this note was his proof of authenticity.

Greg,

I'm asking a big favor of you and a few others I trust. If anything happens to me, please see that the enclosed gets out to the public. If you give it to the media, MAKE SURE it's somebody you can trust.

Look the stuff over and you'll understand why I was asking about your uncle and the OSS.

BUT WATCH YOUR BACK!

Mucho thanks,

Cal

I'm asking you and a few others I trust.
Shelly Sherman — strangled in her apartment.
Danny Mann — highjacked on the way home.

❏

There were about 200 pages in all. On top was a draft of the article he'd written, about 20 pages. The rest seemed to be proof sources, going back as far as the late 1940's. Business memos, letters, old newspaper and magazine articles.

As usual, Cal had begun the project to satisfy his own curiosity: How had the "Beltway Bandit" consulting and defense manufacturing firms grown so powerful so relatively quickly?

He had focused on one of these firms, figuring it would probably be typical, a prototype of the others. By chance — or synchronicity — the one he chose happened to be B-MAR Corporation, founded in 1946 as the Barrington Oil Company, an oil exploration company in Louisiana. Before long, it segued into ocean shipping (to transport the oil it found), then into ship-building, taking over a bankrupt firm. That was just before the start of the Korean War in 1950, and the Barrington Oil Company changed its name to the Barrington Marine Corporation, later just B-MAR Corp.

War work was very lucrative, according to Cal's documentation, and the oil exploration company was spun off, then later sold, so management could focus on following the federal dollar.

Like Willie Sutton (and I), B-MAR went where the money was. Willie to rob banks, and us Beltway Bandits to help the government spend money.

The Beltway was built around Washington in the early 1960's, and it wasn't long before a couple of terms came to the fore. "Beltway Bandits" was one.

Another was "Inside-the-Beltway" — acronymed by those in the know as "ITB." ITB was the self-proclaimed Center of the Universe.

B-MAR grew with the expansion in the federal budget, shape-shifting to accommodate changing budgets. The shipping and ship-building divisions were spun off, again so management could focus on the new action: communications, technology, software, information systems.

B-MAR made a lot of money, but, from what Cal turned up, it gave good value for the federal dollars received. It was a respected company with a good reputation and a track record of getting projects done on time and within budget . . . as much as possible under the bizarre, ever-changing military procurement system, twisted by the vagaries of political expediency.

Over the years, B-MAR's CEO, Hadley Barrington, became a highly respected elder statesman of Washington, a major fund-raiser for one of the parties, but also a contributor to the other, to ensure the channels stayed open.

As a tribute to his clout — and a way of saying thanks for his contributions over the years — he'd been given an Ambassadorship — to Italy — as well as some other lesser posts.

All in all, B-MAR Corporation was the archetype of many of the other similar firms that serviced the federal government on both the military and civilian sides.

If Cal had left it at that and moved on to explore some of the other firms, he would be alive today, and I'd be reading his article a few weeks from now in a magazine.

But he couldn't let go.

By this point, his curiosity had moved from the broader issue of contractors to a more focused issue: How did it happen that the earliest incarnation of B-MAR seemed to spring up out of nowhere back in 1946? Exploring for oil, even then, took major capital, so how did the founder, Hadley Barrington, come up with his grub-stake?

Cal narrowed his focus again, now onto Barrington himself. After college and a year of law school, Barrington had gone to Washington on the staff of one of the state's Senators. When war came soon afterwards, the Senator helped him get into the OSS. Barrington didn't have the Ivy League background that characterized the OSS in those days, but he spoke fluent French — the legacy of parents who had immigrated to Louisiana at the turn of the century. That was when the family name was changed from Bourton to Barrington.

It took weeks of digging for Cal to piece together just what Barrington had done while in the OSS. Katz had dug through OSS archives before without this much difficulty; now he found it puzzling that so many of the records relating to Barrington and the sections he'd served in were marked "Destroyed in a Fire."

He might have moved on to something else had he not come upon a familiar name in one old duty roster: Tapscott. Curious, he pursued that to see where it led.

Always a dogged researcher with the larcenous instincts of a computer hacker, Katz wormed through some old, long-forgotten files, and came upon a letter signed by Barrington's OSS designation — B/F-12 — claiming that Agent Perceval had "absconded with crucial enemy property." That letter had been sent from St. Johann am Fleckensee, Austria, 9 May 1945.

A bit more digging revealed that Agent Perceval had been listed as Missing in Action and presumed dead in Normandy, about a year earlier, at the time of D-Day, June, 1944. That had also been signed by B/F-12.

But then he turned up documents that seemed to say that a dead OSS agent who supposedly died in France had miraculously come back to life in Austria, just in time to steal enemy property — a development that piqued Cal's curiosity even more.

Still another file indicated that Agent Perceval had been dropped, not into Normandy, but instead a couple of hundred or so miles south, around La Rochelle.

Now Katz, a conspiracy theorist *par excellence* was hooked on the new chase: never mind the Beltway Bandits and B-MAR for the moment, what was Barrington, an OSS France specialist, doing in Austria at the end of the war?

The answer seemed to be that he had been chasing his own agent, Perceval. But why?

Then a small bell tinkled in Katz' memory, and he dug up an old clipping from the *New York Times*:

Swiss Banker Claims American Officers Stole Nazi Gold at War's End

The article dated from 1996, around the time documents turned up indicating that Swiss banks had knowingly cooperated with the Nazis in storing and laundering massive amounts of gold plundered from occupied countries and from Jewish holocaust victims.

Somebody, probably Cal, had underlined this part:

It has been a well-concealed fact that certain American military and intelligence officers enriched themselves at the end of the war by grabbing several tons of gold that the Germans had hidden in various locations in the mountains of Austria and southern Germany, most notoriously the cache stored near the Fleckensee (Lake Flecken) in Austria. Until that gold has been accounted for, the Americans have no right to accuse the Swiss of hypocrisy.

Dr. Gniessbach's strange comment: *Schloss Flecken would later develop a certain infamy, once the Americans arrived.*

Once the Americans arrived — that is, after Paul disappeared and after his superior officers arrived in response to the message Gniessbach had forced Paul to send.

Nazi gold stolen by American intelligence officers at the end of the war, most notoriously the cache stored near St. Johann am Fleckensee — where Barrington turned up in the final days of the war.

Which also happened to be the place where Paul Tapscott was last seen — supposedly a decade after the war ended.

My uncle the spy.

My uncle the gold thief?

86

Katje burst into the room. "Greg! I just heard — You look . . . troubled . . . terrible! Has something happened?"

"What was it you heard?," I asked, partly to gain some time to think what to tell her about Cal and this whole new strand.

"Twisted Messiah fans, here and in cities around the world, are staging sudden riots. Actually, not so much riots as flash mobs that suddenly appear, do some damage, then disappear before the police can get there. It's even happening here in Washington. The point is to force the German authorities to back off the siege at Jesse's place. Had you already heard that? Is that why you were looking so glum?"

"Something else," I said, still stalling.

"Your father?"

The best thing was to begin at the beginning. I told her about Cal Katz and that Butterfly fax, then gave her a quick overview of what it was all about. "Cal Katz turned up what seems to be very solid evidence not only linking Hadley Barrington with the theft of the gold from the *Schloss* Flecken, but then going back and tracing how Barrington's share of that stolen gold was the capital that got his empire started, first in oil, then in ship-building, now in multiple areas, including a lot of government work."

She thought over what I'd said for a moment, then shook her head, the hint of a smile on her face. "I don't see why you think that's bad news. I think it's great! What a bombshell that would be for the sons' political opponents! Headline: 'Barrington Political Dynasty Founded on Nazi Gold.' It would be the end of the sons' political career, as well as the end of his companies' ever getting any government contracts in the future."

She paused, then added, "There's also the issue of whether old man Barrington could still be charged criminally for the theft. Is there a statute of limitations for wartime plundering? And what about a civil suit by the government to recover what was stolen, plus all the fruits of that illegal gain over the years? He'd lose everything."

"It makes sense for Barrington to do whatever it took to silence Cal and what he'd turned up."

"And now you're holding that research in your hands. Is it going to silence us, as well?"

I tried to laugh it off. "You have a knack for asking the tough questions. No hard feelings if you set that tea-cup down and run like hell."

"That's not funny. I wouldn't — *would not* — leave you at a time like this."

"I got you into a lot more than you ever expected."

She shrugged. "I have no regrets. No matter what happens."

❑

She spent a while reading through Cal's papers, then asked, "You said that Cal asked you about a relative of yours who'd been in the OSS. Do you think this is why — the link to the Fleckensee gold?"

"I assume so, but can't be sure. Apparently Cal found that Barrington was Paul's commander, but it's not at all clear from these papers whether Paul might also have been in on the gold theft."

"Did Cal actually suggest that?"

"No, there was no mention. Maybe Paul wasn't part of it, or maybe Cal just couldn't come up with proof."

"That must have been a shock for you when you heard Professor Tabersley telling about the gold theft. What are you thinking now? Do you believe Paul was part of it?"

I shook my head. "Maybe it's wishful thinking, but it just doesn't seem like something Paul would do. From all I'd ever heard of him, he was a total straight-arrow."

"Suppose it had been you there, in that place and time. What would you have done?"

"I'd like to believe I wouldn't have had any part of it. Not just because I was so honest, but also because the war was just about over, and I'd have wanted to go home, not risk prison."

She nodded. "From what I know of you, you wouldn't have gotten involved in anything criminal. And if your uncle was at all like you, neither would he."

❑

She walked out onto the balcony and stood for a moment looking at my personal view of the park and the little creek that runs through it.

Traffic was bumper-to-bumper going out Massachusetts Avenue. That seemed odd. Then I remembered: the traffic was normal for evening rush hour. It was my body-clock that was out of whack. Here, in the real-world, it was still early evening.

After a minute or so, Katje came back inside and said, "Cal's note asked you to pass these papers on if anything happened to him. Any ideas how you're going to do that?"

"Not really. I could take them down to the *Washington Post*. Maybe somebody there would pick up the ball."

She was silent a moment, then said, "Color me cynical, but I think the editors at the *Post* would say, 'Very interesting, but we'll do our own independent investigation and maybe get back to you in a couple of months . . . after the election is over and done with.' The election is almost upon us, keep that in mind. The *Post* is not going to run a story based on somebody else's research and risk upsetting the election, only to find that maybe some of this information is wrong or false. And it would be the same with ABC, CBS, NBC — you name it, the result is the same."

My conclusion exactly, but neither of us could think of an alternative. No major media outlet was likely to run with this ball, not now, not in the shadow of an election, not when it involved going up against somebody with the clout of Hadley Barrington.

87

"There's always *The Naismith Letter*," Katje said. "Naismith could move fast on something like this."

The Naismith Letter was one of the e-publications that had sprung up, like the *Drudge Report*, and countless other political "blogs," run by journalists who wanted to make some bucks on the side, and not have to put up with nit-picking editors and publishers. The only limitation came from the risks of libel.

I'd clicked onto it now and then, work-avoidance behavior that sometimes yielded nuggets of useful information or hot Inside-the-Beltway leaks and trial balloons.

The more I thought about it, the more sense it made. Dan Naismith had been an overseas bureau chief for the *Washington Post* way back when, so his blog covered a lot more than just Washington insider stuff. He could move fast, and he had contacts.

Best of all, his record showed that he didn't mind making enemies.

Who better to carry on Katz's quest than another conspiracy-freak, former hot-shot reporter, his career supposedly destroyed by the shadowy "Them."

I didn't remember the details, just that Naismith had left the *Post* under some kind of a cloud a few years back. He'd never caught on with any other big media, but had been one of the first to set up his own newsletter/blog, and now he had a following both among journalists and the general public.

Naismith might be on the outside these days, but he still had connections, and no doubt was hungry for the kind of break that could put him back in the game. Pass it on and let him run with it.

Next question: how to reach him?

I dug out my laptop and logged on, and connected to Naismith's website. With the election coming up on Tuesday, Naismith's usually catholic tastes had narrowed. Now, like the rest of the media, it was all-elections, all the time.

I scanned quickly: no mention of the Barrington brothers, nor the old man himself.

I did turn up Naismith's contact information. He had an e-mail hotline for tips, and I sent him a short note saying I had something "potentially very explosive" to offer him. I didn't mention Cal Katz — I'd save that for later.

But there wasn't time to sit around waiting to see if he'd call back. If he wasn't interested, I wanted to know now, while there was still a chance to scout out other possibilities.

There was no phone listing on his web-page, but Katje worked the search engines, and came up with a number in one of the local exchanges. I tried it and got an answering machine. I gave my name, and mentioned that I had just sent an e-mail.

A man picked up with a growl. "Am I supposed to know your name?," he greeted.

I repeated that I had some "potentially very explosive" information that he could use in the *Naismith Letter*.

"E-mail it to me. The address is on the website. But if it's a hoax, save your time because I've got every kind of virus-catcher going, so you aren't going to sabotage my system."

That's when I knew he was the perfect surrogate for Cal Katz: Naismith and Katz were a matched pair of unsociable paranoids.

"I can't do that," I said. "We need to meet face-to-face. I'll give it to you then if you're interested."

"Too busy. If you want me to look at it, send it. Then we'll talk."

"Cal Katz — does the name mean anything to you?"

A hesitation. "Sure. Never met him, but respected his work. What about him?"

"The project he was working on when he died, so — "

"Katz didn't *die*, he was *murdered*. There's a big difference. So what about that project?"

"The day he died — within the hour before he was killed — he sent me a copy of a draft of his article, along with his documentation. He said if anything happened to him he wanted me to get it out to the public. You seem to be the best way of accomplishing that."

"Has it not occurred to you that perhaps Katz was killed for a reason? And that if you're holding his materials, then you're facing the same risks?"

"Once it gets out into the world, then there's no more risk," I surprised myself by saying. That had been Tabersley's reasoning.

"So you hope." I heard a deep sigh on the other end of the line. "What's the subject?"

"It's complicated."

"Try."

"A certain Beltway Bandit firm and how it got its start on stolen money, way back. Now there's a present-day political link."

"You tell a hell of a bed-time story, my friend. That almost put me to sleep. E-mail it, then maybe we'll talk."

"Hadley Barrington and his days in the OSS, and now his sons. And the family fortune is all built on sham."

"Do you have any idea how many of these calls I get every week, somebody promising the expose of the century? Ninety-percent amount to nothing at all, and most of the rest of the remaining nine and a half percent are somebody trying to plant a phony story either to stab somebody else in the back or to discredit me."

"This is that last half of a percent. When he sent it to me, Katz said it was like that butterfly whose wings set off a storm on the other side of the world. Only he said the storm would be ITB, Inside-the-Beltway."

"You are persistent. And yeah, I do know the acronym. There's a Starbucks in Rosslyn. Take a good look at my picture on the website. You'll have to spot me since I don't know you from Adam. Meet me there in half an hour. And don't come through downtown, those Twisted Messiah freaks have the place in an uproar."

88

Katje insisted on riding along, "even if it's just to make sure you don't fall asleep driving."

The paranoia was getting to me: I was edgy even in my own parking garage when we went down.

But it's not just temporary paranoia — things do happens in garages here, though you don't hear much about it because most of it is small potatoes as crimes go: purse snatching, wallet grabbing, car-jacking. Besides, the corporations that own the shopping malls and apartment complexes don't want those stories getting out to spook the paying customers.

It was dark and rainy out on the streets, and I was feeling spacy between jet-lag and the fact that I hadn't slept in a bed in days, not since St. Johann.

Avoid the flash mobs downtown. So best was back across Chain Bridge, then down the Parkway to Rosslyn. Normally a pleasant drive, but tonight I was having trouble staying focused. I opened the roof; the fresh air helped.

❏

I phoned the hospital again as I drove the Parkway to Rosslyn. Eventually the floor nurse picked up on Dad's line. "Mr. Tapscott seems to be away for tests."

"*Seems* to be away?" That sounded odd. Don't nurses know where their patients have been taken? Isn't that part of the job? Besides, what kind of test would they run in the evening?

Maybe she read my mind: "Sorry, I can't help you more, I've

only come on duty, filling in for somebody who had to leave early."
❑

Naismith was already at Starbucks when we arrived, at a table tucked away in a corner.

He was older and a lot more worn than I'd expected from the picture on his website Late 50's, with a face puffy and creased from hard living. It was obvious enough why he had remained a print reporter: he lacked the hair for TV. What little he had left was combed across the top in a futile attempt to cover a bald crown.

His suit had the wide lapels stylish in the late '70's. An old Burberry raincoat was thrown over the spare chair. It seemed that times had not been good for him lately, not for quite a while if he was still wearing his disco-era wardrobe. *The Naismith Letter* apparently had more impact than profit.

If he was pushing 60 now, then he'd have been somewhere in his late 30's or early 40's as the *Post's* Foreign Service man in Rome. A nice time for expense-account life in Italy, *La Dolce Vita* and all that.

I'd run across people like Naismith: the detritus of Washington – talented people who'd been spit out by the system. People who had never quite made it, or folks who had made it, and then, for whatever reason, lost it. Some had bet on the wrong candidate or wrong issue. Others hadn't caught onto changing circumstances quickly enough, or were shoved aside for "new blood" — just as they had been the new blood that benefitted from earlier turnovers.

He nodded when he saw us, but his eyes focused on the door behind, and I realized he was checking to see if I'd been followed. Paranoid, or just appropriately cautious?

He snapped his laptop shut and put away the sheaf of clippings he'd been working on.

"So you have Katz' last project, and you want me to bring it to the world?"

That seemed a hostile opening from somebody who was getting a gift dropped in his lap. But he was a journalist, and the journalist archetype called for cynical and a little bit seedy.

"So what's in it for you? You're taking a risk holding onto this stuff, you admitted that. Why?"

"Because Cal Katz was a friend of mine, and I owed him this

last favor. Isn't that reason enough?"

Naismith shrugged. "Sure, why not? It's just that in this city I don't run into many people so loyal to their friends. So what have you got?"

I gave him the envelope Cal had sent. He pulled the documents out and scanned them, quickly at the start, obviously primed to dismiss them.

Then he slowed and went back over what he had already seen. He couldn't maintain the inscrutability: it was obvious that he was impressed and excited by what he saw. "Interesting," he muttered a couple of times.

I used the time to put in another call to the hospital so I could tell Dad that I'd picked up a copy of *Joining Miracles* and was eager to get into it.

But he was still out of his room, and a different nurse said she "assumed" he had been taken away for tests.

It still seemed peculiar that the floor nurse could only assume where he'd been taken, but she was in a hurry and I said I'd check back later.

89

"This is interesting material, especially to me," Naismith finally said. "You probably don't have a clue why that is."

I shook my head.

"You have read the stuff? You saw the reference to the gold stolen from *Schloss* Flecken? The Fleckensee gold — *that's* what intrigues me. Know why?"

"I know the story of the gold, but I don't know how you fit into it." I was not about to volunteer that my uncle Paul might have played a role in it; I wanted to get his fresh take on it first.

"Once upon a time, I was a rising young *Washington Postie,* a foreign correspondent with wine, women and song, all on the expense account. I was stationed in London, then Rome, but if there was anyplace in Europe I had a hankering to go, all I needed to do was come up with a story peg and the *Post* would pick up the tab. It was a nice life . . . until I blew it. I got wind of a story about some gold that disappeared at the end of the war — not just the Fleckensee gold, but other caches as well. I wrote the story, in two long articles, and sent it home."

"You wrote about the gold? For the *Post*? I didn't know that." I'd Googled "Fleckensee gold" and nothing had turned up in *Post* archives.

"Damned right you haven't seen it. It never made it into print, because those articles got spiked. Nobody ever said why, they just loaded me up with other assignments, told me not to invest any more time on it, told me that I'd done a good job reporting the basic story, but there were more important things I should be focusing my time on. Word, it seemed, had come down from on high."

"Why? Who would have reason to intervene?"

Naismith looked away, the pain evident in his eyes. "But I was full of fire in those days. I pushed on. That's when things started going sour. I was taken off the foreign beat, transferred back to the States. It seemed like a promotion at the time."

How much of this can I believe? I was asking myself. His face was worn — maybe he'd been drinking too much. Drinkers don't like to face the truth: maybe his boozing had gotten out of hand; maybe he'd become an embarrassment to the *Post*.

"But I wouldn't let it go, not even after I got back to the States. So the powers-that-be set out to crush me. I wrote a proposal for a book on the story of that gold. Would have been my third book, had a track record, should have sold without a problem. But no publisher wanted to touch it. One did hold out a carrot, an offer to do a different book altogether, something that had nothing to do with the gold, and for a very generous advance, too. But I turned it down — damned fool I was then. Could have taken the offer, played along with the game, had an easy life ever since."

He shook his head. "I turned down the carrot, so then came the stick. Charges were trumped up that I'd padded my expense accounts. I hadn't, not really, just shifted things around to fit categories, the way everybody did to satisfy the bean-counters. But it was enough to put me under the gun."

Naismith put both hands flat on the table, as if calming himself. "It was a warning to me. I could have said, Okay, I'll play your game. But I was too headstrong, kept pushing on the gold story. So they set me up and blew me away."

"Who set you up? Why?"

"It doesn't matter. It was a long time ago. We're getting off the point, and the point is Katz and what he turned up. What is it you want me to do?"

I showed him Cal's final note: *If anything happens to me, please see that the enclosed gets out to the public. If you give it to somebody in the media, MAKE SURE they're somebody you can trust.*

"In short, you want me to publish Katz' article in *The Naismith Letter* — is that it?"

"Or at least reference it in your *Letter*, with a link to the full content on your website. That would fulfill what Cal asked, to get it out to the public."

He drained the last of his coffee, then said. "No promises. I'll look these materials over more closely later. Then I'll do some checking. Don't take it personally, but people try to slip me forgeries, crap like that, sometimes to put the shiv into somebody else, sometimes just in the hope that I'll make a blunder. If things fit, then, yeah, I will put it in the *Letter*. This is a hell of a story, I think you know that. And I'll give Katz the by-line, of course, the least I can do for the poor bastard, not steal his last story."

"You did notice references to Hadley Barrington in what I showed you, didn't you?"

"Of course I did. That's what it's all about, isn't it?"

He shook his head. "No, I expect you don't know. I told you I got squashed when I tried to push the story of the Fleckensee gold? It was that bastard Barrington who was behind it. He was pulling the strings. There's nothing that would give me more satisfaction than to get him back. I hope Katz's stuff is all you claim it is."

❑

A heavy rain beat on the big plate-glass window and spattered in little explosions in the lakes that covered the sidewalks. I wondered why Dad's simple request — Go to La Rochelle and find what Willoughby has to say about Uncle Paul — had become so Byzantine.

"Katz' final note to you, what's this he said, look the stuff over, and you'll understand why I was asking about your uncle and the OSS. I see he copied in similar notes he was sending to Dan Mann and Shelly Sherman. I know who they are, and I know what happened to them. Don't you think it's time you told me the whole story?"

He was right. Maybe it would help put the whole thing in context.

I started with that first day: the Butterfly fax from Cal, then that strange letter offering Dad the truth about his brother, provided I went to La Rochelle.

I didn't get into what Paul may have found — "perhaps" the Grail, or "perhaps" something else. I bypassed that for the moment, and told how Paul had been used by a "certain German officer" to propose a trade in the spring of 1945.

"Hadley Barrington was my uncle's commanding officer within the OSS, and it was he who flew down to Austria in response to that message, eager to make a trade. My uncle was being held at a monastery on the Fleckensee, just down the shoreline from Castle Flecken."

I sensed slow excitement building despite Naismith's professional inscrutability. "Let's assume that Barrington and his buddies grabbed the gold. That was Katz' conclusion. Mine, too, back when I wrote that series. So where did your uncle fit in? Was he one of the gang?"

"That's what I've been trying to find out." I hesitated, reluctant to trust Naismith with too much information. But then I thought, At this stage of the game, what's there to lose? So I told him about being kidnaped yesterday by Twisted Messiah.

He shook his head and almost laughed, the first deviation from his characteristic grimness. "Damn! You've *got* to be telling the truth, because nobody could make this up! Okay, I'll look it over in more detail. I'll call you later on, let you know whether or not I want to get involved."

He stood to pull on his raincoat, then sat again and leaned forward. "One bit of advice. You've heard of the AIDS virus, but what about the TMK virus? Are you taking precautions?"

"What's the TMK virus?"

"TMK – Too Much Knowledge. It can be just as fatal as AIDS, but a hell of a lot faster-acting. It's going around ITB."

"You've lost me."

"John Baxter. Gary Whalen. Jack Garnett. Recognize the names?"

"Baxter was on TV, a reporter, I forgot which network. He got killed. Auto accident, I think it was."

"Auto crash, yes, but no accident. Not too far from here on the GW Parkway. He was driving home late one night, somebody cut him off just past Rosslyn. His car slid off the road, and he ended up a floater in the Potomac. Gary Whalen was FBI. Suicide, so they said. But the people who knew him said it was impossible, not Gary. Jack

Garnett was an investigative journalist, one of the best. He drowned in his hot tub one night, just slid under the water and that was it. But strange thing, nobody could ever find his laptop afterwards, nor any of his notes."

Naismith hammered the table with his index finger. "*That's* the TMK virus. They all knew too much. Cal Katz knew too much. I'm getting the sense that maybe you *already* know too much. It wouldn't surprise me if you've already got the TMK virus. For my sake, I just hope to hell you're not infectious."

90

I offered Naismith a lift, but he said he needed to make a stop at his office nearby. Kate and I jogged back to the car though the rain, getting only moderately soaked in the process.

I tried the hospital in Burlington and got cut off by a bad connection as I circled around the high-rises of Rosslyn to get onto the Parkway.

❑

The Parkway, lush and scenic in summer, was bleak now that the trees were bare and wet. The traffic was fast and crazy despite the dark and the rain-slicked roads. Washington drivers don't always know where they're going, but they're always in a hell of a hurry to get there.

I passed a gap in the shrubbery after Rosslyn, a gap wide enough to offer a glimpse down to the Potomac; the grass was still gashed with tire tracks that led to the water. Something Naismith had said about John Baxter, the television reporter: *Not far from here on the GW Parkway, somebody cut him off. His car slid off the road, and he ended up a floater in the Potomac.*

Was that the place it happened?

The TMK virus: Too Much Knowledge can be just as fatal as AIDS, but a hell of a lot faster-acting.

I am the butterfly who sets off the storm that starts Inside-the-Beltway.

But now the Butterfly was getting caught up in the storm.

Was the flapping of the Butterfly's wings spreading the TMK virus?

I was annoyed at myself that I hadn't kept a copy of Cal's materials before handing everything over to Naismith. What if he

backs out? What if he's just playing me along, and has no intention
of taking any action?
❏

Katje flicked on the radio and picked up the all-news station:
downtown Washington had been brought almost to a stand-still by
Flash Mobs — small groups of Twisted Messiah fans appearing at
random intersections to demonstrate and break windows, then
dissolving into the crowd before the police could arrive. A few
minutes later, another Flash Mob would form a block away, or
maybe across downtown, or inside a Metro station.

The message they were sending was clear: If you find this
disruptive, you ain't seen nothing yet.

It was making a mess out of downtown traffic and running
the police ragged.

Which, as things turned out, was calculated, part of the larger
plan, to distract the police before the real attack to come.
❏

The tie-ups were affecting traffic even out by my apartment, a couple
of miles from downtown.   The line to make the turn on
Massachusetts Avenue by American University was blocks long.

I used the time to try the hospital in Burlington again.
Something seemed very wrong. How many tests could they run?

I direct-dialed the number of his room, but an operator
picked up on the second ring. "Who were you calling?"

I told her, and waited while she checked. Probably they had
moved him to another room and hadn't connected the phone there
yet.

Then she came back on, and said, "Mr. Tapscott is no longer
a patient in the hospital."

It took a couple of seconds to process that. "No longer a
patient? He's *got* to be there."

"One moment, while I connect you with the floor."

"You haven't been told?," the floor nurse said when I
identified myself.

"Has something happened to him?" I could barely hear my
own voice.

"Your father is gone."

The word hung in the air. *Gone.*

"He's *gone*? Dead? When did it —"

"Not dead, I didn't say he was *dead*. I said he was *gone*."

"Gone where?"

"He did not confide that in me."

"When?"

"He checked himself out, AMA, at 6:17 this evening."

"AMA? What does that mean?"

"Against medical advice. He left with his son and his brother."

I heard my pulse thundering loud in my ear. "But I'm his son, his only son, and I didn't check him out. I'm in Washington. Besides, he doesn't *have* a brother, not a living brother. I talked to him just a couple of hours ago and he didn't say anything about checking out."

"I know nothing of that. He identified himself as your father's brother. That was satisfactory to your father, and he elected to check himself out of the hospital. Against medical advice, I remind you."

My hands were shaking. It was hard to hit the right button to hang up. What kind of people would kidnap a dying man from a hospital?

Yet *was* it kidnap? The nurse said he had gone willingly with whoever came for him.

But Dad's only brother was Paul, and he'd been dead since Roosevelt was still President.

Unless . . . unless Dad hadn't really been hallucinating the other night. Think outside the box.

What if that *wasn't* an hallucination the other night? What if there really *had* been a visitor? What if that had been Paul?

Suppose, just suppose, it *was* Paul: where could he have taken Dad? To another hospital? Not likely. The only logical place to take him was home, so he could die there in peace.

I tried Dad's home number. No answer, and no answering machine. I dialed his new cell-phone. No answer.

Looking back, Katje must have been mystified by my actions, but I was oblivious. The only thing in my mind was what to do now.

The traffic cleared and I made it around the traffic circle and raced back to the apartment, pulled the car into my space in the garage, and ran for the elevator. Katje kept up with me.

I ran down the hallway, still in panic, still with no idea what to do.

I fumbled with the keys, finally got the door open and hurried inside. The room was just as we'd left it: the lights on, the TV playing.

A form materialized out of the kitchen, and another from the hallway. "Don't move," a third said from behind the front door.

91

A very small woman emerged from the kitchen holding a large black automatic. Tiny and fragile-looking, barely five feet tall, with messy long black hair sticking out from under a baseball cap and pale skin that seemed prematurely fragile. She might be 25, but her skin was already beginning to sag. Too many late nights, too many cigarettes, too much everything bad.

She was messy, her clothes ill-fitting and grungy. The guy who'd been waiting in the hallway was equally a slob, but massive, around 6'4" and strangely top-heavy, like an inverted pyramid. His face seemed misshapen, with a heavy brow-line atop small, expressionless eyes. It was as if he was wearing a rubber Neanderthal mask.

Pierced ears on men were nothing new, but Neanderthal had carried it a step further: somehow he'd managed to expand the piercings in his ears so now each held a wine cork.

As if his size and face didn't get him enough attention.

He pulled a roll of duct tape out of a bag and taped my wrists in front, then shoved me hard, and I fell onto the living room floor. I shinnied myself over to sit up with my back braced against the wall.

"Who the hell are you?," I asked, even though I already knew. "What's this all about?" I wanted to get them talking.

"Tape his mouth," the woman said. "I don't want to hear him. Tape his ankles, too."

She was nervous. Her voice quavered and her hand shook as she set the gun down long enough to light a cigarette. Gaulois — a French brand. But her accent was not French.

She signaled to Katje to sit on the sofa. They didn't tape her up. Why not?

I still hadn't gotten a look at the one by the front door. He was out of my line of vision, still guarding the door.

I heard the man's heavy steps moving through the apartment, checking things out. She turned the TV louder and flicked channels, obviously looking for something.

CNN came on with breaking news. A videotape with the jerky, un-synched quality that said it had come in via the internet.

Jesse Cripes talked to the camera, looking more haggard than usual, eyes fiery inside deep gray circles, haranguing the world, and gloating that he was still alive.

The crawl at the bottom of the screen brought things up to date:

> *Jesse Cripes emerges alive, was not killed in copter crash. . . . Claims his "world-wide army will punish every nation" unless German police withdraw from his convent.*

After saying again that Twisted Messiah supporters were ready to strike out at "the illegal and oppressive governments in every nation," he went on to claim that,

> *. . . it has been obvious for some time that the entrenched system of interlocking governments has been plotting against Twisted Messiah and its followers. That is why our supporters have been donating weapons, both of conventional types and weapons of mass destruction. And I warn the world and every person in it that those weapons will be used unless the German police and military withdraw immediately from my home, and back off from any more investigations.*

She flicked to another cable news channel. It had a different segment of Jesse's tape. Maybe it was the poor quality, coming as it had via the internet, or maybe I saw what I was looking for, but Jesse seemed to crackle with anger and a chilling, crazed intensity. He came across the tube as someone who wouldn't hesitate in pushing the button to blow up the world.

But did he really have any force behind the threats?

Back to CNN and a post-mortem by some talking heads. For once, all agreed on something: Jesse's claim that Twisted Messiah fans had conventional weapons was plausible. Guns, explosives, and even WMD — Weapons of Mass Destruction — were easy enough to obtain for a group that possessed Twisted Messiah's money and connections.

As one of the panelists, a terrorism expert, pointed out, Soviet General Lebed had once told *60 Minutes* that Soviet special forces had hidden 100 atomic "suitcase bombs" around the United States, most of which could no longer be accounted for. Where were they now?

Another expert pointed out how relatively simple it was to construct a "dirty" bomb — wrap nuclear waste, even atomic-charged medical waste like the effluvia from X-ray machines, around a few sticks of explosives, and the fall-out from the explosion could render a city uninhabitable for decades to come.

A third talked about the varieties of biological weapons that could be made relatively easily, or bought from renegade scientists and even governments operating under their own agendas. Ricin was relatively simple: grind up some castor beans, do some other hocus-pocus, and *voila!* you have a strong poison.

Even the weather outside was grim: wind, and intermittent rain.

Let your imagination run wild — then realize they can do worse, much worse than that. Look at it, they've got an army of dead-end kids around the world, all willing to drink the Kool-Aid, and they've got tons of money and contacts to buy any kind of damned weapons, even WMD. Play with those possibilities when you wake up in the middle of some dark night.

❑

A light tap at the door. A short, wiry kid slipped in, maybe 20, with the head of snakes tattooed onto both hands, and two more on his neck, as if closing in on his jugular vein.

Two others came in with him, but they were out of my line of vision. Just as well: I wouldn't have to see what bizarre markings they were flaunting.

They stood in the front hallway, talking intently. They all chain-smoked, and the air quickly filled to a thick fog. The woman seemed to be in charge, and it seemed the big Neanderthal guy was not happy about that. She seemed intelligent, so what was she doing as a Twisted Messiah captain?

I picked up that her name was Elena, and the Neanderthal guy was Horst.

A phone rang; it took a second ring before I realized it was my own cell-phone. Elena came in to see what it was, ripping the tape off my mouth. "My father is in the hospital, near death," I said. "I'd like to take the call."

That sounded more believable than saying my father had been kidnaped from a hospital.

But maybe it was another branch of Twisted Messiah's gang that had grabbed him.

She unclipped the phone from my belt and warned me to "be very, very careful," then flicked it on and held it to my ear. She bent over to eavesdrop. Her breath exuded the aroma of a tar pit.

It was Dan Naismith. "This stuff you passed me — are you out of your mind? Or are you just plain damned dense?"

His words were slurred, and I figured he'd been drinking. Not a promising sign if he was going to pass the word on to the world.

"I thought you'd see it as an opportunity to — "

"What the hell *is* this stuff? Goddam, can't you see how sensitive it is? How damned *dangerous* it is?"

"I'm hoping you can help me — "

"*Help* you? Hell, I'm going to forget I ever *saw* this stuff. You'd be smart to do the same. Provided it's not already too late."

"Those memos are the real thing. Cal Katz sent them to me, the morning he was killed. He said if anything happened to him he wanted me to pass it on. I can't think of a better way of doing that than via your newsletter. I'm hoping you'll take them and run — "

"So you weren't lying? Katz really sent this stuff to you?"

I felt a surge of hope. "He dropped it in the mail to me the morning he died. I just got it because I was out of the country until today. There was postage due."

"The morning he was killed? Doesn't that tell you something? You still don't *get* it, do you? This isn't stuff to play around with. This isn't a computer game, you don't just hit Restart and come back to life. Don't tell me you've forgotten what I said about the TMK virus that's going around? Look what happened to Katz himself."

"We need to get those papers out into the world — that's what Cal asked me to do."

"We? *We?* Remember what Tonto said to the Lone Ranger when they were surrounded by that Indian tribe?, 'What you mean *we*, Kemosabe?' Maybe that show was before your time. No matter. This stuff got Katz killed. My life may not be the greatest at the moment, but it happens to be the only one I have, and I'm not about to sacrifice it on a lost cause."

"It's *not* a lost cause," I tried, wishing it were true. "There's still time to — "

"Billions of dollars ride on elections these days, and you better believe they play hardball with that kind of money at stake. Katz was a pesky little bug, and they swatted him. You're next, if you don't watch out."

I didn't see how I could get into much more trouble than I already was, surrounded by five of Twisted Messiah's foot-soldiers. "Look, something else has turned up since we — "

Naismith sighed into the phone. "You don't know when to quit, do you? Well, you do what you want, but count me out. Period."

"You want a story to bring your career back to life. This is it. This would really put you back on the map."

"Maybe so, but it would put me into the grave a long time before I made it onto any map. Martyrdom was never one of my career objectives."

"Why? What's changed your — "

"A couple of guys were waiting for me when I got home after

seeing you today. They beat the shit out of me, feels like they cracked a rib or two, broke my nose, gave me a pair of fat lips. It all hurts like hell, but I'm grateful. It could have been worse, could have been fatal. You might think about that yourself, especially before getting anybody else involved. They took Katz' papers, of course, so there's nothing I could do, even if I wanted to become a martyr to his cause."

92

"What was that about?," Elena asked when she clicked my phone off.

I told her everything, starting with Cal's fax that first day, and the packet of materials on Barrington and sons. If Naismith wouldn't run with that ball, maybe they would. They already had the attention of the world media. It might work out even better than Cal could have imagined.

She didn't seem interested until I explained that Barrington had been my uncle's OSS commander. Then she got very interested.

"This Barrington — he worked with your uncle? Did he know what it was your uncle found? Does he know where it is now?"

"Is that what you people want? What my uncle found?" That was no revelation to me, but I wanted to get her talking.

"Of course. You know that already. But it is I who will ask the questions. Does Barrington — "

"I don't know what Barrington knows about my uncle and what he found. I do know that he has two sons running for office."

She shook her head. "Elections? Who cares? After today there will be no elections."

Neanderthal ran into the room, his heavy footsteps shaking the floor. "Elena! Elena! Something new!" He flicked on the TV, and the others gathered to watch.

The tube came to life showing another live stand-up from Jesse's Convent of the Sensuous Virgins. Germany was six hours ahead, so it was already dark there. It was the same reporter as earlier, now looking even more troubled:

> *To recap, the German authorities have just concluded a press conference here at which they revealed that home-made videos, so-called "snuff films," have been found in this former convent, clearly showing Jesse Cripes and other members of the Twisted Messiah group performing sexual acts with what appear to be under-age fans, some evidently barely more than children. The videos also appear to show these young people being killed, or 'snuffed,' as it is termed, in most cases by strangling. Stills from those films were shown to media representatives here, and I can say —*

The reporter's voice broke, and he turned away from the camera. His body heaved. Finally he managed to add:

> *Given the graphic, extremely disturbing nature of these videos, it seems unlikely that they will be released to the media soon, if ever. In the press conference, we were told that it is believed that at least 50 victims have been counted on the videos. Meanwhile, we are told, German police are rushing specially-trained dogs here to determine whether any of these alleged victims are buried on the convent grounds. Infra-red aerial photographs, taken earlier today, indicate the presence of a large area of disturbed ground that may — repeat, may contain decaying organic materials.*

The CNN anchor in Atlanta could only shake her head. The camera cut away to a public-service announcement for seat-belt usage.

Now I understood those blood-chilling screams in the night.

The others were silent, staring at the screen. Their faces told me that Elena and Neanderthal and a couple of the others knew what had been going on there. Maybe they were even in the tapes. The others seemed stunned.

"It was good while it lasted, yes?," Neanderthal finally said, his face expressionless. I wondered if he was capable of feeling anything.

Elena snatched her cell-phone out of her pocket and stomped out of the room. "Yes, Horst, perhaps it is finished for us. But we will make them pay! Oh yes! If we go, then everything goes!"
❏

"Christ! Now it's really going to hit the fan!," Barrington grunted. "These Twisted Messiah shit-heads, what do we know about them? Do they really have WMD?"

"Conventional weapons, of course, would be easy enough for them to obtain," Fackson said. "As for WMD? Possible, though not likely. Certainly they have the financial resources, and the weapons are available on the black market, but I question whether they'd have been smart enough to plan something like this in advance. Query as well Jesse's claim to have an 'army' ready to act. That army is really nothing more than a hardened inner cadre, scummy kids who have nothing to lose, people who are complicit in the killings shown on these tapes. I expect there are videos of members of this inner cadre shown on the tapes, doing the killings. That would be a way of ensuring their loyalty."

"Maybe Jesse and his gang have more brains than we've credited them with."

"It seems the whole world has been failing to take them seriously enough. It's another instance of the generals preparing to fight the last war. In this case, eyes were too focused on the last enemy and we missed what's been right in front of us."

"Christ! I've got a son who'll be President in two years' time. Provided this election doesn't get messed up by this bunch of trash. We can't let that happen."

93

Horst motioned Katje to come with him and two of the others.

Katje's eyes met mine, and she managed a smile. "I'm sorry I got you into this," I tried to say, but Neanderthal had slapped tape back across my mouth, and it came out as grunts. She nodded, as if she understood.

It was deathly quiet after they left. From time to time I heard Elena on the phone in my bedroom. I could hear only enough to know that she wasn't speaking in English.

She came out after a few minutes and nodded, and Snake-man cut the tapes binding my ankles and then my wrists. He left the tape across my mouth.

"We are going to free you soon," she said, "but first you must drive us in your car." Her eyes told me that was a lie. "Will you cooperate? Will you be silent if we take the tape off your mouth?"

I nodded. The alternative was to stay here, silent and dead.

We went down to the garage level, meeting no other tenants.

Elena handed over my car key and told me to drive. Snake-man climbed into the back seat. She sat beside me, holding one of the Uzis under a towel she'd taken from the apartment.

"Drive. You will see a blue van. Follow it," she said.

I pulled out of the garage. Katje's white car was gone from the visitor lot.

We picked up the blue van where it was parked just off MacArthur Boulevard. It was an ordinary, blue Mommy-van, the ubiquitous vehicle for the school-to-soccer-to-skating shuttle.

"Is Katje in the van?," I asked, hoping the answer would be no.

"You don't need to know that," Elena said, lighting another cigarette. I guessed she was maybe 25, yet her lungs already were probably as black as her leather jacket. If what I'd picked up earlier was true, it didn't matter much. Cancer wasn't a concern since she wasn't planning to live longer than another hour or two. But what about Katje and I and the rest of us?

She punched a speed-dial number on her cell-phone and spoke rapid German, too fast for me to pick up any of it. I followed the van as it led the way back across Chain Bridge and onto the George Washington Parkway headed toward downtown Washington. I was retracing my journey of an hour ago when we went to meet Naismith in Rosslyn.

She clicked off her phone and I said, "Where is it you want to go? I know Washington, maybe I can help you find better routes."

"You just follow the van, that's all you think about. Move up closer to it."

The CIA guy back in Munich. *Let your imagination run wild — then realize they can do far, far worse than that. They've got an army of dead-end kids around the world, all willing to drink the Kool-Aid, and they've got money and contacts to buy any kind of damned weapons, even WMD.*

They weren't headed into the District for sight-seeing, not this crowd, not with Uzis.

"Drive faster, get closer, don't let any cars come between us and the van."

If the van held explosives, closer was not where I wanted to be. "There are laws against tail-gating, driving too closely. Do that, and we're at risk of the police pulling us over."

"Good. Then I kill one of the pigs sooner. The first of many."

"What are you going to do?"

"Be quiet!"

"You strike me as too intelligent to be a suicide bomber."

Silence.

"You could still get away. Break off now, before anything happens. I could drop you at the train station, you could get away and live a normal life."

Silence.

"At least tell me where Katje is."

Snake-man giggled from the back seat. "Horst killed her. She is dead already."

"Then I have nothing to live for," I bluffed, hitting the gas and coming up fast onto the van.

"Stop! Slow down! It's a bomb on wheels. You hit it and we all die."

"You killed Katje, so —"

"No! He lied, he did not kill her!," Elena screamed. "She is in another car! You will be with her soon!"

I pulled back. I didn't believe her, but there was nothing to be gained by going out with a bang.

"So the plan is to blow up something?"

"I have no desire to live out my life locked in a cell. Nor do the others. We will die, yes, but we will take as many with us as possible. Why not?"

I had no idea how to respond. The 9-11 killers were willing to die because they were hoping to get to paradise, however they saw it. These people seemed just as willing to die, but what could they be hoping for in another world?

"Why? Why choose to kill?"

She turned to look at me. Our eyes met. I saw fear and hopelessness. But even more I saw anger, not just a sudden flare-up, but the kind that had been simmering for most of a lifetime, a malevolence seeking satiation.

"Why? Because the world is shit, and Twisted Messiah was our chance to rub the world's face in its own shit. Now stop talking and drive. I need to think."

"I'll stop asking questions when you tell me where Katje is."

"I told you, she's ahead of us. You'll see her. Now be quiet."

"Ahead of us in the van?"

"Shut up." We were still close behind the van, in that stretch of the parkway along the side of the Potomac palisades where the road rounds a bend and the incoming lane is on a grassy hillside above the oncoming traffic. The road here is high, and the view opens up of the river and the lights of Georgetown and the gleaming marble monuments across the city.

It had always been one of my favorite views, and I wondered if I was seeing it for the last time. Then Elena hit speed dial on her cell-phone and in a flash everything changed.

What is luck?

What is random chance?

What is coincidence?

What is synchronicity?

What is the way things work out when you have side-stepped into an alternate version of the universe?

The van exploded into a roiling ball of orange and red flame. I swerved to avoid it, but the flaming van, still speeding, rocked from lane to lane, forcing me off the pavement onto the slippery, grassy edge. The wet grass was slippery, the bank as steep as a ski-slope. I pulled the wheel back, it was like driving on glare ice, and momentum carried us back up the slope.

The van's tire blew, and the front-end dropped to the pavement. The van tipped, rotated, and bounced along the pavement. I swerved again and missed it by inches, and we were past. The tail broke loose and we spun 180 degrees to a stop, looking backwards, in time to watch the ball of flame bounce down the slope, explode on the lane below, and disintegrate along the riverbank.

Flaming debris blocked the traffic in both directions, and we sat there, stunned.

Had Elena's phone call short-circuited some kind of timer in the van? Or had one of the passenger been stupid enough to flick a lighter?

Then I managed, "At least tell me . . . was Katje in . . . in the van?"

Elena's voice was barely more than a whisper. "I do not know, I honestly do not know. That was up to Horst, he arranged that part of it." Her voice was shaky, she seemed hardly able to breathe, yet she lit another cigarette. "Now go. Turn around and continue toward the center of the city."

"It's time to give it up," I said. My voice sounded strange, as if it were echoing down a concrete tube.

"No! Never! We continue!" She uncovered the Uzi, the barrel pointed toward me. "Now drive, or I shoot you and we drive ourselves. Do it fast, before the police arrive!"

The car had stalled in the spin-out, and it took a couple of tries to get it going. If I went along, there might be a chance to stop them before it was too late.

94

Most of the rush-hour traffic flow was outbound from the District. Police cars, fire-trucks and a couple of ambulances tore past in the outgoing lane, headed for the explosion.

We crossed the 16th Street Bridge, then passed the Mall, toward the marble dome of the Capitol gleaming in the spotlights.

The Capitol would be the target, I figured. Then Elena surprised me. "Turn here, go to Union Station."

The traffic slowed as we encountered the usual contingent of tour-busses and taxis and travelers towing suitcases. A police helicopter whirred overhead, but in DC that was normal.

Union Station, built in the glory days of the railroads, had been modeled on the great rail terminals of Europe, which, in turn, had been modeled on the massive public baths of the Roman Empire.

Like the railroads, Union Station had fallen on hard times after World War II. Now, thanks to the generosity of Congress and its infusion of a few hundred million federal dollars, the station had evolved from a shabby transportation hub into an upscale shopping mall of boutiques and eateries that also happened to be one of the major crossroads of East Coast transportation. The interior, once spacious, even grandiose, had been chopped into galleries and mezzanines that created new rental possibilities.

"Drive around the corner, then pull over," Elena said. I did, and nosed into a loading zone. She jumped out, still holding the Uzi under the cover of a folded jacket. Snake-man scrambled out, pulling with him a heavy canvas bag, the twin of the one Horst had carried.

She held the door open and leaned back inside. I flinched, expecting the rattle of the Uzi. "Go! I told you I'd let you go, now go. Get out of here!"

"Where's Katje? You said —"

She slammed the door and I drove away, my hands shaking, my legs wobbly on the gas. *I'd survived! I was going to live!*

But I couldn't just drive away and let things happen.

I did a double U-turn and pulled back into that loading zone and jumped out.

A policeman appeared and told me I couldn't leave the car unattended.

"Have you got a radio?," I asked. "Get on it, spread the word, there's about to be a terrorist attack here."

"Mister, I'm telling you, you got to move that car, this here's a loading zone, no unattended vehicles."

I took a second look at him. He wasn't police, he was a security guard. With a securely closed mind.

I grabbed the tire-iron from the trunk, slid it up the sleeve of my jacket, and ran around toward the front of the station, leaving the guard screaming that he was going to have the car towed.

It wouldn't be the first time I'd been towed here. Towing was a major profit-center both for the DC government and for the towing companies that had the contracts.

Union Station was the hub for the trains that snaked up and down the eastern seaboard, as well as commuter lines to the far suburbs of Maryland and Virginia. It was also a key link for part of the District's Metro system.

On a normal Friday at this time, the commuter crush would have eased off, but this wasn't normal: the Twisted Messiah Flash Mobs forming and dissolving downtown and within some Metro stations upset the schedules, and the station was crammed with weary, frustrated folks in business suits, tourists, and bunches of high-school kids coming back from, or maybe headed out to, football games.

I fought my way through the crush, for once looking at the faces, realizing this wasn't just a moving barrier mindlessly blocking my way; this was a collection of humans with homes and families and jobs and memories, a cross-section of America — all in Elena's cross-hairs.

Unless I found a way to stop her and her team.

I looked for a policeman, a real cop, not just another narrow-focus rent-a-guard. But there were none in sight. Maybe they were all up-town shepherding the marchers. Bad planning.

I pushed my way through the masses, irritating some, but too bad. Somewhere in this place there had to be a real policeman, somebody who could make things happen.

And if I found a cop, then what? Would he listen to me? Would he believe me? Would he act?

My eye was caught by a head sticking out from the crowd. Horst the Neanderthal, moving with a strange, loping stride, his head bobbing up and down as he moved. He was surrounded by a phalanx of high-schoolers coming back from a football game, big rowdy kids blustering a path through the crowd, hanging with them, using them as cover, using them to open the pathway.

I broke out of the knot of commuters and reached for my cell-phone. The belt holder was there, as usual, but the phone was gone. Elena had kept it after Naismith's call. I was on my own.

Neanderthal, now half-way up an escalator to the mezzanine level, turned to look behind. I lowered my head — an instant too late. His eyes locked on me, and I saw the shock on his face.

He spun and pushed his way up, two steps at a time, knocking people aside. As he moved, he unslung a heavy back-pack and reached inside.

I ran after him, trying to thread though the lethargic crowd.

Somebody grabbed my arm, and the tire iron slid of out my sleeve and clattered on the floor. A woman, nearly as tall as I and twice as wide, locked me in a beefy hand. One of the station's security force, a rent-a-cop in a gray straw cowboy hat.

"No running here, mister."

"That tall guy in black, going up the escalator — he's carrying a bomb." Bomb was an easy four-letter word, something that would register fast.

It didn't register. "Make no difference, no running in the station. Lot of old folks —"

"Are you hearing me? He's got a *bomb*! Stop *him*, he's running."

"It's you I got, so settle down or — "

She turned when a small girl tugged her arm. I twisted out of her grasp; she lost her balance and stumbled backward, then thumped on her rear as she hit the ground. I couldn't find the tire iron.

I pushed through a scrum of nuns to get to the escalator.

Neanderthal, now at the top, glanced back over his shoulder, then suddenly disappeared.

I raced up, pushing past angry people. Neanderthal lay face-down on the floor, held down by a lean older man in a burgundy Redskins cap, holding on like a rider on a bucking bronco.

I froze for an instant. It couldn't be! The man holding Neanderthal down was my father!

Neanderthal heaved, rolling sideways and Dad tumbled off. I dove to help, but another terminal cop grabbed me. "Stay out of it."

"It's my father, dammit. The other guy's a terrorist."

"He's a terrorist, and I'm the President." With one quick motion he snapped a handcuff onto my wrist. I slammed him with an elbow in the fat belly and he doubled over and went down.

Neanderthal was on his feet now. In one hand he held an Uzi, the little grease-gun that can spray slugs faster than an auctioneer can talk; in the other what looked like a bottle of wine. It struck me: You don't carry bombs in glass bottles; in bottles you carry poisons and biological weapons.

The crowd backed away, giving him space and a clear shot at me. Time stopped.

I glanced at Dad and knew that it wasn't really my father, only a replica. He managed a wink, and unspoken words passed between us: *Are you who I think you are?*, and the response, *Hello, nephew, good to meet you at last.*

I looked back at Neanderthal. He seemed frozen in place, his stubby gun pointed directly at me. Where were the police? Where were the fire sirens? Didn't anybody understand what was happening here?

I sprang at him, the handcuff still dangling from my wrist.

Maybe I could use it as a weapon. Better than waiting to be shot.

Was it random chance that saved me, sheer luck that a bunch of guys from Quantico were in transit?

Or was it something more?

Neanderthal jolted forward and hit the floor, propelled by the full force of a Marine in dress blues tackling him from behind. One of the wine corks popped out of his ear, and the Uzi clattered away across the tile floor.

Uncle Paul and I moved together. He fired a blast of pepper spray into Neanderthal's face, and I grabbed the bottle, catching it an instant before it hit the ground. The Marine — with a bunch of gold sergeant's stripes down his arm — grabbed him in a hammerlock.

I rolled away, cradling the bottle with my body. My ribs exploded with pain, the wind knocked out of me. The fat station rent-a-cop stood over me, ready to hit again with his night-stick. His eyes said he hoped I'd give him the excuse.

Another cop materialized and grabbed my arm, and I lost hold of the bottle and it rolled away, headed toward the edge of the balcony. The cop ignored it, determined to force me into the other handcuff.

I kicked his leg and he fell backward, pulling me down on top of him. A blast of stale onions, french-fries and coffee told the story of his day.

Paul hit him with a jolt of pepper- spray, and he rolled away from me, clutching at his eyes. I grabbed the nightstick from his belt and started to roll to my feet.

No time: Neanderthal had slipped away from the Marine and loomed over me, moving fast to grab the bottle rolling across the floor. I lashed out with the nightstick, whacking his shin with a satisfying crack.

He bellowed, tottered an instant, then pitched forward, slamming into the metal guard-rail. But the railing had been designed to protect normal people, not top-heavy giants. The railing came only to his groin, not his waist, and he pitched forward, momentum pushing him out into space. His big hands reached out, desperately flailing for a grip, but the rail eluded him, and he disappeared over the edge of the mezzanine.

The screams began an instant later. I scrambled to the edge and looked down. Neanderthal lay on the marble floor, his head twisted out of sight beneath his body.

He was dead. I'd killed him. But that didn't register then. The glass bottle was all that mattered, and now it was gone.

"That bottle — what happened to the glass bottle?," Paul shouted. No one answered, no one wanted to get involved.

At last a small girl spoke up. "Those boys, they grabbed it." She pointed to a pair of kids, maybe 17.

"What's it worth to you?," one taunted, holding it by the neck. "It got any —"

The kid winced, his knees buckled, and he dropped to the ground, a knife sticking out of his back. Tiny Elena appeared from behind him as he fell, Uzi in her hand. She grabbed the bottle from him.

A flash of red emerged from the crowd, a bright candy-apple red rain jacket that I recognized. Katje! She was alive! Elena spun and fired a rattle of bullets, and Katje hit the floor hard and slid across the tile.

Elena stumbled, blown backward by the Uzi's recoil. The gunshots echoed off the hard stone walls, drowning out the screams for a moment. Bullet fragments, dust and plaster showered down.

Panic exploded through the crowd, and the moving wall of bodies blocked me from getting to Elena and the bottle.

Elena had caught her balance now. She pivoted to throw the bottle over the railing. It would shatter on the hard marble floor of the lower level, and —

Two more Marines in dress blues burst out of the crowd, grabbed her, and pulled the gun out of her hand. The bottle hit the floor without shattering, and rolled toward the open spokes beneath the guard-rail.

A hole opened in the crowd. I dove through, scooped up the bottle and rolled, cradling it with my body. I felt the guard-rail behind and braced my back against it.

Now police swarmed the area, led by the wide-bodied lady-cop I'd tangled with downstairs. Before I could pull away she grabbed the open handcuff and snapped it to the metal guard-rail.

She tried to pull the bottle out of my other hand. Paul hit her with a blast of pepper-spray and she turned away.

"Stay back, stay back!, he shouted. "Somebody call the FBI, call a CBW Response Unit. There may be more of these people — they're Twisted Messiah!"

I looked through the forest of legs and got a glimpse of Katje de Vriess, in her candy-apple red rain-jacket, on the station floor.

A blast erupted somewhere on the lower level, a clap that echoed and magnified off the stone walls of the terminal, and masses of people were screaming and running wildly in all directions.

95

Paul turned to me and said, "I expect this handcuff will pull right off you."

Expect — I'd learn later that in usage that was a word of art.

He tugged at it and the lock slipped, and my hand was free.

The two marines carried Elena, kicking and screaming, to this railing and snapped the loose cuff around her thin wrist.

"Dumb-ass security guard," one of them said. "You're the damned hero in this, and she's trying to lock you up."

"What's in that bottle?," the other one asked. He was the sergeant who had saved me by tackling Neanderthal before he could shoot.

"We don't know for certain," Paul said. "It could be WMD, or it could be a bluff."

"We'll take care of things, sir," the marine sergeant said. "My advice, you better get the hell out of here before that guard comes back with reinforcements."

This upper level had emptied. I didn't see Katje now. She wasn't on the floor where she'd fallen. That was a good sign, maybe. Then she waved from behind a pillar where she had sheltered against the panicked crowd racing for the stairs.

"I'm fine," she said when we got to her. "Synchronicity: I tripped just as she shot at me. It's not very dignified to fall flat on your face, but it saved my life."

Paul led us down a back stairway. He told us to take off our jackets, so it would be harder to link us to what had happened upstairs. We had, after all, assaulted a couple of rent-a-cops.

Now sirens were converging from all directions, fire, police, ambulances. We merged with the crowd pushing to get away from the station, then headed to the loading zone where I'd left the car. Paul was pushing 85, and moved as easily as Katje and I. Good genes, or good living?

"Tennis," he said. "You're wondering how I keep in shape — I try to play tennis three or four days every week. Things kept me too busy this week, though."

Good news: my car was where I'd left it, not towed, not even ticketed. That *was* synchronicity.

❑

"He is the luckiest damned guy alive," Fackson said when he got the report of what had happened at Union Station. Someday he'd explore this some more, how many times young Tapscott had slipped through the cracks through sheer dumb luck.

But right now there was a job to finish. "What I want is for the two of you to hustle ass and get back to his place before he does. You've got the beeper that lets you in the garage. Be there, waiting for him, and bring him and the old man to — "

He cut himself off before saying the name. It was just possible somebody might be tapping in. "Bring him to the client's residence. I'll be waiting there."

He clicked off, poured himself another in an endless series of black coffees. And then he thought: Nobody can be that lucky. It wasn't just luck, young Tapscott really *did* have something special going for him.

What if there really *was* something to all that?

If that was a real power, then no damned wonder the Nazis had been after it. No wonder Twisted Messiah, too.

No question about it, that really would be the most powerful force, ever.

He gulped the coffee, excitement building.

This was just the kind of off-the-wall thing that the out-of-the-box thinkers at DARPA were on the look-out for.

Now the pieces were making sense. The old man at the railway station wasn't Greg's father, it *had* to be his uncle.

He was Perceval.

Who had found the knowledge — whatever the hell it was.

Worth exploring.

96

The after-shock hit me as I climbed behind the wheel, and my hands were so wobbly I couldn't fit the key into the ignition.   We'd survived, we'd pulled it off, Katje was alive and so was I — and so was Uncle Paul. And Elena and her team had been stopped.

We could all have been dead — we and thousands of others — if things hadn't fallen the right way.

Paul, in the passenger seat, took the key and fitted it in for me. "That's normal, a reaction to stress. Just take some deep breaths and you'll be fine in a moment. I'd offer to drive, but I don't have an American driver's license. I don't exist, officially."

"I'd offer to drive," Katje said, her voice quavering, "but I'm in worse shape than you. I wonder how that boy is, the one she stabbed."

Paul was right: in a minute I had it under control, and was okay driving.

Sirens were still converging from all directions. The last thing we wanted was to get caught in a check-point, so I navigated a labyrinth of back streets and picked up Massachusetts Avenue at Du Pont Circle. From there, it would be a straight run to my apartment.
❏
As if reading my mind, Paul said, "There's no need to be concerned about your father. He's safe and in good hands."

"He's with your people?"

"He was not hallucinating. You probably understand that by now. I did visit him in the hospital that night."

"He claims you healed him."

"I *helped* him. I helped him understand how he had chosen the track he was in, and I helped him join a track that was better for him."

As he talked I picked up an undercurrent of an accent. His English was still American, but slightly mixed with something else. Probably from living overseas for all these years.

"There's a book Dad keeps mentioning, *Joining Miracles* — did you write it?"

"Let's just say I translated the Knowledge into a form that was more accessible to today's readers."

❏

I hit the remote, and the garage door opened onto the familiar subterranean gloom beneath my building. I pulled into my assigned space, and led the way to the elevator, wondering whether I had enough in the refrigerator to —

A man stepped out from behind a pillar. He wore sunglasses in the dark garage. A baseball cap was pulled low over his face. Most noticeable was the large black automatic in his hand.

Something about him, about the way he stood, seemed familiar.

From behind I heard another voice: "You're covered from back here, too, so don't try anything dumb. We're not going to hurt you, we just want to go for a drive, there's somebody that wants to meet you."

"Tell Barrington to go to hell," Paul said, his voice as calm as if he were buying a newspaper.

"You can tell him that yourself," the voice behind said. "Hands over your head, then step apart so I can come in and frisk you. But I warn you, don't try anything."

I wondered how long before someone would come down from the apartments above, and what would happen then.

He frisked me, then moved to Paul. I heard a grunt and a thud. I turned. A rangy black guy lay on the ground, face down. Paul held the gun in one hand, and his Redskin cap in the other.

He tossed the cap, frisbee-style, at the man by the pillar, and it was as if it floated slow-motion across the space, shape-shifting from hat to a discus. It hit the man in the face. Whether the force of the hat knocked him back, or he tripped on the concrete, there was no telling. It didn't matter: he went down, hard, his feet flying upwards with the force.

"It's him!," Katje said as I recognized those giant feet, the feet that had followed me to the bookstore in La Rochelle, to the pub in London, to the Alps.

Paul moved fast and grabbed his weapon, then turned as the first one rolled to his feet. Something crackled, and the black guy hit the concrete floor and lay twitching. A Taser.

Their car, a big gray Crown Victoria, was easy to spot, as drab as an unmarked police car. The trunk was ajar. To hold us, I suppose. A friend of mine in New Jersey says up there the local name for Crown Vics is Mafiamobile — they've got a four-body trunk. The two big guys fitted with room to spare.

"You drive," Paul said, and recited an address in Georgetown.

97

Georgetown was only a few blocks away: down Massachusetts, down Wisconsin, then into some side streets, and we were there before I could begin asking Paul the questions I'd been saving up, not just this past week, but for most of my life.

It didn't matter: he spent the drive speaking rapid French on his cell-phone. I wondered who was on the other end, but he didn't say.

He pointed the way by hand-signals as he talked. Here left, then straight, now right. This was a route he had scouted out before.

Finally, he signaled to stop, and clicked off the call.

"This is the Washington residence of Barrington's son, Harmon. He's the senator, up for a second term this election, and looking like a very serious contender in a presidential run next time around."

The gate swung open and I drove through. This wasn't just one of the run-of-the-mill $6 or 7 million Federalist townhouses that the ordinary senators and millionaire lobbyists lived in. This was one of the grand old estates that went back to the era when Georgetown was an independent village, a port along the river, not just an upscale semi-burb of Washington. There was probably an acre inside the fence, maybe more, and well-manicured.

I didn't have a good feeling about this, not at all, and I was reminded of one of Aunt Ursula's sayings, back when I was a kid visiting her in the house in Burlington: "'Come into my parlor,' said the spider to the fly."

Why are we doing this?, I wanted to ask. *Why are we looking for trouble?* But I kept quiet. It was Paul's show. I just hoped he had — literally — an exit strategy in mind.

I parked in the circle in front of the house, and the front door opened. A man emerged, dressed in blue blazer and tie — Sunday evening attire in Georgetown mansions, apparently. Or was he the butler?

He froze in place when he saw Paul and I in the front seat.

"You look surprised," Paul said amiably. "Were you expecting someone else?"

"I — "

"If you're shocked, imagine how shocked your men were when we turned their Tasers around on them. They're in the trunk, resting up. You are Mr. Fackson, I believe?" He handed Fackson the keys and started to walk past him into the house.

Fackson backed up quickly and closed the door. "Wait! You can't go in yet. We need to check for weapons."

"You should have checked your boys for weapons before you sent them to pick us up. Barrington is waiting. Let's go."

"Give me the guns — the Tasers."

Don't give up the guns, Uncle Paul. Don't trust him

"How do we know you don't have a gun?," Paul asked.

"I don't. Greg can frisk me."

"I'll take your word," Paul said. He spun one of Tasers into the shrubbery; when Fackson looked that way, he tossed the second one into the shrubs on the other side.

98

A woman met us as we stepped through the front door. She wore tailored slacks and a feminine-cut blue blazer with a rainbow scarf around the neck — a trick, I'm told, for hiding the ravages of age and turkey-wattle. "My name is Sharon, Mr. Hadley Barrington's personal assistant."

I guessed she was maybe 50, with attractive features that had hardened into a tightness that make-up couldn't soften. Maybe that was the price paid for working for Barrington.

Still, her look softened for an instant as her eyes made contact with Paul's. Did I detect a trace of a wink?

"Will Katje be going up with you, or would she prefer refreshments in the conservatory?"

"With us," Paul said.

My eyes met Katje's. If they knew her name, what did they *not* know?

Sharon led us up the central staircase to the second floor, into a large room overlooking the front of the house. Maybe it had been a ballroom in the old days. Now it was set up as an office, and an old man was hunched at a desk in the corner, speaking softly into a phone.

The blinds were drawn; despite the size of the room it seemed claustrophobic. I wished Paul hadn't given up the Tasers.

Barrington continued talking on the phone. He gave no indication that he had heard us enter, and Sharon made no move to alert him.

The one interior wall was lined floor-to-ceiling with framed photos: the Barrington dynasty Ego Wall. It was impressive, because it was designed to impress: Barrington with everyone who ever *was* anybody in Washington from the Truman Administration onward, along with his sons and their photo conquests.

In the pictures, Harmon, the older son, a Senator now up for re-election after his first term, had the full head of well-coiffed hair that looks good in photo ops.

Henley, the junior son now hoping to become governor of Louisiana, was a decade younger, with an even more luxuriant growth of hair.

Barrington senior finished the call, pulled himself out of the chair, and scrutinized the three of us, though most of his attention went to Paul.

His eyes, dark and penetrating, were hooded like the eyes of a lizard, and dominated the face. His body was stooped, and his skin had shriveled into sallow, wrinkled parchment.

"It's been a lot of years," Barrington said. His voice, still mellow and deeply resonant, hadn't changed from the times I'd seen him on the evening news and Sunday morning talk shows. Paul stared back, saying nothing.

Barrington was only a few years older than Paul, but looked a couple of decades more aged. Or maybe it was that Paul looked and moved 15 years younger than his actual age.

Barrington nodded, leading the way to the arrangement of sofas and chairs at the far end of the office. "You're Greg, I've heard a lot about you, a very resourceful young man, they say. It's true what they've been telling me, you look so goddam much like your uncle did in those days that it's like seeing a ghost."

He made no offer to shake hands, just pointed to seats opposite his own, then turned again to me, "Your uncle was a hero. You should have left well enough alone."

Then he turned to Paul. "You wasted your whole damned life chasing a fairy-tale — do you understand that yet? You didn't have to run away with that damned chest. We didn't give a shit about that, we'd have let you keep it."

"Untrue, and you know it," Paul said. "The truth is, you wanted me on the run to cover up your theft of the gold. You'd have killed me if you caught me. Even better than a missing scapegoat is one who can't talk. But I have no regrets. You got the gold, but I ended up with something infinitely more valuable."

"Valuable only to you. We never gave a damn about it, and that's the truth."

"But now times have changed. What you missed then is coming back to destroy you."

"Destroy me, hell! Looks to me like I've won the game."

It was like watching two Japanese Sumo wrestlers at the start of a match — circling, feinting, testing, looking for weaknesses, trying to psych and intimidate the other. Would one of these Sumos back away, conceding defeat?

Barrington shook his head. "You're still a dreamer, Paul, still naive. It's over, the election is almost here, and my boys are way out front. I'm going to have a governor and a senator, and in two years time, a president."

"You're wrong. It's not over yet."

"It's all over as far as you three are concerned. You don't think I'm going to let you walk out of here, do you?"

You shouldn't have given up the guns, Paul.

Paul was silent. After 60 years waiting for this confrontation, after investing most of his life in a cause, after coming so close, it seemed that Paul was the Sumo coming to realize he was outmatched. And Katje and I had bet our lives on him.

"Tell me this," Barrington said. It sounded more like a command. "My people tell me you didn't have anything to do with Cal Katz and what he turned up. Is that right?"

"I never heard the name Cal Katz until Greg was well into this project."

"So it was just a damned coincidence? Amazing."

"It was no coincidence. It was part of the way the elements fitted together to achieve the outcome we selected."

"You're talking mumbo-jumbo. Who's this 'we' you're talking about?"

"A group of linked minds. If you've done the research you'll know who I mean."

"The readers of your little book? We've taken care of that; that's what I was on the phone about just now. I gave the order, and we're blocking your web-sites, the ones for your book, as well as all the related ones, every damned one of them. 'Technical problems,' that's what the error messages will say. You have your readers, you have the study groups for the book — but they don't have leadership or communications. By the time things get fixed, the elections will be over, and my boys will have won."

99

Barrington turned his lizard gaze to me again. "You gave Naismith Katz' memos, but we took them away from him. I expect he didn't get around to telling you that. Now Naismith, the gutless bastard, has gone into hiding, scared shitless. Whether you know it or not, that means we got hold of all three copies Katz made. The game is over, and we won."

"There's another set you missed," I bluffed.

"No there isn't. And even if there were, it wouldn't matter because you aren't going to get to it. I'm not dumb enough to let you walk out of here. As for Naismith, he's on the run now, but he won't survive long, not with the TMK virus going round."

Barrington let that sink in, then he said, "Bottom line, it's all over. I've won. Again." He shook his head, and the sagging jowls rippled. "I *always* win. You should have known that by now."

It was naive to give up the guns, Paul.

Barrington had just admitted a murder before it happened: Naismith was going to die. He'd all but admitted that he was behind Katz' murder, and the others who had held those memos. He wasn't going to let us walk, today or ever, after telling us that. I looked at Katje. She looked back, her eyes telling me she was thinking the same gloomy things I was.

"Any final thoughts, Paul, Greg, Katje? Any last questions? We won't be meeting again, ever, you know that."

"You're wrong," Paul said, his voice preternaturally calm. *What? Me worry?*

I looked across at Katje. Oddly, Paul's confidence seemed to have energized her, and now she smiled back at me, apparently serene in the knowledge that things would work out.

I felt a surge of the same energy. I'd survived two kidnapings, a shoot-out at Union Station, and too much else to fold now. I'd gotten Katje into this, I had to do whatever I could. Barrington was maybe 15 feet away, and didn't have a gun — at least not visible. I could get to him in a second, grab him as a hostage, and —

A discreet knock at the door, and Sharon stepped in. "Sorry to interrupt, Mr. Barrington, sir — "

"You *are* interrupting, and at a damned inconvenient time. What is it?"

"The *Washington Post* is on the line. They're asking if you want to comment on an article they're about to run. Also, your son the senator called, and will be calling you back. It seems the media in New Orleans are after him on the same subject, wanting a comment."

"Dammit, what's this all about?"

"*The Naismith Letter* has come out online with a very long special report, and now the *Post* wants your feedback on it for a story they're working on. It seems that part of the Naismith piece relates to something he referred to as 'the Katz memos,' and another part of it has to do with allegations about your sons and some business dealings."

Barrington sat deathly still for what seemed like a very long time. His jaw moved, but no words came. I wondered if he'd had a stroke.

Then he pointed at Paul. "You son of a bitch!" His voice was suddenly quavery. The anger was there, but the strength had been knocked out of him. "You arranged this! You're *dead*. Painfully as I can damned well make it!"

Paul chuckled. "The fact is, as I told you, I'd never heard of Cal Katz in my life, until Greg became involved in this, and then I saw how that strand was dovetailing with this."

Barrington turned to Sharon. "Take these two out of here, but keep them handy — and out of sight. I'm not finished with them yet. We definitely don't want anyone knowing they ever came here. And we sure as hell don't want them making a run for it, so tell Fackson to make sure his guys stay alert."

1 OO

Sharon led us to a smaller room on the same floor.

The two men who'd tried to jump us in the parking garage glared at us, though the tall one watched Paul with what I took to be an expression of awe in his eyes. Finally he spoke: "I don't know who you are, but you are one hell of an amazing old guy, I hand you that."

"You'd like to know how I managed it?"

The short one grunted.

"It's all in the mind. Read my book."

"You embarrassed them professionally, you know," Sharon said after she had closed the door. "I liked that."

"I was in the OSS, a long time ago," Paul said. "As was your boss. Some tricks you don't forget."

But the OSS never taught the trick of turning a cap into a discus.

Or did you hypnotize us into believing it was a discus?

"I know you've had a long day," she said, "so I arranged sandwiches and refreshments for you." Her eyes met Paul's and again it seemed as if some signal passed between them.

❏

Sharon slid back a wall-panel, revealing a big plasma television screen. "There have been some significant developments in the matter of Jesse Cripes and his threats. I'm sure you'll want to see."

She flicked the TV on, then handed Paul the remote. "The windows are wired to the alarm system, and one or both of the security gentlemen will be guarding the door, so there's no point in trying to leave."

Did I hear her whisper "yet" at the end of the sentence?

She left, and I heard the key turn in the lock. Paul picked up some of the small sandwich squares, and poured tea into a china cup.

"But this food could be drugged, even poisoned," I said.

Paul shook his head and smiled. "I expect it's perfectly safe. Have some. There's an old military saying, Never pass up the chance to eat, because you don't know when you'll get the chance again."

How many times had I heard Dad say the same thing?

One commercial followed another on the TV; I used the interval to study the uncle I'd waited all my life to meet. He looked like Dad, though leaner. What I hadn't expected was how much he still looked like me — rather, as I would look a half-century from now. That augured well for my future.

But how much future did I really have? Despite the courtesy of finger-food and fine china, Barrington was not going to turn us loose, even after the election was wrapped up. He didn't have a choice: we knew too much, we could go to the police and claim that his agents tried to kidnap us. Even if the police and the media laughed us away, our story would get out, and it would be a shadow on his sons in this final weekend before the elections.

And if the media took an interest in the story of what happened to the eight tons of gold that disappeared from Flecken Castle, then the Justice Department, or maybe the CIA would be forced to investigate. Then what? It could be one of those stories that rolled on and on, revelation after revelation. He wouldn't want that, either.

❑

The clot of commercials out of the way, the network special report continued.

A shot of a small apartment house in Munich, indistinguishable from others on the street.

This is the final hideout of Twisted Messiah lead singer Jesse Cripes. He and approximately 20 of his closest associates and security personnel were trapped here before dawn, local time, when the building was surrounded by German police units. According to unofficial reports, it was Jesse's intention at that point to commit mass suicide by throwing a switch that would have ignited several pounds of explosive. The switch was apparently defective, giving some of the others who were not willing to die a chance to overpower Jesse, and drag him out of the building where he and the others were arrested.

Even before this, however, the demonstrations in support of Twisted Messiah had largely ended in several cities — apparently a reaction by the young supporters' shock and disillusionment upon learning of the more than 70 corpses of people like themselves who had been tortured and buried in Jesse's German residence.

Shots of scraggly kids bunched together, crying and wailing followed. In one, a pro-Jesse sign had been turned around and one of them had crayoned,

**Jesse
How could you do that to us?**

101

It was my childhood fantasy come-to-life, sitting with Uncle Paul.

Yet, from the first moments, it seemed as if I'd *always* known him — maybe because he was so much like Dad in little mannerisms, in the ways of expressing things, even in the same hand-gestures as he talked.

I had no idea what was coming next, so I asked the questions while I had the chance.

What I'd pieced together about his mission to La Rochelle and the aftermath turned out to be mostly accurate. It was true that Hadley Barrington had sent him to France to be sacrificed on a decoy mission: to recover the Holy Spear, which, of course, was never there.

What Dr. Gniessbach had said was also true: Gniessbach had hidden Paul and the chest in the monastery in St. Johann on the Fleckensee for nearly a year, then used him to try to broker a trade: immunity from prosecution and some money in exchange for the chest.

"I met Dr. Gniessbach, and —"

"I know you met him. The Twisted Messiah people had been watching him for nearly a year."

"That long? How did they know?"

"It was they who sent that first letter to your father, the one supposedly signed by Willoughby — to stir things up again, in the hope that you might turn up a fresh lead to me and what I found in the Templar Chest.   Apparently they heard rumors about the Templar Chest — very likely from some of the old Nazis. The Twisted Messiah group had enormous amounts of money to work with, of course, and hired researchers who picked up the basics. That's why they placed one of their people in Gniessbach's retirement home, to see what he might know."

That would have been Grim Fraulein Elfriede, who killed Dr. Gniessbach after he gave me the materials.

"They also sent a couple of undercover teams to St. Johann, even to the monastery, posing as visitors. Once we knew they were interested, we looked for ways to use it against them. We joined the track to the perfect outcome, and events came together to achieve it."

"Brother Augustus told me you hadn't been back to the monastery since about 1955."

"True, I was not there in person. But I kept in touch."

Old Brother Augustus at the monastery when I asked what had happened to Paul: *After that I cannot say.* Not quite a fib: he "could not say" in order to keep the secret.

"But why would Jesse's people care what was in the Templar Chest," Katje asked. "They're not religious, far *from* it."

"Ah, but they *are* religious — in their twisted way. Hence the ceremonies and rituals built into their performances. But their ceremonies were not to worship the Creator, theirs were set up to tap the *destructive* force. They wanted what I found in the Templar Chest for the same reasons Hitler and Himmler and some of the other top Nazis were obsessed by the dark side of the occult. They wanted to learn how to access those powers. They hoped to harness the energies of the fans, young and malleable as they were, and direct those energies to destructive ends."

❑

I heard voices and movements outside; no telling how much longer we'd have together. So I asked, "Dr. Gniessbach told me that, in the last days of the war, he directed you to contact OSS headquarters and offer a trade."

"Correct."

"He said that, in response to your signal, Barrington jumped in a plane and raced to Austria in hopes of making a deal."

"Barrington came to Austria, that's true, but only because he had deluded himself. In the message I'd sent from La Rochelle in June of 1944, I'd used the term 'greatest power.' When I was allowed to make contact again, to convey Gniessbach's offer to turn over what I'd found in La Rochelle in exchange for immunity, Barrington convinced himself that could only mean some Nazi super-weapon. Mind you, even in the spring of 1945, no one outside a small contingent of scientists had heard of atomic weaponry, so he had no idea what I'd turned up. It never occurred to him that I was referring to a spiritual force, to an inner human potential."

He paused, took a deep breath, then added, "Had he understood that, Barrington would never have bothered to come. And everything would have turned out differently."

How differently things *could* have turned out. Paul could have come home after the war, could have lived a normal life. But I didn't detect any regret in his voice.

"Barrington hustled down to Austria because he saw Gniessbach's offer as an opportunity to score a big win, a chance to seal his reputation as the man who secured the Nazi super-weapon before the Russians got there. The Americans and British and French had teams out all over Europe looking to recruit Nazi scientists with expertise in rockets and atomic weapons. Barrington convinced himself that he had a unique lead on another kind of Nazi super-weapon, and he figured a success like that would be his ticket for life after the war."

Paul paused, looking off into space. "Naturally, Barrington was devastated when he got to the Fleckensee and found that I was gone, along with the supposed super-weapon that he'd come for. Instead of being a hero, he was going to come off as a fool, as the officer who let the big secret slip through his fingers. He pushed very hard, *brutally* hard, to find me. I knew the kind of person he was, and *could* not, *would* not let the Templar materials fall into his hands. I had barely begun to learn to apply the knowledge at that point, so could only hide and hope."

He paused to sip some tea. "But, call it luck, call it *synchronicity*, or, as I do, call it my first success in applying the Templar wisdom to join a different reality track. Whatever it was,

Barrington picked up the rumor that several tons of gold were hidden in the castle just down the lake from the monastery where I'd been held. It would seem to be a total coincidence, except that there *are* no coincidences when things really matter."

"Had you known that Nazi gold was stored in the castle?"

"If the monks had picked up the rumors, they hadn't told me. Barrington apparently learned about it when he interrogated some of the locals. Maybe even Dr. Gniessbach told him. I don't know."

"Cal Katz turned up the story of the stolen gold in the course of investigating Barrington's firm as an archetypal Beltway Bandit. Dan Naismith, the former *Post* correspondent, said he picked up rumors of it back in the 1970's."

"The story was out there, no question of that, but there was — *could* be — no proof. Barrington's crew had torched any files that could implicate them, along with a warehouse full of other documents. From that point, there could be only rumors and suspicions. Barrington and the others had covered their tracks very well, partly by bringing some people into it, buying off others, and killing those who didn't want to go along. They set me up as a scapegoat, which is one reason I could never go home after the war. The affair was an embarrassment to the American government — American officers stealing the gold the Nazis stole. It was shoved under the rug as quickly as possible."

"You told Barrington that you hadn't heard of Cal Katz until a few days ago."

He chuckled. "This is Washington. I cannot tell a lie. That is true."

"So it was just random chance that Cal stumbled on the story of the Fleckensee gold?"

"Random chance? I wouldn't call it that. It was more the working out of the track that actualized. I'm sorry your friend was killed. But he died doing what he considered important. He knew the risk he was taking. The fact is, Katz and what he was up to came as a total surprise to us. We'd never heard of him . . . until he faxed you that first morning. From that —"

"You knew that? You were tapping my lines?"

"*Joining Miracles* has created a band of readers everywhere, all willing to help. We've even had people feeding us information from close to the Twisted Messiah inner cadre. That's how we knew they were interested in you. So, yes, we did tap your lines, but only for the few days immediately before it all started up. Katz' calls to you that first morning puzzled us, but things were already underway on other fronts and there was no going back."

"Who killed Cal Katz?" I figured I already knew that, but wanted his take.

"Not us, of course. Presumably some of Barrington's people. In a way he could never have dreamed, Cal Katz played a part in bringing it all tumbling down. I think he would have liked that as part of his epitaph."

Barrington's visions of a political dynasty had not yet tumbled down, by no means. Was it going to be part of my epitaph? Would anyone ever know?

"I was told that the CIA got onto Twisted Messiah's plans by intercepting their communications. Did they alert you?"

Paul smiled and shook his head. "Not at all. We have no links with the CIA, none at all."

❑

Fackson waited until Sharon was on the phone, then got together with the two men he had with him. They weren't his best people, just the best available this final weekend before the election when all of the first team was spread around the country putting out last-minute fires for clients.

But they'd do exactly what he told them and ask no questions. That's what mattered.

"Circumstances have changed," he told them. That was for sure. In an hour, the Barrington dynasty had cracked wide open. "That means our mission has changed. Here's what's we're going to be doing now."

102

We sat in silence for a while. It had been quite a day, starting at Jesse's convent, 3500 miles across the Atlantic, and now ending here, in Barrington's lair . . . and the day was a long way from done. I was tired, though Uncle Paul seemed surprisingly fresh.

Better to ask the questions now, as there may never be another chance.

"You started to tell me about *Joining Miracles*. You said you didn't really write it, just translated it?"

"I put the words on paper, that's true, but I don't claim I was really the author. What I mean is that I translated into modern context some of the ideas I came upon in the Templar Chest. I did have one very large advantage, as I had the insights of quantum physics as a framework for understanding the knowledge."

"Why didn't you just send me a copy of the book back at the start? It would have made things easier. Then I'd have known what was going on."

"It was better that you did not know, that you discovered things for yourself, as that led the others into the open. In any case, I expected the book would be presented to you in the perfect way at the perfect time . . . and it was."

"It seems to be saying that we can simply select some outcome we want, and we somehow sidestep into an alternate version of reality — is that a fair statement?"

"Alternate version of reality — but what *is* reality?"

"You tell me."

"It's *all* reality. If we listen to what the quantum physicists are saying, every possible reality exists, every potential twist of fate is out there in the universe somewhere. All potential realities already exist in a latent form. We're not aware of them, but nevertheless those various potential realities do exist, in a latent state, waiting to be brought to actuality. The Templar Wisdom – which I've tried to convey in *Joining Miracles* – suggests that we have a power within that enables us to join whatever version of reality we choose. Since all potential versions of reality already exist, why not step into the version that's best for us?"

"You're saying that I can join – step into – an alternate version of reality, just like that, and events will necessarily come together to bring it about?"

"Not necessarily, not with absolute certainty, of course — the physicists tell us there is only *probability,* not certainty, in this physical world in which we live. True, they're referring to things at the quantum level. But, as below, so above. By making a conscious choice, a clear, focused intention, we greatly increase the probability of that version becoming the one we experience. And if enough of us join in that expectation, then the probability increases even more."

"How can that be?"

"The people who explore this field generally agree that the human mind does somehow play a role in determining which potential outcome actually manifests – in other words, becomes the reality we experience. But they haven't yet come to agreement on *how* that can be. No matter, even though we can't explain *how* or *why* it happens, the fact is that these principles *do* work in predictable ways, and the results can be applied to practical ends."

I tried to make sense of that.

Then he added, "There's a phrase among those who work in the field, 'Shut up and compute,' meaning, Don't waste energy trying to understand what is presently not knowable, don't fuss over why things work as they do, just move on and apply the knowledge in practical ways."

Shut up and compute — the phrase Dad had used.

"In *Joining Miracles* I suggest much the same mindset. Be humble enough to accept that we humans don't now, and maybe never will, understand the why and how. But, understand it or not, the fact is that you are free to experiment and test it for yourself, and see how it works in your own life. Shut up and compute; shut up and join the miracle."

"Is this the knowledge you found in the Templar Chest at La Rochelle?"

He nodded. "The Knowledge, as translated to modern terminology and understanding. Of course, the people who put it together back then were totally unaware of what we've since learned about quantum physics and the fact that 'solid' matter is really 99.99% *not* solid, rather mostly empty space and energy. Nevertheless, they seemed to have an intuitive prefiguring of that deeper reality, though their orientation was toward applying it."

"The Knowledge in that Templar Chest — is *that* the Holy Grail?"

He smiled. "Ah, but what *is* the Grail? Who is it to serve?"

"Those are the classic questions of the Grail quest," I said, puzzled by his response. "So how would you answer them?"

"Second question first, and my answer is the same as the traditional one. Who is it to serve? It's to serve all."

He stopped there, so I said, "But you haven't answered that first question: What IS the Grail?"

He looked at Katje. "I think you already know the answer."

"What I've been calling the Latent Miracle Power?," she offered.

"The power within us, within human minds, that we're just beginning to learn to tap. The power of focused intention, the power to select among the alternate potential tracks in reality. The power, if you will, to induce what we call synchronicities."

"The power to *induce synchronicities*?," Katje echoed. "That's it?"

103

We heard voices in the hallway outside and waited, expecting the door to be opened ... and then what? Resume the conversation with Barrington? Or take a one-way trip with Henson's guys?

Nothing happened, which gave me the chance to ask some of the other questions that had been building for days. "I had the chance to talk with Professor Larkwood — principal researcher on the legendary report that bears his name."

Paul nodded. "I know."

"He said that he came upon various references to Agent Perceval and what he turned up, but never got cooperation in getting the facts."

"I'm not surprised. Of *course* they tried to keep Larkwood away from the facts. They *had* to keep him away. He might have uncovered the truth about who stole that Nazi gold. That was Barrington, as you've doubtless concluded by now, along with some others he brought into the scheme."

"Larkwood also said that he believed that you – in uncovering the Templar Chest – had found what the Nazis had been looking for in their drive to investigate so-called 'intangible science.' That you had, as he put it, 'uncovered the key to a power within the human mind for directing and focusing energies from other dimensions.'"

He nodded. "That's a reasonable way of expressing it, another term for the capability within us that can connect us with the universal power, the key to tapping our highest human potential."

"It sounds like magic," I said, to draw him out.

"If that's magic, then we're all potential magicians — in the sense that we all have the power to affect reality beyond the tangible world. We're all possessed of a power latent within us to affect reality beyond the tangible and material."

He paused to sip some more tea, then added, "Look at it from the other direction. Surely you know people who seem to have a knack for bringing about what they *least* want? *They* are magicians, but with the knack for manifesting the undesired."

"But isn't that just coincidence?"

"The pattern happens too often to some people for it to be just coincidence. Once is a single event, twice might be a coincidence, but for the same pattern to recur month after month and year after year is something quite different. The Templar Wisdom tells us that we have within us the power to set up the conditions for synchronicities — coincidences that are more than mere coincidences. In short, that we have the power to facilitate serendipity — or the reverse."

"How?"

"By using the power of focused intention. That is, by choosing the expectation that a certain desired track in reality will come about . . . which, with high probability, *does* come about."

"*Choosing* an expectation? How can you choose what to expect?"

"It's becoming *active*, rather than merely *passive*. The power is unlimited, but if we're to tap it, we must be open to a different awareness of reality — an awareness that all alternative possibilities *already* exist, and that we are free to join them."

"How is that different from prayer?"

"I'm not saying it *is* different. At most, it's more like a different language, a different manifestation of the same effect."

"But prayer . . ." I paused, groping for the words to express the question. "We normally think of prayer as *imploring* God, as asking for something — health, safety, whatever. Asking God to grant a favor. What you seem to be suggesting is not imploring, rather more that we have the power to answer our own prayers. Almost as if you're saying that we ourselves *are* God."

"No, not that. By *no* means am I suggesting that. I think the difference is in the paradigm — the mental model we use to try to understand."

He paused. "You *are* familiar with the term 'paradigm?' Think of a paradigm as a mental framework for trying to make sense of a variety of elements that we don't fully understand.

Scientists use paradigms, or models, for trying to fit facts and theories together, shuffling them around in different ways until they find one where everything seems to tie together. Then they use that model . . . until a better one comes along."

I didn't grasp what this had to do with prayer, but I nodded.

"From the dawn of time, we envisioned the world around us as solid. But just in the past century or so, largely from the work of the people exploring the world within the atom, we've come to understand that that 'solid' model of reality is not accurate. The supposedly solid things of this earth are in reality more than 99% *empty* space, and less than 1% solid. Nonetheless, in our everyday use, we mostly still use that paradigm that pictures the world as solid. It's a useful illusion."

Useful illusion — a phrase Dad had used in one of those puzzling phone conversations.

"But from our new understanding of the nature of reality — as mostly energy and empty space — flows the possibility of a different paradigm. Now we have learned that the world is not really solid, not really fixed, and — very important — that our minds appear to play a crucial role in the unfolding of the version of reality that we come to experience. That changes things. That opens up wonderful new possibilities . . . as I've described in *Joining Miracles*."

"Sorry, but I haven't had the chance to read it yet."

"You will. Once we're past this."

I hope you're right, I wanted to say. I hope we survive.

Paul smiled. "You're wondering whether you'll live long enough to read it. Well, there's my point. Our minds, our expectations play a key role in opening up one version from all of the potentials — by inducing the synchronicities that bring that version to actualization. So, in short, it behooves us all to join the track in which we *do* make it out of here alive. The track we expect, the track we consciously choose to join, *is* the track that becomes."

"Somehow we conjure up a way out of this situation?" I didn't like the way I'd said that, I didn't mean to come across as so cynical. But I was tired . . . and scared for my life.

"There's no 'conjuring' involved. All potential realities

already exist. We're simply choosing — or *electing* — to step into one of those other versions."

"So I should simply *expect* we'll be okay? That still sounds like praying for a miracle."

"'Miracles happen, not in opposition to nature, but in opposition to what we know of nature.' That's from St. Augustine, by the way.   Conventional prayer, or supplication, fits one paradigm. But there's another paradigm — that we're not imploring God 'up there,' but *rather are utilizing powers that the Creator already placed within us*. After all, we now understand that the human mind plays a central role in determining which version of all those potential realities comes to be."

Again, that echoed more of what Dad had been saying. I thought of how he'd cited Moses and the staff that turned into a snake. Was that because Moses chose to shift from one version of reality to another? Had Moses, way back then, understood that there was more than one paradigm for understanding our relation to God and the rest of creation?

Paul went on. "Most of the traditional paradigms set up a chasm between us and the Creator, with God 'up there,' so to speak, and us 'down here.' I think that's a remnant of the days of the kings and chieftains, when the system was that the people did have to implore favors of the ruler. People thought in terms of that mental model back then, and it has carried over till now."

Again I nodded, my usual response when I wasn't quite understanding.

"True, that hierarchical perception is the usual, the *traditional*, image we call upon in viewing our interaction with God. But, in reality, we just *don't* know, and *can't* know, because God, the Divine, the Creator — whatever term you use — is far beyond our human powers of visualization and understanding.   Certainly, millions of people through the ages have found that hierarchical paradigm helpful. But it seems presumptuous to present one model and claim that *that* is the one and only way of interacting with the Infinite Power in the universe. If God, the divine, is infinite, then how can we with our finite minds presume to limit what is beyond our human capabilities to understand?"

I glanced at Katje. This was her area of expertise, and she was obviously captivated.

"Maybe God *is* like those kings in olden days, and we are the supplicants," Paul said. "But let me propose a different paradigm, one that is perhaps no less valid. Maybe God is like the ocean, and maybe we are like the fish that have been given existence in that ocean. Maybe there is not that chasm between God and us, and maybe we are much closer to God than we have understood. Maybe God is not sitting 'up there,' watching us act out our lives 'down here' on a stage. Maybe we are swimming *within the Creator,* and maybe *the Creator is in us* as the sea is in the fish. Perhaps the way it works is that certain of the Creator's powers of mind permeate us as the sea water permeates the fish."

"What would that mean?," Katje asked.

"It would help us understand how it is that we have the potential to co-create the version of reality that we encounter."

He turned to me. "You asked how this differs from the conventional perception of prayer. The difference is that we are not imploring God to grant, rather we are using God-given powers within our minds in order to actualize one among the variety of potential versions of the world that exist."

He looked at Katje, as if expecting a question. She shook her head at first, then said, "By inducing synchronicities via our expectations?"

He nodded, then went on: "In this analogy, in this *paradigm,* God actualized this figurative sea, and God actualized, or created us as being like fish that swim within it. But we are *not just* fish, we are *also mind and consciousness.* That gift of mind enables us to play a key role as the creation continues, and we can select which of all the potential versions is to become actual. We can elect to actualize constructive things, or destructive, peace or war, learning or ignorance, cooperation or conflict."

He gave us a moment to absorb that, then added, "Similarly, call it praying, call it joining miracles, call it tapping unknown powers — call it anything, or call it all of the above, and we *still* can't begin to express the totality of what is so much greater than we can conceive, let alone access."

104

I wanted to pursue that, to explore what Paul meant, but the door opened and Brad Fackson entered. His face was flushed; he seemed more energized than earlier.

He dropped into a chair, popped a couple of the small sandwiches in his mouth, then washed them down with some tea.

Then he got to the point. "The game has suddenly changed, my friends. Barrington's dreams are shattered, his sons are history — and you can take most of the credit. You and the late Cal Katz. And of course Naismith, who you brought into this."

"Are you giving us credit, or fixing the blame on us?," I asked. I was too tired for games.

"Depends on your point of view, doesn't it? You can bet Barrington doesn't like that, and he's madder than hell. Mad at you *and* at me. Turns out that Naismith copied all the Katz materials you gave him onto a microchip, and hid it in his shoe. We missed that. So he ended up with a complete copy of Katz' article and all his backup proof. He copied it all onto his online newsletter and website and — "

"Fantastic!"

" — along with that, Naismith added in a shit-load of other dirt on the two sons that we didn't know about. Seems they'd played some money games with the gambling interests down there, something their old Daddy didn't know about and we hadn't turned up. Somebody got the goods and forwarded them to Naismith. Once he managed to get his *Letter* back on-line, he hit a grand slam — a big, big story. Katz' documentation on how the old man got his start with stolen Nazi gold, way back when, then this new stuff on how the sons were willing to get into bed with some really dirty gambling enterprises. Now the *Washington Post* is all over both stories, as are some of the big papers back in Louisiana. The networks, too, of course. This time, no amount of Barrington clout is going to bury it. My feeling, the mangiest stray dog in New Orleans has a better chance of getting elected than those two boys."

"Why are you telling us this?," Katje asked.

"Because I'm here to offer a deal. Barrington is finished, and so're his sons, and so're most of his business enterprises. You can bet the feds are going to be all over everything, going all the way back to the war. He's going to spend the rest of his life fighting lawsuits, trying to stay out of jail and salvage whatever he can."

"What kind of deal?," I asked. Was Fackson really so quick to shift loyalties, or was this just another trick?

"I've been watching you these past few days. At first, I was thinking you had to be the luckiest SOB alive, the way things just kept falling the right way for you. Then I began to understand what all this is really about — kind of a technology of magic, just as you said. And I started thinking, What a hell of a powerful weapon."

He turned to Paul. "Just like you said in the message you sent back in '44 — about that most powerful weapon ever known."

He gobbled another sandwich before going on. "A week ago, at the start, if you'd told me about this, I'd have written it off as a crock of crap. But now I know I was wrong, and I know who we can sell it to."

"I hear Twisted Messiah is out of the bidding," Katje said.

Fackson missed the irony. "Forget Twisted Messiah, they're a bunch of screwed-up losers. They're history. I'm talking about DARPA — you've heard of DARPA? Defense Advanced Research Products Agency. It's their mission to think out-of-the-box. They're always exploring looney ideas on the chance some of them might work. What I'm saying is, I've got contacts, and I've got credibility. You've got the kind of product they go for, and I've got the entree that can get us listened to. If there's anything to what you've got, if it holds up, then we're talking big money. Big, *big* money, split down the middle."

"You've got a going concern, you're the respected private eye for the political class," Paul said. "You wouldn't want to let go of that, would you?"

"Shit, after this, there's not going to be much left. People will blame us for Barrington's problems. They'll avoid us in droves."

Paul nodded. I couldn't believe he was actually listening to any of this. If Fackson was willing to turn on Barrington at the drop of a coin, then how long would he keep us around?

"I say DARPA, but that's just for the government money. Based on what I've picked up, there are some really strong commercial opportunities, as well. We need you, Paul, to help us get set up, then you can go live in Hawaii, or any damned place you please."

"If that's what you're thinking," Paul replied, "then you don't understand it at all. We can't very well bottle it up and sell it, not to the military, not to industry. It doesn't work that way."

Fackson reached into his jacket and emerged with a pistol in his hand.

"Matter of fact, I *do* understand, understand a lot more than you. I understand that the game has changed, Barrington is out, and now I'm the one making up the rules, not you. Rule One is we're going to get out of here while the old man's still preoccupied with damage control. On your feet, let's go. My guys have a car waiting."

The voice, coming from the ceiling, startled us all. It was Barrington, on an intercom I didn't suspect was there. "Fackson! I've been paging Sharon. She doesn't answer. Where the hell is she?"

"I don't know, Mr. Barrington, sir, but I'll check on her right now."

"Never mind that. You come in here right now. And bring Paul with you. Just Paul, not the other two. And leave your men outside. Just you and I and Paul — got it?"

Fackson thought a moment, then shrugged. "Sure, let's go see the old bastard one more time." He waved Paul to the door with his gun.

105

"I'm going to leave you two here, with the door unlocked," Fackson said to Katje and I. "That's a show of good-faith on my part, just to show we can work together on this and all come out in great shape."

I got a glimpse into the hallway as they left, and didn't see Fackson's two heavies. Not that it really mattered. We wouldn't get far before they spotted us. In any case, we were not going to leave without Paul.

"I wish Paul had hung onto those guns," I said.

Katje shook her head. "Your uncle knows what he's doing."

"I don't trust Fackson. He's not about to let us walk free."

"The track we expect is the track that becomes. *Expect* a solution to present itself, and be open to it when it comes. That's his message: focus on inducing the synchronicities that slip us into a better track in the universe."

I must have had a blank expression. She added, "That's from Paul's book, in case you didn't get to read that far yet."

I wanted to tell her to cut the mumbo-jumbo and come down to earth. But I didn't see any practical way out. Maybe expecting, or praying — whatever you wanted to call it — was really the only hope.

A gunshot — no mistaking that sound — shook the old house. Then a second shot, and the bullet punched a gaping hole in the wooden door, then buried itself in the wall, releasing a cloud of dust and plaster.

I dropped to the floor and pulled Katje down with me, then crawled on my stomach out to the hallway. No sign of Fackson's men. The top half of the door to Barrington's office was splintered.

Paul had been in that room.

I half-crawled, half-slithered down the hall. Two more shots. I felt the impact as they hit the walls.

I reached up and turned the knob and shoved the door open. A body lay on the floor inside, bleeding onto the oriental rug. Fackson.

Barrington sat at the desk on the far side of the room, holding a large automatic. I didn't see Paul.

"You've haunted me all my life, you bastard," Barrington said, his voice heavy and rheumy. "I always had the feeling you'd show up like this, and ruin every damned thing that I've spent a lifetime working for."

"You *expected* to get caught one day, and so it came to be," Paul said. "You knew it was coming."

I saw Paul now, still standing. He'd been blocked by the door.

"I've created hundreds, hell, *thousands,* of jobs for people. I've made a lot of people rich, those who stuck with me. And yet somehow in the back of my mind I always knew you were there, watching, waiting to get your revenge."

"You're wrong on that. I have kept track of you, that's true. But not for the sake of revenge. My only interest in you was to make sure you weren't coming after me. I've been blessed with a mission in life, and I didn't want you destroying it."

"The hell with what you say, that's sanctimonious crap. You've wanted to get me back, that's just human nature."

"It doesn't *have* to be — that's one thing I've learned. You lied to me when you sent me to La Rochelle, but it was wartime. I couldn't hold that against you. I was a soldier, and I was sent on a mission. Besides, look at what it started — the synchronicity that brought events together and opened the way to finding the Templar Chest."

"Shit! That really *is* all you care about, isn't it?" Barrington gripped the gun in both hands, and braced it atop some books on the desk. "You've screwed everything up for me, brought about this goddam mess, my boys are going to lose, it's all over for me."

He leaned down to sight along the barrel, still braced on the desk-top. It was an old World War II .45 automatic, probably one he brought back as a souvenir.

"Fackson is bleeding," Paul said. "He needs an ambulance. Call 911."

"Let the bastard bleed. I had the intercom on, I was listening in to what he was saying in the other room. He was double-crossing me. I *made* him, and at the first sign of a problem he was ready to cut and run."

"I don't have a gun," Paul said. "I'm reaching into my pocket for a cell-phone."

Barrington fired. I saw now why he braced it with two hands: he was weak and frail, and the recoil jolted him back. The bullet jolted the house, but missed Paul, who remained standing where he was, talking to the 911 operator.

"Uncle Paul," I called, sticking my head around the door so he could see me. "Just get out of there. Run!"

He shook his head. "Barrington and I need to have this talk. We need to clear the air."

"You get out of here, boy," Barrington growled, waving the gun in my direction. "This is between Paul and me, and you don't want any damned part of it."

I felt a tug on my ankle. "Greg, get out of there," Katje said. "Don't be crazy. Paul, listen to Greg. Run for it. There's so much good you can do if you stay alive."

Barrington fired. Again the shot went wild, and I heard glass shatter.

He fired again, and again it missed. The room reeked of cordite. Why hadn't somebody heard the shots? Where were the police?

"Damn it all! You are one lucky sumbitch! I've never missed that many times in my life all put together. But if I'm going, then dammit, so are you."

He fired again. Paul didn't flinch. The bullet punched a hole in the wall behind him, and plaster dust floated down, marking the spot.

Paul was still standing, unhurt. Barrington *had* to have missed. But that hole seemed to be directly behind Paul. How could that be?

Barrington fired still again.

Maybe I blinked at the noise, maybe whatever. I *know* I saw Paul before Barrington fired, and I *know* I saw him standing there an eye-wink later — in almost the same spot — after the bullet hit and that puff of dust marked where the bullet slammed into the wall.

But what did I see in that instant between?

I think I *did not* see Paul.

I think Paul was *not there* as the bullet passed between Barrington's gun and the wall.

But if I didn't see him, where did he go? No human could have danced aside and then back in place faster than a bullet.

Maybe I'm wrong, and it's probably something I'll wonder about till the day I die, but what I think happened was this: somehow Paul joined another track in reality for the duration of the bullet's flight, and then came back to almost the same spot.

True, that doesn't make any sense, no sense at all — no sense in our usual paradigm of reality.

But what happened made me think again that maybe our usual paradigm isn't quite accurate, that maybe there are other ways of perceiving — and acting — in our world.

Was it just random luck that those Marines happened to be on the Mezzanine in Union Station at just the right moment to grab Horst and then Elena?

Or was their appearance at the right place and time a synchronicity that opened up as the normal course of events in the reality track Paul had joined?

Who knows? I sure don't.

But I know enough not to dismiss it as impossible.

Now I'm open to the possibility that maybe reality is wider and richer than we will likely ever grasp. So maybe it's best, as Dad was saying in that phone conversation, to not get bogged down on trying to understand, and instead just use the gift of the wider reality. In IBM-speak, Shut up and compute.

"Aw shit," Barrington said, "I don't know what it is, but you are one lucky sumbitch."

I held my breath, waiting for the next shot.

Barrington grunted, then stuck the big .45 in his mouth and

pulled the trigger.

I looked away. This I definitely did not want to see. A click, no gunshot.

"You didn't really want to die, did you?," Paul said. His voice was still calm after all this.

"Maybe," Barrington said, his usually impassive lizard eyes now wide with shock. He turned and threw the heavy pistol at the window, nearly knocking himself over with the effort. The glass shattered, and I heard sirens.

Paul said something to Barrington that I didn't hear, then he turned to Katje and me. "Police are coming, time to get out."

He led the way back down the hall, then ran down the stairs so fast it was hard for us to keep up with him. Fackson's men were gone, and the front door swung open. Paul jogged through the rooms until he found Sharon in the kitchen, duct-taped to a chair.

He cut her loose, using a steak knife, and stuffed the tape into his pocket. He wiped his fingerprints from the knife and dropped it back into the drawer.

Sharon mumbled something I couldn't hear. He touched her affectionately on the shoulder, and beckoned us to follow him.

He hit a light switch by the door, killing the outside lights. Out the kitchen door, across the dark yard to the row of hemlocks that bordered a wire fence. He pulled himself over it. I offered a boost to Katje, but she was across before I bent down. I followed.

Now we were in what I thought was a park, but turned out to be a cemetery. Sirens from all directions were converging on this area.

The cemetery gate was locked, but we managed to pull ourselves over the wrought-iron fence, and found ourselves on a quiet residential street, lined with Victorian era brick townhouses and small apartment buildings.

Paul pulled out his cell-phone and punched the speed-dial. They answered on first ring. He said a few words, listened, then clicked the phone off.

Day Seven

"WHAT YOU'RE SUGGESTING WOULD BE NICE, but it's simply not possible — not in the real world. There's no connection between what I 'expect' or 'select' and what occurs in the world outside me. I can't just select for a miracle to happen."

Brother Freddie wagged his finger. "It would be more accurate to say that there is no apparent connection. Even better would be to say, 'there is no link detectable by our present methods.'"

"It can't possibly be true! There's no way my thinking could affect outside reality!"

"Ah," he said, raising one finger, "but what if it is true? What then?"

I didn't realize then how that phrase would keep nagging at me for days to come. "What if it is true? What then? What if the human mind does impact matter? What then?"

"What if the new ideas are right?" he continued. "What if the conventional wisdom is wrong? It wouldn't be the first time. The conventional wisdom claimed that the earth was the center of the universe. The conventional wisdom insisted that the earth was flat. The conventional wisdom scoffed at the idea that there was such a thing as germs, or that sanitation made a difference. The conventional wisdom said that it was absurd to think that man might fly, then that it was ludicrous even to suggest that man might fly to the moon. Now the conventional wisdom rejects the idea that there might be more to a human being than the instruments of today can measure."

He paused, a bemused expression on his face. "One might think that the proclaimers of the conventional wisdom would learn how often reality dares to contradict their certainties."

"BUT IF THIS WERE REALLY POSSIBLE, then wouldn't everybody already have done it? Wouldn't everybody be 'joining miracles' all the time?"

He shook his head. "It's been my experience that 'everybody,' as you say, follows what 'everybody' else does. 'Everybody' assumed that it was impossible to run a mile in four minutes. Then Roger Bannister made his run in 1954, and since then 'everybody' has known that a four-minute mile is possible. Now more and more people do it every year, so a four-minute mile is almost a commonplace event today, no longer a miracle."

"But miracles — I always thought of a miracle as from some higher dimension. It doesn't seem right to classify setting a record in a footrace as a miracle."

He shrugged. "In the view of the experts of the time,

before Bannister, a four-minute mile was completely out of the question, something utterly beyond the physical limits of a human being. Therefore, that first four-minute mile transcended the laws of nature — as they were then known. Bannister's achievement fit the definition of miracle: an event in the physical world that deviates from, or transcends, what we believe to be the laws of nature."

"But a four-minute mile wasn't so much a miracle as a matter of underestimating the capabilities of a well-trained individual."

"Exactly so! But is there a difference?"

"I don't follow."

"Perhaps it is not only in the area of athletics that we underestimate human capabilities. Perhaps, if we would only allow ourselves, we could transcend in other ways what we assume are the known limits."

"Are you suggesting that even I could work miracles — if I'd only 'allow' myself to do it?"

"Only you can answer that for yourself. . . and for that answer to be correct, then you must try it with an open mind. Expect, not merely wish for, but expect the outcome you desire, and then be open to recognize the form in which it actualizes."

From
JOINING MIRACLES:
Navigating the Seas of Latent Possibility
by "P"

106

I woke, and for a moment had no idea where I was. A small bedroom, not my own, a room I didn't recognize. A clear sun shone in, and then it came back to me. A house in the Virginia suburbs, a large place we'd been driven to last night.

The car had pulled up soon after Paul made his call, and we climbed in quickly. The driver made a quick turn and we were on Wisconsin Avenue before I recognized him: Brother Jack, the young American at the monastery in St. Johann on the Fleckensee, the monk in the green robe who had greeted me then with, "We've been expecting you, Greg."

The other man in the front seat was the silver-haired monk, Brother Theo. Now both were dressed in street clothes, and looked like a pair of Redskins fans heading home from the game.

Paul introduced them to Katje, calling them just Jack and Theo.

No one said much. Jack headed up Wisconsin, and I thought we might be headed for my apartment until he kept going, then turned at River Road. "The further we stay from downtown, the better," Theo explained.

Back around the Beltway, across the Potomac, then down winding Georgetown Pike, little changed from the trail it had been a couple centuries ago, apart from some asphalt paving, ten or twenty thousand commuter cars daily, and a succession of secluded mansions, estates, and even a horse farm or two — each probably equal in value to the Gross National Product back when Washington was President.

We went a while, then turned off the Pike, and turned again onto a gravel driveway until we came to the end of the line, a French farmhouse nestled in woods. "It's the home of a friend, someone

who liked the book," Paul explained. "They're away and we're house-
sitting."

    None of us were hungry, just bone-weary, drained by the
events.

    I dropped into the bed, and woke ten hours later to clear
sunshine.

❏

Someone had slipped a copy of this morning's *Washington Post*
under the door. Two headlines competed for space on page 1 above
the fold:

Jesse Cripes Captured
Fans Shattered on Hearing of 76 Mutilated Bodies

    The body-count had risen overnight as police found more
bodies and tapes in Twisted Messiah enclaves in other countries.
Most of the inner cadre and security people have been rounded up.
That seemed to be the end of the Twisted Messiah movement.

    The other story rated three linked headlines:

November Surprise Devastates Barrington Brother
Candidacies

Senior Barrington Charged with Attempted Murder
of Investigator Brad Fackson

Possible Link to Story Uncovered by Murdered
Journalist, Cal Katz

    Yesterday's *Post* had proclaimed **No October Surprise
this Year?**, with a question mark. This year, the big election
surprise came a day late.

    Brad Fackson was expected to recover after having been shot
by Hadley Barrington. But there were unanswered questions, not
only on how and why the shooting occurred, but also on how that
incident at the home of Senator Barrington may have related to some
of the other events of the day.

Other questions had been raised by Cal Katz' article, as published by *The Naismith Letter*, offering evidence that Hadley Barrington had been part of a team that stole eight tons of Nazi gold at the end of World War II.

Still other questions had been raised about the Barrington sons' links with organized crime and gambling interests.

A pull-out chart on an interior page tried to lay out the chronology and links among these sudden Barrington scandals.

Out of respect for his age and physical condition, Hadley Barrington had not been arrested yet; he was being held under police guard at Georgetown University hospital.

❏

The final article of particular interest was buried on page 3 of the Metro section, buried so deeply that it took two readings to recognize it for what it was:

Lovers' Quarrel Turns Deadly at Union Station

If reality is in the eye of the beholder, then those of us who were there saw a very different reality than the police fed to the *Post* reporter.

According to this article, an unknown man leaped to his death from the mezzanine level of Union Station last night following a violent argument with Elena Larcotti, 26, an Italian citizen, if her passport was authentic.

Though witness accounts varied, it appeared that the deceased man fired a weapon several times, though there were no injuries. In the scuffle to subdue Larcotti, Letrainer Washington, 15, suffered minor knife wounds.

According to a police spokesperson, the motive for the violence was not known, and Larcotti was refusing to cooperate.

What about that explosion? I was sure I heard it, but no mention here.

A request by a *Post* reporter to view the security tapes had been denied on the ground that the relevant camera had been out of service, awaiting repair.

Strange. I remembered Horst, the deceased Neanderthal guy,

Michael McGaulley

holding a bottle that may have contained some kind of biological weapon, or maybe a poison. But there was no mention of that bottle, so I guess I'll never know what it held. Was it real WMD stuff, or just a bluff?

And I'd never get to see the videos of Uncle Paul and I teaming up to secure that bottle.

But I'd been around Washington long enough to know that the allegedly broken camera wasn't just a matter of random chance. Nor was it synchronicity. It was a cover story. It wouldn't be politically prudent, with an election looming, to let the citizenry know how close it had been last night. Float this account as a trial balloon and hope nobody pricks it.

Just as well for me, though: now I wouldn't have to think about being charged with assaulting a couple of wide-body rent-a-cops.

❑

It was after ten. I hadn't slept this late since high school. I smelled the pungent draw of bacon, and realized how hungry I was.

There were fresh clothes on the chair and I threw them on and headed down the long white staircase.

Katje must have heard me, and came to meet me with a hug. "I'm so glad you finally decided to wake up and join us." She took my hand and led me down the glass-enclosed corridor to the source of the cooking aromas. "Some people are very eager to see you."

A striking, silver-haired woman turned from the stove when she heard us coming. "Ah, you must be Gregory." She held out her hand. "It is so good to meet you at last, after all these years of hearing about you. I am Cecile."

"Cecile," I echoed, trying to absorb it. But Lili had said her aunt Cecile had died years ago.

Then I saw Dad, sitting at the table, his hand outstretched to take mine. "I *told* you I was healed, but you thought I'd been seeing pink elephants." He looked good, a little pale, thinner, though still lacking hair.

"You're really here?," I blurted, at a loss for anything else to say.

"You bet I'm here. Against doctor's orders, at that. Annoyed the hell out of him, my getting cured. Spontaneous remission, he termed it. I termed it being sick and tired of being sick, and making up my mind to change tracks. He didn't like my saying that — guess he saw it as a challenge to his doctorhood. Anyway, enough of that, Paul's around here somewhere."

He stood and hugged me and I saw the tears in his eyes. "Greg, I can't tell you how happy this has made me, your turning up Paul and his wife after all these years."

"Wife?"

Paul had come in now, and he stood with Cecile, arms around each other, smiling.

"I expect today is going to be a day to remember," Katje said.

The Grail Conspiracies

Know others — maybe friends or family ---- who might enjoy The Grail Conspiracies? You can order from your local bookstore, or through **www.TheGrailConspiracies.com**. (ISBN 0-9768406-0-X)

Have you logged onto the **scenic, motivational slide presentations** that provide background to *The Grail Conspiracies*? The first two in the series are already on-line. See them at www.TheGrailConspiracies. com:

> *Part one:*   *Ah! What then?*
> *Part two:*   *Synchronicities?*

If you'd like to be **notified** when the **next slide shows in the series are ready**, send an e-mail to NotifyMe@TheGrailConspiracies. com

Please *feel free to pass this* **www.TheGrailConspiracies. com link to others** *who you think would find the materials of interest.*

JOINING MIRACLES:
Navigating the Seas of Latent Possibility

Each "Day" in *The Grail Conspiracies* began with an excerpt from *JOINING MIRACLES: Navigating the Seas of Latent Possibility*. That companion book to *The Grail Conspiracies* is scheduled for publication, fall, 2005 (ISBN#-9768406-1-8).

Register now at NotifyMe@ www.TheGrailConspiracies com, and receive personal notification *when JOINING MIRACLES* is available.

The Eternal Life Chimera

On the following pages, you'll find a preview of the new thriller, *The Eternal Life Chimera*, by the author of **The Grail Conspiracies**, Michael McGaulley. *The Eternal Life Chimera* is scheduled for publication in early 2006. (ISBN# -9768406-2-6.)

Register now at NotifyMe@ www.TheGrailConspiracies com, and receive,

- Personal notification to your e-mail address when the *slide presentation* for *The Eternal Life Chimera* is ready for on-line viewing, and,

- Personal e-mail notification *when the book is available*.

Sample

The Eternal Life Chimera

Michael McGaulley

Author of
The Grail Conspiracies

Chimera (def): 1. Fantasy. 2. Hybrid creature, often part human, part animal.

1

University Hospital. Chicago. 6:10 P.M.
Take me to the cannibal, Daddy. Please!
Jenny's words echoed in Doug Daulby's mind. By now, Jenny and Jackie would be headed to the carnival; he wished he had gone with them to see the big smiles as Jenny swept past on the rides. She was already seven; how many more years would the carnival interest her?

He pushed the thought away to focus on the tiny creature on the operating table. Draped so that only the top of the head was exposed, it could almost pass for a human infant.

They were calling it Chimp Donnie.

He sliced across the shaved skull from ear to ear, then loosened the fascia, teasing the scalp to separate from the bone.

Daulby's prematurely white hair, his size — 210 pounds spread over six feet — and his booming voice, had earned him the nickname Doc Polar Bear.

But he still moved with the grace of the athlete he'd been, and his fingers, long and supple, had a sensitivity that amazed students. They seemed to function independently of his mind, allowing him to work fast in close tolerances without missing a beat in a conversation.

Tonight, he didn't feel like conversing. Tonight he just wanted to finish and get the hell out of there. He was wishing now that he'd never gotten into this, never even come up with the idea.

But now there was no going back.

When the incision was complete, he lifted the entire top of the chimp's skull free and put the skull section in a pan of Betadine solution to keep it sterile for replacement when the operation finished.

Take me to the cannibal, Daddy.

Evanston, Illinois. 6:15 P.M.
Jenny was Mrs. Benson's last student of the day, and when she saw
her mother, she begged to stay "just another minute" to play the new
piece she had learned.

Jackie blinked away tears as Jenny played. It was such a
privilege to see a replica of herself as she'd been at seven, the same
golden hair, the same angelic face she knew from her own old
photos.

But Jenny, thank God, didn't have her tendency to
chubbiness; that would make her life easier.

Jackie loved the elements of Doug she saw blended into their
little creation. Definitely Doug's eyes, everybody said so. Maybe that
meant she'd grow up to have Doug's intellect. But hopefully without
his compulsiveness. That would really be the ideal combination.

"She has remarkable talent for someone so young," Mrs.
Benson whispered to Jackie. "She's such a wonderful little girl, such
a wonderful personality, such a bright future ahead of her. You and
Dr. Daulby must be very proud of her."

"We are," Jackie said, "she's the most wonderful thing that's
ever happened."

■

"Let's have dinner at Baskin-Robbins, then we can go to the
cannibal," Jenny said as they left Mrs. Benson's. It was a quiet, tree-
lined street of older, well-kept homes. There was little traffic here
away from the main commuter routes.

"We need vegetables with our dinner," Jackie said, thinking
how much she and Jenny would miss Doug tonight.

"We can have banana splits. The bananas and cherries will
be our vegetables. Then we'll go to the cannibal."

She dug out her car keys. What difference would it make if
they lived it up on junk food for one night? Life is short. "Okay,
sounds good to me. But it's just this one —"

She broke off when she saw two men materialize from behind
a van. One held a gun.

This can't be happening! a voice inside her head screamed.
Not to us!

"Just give us your purse," one of the men said. He was thin, almost frail, with light blond hair and wire-framed glasses. We just want your money. Give us that and we won't hurt you or little Jenny."

Jackie fumbled for her wallet. Then it struck her: Jenny! Why did a mugger know Jenny's name?

She kicked, connecting with the man's leg, and he went down. She dove to swoop up Jenny. The second man grabbed her from behind and slapped a white cloth over her face. She sniffed the bite of ether. She tried to scream, but it was no use.

As her world went dark, she saw Jenny struggling against the grip of a third man, dressed in black. He pushed a white cloth against her face, and Jenny's movements slowed. Then her body went limp.

"Doug! Help us! Jackie gasped as she blacked out.

■

Take me to the cannibal, Daddy. Please!

Jenny's voice still echoed in his head. That had never happened before, never broken through his concentration, and he wondered why tonight.

Cannibal — carnival. The last vestige of her baby-talk, a family joke now.

But he couldn't take her to a carnival tonight. Not tonight, of all nights.

Tonight's work had taken months to set up. It *had* to be tonight. Tonight, or maybe never. The window of opportunity was open, and he had to slip through that window before the politicians and bureaucrats slammed it shut again.

Take me to the cannibal. Please!

Cannibals! The word struck him. Is *that* what we are tonight, feeding on one for the sake of another?

"Dr. Martinson is extracting the donor tissue now," one of the surgical nurses said.

He glanced through the glass wall to the second operating room where Martinson was working on the other subject, a human fetus aborted moments earlier.

Martinson's role in opening the tiny soft head of the fetus was as exacting as his own. The fetus was 18 weeks, and weighed about a half-pound, with a head smaller than an orange. It would provide the material to implant into Chimp Donnie's brain.

The operation itself — implanting the human fetal brain cells into the brain of a young chimp — was certain to succeed: the two little creatures were nearly 99% genetically identical, so the human tissues would quickly grow into and become part of Chimp Donnie's brain.

Cross-species implants, human to animal and the reverse, were becoming common in the scientific community. There was even a term for the living creatures that resulted: *chimeras*, creatures with living parts from multiple species.

As far back as the 1980's there was the "geep" — an animal created in the laboratory by combining the embryos of a sheep and a goat. It grew up to look like a goat, though covered in patches of sheep's wool.

In another lab, they successfully grafted part of a quail embryo into a chicken embryo, resulting in a chicken with a quail's brain and characteristic sounds.

Who could forget the picture that went around the world of the mouse with the human ear growing on its back?

More recent experiments with chimerical creatures included the lamb fetuses into which human stem cells had been infused, resulting in the possibility that in time human livers could be grown in sheep for transplantation to ill humans.

Other researchers had transplanted human stem cells into the brains of baby mice, and the human cells had grown to make up about one percent of the mouse brain.

In 2001, a team had implanted human stem cells into the brains of monkey fetuses and allowed them to grow there for a month. Autopsies conducted after the monkey fetuses were aborted revealed that the human neural cells had spread and grown throughout the monkey brains.

Most of those experiments had involved creating the chimeras at an early, fetal stage. But that would mean finding a pregnant female chimp, opening her under anesthesia, and operating on her fetus while it was still in the womb. That added layers of complexity that Daulby was not prepare to deal with now.

So he resolved to vault several steps, and implant from human newborn, just aborted, to chimp newborn.

Since human and chimp were genetically so close, it was virtually certain that the human cells would grow within the chimp without rejection. Hence the real question was whether the *larger* experiment would succeed. Would Chimp Donnie grow up to prove Daulby's hypothesis?

And if the experiment *was* successful? What then? What doorways would that open?

He knew he was risking his career as a researcher. He had set this experiment up in secret, he had not followed the protocols, he had not gotten clearance from the ethics committees and the layers of university and federal bureaucrats — and the politicians to whom they were beholden.

"Let's just do it!" he'd finally decided at the end of the meeting with his core group. "If it succeeds, then our transgressions will be forgiven."

The members of the team had laughed at the joke — hoping he was right.

∎

The implants were in place, and Daulby was fitting the piece of skull back into Chimp Donnie's head when the phone rang in the OR. Betty Reed took the call. They were short-staffed tonight — just the core team, for security — so work paused for the moment.

"Oh God!" she said, stumbling back against the wall. She looked across at Daulby, the color draining from her face. "It's for you, Dr. Daulby. It's about your wife."

"A divorce lawyer at this time of the night?" he joked, hiding his concern.

"It isn't that. Two policemen are outside to see you."

"Jesus! Get that fetal tissue out of sight," Martinson said. "Don't let the cops see that."

"That — that's not the problem," Betty said, slumping against the wall. "They found your wife's car, and she's — she and Jenny. Oh God!"

2

San Diego, California.

"But I don't *want* to go! I like it here!" Sexy Sally said. "I like partying and drinking and screwing. I don't want to go, and you can't make me."

"But that life as Sally is finished," Kate Remington said gently. "It finished in the car crash. Now you must leave so that Linda can be healthy. Your mother and sister are waiting to guide you over. Just relax and let it happen."

"Sally" was stretched out on a recliner chair in the darkened office, while Kate — Katherine Remington, Ph.D. — sat at the edge of the room.

Kate was 32, tall and lean, with an attractive, gentle face, striking high cheekbones, warm brown eyes, and shoulder-length dark hair. She wore one of her trademark jogging suits, today pink. Jogging suits were comfortable to wear, and comfortable for the clients to be around.

Kate's friendly smile and easy manner put patients at ease, so rapport built sooner. She gave no indication of the way her life had been shattered a few months earlier when Karen, her twin sister, was mugged outside her apartment. Days later, Kate's fiancee was killed in a drive-by on his way home from the hospital.

Kate had begun the session by leading Linda through an hypnotic induction, first relaxing her until she was almost oblivious to her present body and the present time, back to when it had all begun: A stepfather she called "Newdaddy." A little girl, then aged eight, who hated the things Newdaddy did to her.

Then that little girl, the child Linda, found herself outside her body, watching what was happening. It didn't hurt now, didn't shame her any longer, because now it wasn't happening to her.

Now it was happening to someone else, to someone who called herself Sally. Sally didn't mind the things Newdaddy did. Sally was always ready to step in when Newdaddy was doing the bad things. Once Sally arrived, Linda could go away.

"Now I'd like to speak to Sally," Kate said.

"The hell you want?" came the reply from Linda, but it wasn't Linda's voice, nor was it Linda's tone. Linda's normal voice was soft, so gentle and sweet it could barely be heard. This voice was brassy, the pronunciation coarse. This was the voice associated with the Sally personality.

"How long have you been with Linda?" Kate asked.

"You heard her, ever since Newdaddy started messing around with her."

"Why did you come to Linda?"

"The hell you think I came for? To have some fun again, get drunk, get laid."

"Where were you before you came to Linda?"

"Don't know where the hell I was. Lost somewhere, all confused, like some crazy dream."

Kate held a mirror in front of Linda's face. "Sally, I'd like you to open your eyes and look into the mirror. Is that your face you see?"

She pulled back from the mirror. "Hell, no, that's not me, not really me. That's Linda."

Kate eased back to her chair. This was the crucial step in bringing them out. "Tell me about the last time you saw your other body," Kate prompted.

"It was all – all tore up in the car, all bleeding and twisted. My – the face – it went through the windshield, and the head, it's turned almost clear 'round to the back."

She broke off and sobbed, convulsing in the chair. "It hurt so much at first, I couldn't stand it. Like I was being just tore apart. So I just kinda let go, y'know what I mean? Then it didn't hurt no more."

"I'd like you to look again at the body there in the car," Kate said. "Why is the head twisted around?"

"I don't want to look. It's weird seeing my body all tore up like that, a real bad dream."

"I'm sorry, but it's very important for you to look closely. Why is the head twisted around?"

"I think it — I think the neck's broke. But it *can't* be. I mean, I feel all right. My neck's not broke, *hell no!*"

"Now go in closer, and look at the eyes of the person in the car."

"No! I can't look at them eyes — they're . . . awful. Spooky!"

"What is it about the eyes?"

"They don't focus, they're just staring off into space!" She rocked with sobs. "Oh God! There's nobody *there* behind the eyes! It's *empty!*"

"Watch Sally's body there in the car. What happens next?"

"The men, they come'n put me — I mean, back then, after the accident, they put that body — onto a stretcher and — "

When she got control again, she went on, "And they put a sheet over it all, even up over the face."

"Do you understand what that means?"

Moments passed, and Kate was about to repeat the question when the reply came, "It means she's dead, don't it? But how can that be? I'm Sally, and I'm still alive."

"Look around you," Kate suggested softly. "Do you see any people you know?"

"Yeah," she said, and now her voice was softer, brighter. "Yeah, I see my mom. And my sister. They're there, just like —" She shook her head. *"But that can't be! They're dead!* They been dead for years! *The hell's going on?"*

"Ask them why they're there."

"Something about they've come to guide me."

"Guide you where?"

"Across, to the other side — that's what they tell me."

She jerked in the chair. "But I don't want to go! I like it here! I like having fun. I like partying and drinking and, hell, I like screwing. I don't *want* to leave here! *I don't want to go!"*

"But that life as Sally is finished," Kate said gently. "It finished in the car crash. Your mother and sister have come for you."

"You *stop* this! *I don't want to go, and you can't make me!* Leave me alone!"

"Is anyone else with them?"

"I don't want to go! I don't! I *don't!*"

"Do you see a tunnel? Do you feel the energy pulling you into the tunnel?," Kate asked.

"It's pulling me, it's pulling me, and there's a light way up at the end. Mom has her arm around me now, and it's so good to see you again, Mom. It's pulling me up and —"

■

After the session, Kate stopped by her office to check messages. Only one: a call from a Dr. Rausch of the Grafton Foundation. She had never heard of either Rausch or the Grafton Foundation, but foundations funded grants, and she desperately needed a grant.

She was on contract at the Clinic, and the contract was up for renewal next month. Not a good time, with talk of major cutbacks coming soon. Her approach to treating Multiple Personality Disorder was controversial, and might be one of the first to be cut . . . unless she could come up with independent funding.

When she returned Dr. Rausch's call, he mentioned that he was intrigued by what he had heard of her "unorthodox but very intriguing therapy for Multiple Personality Disorder," and "believed they had some shared interests, based on her very interesting work."

He suggested lunch on Friday to "discuss some career possibilities that you may find of extreme interest."

About the author

A graduate of Le Moyne College (a Jesuit college — there really *are* no coincidences!) and the Cornell Law School, Michael McGaulley was admitted to the bars of New York, Virginia, and the District of Columbia before leaving law practice to focus on management consulting, where his clients included the U.S. State Department, various Xerox operating companies in the United States and other countries, Kodak, Bank of America, and other organizations in government and private industry.

Formerly based in the Virginia suburbs of Washington, he now divides his time between upstate New York (brr!) and Florida.

Printed in the United States
50453LVS00003B/21